PRETERNATURAL
by
Matt Hilton

MATT HILTON

PRETERNATURAL
by
MATT HILTON

Published by Sempre Vigile Press

Also by Matt Hilton

Dead Men's Dust
Judgement and Wrath
Slash and Burn
Cut and Run
Blood and Ashes
Dead Men's Harvest
No Going Back
Rules of Honour
The Lawless Kind
Six of the Best (E-book)
Dead Fall (E-book)
Red Stripes (E-book)
Instant Justice (E-book)
Dominion
Darkest Hour
Mark Darrow and the Stealer of Souls
Preternatural

PRETERNATURAL

ONE

Within

"Conventional wisdom dictates that my skin should be sloughing off by now. Am I supposed to thank you for the mild day, Carter, or was that simply a mistake on your part?"

"Shut up, Cash. I'm in no mood for any of your rubbish talk today." I scanned the distant mountains; they were lavender in the coruscating heat haze. Beneath my boots, sand as white and fine as talcum powder swirled on the ghosts of eddies kicked up by my approach. Without looking I knew that the sky would be stark brightness, the sun an infernal ball of fire against cobalt blue. "If you'd rather, I'll crank up the heat if you think it'll make you more amenable."

Cash lifted his manacled hands, shook the chains that stretched off into a haze of their own. "No, I'm quite comfortable as it is. But, hey, thanks for the offer." Feigning satisfaction, he placed both palms behind his neck and lay back as if catching rays on a Mediterranean beach. "Mind rubbing me down with some oil? I may as well make the most of my time here, huh?"

I folded my arms, eyeing him with disdain. "Sit up, Cash."

Cash glanced down the length of his naked body, seemed particularly impressed with the tangle of ginger pubic hair, as unruly as an academic's hairstyle. His mouth quirked downwards in what passed as a smile in his repertoire of five expressions. "Would you just take a look at that? Goddamnit if I ain't naked again!"

I snorted. "Sit up."

"Y'know something, Carter? I'm beginning to gain the impression that you enjoy seeing me like this." Cash raised an eyebrow. Expression number two. "Hot, naked and sweaty…you sure this ain't some sort of latent homosexuality thing you've got going on?"

"I told you I'm in no mood for your nonsense."

"Actually, I think the word you used was 'rubbish'. You know, I don't like to contradict, but what I think you were really getting at was *trash* talk. That's the *happening* slang these days, ain't it, *dawg*?"

Exhaling my impatience, I snapped up my chin. And, marionette-like, Cash followed the gesture, folding up from reclined to seated with no hint of volition from one position to the other. Again he hit me with expression number one, his lips down turned. "Christ Almighty, Carter," he said. "You could have given me whiplash there."

"I could do a whole lot worse than give you a stiff neck, believe me," I snapped. "Now shut the hell up and listen to me."

Eyebrow up, lips down, didn't count; it was a blending of expressions one and two. Cash opened his palms, creating emphasis. The manacles were making his wrists raw: one of the minor details I hadn't neglected.

"I have to tell you, Carter, when I found out where you'd brought us this time, it got me thinking." He squinted up at the sun and for good measure I made sure that it seared his eyes. He grunted, searched the horizon behind me. "For the first time it made me wonder about you."

"I'm not interested."

He shrugged. "Carter, call me a captive audience. I've no option but to sit and listen to you jabber on. The least you can do is hear me out for once."

"I've told you…"

"You're in no mood for any of my nonsense. I know. I know. But I think this is important…for both of us."

I lifted a hand. Cash's mouth snapped shut. Around him flames the colour of the sky broke from the magnesium earth, encircling him with heat that would burn this time. I allowed him to squirm back from the blaze, to tuck his feet beneath his

8

haunches in an effort to escape a roasting. After half-a-dozen racing beats of my heart, I blinked. The flames went out and with them the heat. The sand was as titanium white as before.

"Next time I'll start the fire between your legs, Cash. See how your dick looks when it's all shrivelled up and flaking ash."

"Whoa! Latent homosexuality I can understand, but Carter, sado-fetishism?" He folded his hands in his lap. "You surprise me."

I ignored him. I turned my back and walked away. I suspected that in that instant that he'd be straining at the shackles like a manic beast, slavering and jerking in animal-like ferocity. I snapped my gaze over my shoulder. He was sitting swami fashion, as if lost in meditative-tranquillity on a mountain top perch. He didn't fool me for a second.

"I told you that I wanted you to listen. Are you ready to do that, yet? I'm warning you Cash…one more word of bullshit and I leave you here." I reached my fingers to the heavens, plucked at an invisible cord as if pulling on a bathroom light. The sun became Saharan hot. "A couple of hours should do it."

Cash's eyelids drooped. Finally, expression number three: resignation.

"Good," I said. I didn't bother with the theatrics this time, merely allowed the heat to subside.

But he wasn't finished yet. "All I was gonna ask was if you'd finally found religion."

It set me back on my heels. Against my better judgement, I asked, "What are you talking about?"

"Just what I said. Something that's important to the two of us."

I shook my head. "Where are you going with this, Cash?"

"Well. All you gotta do is look around yourself."

I didn't bother looking. I knew the landscape intimately.

"Straight out of the Bible, no?"

"No," I said. "Straight out of *Lethal Weapon*. You know that scene where the bad guys have Murtaugh's daughter in the back

9

of the Limo? Riggs is about half-a-mile away with a sniper rifle, about to blast them all to hell."

Cash glanced skyward, head shaking. "In that scene the bad guys had a helicopter, didn't they? Well, I don't see a helicopter. You can say what you want, Carter. You've fed off another subconscious influence here. This is the scene from the Bible where Jesus is alone in the wilderness and is being tempted by the devil."

"Uh-uh," I said. "Lethal Weapon. Believe me."

"You can't fool me, Carter. This is the temptation of Christ. Only thing is, I can't get it straight in my head what part you're playing in this scenario." He lifted his manacles. "A little role reversal going on, no? I mean, hey? Who's looking like Old Nick these days?"

I spat on the sand. "There's only one devil here, Cash. And it sure as hell isn't me."

He jangled his manacles.

I shook my head. "Whatever you think, it isn't torture for torture's sake. You know that."

"So what do you call it, Carter? Justice? Punishment? What?"

"I don't call it anything. The chains are a means to an end. Anyway, nothing I could do to you would be punishment enough."

Cash showed the tip of an eyetooth. It was neither smirk nor smile, but disdain. "And here was me thinking you were about to go all Christian on me. I thought that…well, perhaps you were ready to forgive and forget."

"Never."

"Never is an awfully long time."

"Not long enough."

Cash fully smiled this time. His eyes were like collapsed stars in the void of deepest space. "You'll die one day, Carter."

"Not for a long time, arsehole."

"Says who?"

"Says me."

He laughed. I allowed him his little moment.

"But it will happen one day. What do you suppose will happen then?" In defiance, he cupped his neck and lay back. Instead of forcing him upright as before, I decided he should be clothed. An orange prison jumpsuit was the most fitting garment I could imagine. He grunted. "At least it matches my complexion."

"Cash...shut the fuck up. I want you to listen to me."

Perplexed, he actually sat up of his own accord. Something in my tone perhaps, or maybe he knew me better than I realised. He crinkled his nose as though he'd stood in something foul and tracked it indoors.

Hollow-eyed, I stood over him. Admittedly, it was perhaps a weakness on my part. But I knew I had little option. "Cassius," I said, giving him his full name. "I need your help."

TWO

Connor's Island, Shetland Isles.

Bethany and James crouched over the bird, watching as it fluttered in a broken circle, one wing at an unnatural angle. Its head was tilted to one side, its single visible black eye accusing.

James poked at the bird with a finger that was striped red with ink from a marker pen, his bony knees flanking his equally bony elbows.

As though giving the bird voice, Bethany squawked, "Leave it be, Wee Jimmy."

"A cat must have got it," James said. "Look!" He poked the bird again, attempting to flick it over on its back. "There's blood all over it."

"Leave it be. You ken what Ma said about touching dead birds."

James gave her the look. The one reserved for older brothers disdaining their siblings. Especially when the sibling was his little sister. "It's no' dead, you Muppet."

"Ma said you'll catch the bird flu, and you're no' to touch."

James rose up to his full height: all four-feet ten-inches of it. He fisted his hands on his hips, frowned down at the bird. He could see its heart beating in frenzy against its chest. "Does that look like the bird flu to you, idiot?"

"Poor wee thing," Bethany offered. "Do you think its wing is broken, Jimmy?"

"I don't ken, do I?" James nudged it with a scuffed shoe. The bird made another futile circle in the grass. A bead of scarlet edged between its open beak. "We should put it out of its misery," he said. By the flat planes his features took on there was little thought of mercy in his adolescent mind. Bethany recognised that face all too well.

12

"Don't you dare harm it!" She pushed by him, interjecting her small frame into the space between Jimmy and the bird.

"Hey! Get out of it!" James grasped the strap of her schoolbag, tugged her and watched as she sprawled on her backside, an ignominious bundle of grey school uniform, white socks and straw-coloured pigtails. "Do that again, Beth, an' it'll be you who'll have something broken."

"I'm telling Ma on you!" was Bethany's answer, that universal cry of all wronged youngsters.

James rounded on her. Skinny, pale, chewing a lip scarred with a week old cold sore, he was still the dominant figure in this picture. Bethany scurried backwards. Not quickly enough to avoid the nasty intent of the jab James aimed at her with his shoe.

"Oww!" she shrieked, rubbing at the sore spot on her shin. "Stop kicking me, Jimmy."

"It's what I do to squealers," he said, with all the vitriolic rancour of an eleven-year-old bully. "You dare tell Ma an' I'll kick your greetin' face in."

"No you won't. Ma will tell you off."

"I'm no' afraid of Ma," James said, his chin jutting. "Not like you, you cry baby."

"I'm no' crying," Bethany pouted.

"Aye you are. Cry baby."

"No I'm not." Bethany scrambled up. She was three inches shorter than her brother, and he outweighed her by ten-or-so pounds. She wasn't afraid of him, though. Not really. Not when she knew his secret and could hold it against him. "I'll tell everyone at school that you still pee the bed."

James shivered as if water had just been dashed in his face. His voice came out as brittle as ice-crystals. "I don't."

"Yes you do. You're a pee the bed." She danced away from him. "Pee the bed, pee the bed, one, two, three."

Panic. Shame. A thousand raw emotions. James glanced around, his breath short and rasping in his throat. The hillside remained empty of observers. Only the injured bird bore witness to his sister's *lies*. He stared at it, reading the accusation in its eye. Knew that look for what it really was. Mockery. Even the bird knew what it was he'd so long tried to hide. If this got out, school would be even more of a hell on earth than it already was. James howled. Not at Bethany. She was beyond his immediate concern. He couldn't do anything about her. But he sure could do something about the bloody bird.

One stamp was all it took. Logic, alas, meant little to James. He kept stamping and stamping. Then, for good measure, he kicked the shredded carcass in the air in an explosion of feathers and guts. And if his mother had heard the curses he screamed, she'd have grounded him for a month. Plus, she'd have more than a harsh word to say to the parents of his friends, Rory and Gregor, for, in her wisdom; where else could he have learned such profanity?

The bird rolled down the hillside, coming to rest by a tuft of couch grass rising from the hillside like the snatching fingers of purgatory. Breathless, James stared at it. He was set to resume his attack if the bird gave even the slightest hint of life. The bird - obviously prudent - remained dead. Finally James could breathe again. He turned to Bethany and his bearing screamed gloating. After all…he was proud. He'd shown her what he could do to those ready to even whisper his secret.

His features slackened. Bethany's face was painted with the horror and loathing of the moment. But she wasn't looking at him. She wasn't even looking at the pitiful wreckage of feathers and blood-streaked bones of the blackbird. She stared wide-eyed beyond her brother, towards the summit of the hill beyond which lay their home.

James couldn't look. He knew. Ma had seen what he did to the bird. She'd heard him swearing. There was going to be unholy retribution to pay for his sins. He looked back at Bethany, mind tumbling in an effort to find an excuse for his actions, or someone to pin the blame on. Anything. Anybody at all. Bethany shivered. Her schoolbag drooped from her shoulder as if it was the burden of both their sins. She took a faltering strep backwards and the noise she made was more pitiful than the squawks that had originally led them to the injured bird.

What's wrong, Beth? The words formed in his mind, but James could not give them voice. He turned, searching for the source of her terror. He saw it immediately. And in that instant, he so, so, begged God that it had been his mother silhouetted against the northern skyline.

THREE

Norwegian Sea

Pain thrummed a beat through my senses. The fistful of paracetamol I'd swallowed did little to dull it. The growling engine, the stench of diesel oil, the shouldering of anxious passengers did little to assuage my discomfort, neither. The faded orange plastic seat I sat on was as uncomfortable as perching on razor wire, yet it was the more alluring prospect than standing at the rusty handrail listening to sweaty-faced landlubbers dry-heaving the remains of their dinners into the murky sea. What should have been a pleasant ferry ride over to Connor's Island was fast becoming my own private journey into Hades. Not for the first time, I glanced up at the captain jostling with the controls, half-expecting to see Charon at the wheel as he guided us across the turbulent Styx.

One small grace, there was a roof over my head. Not that it deterred the pummelling weather from soaking me to the core; the window mechanism had long ago given in to the corrosive sea air and remained open come hail, rain or shine. Around me, other passengers huddled together, their exhortations for respite from their discomfort only adding to my misery. I suffered in silence, chewing at the flesh of my inner-cheeks every time the prow of the boat lifted and plunged amid the surging waves. I would have closed my eyes so that I didn't have to look at the fear-streaked or nausea-pasted faces of the fellow doomed souls bound with me for Tartaros. I would have, but I resisted. When I closed my eyes I was often transported to worse places than this stretch of the Norwegian Sea in the north Atlantic.

Through algae-pitted windows I searched out our destination, but Connor's Island remained an indistinct shape in the murk. Twenty-two miles behind us was the Shetland Isle of

Yell, and about ten to the east was Unst, commonly marked on maps as the most northerly of the Shetland chain. Only eight miles in length and two across its middle, Connor's Island didn't bear the distinction of being named on too many cartographers' charts.

Once over it had been the anchorage of Vikings, later on a stronghold of the eighteenth century pirates and smugglers who plied these waters, most notably the notorious John Fullerton - ironically dubbed The Pirate of Orkney - who once sheltered there when evading capture by the Royal Navy. As recent as the early twentieth century the island had become the domain of farmers and fishermen, who made a living bartering their produce of eggs and butter for the more potent gin of French and Dutch sailors. However, come the advent of the two great wars, and the intervening sixty-odd years since, Connor deliberately faded into obscurity and was purposefully left off maps. The fact that a secret nuclear submarine tracking station took up a formidable northern chunk of the island had nothing to do with it. Allegedly.

I scrutinised my watch, had to brush away beads of moisture. It was barely after six in the evening. The sky was telling lies. Again I searched out the captain at the helm. His jaw was set in a rictus grin. Nothing in his face gave any hint that we were nearing our destination. Finally I could hold it in no longer. I groaned.

"First timer, huh?"

It wasn't admonishment. More a statement of fact.

I swivelled to look at the woman sitting to my left. It was the first occasion I'd acknowledged another's presence in hours.

I gave a strained laugh. "Does it show?"

A smile fluttered at the corners of her mouth.

I nodded sagely. "I suppose it does."

She looked to be in her mid-thirties, small within her quilted parka. She had dark hair pushed behind her ears and held back from her forehead with one of those multi-coloured *scrunchie* things that had been popular two decades ago. Her face, highly coloured about the cheeks, was what may be called handsome in some circles, or simply plain in others. Either description would have done her a disservice; I saw a face of intelligence and character, and, yes, a step above the average in the pretty stakes. Out of these grim surroundings un-assaulted by brine and buffeting winds, I guessed she could turn many a man's head.

"I do this trip twice a month and it still manages to turn my stomach," she said. Her voice held the soft burr of a Scottish ancestry, but I didn't believe it was of this locale. More cosmopolitan. Edinburgh, perhaps.

"Do you live on Connor's Island?" I asked.

The woman cocked her head to one side, watching me with eyes the colour of Lakeland slate. Apparently, striking up conversation with a stranger wasn't the norm for her. She studied my face, decided that my question was innocent enough, that I wasn't a crazed stalker who'd pursue her for the remainder of her days.

"No. I just work on Conn."

I nodded. As though her answer was obvious. Conn? Local colloquialism, I decided.

"What about you?" she prompted. "Why are you doing this journey? It can only be for one of two reasons; either you work there and have to get on this excuse for a ferry, or you're insane."

I couldn't very well admit to the second option, could I? "I'm looking for someone."

She shrugged her shoulders. "If they're on Conn, they shouldn't be too difficult to find. There are barely a couple thousand people there at the best of times. This late in the year, figure drops to below a thousand resident islanders."

"Should make things a little easier." I must have said it with little conviction, considering what she said next.

"Who is it you're looking for? Family member? Old friend." Her eyelids flickered, hinting at subdued humour. "Lover?"

My smile was sad. "An old acquaintance."

"What's their name? Who knows, I might know them. Could maybe even point you in the right direction."

I did a quick mind spin. Did I tell her his name? Would it hint at my reason for coming all this way to the island? Did it really matter that I told her? Considering I didn't fully understand why I was here, it didn't make sense to lie to her. "He's called Paul Broom. Ever heard of him?"

A small click in her throat. "Can't say I have, no."

I was stuck as what to say next. I hadn't actually talked with a woman for a long time. Wasn't good at making polite conversation with the opposite sex. But I had to say something if I wanted to keep the conversation going. Maybe I should have told a little white lie, said I was here on an impromptu visit of the island. Maybe she'd have offered to be my tour guide, show me the sights. That was a distraction I couldn't possibly afford. "He's just an old friend. A writer. He's come up here to write a novel. To get away from it all, so to speak."

"To get away from it all," she echoed. I detected a note of pathos. "Well, he has certainly come to the right place."

Just at that, the sea, the wind, maybe even Charon's hand at the wheel, conspired to throw us together. The woman reflexively gripped my forearm to stop her pitching all the way across my lap. Equally as reflexively, I glanced down at her slim fingers; saw the dull gleam of gold on her second finger. Inextricably, I felt a phantom knife wrenching my guts. Quickly, she retracted her hand, sucked the fingers up into the sleeves of her coat as deftly as any sleight-of-hand, leaving me to wonder if I had seen the wedding band or if it was merely a trick of the light.

"Sorry."

"It's okay," I said. Awkward words between two strangers caught in an intimate moment with neither of them able to handle it, and perhaps reason for both to avoid it.

PRETERNATURAL

The woman cleared her throat. She straightened herself without any perceptible effect on the shape or dimensions of her over-sized coat. The silence between us became tangible. Uncomfortable. After a few more minutes, I excused myself, stood up and swayed and pitched my way to the prow of the boat. I could feel her eyes on me the entire way.

The sea was the shade of damp ashes, with splashes of phosphorous where the prow split the waves. The waves towered, folded and crashed all around us. It was an idiot's folly to attempt the crossing from Yell to Connor's Island in a boat as decrepit as this, and only the woman's hint that there were only two reasons you would go there gave the voyage any credence. Either you had to do it because you lived there - there was no fancy helicopter or airplane shuttle to the island - or you were insane. I wasn't seeking employment, so it didn't say much for me. Though, I suppose, you could say I had work to do. Of course, considering the task I suspected waited for me, that also designated me insane.

The pain in my head wasn't subsiding. I rubbed at my temples, alternating hands while I gripped the rail with the other. The boat shuddered and yawed to the left and I had to hold on with both hands to avoid tumbling into the Atlantic. Behind me, a chorus of cries went up. Even seasoned travellers to the island weren't used to this hazardous a journey. The boat dived into a trough, blasted skyward the next instant as it crested the following swell. I tasted salt as seawater invaded my senses. An intelligent person would have decided that it would be best to return to the cabin. I stayed put, riding out the storm, feeling strangely invigorated in a weird masochistic sense.

Though it was barely evening, the heavy rain clouds, the autumn month and the northern latitude conspired against the day. Already the sky was the same hue as the sea, and if it hadn't been for the whitecaps it would have been difficult differentiating one from the other. Something else caught my eye: a series of upright antennae reaching hundreds of feet into the air, their red blinking lights were a warning beacon to low flying aircraft. Had to be the masts of the submarine tracking station. Though I couldn't swear to the fact, I guessed that the bulk of Connor's Island now lay to the west of us, and we were in fact fast approaching the bay mid-way up the eastern side of the island. As if to applaud my deduction the captain gave a series of blasts on his horn, and then the boat slewed towards the harbour. The boat jounced and rocked over waves half-a-dozen times before I could pick out the darker bulk of the island against the twilit sky, then another half-dozen before the pinprick of lights betrayed the presence of Skelvoe, the settlement built around the harbour.

"Home sweet home," a voice breathed beside me.

I hadn't been aware of her approach, but when I looked, the woman was beside me at the rail. She was standing with her legs braced against the pitch and roll, arms slack against the rail so that she rode each motion rather than fought against it. She was wearing a smile, one that was laden with as much sadness as relief at our impending landfall. I couldn't help it: I wondered what her story was. I really should have cautioned myself, because I simply had no right to be thinking about her. I had enough reason to avoid making any contact with the islanders that went beyond superficial, but something about her intrigued me. Contrary to myself, I asked, "What is it you do on the island? Your work, I mean."

She expelled air, eliciting a noise somewhere between a grunt and laughter.

"I dig holes."

"What? Like an engineer or something?"

"Or something," she said. "I'm with a team from Edinburgh University. We're conducting an excavation of a Viking settlement over on the western side of the island."

Despite myself, I was surprised. I studied her face. Again I decided she was in her mid-thirties. "Don't take this the wrong way, but aren't you a little old to be a student?"

She shook her head, amused at my ignorance. "You're never too old to learn."

"Oops!" I blew out my cheeks. "You did take it the wrong way. I didn't mean that you were old, just that…."

She rocked to-and-fro with the motion of the sea. Again her eyes flared with humour as she tilted up her head to study me. "What about you? Aren't you a little too young to be on a sabbatical?"

Sabbatical? I searched my memory for what she was referring to. Oh, yes: my story about searching for my author friend. "Hey! I'm only visiting. It isn't me who's put himself into self-imposed exile to find his muse."

Her chuckle was like water over pebbles in a stream. Unconsciously she ran her tongue over her teeth. There was nothing lascivious about it, merely an unconscious quirk. One that I liked. It was as intriguing a detail as was her out of fashion scrunchie and her too-large coat. Before I could catch myself, I asked, "What's your name?"

She shrugged. "Depends."

"On what?"

"Whether we're being formal or not."

I looked down at my rain-drenched overcoat, my equally soaked chinos, the froth squelching out the tongue of my boots. "Do I look the formal type to you?"

She chuckled again. "Well, in that case, you'd best call me Janet."

"Janet," I echoed, tilting my head to one side. "And say I was the formal type, what would I call you then?"

Her lips crept up at the corners, giving her an elfin look. She winked. "Then you'd still call me Janet. But you'd have to be a whole lot more respectful about it."

She left me pondering that one. She walked away. In fact, glided away would be a better description for the way she negotiated the surging deck. I considered following her, but that only lasted a second or two. Connor's Island was a small place.

22

Not that large a population. And - if you discounted the possibility of private charter - this ferry was the only way off the island. I didn't doubt that I'd come across Janet before too long.

Satisfied with that, I concentrated on our approach to the harbour. The town of Skelvoe was built around an existing natural cove, the buildings hugging steep cliffs. At the furthest reaches of the cove, which to be more than fair was little over eight hundred metres in length, quarried rock fortified natural buttresses of stone to form a croissant-shaped harbour. The promontories of stone fought the angry seas, offering respite within. To my left, fishing boats and larger trawlers bobbed at their moorings, while smaller craft were drawn up on the pebble-strewn beach encompassing the remainder of the harbour. Beyond the beach was a single road, devoid at a glance of any traffic other than a lime-splashed police car that was parked with its two front tyres on the beach. Its headlights were dipped. I guessed a conscientious copper had been keeping vigil for the ferry's arrival. As if on cue, the main beam flicked on and the car reversed onto the road, then crawled away, disappearing from sight beyond the houses built along the northern cliff. Vigil over, the police officer could get on with more pressing duties. Though, on so remote an outpost as this, what those duties could be was beyond me. Barring the reason I'd come here of course.

Within the harbour the sea was calm. Talk about sea legs. After riding the tumultuous waves on the way over from Yell, the relative stillness of this water made me feel queasy and unbalanced. Passengers were beginning to gather their belongings, excited now they'd survived all the hazards Charon had brought them through, full of chatter and relieved laughter. En mass they moved towards the disembarking point, anticipating blessed land even though we remained minutes away. The engine went into overdrive, the roar harsh against the night. An answering clamour went up as gulls and terns broke from their roosts and pin-wheeled into the sky in angry protest.

I didn't have much luggage with me, only a single backpack I'd earlier secreted beneath my chair in the cabin. Pushing against the flow of exiting bodies, I returned to my seat, reached beneath it and pulled free my pack. It was damp and gritty with sea-spray. Standing, I swung it on to my shoulder. I considered following the flock to the off-boarding ramp, but decided I'd only have to stand in line with all the others. Instead, I sat down to wait the queue out.

Expertly the captain guided the boat one hundred and eighty degrees, and the engine thrummed into reverse, then silenced. The boat slid smoothly into dock with only the faintest thump against the pilings. Next instant there was the clatter of feet down the ramp and on to the dock. As the line diminished I stood up and tagged on the rear. Shuffling forward, I realised that my headache was gone. Just like that. Perhaps stress induced by the fraught boat ride had triggered it. And now that the trip had ended, then the headache had no place in my psyche. Or, maybe, like my other supposed psychological problems, the headache had been nothing more than a figment of my imagination. Either way, I was glad it was gone. I required a clear mind for what I suspected was waiting for me on Connor's Island.

As I approached the gangplank, I noticed that the captain had come down to see his passengers off the boat. He was a short, fat man, florid-faced below a flat cap. Nothing like the ferryman of ancient legend. I snorted derision at myself, even as I handed him a five pound note gratuity. He nodded, smiled at my generosity: it wasn't payment in silver, but it would do.

I clumped down the ramp onto the dockside. In mass ensemble the other passengers were moving to the left and I followed suit. They had an immediate destination in mind. I didn't. But left was as good a direction as any.

The dock led up a ramp onto the road. I saw Janet at the head of a group of perhaps five others, faces I recognised from the boat trip. Now, they did look like archaeological students. I wondered why - considering she'd had colleagues on board - she'd bothered to strike up a conversation with me instead of spending time with them. Or why she was apparently waiting for me to catch up to their group. Another woman, this one red-haired and no more than twenty years old, said something to her, and I saw Janet flutter her hands, beckoning the group on. I continued towards Janet and our gazes met and stuck.

I lifted my chin.

"I feel like I'm at a disadvantage," she said.

"How's that?"

"You know my name."

"Only your informal one," I teased. "For when I'm not being respectful enough."

She laughed through her nose. "So what do I call you?"

"Carter."

"First or last name?"

Lifting my shoulders, I said, "It's the only one I answer to."

"Carter," she said, as though tasting my name on her tongue. "Sounds very formal to me. What about your family, your friends, what do they call you?"

"Carter."

Again her slate grey eyes turned effervescent. "Oh…Kay. So what about your enemies?"

"Enemies? Who says I have enemies?"

"Carter," she said. "Everyone has at least one enemy."

"I suppose you're right."

"So? What does your enemy call you?"

Oh, that was easy. Though I couldn't tell her. My enemy calls me *Brother*.

FOUR

Skelvoe, Connor's island

The Sailor's Hold was one of those establishments that cater not for tourists, but rough, hard-working labourers who rent the small billets above the common room by the season. There was nothing fancy, none of the mod cons you'd expect in hostels catering for the refined traveller, but what there was on offer was serviceable. I had no foreknowledge of how long I'd need the room, so I paid a week up front with a promise to the landlord that I'd inform him should I require the room any longer. My room was at the top of a narrow flight of stairs, way up in the roof gable of the house. Above my sagging ceiling were only timber and slate, and the occasional rattle of gulls' feet. A small gas heater fed from an unsightly red canister barely made the room comfortable. I dare say, come the onset of winter, only the toughest and most weather-bitten seadog would be snug in there. The bed was originally designed for someone shorter than my six feet one, but it was as welcoming as the soft hiss of the heater. I kicked off my sodden boots and lay back, linking my hands behind my head.

Studying the room, I noted the uneven plaster on the walls, the slightly warped doorframe, the nicotine-stained curtains over the single window. It was basic, sure enough, but I felt right at home. Once I'd been used to better things. But this room served my present disposition nicely. Also, I reminded myself, it was probably all I deserved.

I'd watched as Janet climbed aboard a mini-bus with her small entourage of colleagues. I didn't say goodbye as such, but we'd both waved as the van drove away, a big man with a matted beard at the wheel. I watched as the van picked its way past stragglers from the ferry. Janet also watched me, her gaze on mine until distance and the curve of the road intervened. When I'd nothing further to look at, I spied out the first building offering accommodation. For no other reason than the Sailor's Hold was the nearest, that was why I found myself lying on a rickety bed in an attic crawl space. Thinking about Janet.

A spark of attraction existed. Even blindfolded it would have been easy to recognise. It wasn't anything we'd said. After all, little more than small talk had passed between us, and we hadn't exactly flirted, but I definitely sensed a stirring of interest on both sides. Probably due to her line of work Janet had deliberately dressed down - you don't wear Prada to dig holes - but beyond the plain façade she couldn't conceal the natural beauty that had leapt out and gripped me the first time I looked at her. Something about the fullness of her bottom lip, the curve of her nose, the smoothness of her brow as I'd studied her in profile. Or, more probable, it was the way her eyes shifted from cool grey to sparks of rainbow when she laughed. Eyes do that for me. Whatever, I was hooked. I knew it without even the slightest attempt at self-analysis or psychobabble. I knew I was attracted to her the instant I saw the wedding ring and realised the twisting in my guts was jealousy.

Crazy. I had to be. My sole intention for coming to this God forsaken outpost wasn't to search for Miss Right. Anything but. However, I couldn't deny what my senses were telling me. Fanciful as it may sound, I know now that there is a greater power out there that rules the fickle lives of men. I know that every act we do, every thought, both kind and wicked has a purpose in the grand tapestry of the universe. Quite simply, I don't believe in coincidence. I believe that things happen for a reason. Janet and I were destined to meet on that ferry ride, and that meeting held great portent for things to come. Good or bad. Sadly, considering my history, I couldn't help but fear that events did not bode well for pretty Janet. The outlook, as they say, was grim.

So? I asked myself. Why was Janet attracted to me? Fair enough, as men in their late thirties go, I suppose I'm not too far gone that I can't catch the eye of a woman any longer. Some women, I've heard, like their men to have a rough edge, so maybe my slightly misaligned nose and the scar over my right eyebrow adds to the attraction. I am moderately tall, another thing that some women go for, and I've kept myself in the best shape my nomadic lifestyle allows. But couldn't she see that I was damaged goods? Couldn't she detect the hurt in my eyes? The stoop in my shoulders from the weight of despondency I carried? More importantly…couldn't she detect the monster that lurked within me?

"Feeling sorry for yourself, Carter? Now isn't that unusual?"

I ignored the voice in my head.

As I rose from the bed I straightened the throw. No point in adding to the mess. By the single window was the en suite bathroom that the proprietor promised - a thankfully clean toilet bowl, a chipped porcelain sink, replete with dingy bar of scummy soap, and a mirror screwed directly to the wall. Hitching my chinos I stepped forward. I turned on the tap and listened to water straining its way through a system under demand from the lower floors. Finally, a weak trickle of water began pooling in the sink. I left it running, walked away to fetch my backpack and rummaged through it to find my razor. No hurry. By the time I was back at the sink, it was barely half full - or half empty depending on your outlook. I turned off the tap, tested the water: tepid at best. It would have to do. There was a film of salt on my face and hair courtesy of the ferry trip over. A shower would have been wonderful, but this sink was all that was available to me right then. Apparently there were communal showers in a separate building at the rear of the hotel, but I was in no mood for sharing my ablutions with a load of men smelling of fish guts.

In front of the mirror I stripped down to my chino's, hanging my coat on an 'artfully' placed hook on the wall, but

28

allowing my wrinkled shirt to fall at my feet and kicking it to one side. I turned on the tap again and found the water a little warmer. The mirror had been fixed in place with shorter guests in mind, probably for the bow-legged seamen of decades past, and I had to lean down to see my face. The patina beyond the glass didn't aid my appearance any, made me look twenty years older. I didn't look away. I continued to stare at my reflection, settling my gaze so it grew unfocussed, fuzzy. And in that state I could see him. Like staring into one of those Magic Eye puzzles. Whilst I was awake he only appeared to me when I was in that altered state. He was nothing more than a scarlet blur, but he was there. His cold eyes were as red as the rest of him, his red tongue flicking at the lobe of my left ear. Taunting. In a pointless gesture, I batted backwards over my shoulder. Of course, it had no effect on the mirror man.

"Give it a rest, Cash."

Laughter. Not my own.

I snapped back to the here and now. Only my face stared back at me. Breath tore from me in a ragged exhalation. The tap had finally delivered a passable amount of warm water, so I twisted it off. Then I threw water over my face and hair. I again tasted salt. Threw more water. The cake of soap was just that; caked with someone else's grime and bristles of grey hair. I nudged it into the water, actually hand washed the soap before I was reasonably happy enough to lift it from the water and lather it between my palms. I scrubbed the traces of my voyage from my face, my neck, down my chest, avoiding observing as best I could the progress of my hands. As ever, it was a pointless exercise. Standing, my chest was reflected in the mirror, and the suds did little to hide the crisscross of puckered scars that marred my body from collarbones to upper abdomen: my genuine reason for avoiding the communal showers.

"You've no appreciation for art."

I concentrated on lathering up again. Patted the scummy suds onto my two days old beard, then used my razor to unveil a fresher face. Finished, I used the same water to clean the sink as it drained equally as slowly as it had taken to fill.

There were towels folded in a neat stack on a chair next to my bed. Surprisingly enough they were soft and smelled of fabric conditioner, and I supposed clean towels were in the domain of Mrs Proprietor whilst the remit of interior decoration was the realm of her less-discerning husband. But who knew?

In my backpack I had only the essentials. A couple of T-shirts, a pair of jeans, underwear, socks. Not the classiest wardrobe by any stretch of the imagination. I pulled free the black T-shirt, saw that it was less wrinkled than the green one, then shucked into it, stuffed it into my waistband. On went my damp boots. Then I ran a comb through my hair. Presentable enough, I decided.

My coat was wet, but I was a fatalist. It could only get wetter. I pulled it on. Left the room. I didn't bother locking the door with the key on its kipper-sized fob that I'd been supplied with. I had nothing to steal. If anyone was desperate enough to need the meagre clothing and backpack, then they were in far greater need and welcome to them.

The stairs creaked beneath my weight. I could hear the tinny strains of a radio from one of the rooms a floor down, someone barking out a cough that spoke of a sixty-a-day smoking habit. The light was muted, but it wasn't deliberate ambience, more the result of grime congealing on the lampshades. I steadied myself on a banister worn smooth by the passage of hands over more than two centuries, wondering about whose fingers had lingered where mine now passed. What memories the house could replay, what ghosts wandered its labyrinthine passages. My lips quirked at the memory of a previous visit to Paul Broom, the yellow 'post it' note fixed to his computer monitor, home of his tales of terror and imagination.

I'd read it out loud. "W.W.V.H.D.?"

Broom had glanced over his shoulder, offering a sly smile. "It's a prompt," he said. "For when I don't know which direction to take the story."

"Yeah? What does it mean?"

He shot me a cheesy grin. "What would Van Helsing do?"

I didn't own a mobile phone, but found a telephone in the small dining room. There were no patrons, only the lingering odour of their meals, so the telephone was situated privately enough for my needs. It was one of those bulky cream affairs with large buttons and a slot to feed coins into: as ancient a relic as the rest of the hotel. I dropped fifty pence into a hollow-sounding receptor, even as I read the security advice that the phone was emptied daily. I jabbed buttons, listened to the electronic beeps and blips, then the sound of a ring tone that was echoed a bare two miles away.

"Verbalise."

"Verbalise?"

"It means 'speak'. I prefer 'articulate' but another author already holds the monopoly on that greeting."

Frowning at the receiver, I said, "I'm on the island."

"I know that."

"I thought that might be the case."

Paul Broom clattered something at his end.

Sounded like one of them old-fashioned football rattles. "Didn't take too much deduction," he admitted. "You called me to say you were boarding the ferry from Yell. The ferry didn't sink. Ergo, you are now on Conn."

"I could have jumped overboard," I said.

"But you wouldn't now be on a telephone to me, would you? Ergo - I say again - you are on the island."

Our conversations were often as pointless as this. Light, stupid, harmless fun. Kept our minds off our real reason for *verbalising.*

"You want me to come on up to your place?" I offered.

"Good a place as any."

"I'll set off now."

"Do you want me to come and pick you up?" There was no enthusiasm in his offer.

"No. I'll walk."

"It's raining."

"Helps clear the mind."

Broom, one of only a few people who knew my secret, made a sound in his throat. "Yeah," he concurred. "Maybe best you come with an *open* mind."

And that was the end of our conversation. Not exactly value for money for my nice, shiny, pointy-edged coin.

I left the Sailor's Hold without setting eyes on another living soul, stepped out into rain that wasn't any heavier than when I'd done the ferry crossing, but it was a whole lot colder now that the night had settled in. Up went the collar of my coat. I stuffed my hands in my pockets. There was only the one main street. Didn't matter which way I headed, the road led around the tiny harbour town in both directions, picked up spurs that went up and over the cliffs behind Skelvoe, then joined the coast road that circumnavigated the island. If I went to the right, it was a marginally shorter trek to the coast road. I turned left. Call me Mr Gauche; I don't care. The longer I walked the more head clearing I could do.

Having previously studied a Google Earth image of the island, I knew that Broom's rented cottage lay two miles to the northwest. But that was as the crow flies. If I followed the coast road north, then cut across the island on a feeder route, it made the journey almost three miles. Much of that was at a steady elevation, too. A good work out, even without the extra burden of carrying around sodden clothing. But I was up to the challenge; choosing to walk, I suppose, is another of those penances I've frequently set myself in order to redeem my failure.

My walk took me past more harbour front hotels, a couple of which appeared less run down than the Sailor's Hold, but also a couple that held even less appeal, and I came to the conclusion that I hadn't done too poorly out of my choice. A post office-cum-general store was in darkness, as were a few other shops and, to my surprise, a tiny branch of WH Smiths. No Marks and Spencer, though. The remainder of the harbour side buildings was privately owned dwellings and workshops. A couple of alleys led on to side streets, but I didn't venture into them. I followed the main route where it passed between a fishing tackle shop on one side and a bank on the other, then found that it swung to the right and climbed steeply. Mid-way up the hill I was looking down on the rear of the harbour buildings, whilst to my left smaller houses climbed the hillside like disarrayed rows of packing crates. At the top, the road continued to the right, and I wandered along the narrow pathway, blinking the rain out of my eyes. From this high vantage I could see the red, blinking lights from the submarine tracking base way off on the horizon. Four or five miles of rugged terrain separated us. At the spur road I again lost sight of the masts. Here a bulwark of stone jutted high in my vision, forcing the harsh angle the road took. I continued on along the road, a brief respite from the rain afforded by the sheltering rocks. At the coast road the rain returned with a vengeance. I was once more in open country, not even a shred of shelter offered by the stunted bushes hugging the roadside. Connor's Island was about the bleakest of bleak. There was the occasional sparse tree, uncommon this far north, but most of the indigenous flora was in the way of short, tough grasses, moss and a spiny form of bracken I couldn't identify. There were no street lamps. There wasn't even a moon in the sky to light my way. There was nothing in the sky but the slanting rain that twinkled like slivers of broken glass.

I didn't care. I wasn't afraid of the dark. There are far worse things to fear than the insubstantial shadow of night.

I plodded along for perhaps half-an-hour, found the road that cut across the island. During my march I cleared my mind of all outward influences, got into 'The Zone', as they say. I put out of mind that which had haunted me these past four years. Even *his* constant murmuring subsided to the faintest of buzzing in the far reaches of my senses. Cassius's voice was quieter than the patter of rain on my head, inconsequential. I was actually beginning to enjoy my walk.

Then I saw the headlights.

A single set of them about a quarter-mile ahead. In reflex I glanced down at my wristwatch. The fluorescent dial showed me it was twenty past nine. Not exactly late, but around here, in this weather, who would be out driving unless they had to be? Only one answer: conscientious copper. I sighed because I knew what to expect.

Sure enough, as the vehicle approached it slowed down. Paying it no mind, I continued walking, head down, hands fisted in my pockets. The car came to a halt beside me. When I was a kid, police cars were predominantly white with a central red band. We called them 'jam sandwiches'. This vehicle was more akin to a lime marmalade sandwich where the filling had erupted in all directions. Still, it remained a police car. I continued walking, feeling the eyes scrutinising me from within. The gumball lights came on, followed by the short bleat of a siren. I stopped, gazed unconcernedly back at the car. Rather than climb out of the car where it was, the driver reversed so that it was again level with me. I leaned down as the policeman inside cracked open his window.

"Evening officer," I offered.

"Evening." The cop was older than me, with sandy hair, freckled features, and thick around the neck and shoulders. Next to him was a woman, fifteen or twenty years his junior, but it was her who wore the stripes on her shoulders. I wasn't surprised to see two officers; in Scotland police always come in twos: due to that corroboration of witnesses thing that doesn't apply to English or Welsh law.

"What can I do for you?" I tried for amiable, without concern. The way I hoped any innocent person would react to being stopped by the police.

"We don't get too many people walking way out here at this time of night." The policeman's accent was of the islands; similar to that I'd heard spoken in the hotel. "Especially on a night such as this."

I did the old look up at the sky, blink of confusion, shrug and lift of the palms, the rain's not that heavy, kind of thing.

"Where are you going?" It was the sergeant. Her tone was lighter, more lilting in its pronunciation, more Scottish lowlands. I placed her as hailing from Ayrshire, or maybe Dumfriesshire.

"I'm going to a friend's place," I said.

"What's your friend called?"

"Paul Broom."

The constable said to his sergeant, "Is that no' the writer out at Mrs McClure's place?"

She glanced over at me for confirmation. I shrugged. "I've never heard of Mrs McClure, but, yes, Paul's a writer."

"He's quite famous, too," the constable noted. The sergeant nodded in agreement. The man said, "What's your name, then?"

I told him. He said, "Date of birth, please. And your home address."

I told him those details, too. He leaned down and started punching buttons on an in-car computer. As remote as the island was, I didn't believe they'd be in touch with a dispatcher based here - probably over on the mainland - but they weren't short of the technology to keep tabs with the rest of the world. Probably had to be hi-tech due to the presence of the submarine tracking base being situated here. Blue light pulsed from the screen as the readout of my personal stats came back. Clean.

"Any warrants out on you?"

I shook my head. "No. But you can check, if you want?" He was going to anyway. A few more buttons were pressed. The cop sniffed, almost as if he was disappointed.

"Got any identification on you?"

I didn't complain. I was used to this. Kind of comes with the territory when you move around a lot. Doesn't help when your accent denotes you 'not of these parts'. I have to admit, though, even this was a bit of a record for me. I'd barely been on Conn three hours and already I'd attracted the eye of the law. I scratched in my back pocket, pulled out my wallet and fished out my driver's license. I handed it to the officer and he scrutinised it as though it was an original Dead Sea Scroll. Sniffing again, he passed it back to me.

"All appears in order," he said, more for the sergeant's sake. She didn't answer. She was staring at me. I stared back. Her pupils dilated and her gaze flicked away.

The policeman handed me my license. "Thanks," I said, returning it and my wallet to my pocket. "Is it okay if I get going again? Like you said, it's not the best weather to be out walking."

"We can give you a lift," the man said. I looked to the sergeant, saw her eyes dart to mine, flick away again. She didn't seem keen on the idea.

"No. That's all right." I gestured up the road. "Can't be too far off, now."

"Still a good distance off. But if you'd rather walk, well, so be it. There's no law against it." The officer sniffed again. Earlier I thought the sniffing was all part of the package, all part of the condescending copper act. Now I could see a bead of mucus trembling on the tip of his nose and realised he was suffering a cold. I think he caught me looking, because, next second, he batted at the end of his nose with a thick wrist. Sniffed again. "Just be sure to stay on the roads. I don't want to be traipsing over the glen half the night if you get yourself lost."

I flicked a finger alongside my head, a salute of sorts. "Stay on the roads. Yes, sir."

He gave me a smile full of teeth, but no humour. "Good night…sir."

"Good night, officer." I leaned down, saluted again. "Sergeant."

Her smile was pinched. Not one for wasting her valuable time with obviously crazy Sassenachs. All down to an impression formed from what she'd read off the computer screen, no doubt. I walked away. They idled in place and I guessed they were watching my progress in their mirrors. Maybe they expected me to start making chicken noises and bobbing my head or perhaps throwing my arms skyward and praising the Lord or something. It was probably disappointing when I simply carried on my way, looking as sane as could be whilst walking in the middle of a storm with very little protection from the elements. After a further ten seconds-or-so I heard the growl of the engine as the police car continued on towards Skelvoe harbour. I guessed a pot of tea was calling them.

After that I found it difficult to clear my head. The confrontation with the officers had undone in minutes what my walk had tried so hard to erase. I was back to square one, and I walked on with agitated strides. Maybe if they'd hung around a little longer I'd have confirmed what they'd read on their computer; that I'd spent time in a psychiatric hospital fighting the spectres of my horrific past, and was still suffering the schizophrenic delusions associated with some forms of Post Traumatic Stress Disorder.

FIVE

Four years ago...

"Mr Bailey? Mr Bailey! Karen's on the phone for you."

I looked up from the stack of reports I'd been busy with the past five hours, a stack that - like some magical replenishing pot - didn't diminish, regardless of how many I shoved into my out tray. I was almost done for the day, physically, mentally, but not exactly productively. Unfortunately, the bills outweighed the orders, which wasn't very comforting this close to Christmas.

I stared somewhat cross-eyed at my assistant, Rebecca Woods. She stood in the open doorway of my office, head lowered, mouth gaping around a wad of chewing gum as she waited for my acknowledgement. I blinked. Rebecca cocked her head.

"Sorry, Rebecca. What did you say?"

"Karen's on the phone," she repeated, enunciating clearly. "She says she can't get you on your mobile."

Raking through the contents on my desk, I found my mobile phone beneath a bulging catalogue I'd first perused hours earlier. Vaguely, I recalled turning off the ring tone to avoid unnecessary distractions. I saw that I had four missed calls, all of them from my home number.

"Oh, shit," I whispered.

"She sounds pissed off," Rebecca said. "I thought I'd check with you before I put her through. Y'know, just in case, like?"

I made a face. I considered returning the call on my mobile. Rebecca noted my dilemma. "I'll put it through, okay? Cheaper using the work's phone than your personal mobile."

"A little bit of leakage there, Rebecca?" It explained why the company telecommunications bill had jumped exponentially in the three months since Rebecca had joined the firm. But I nodded anyway. Didn't make much of a difference to my pocket either way; I'd be paying the bill for my home phone, my mobile, or the office phone, whichever way we did it.

Rebecca stepped into the outer office, clumping like Herman Munster in her huge wedge-heeled shoes. The shoes were hideous, the latest attempt of the fashion industry to bring back the Glam Rock of the Seventies. Rebecca was a sucker for fads. But she was a pleasant enough kid as far as sulky teenagers with more metal piercings than sense goes. Her youth, and her eye for the latest trends, were actually a great help when choosing what stock to carry. Plus, she was a half-decent receptionist, *usually* with my best interests in mind.

In the next couple of seconds I sucked air into my lungs, building my fortitude. Karen wasn't going to be pleased that I'd ignored her calls. She wouldn't believe that the silent phone was an oversight on my part. Trust wasn't one of Karen's strongest points these days. Not good in a relationship destined for marriage not more than three months hence.

She came on the phone, and immediately I picked up on her tension. "Carter? Where have you been?"

"I've been here at work," I answered. "Where do you think I've-"

I was cut off.

"You'll have to come home."

"I can't, Karen I've still got a mountain of-"

"You *have* to come home, Carter. Please…come *now*."

I didn't argue. That wasn't mistrust or jealousy or anger in her tone. It was desperation.

"Karen? What's wrong?" Subconscious volition threw me to my feet. I stood hunched over the phone, nerves doing somersaults in my guts. "Are you ill? Is it…wait, I'll get a doctor."

Karen sobbed. "Just come home, Carter. Please. Come home *now*."

"Where's Cash?" I asked. "Tell him to come to the phone."

"He won't. He said I had to call."

"What? Karen, put him on."

"Please, Carter…" Her voice faded, replaced by the dial tone.

I looked at the handset, mystified. I quickly stabbed out my home number and got the engaged line tone. I thought that perhaps Karen was trying to ring back. I quickly hung up. Waited. Nothing. Pressed redial. Again I got the engaged tone. I hung up with more force than intended, almost catapulting the phone and my out tray off my desk. I had to grab at the tottering tray to avoid upsetting all my hard work.

"Rebecca," I shouted, realising that this was an extension phone.

From the other office Rebecca said, "What?"

"Have you got Karen on that phone?"

"I put her through to you."

"I don't mean before…" We were getting nowhere. "Never mind."

I tried again but my home line was still engaged. "Fuck!"

There was movement in the doorway. Rebecca watching me. She was chewing a piercing in her bottom lip, her teeth clicking on metal. She flinched as I lunged towards her.

"I gotta go," I said.

"What's wrong, Mr Bailey?"

"I don't know. Something. I don't know."

"Is everything okay with Karen? With…you want me to-"

But I was already shoving past her. "Tell James I've had to go home. Family emergency."

James Pender was my business partner. As an ex-international tennis champion he was the poster boy for our sports clothing line. He was only encamped in the office next to mine. I didn't have time to stop and explain myself. Well-meaning people took up way too much precious time during any emergency.

Just as Rebecca was doing now.

"Mr Bailey! Your jacket." She stepped into my office, unhooked my jacket from behind the door, swung it after me. I didn't stop. My jacket was surplus to requirement regardless of the snow outside.

I was jogging by the time I reached the stairs down to the lobby, but as I hit the street I was running full-tilt for the car park adjacent to the office block housing *Rezpect Sports*. Beneath the feet of passing pedestrians the snow had turned to brown slush. It splattered my suit trousers as I ran, but my dry cleaning bill was the last thing on my mind. The snow didn't aid stability. Twice I almost went on my backside before I reached my car. Then, wheels biting for traction on the slick road, I spun out into the traffic. Someone blew their horn at me.

The next five miles were a blur as I negotiated the late afternoon traffic. Luckily it was Friday. Rush hour was always early on a Friday as commuters made an early dash for home, so the roads weren't as congested as normal. I still had a couple of near misses, and this time it was me honking my horn at the inconsiderate bastards who wouldn't get out my way. Couldn't they recognise my urgency, my desperate need to get home?

Finally, I hit the dual carriageway and the way was a little easier. The snow had intensified, and the wipers beat a rhythm with my heart as they battled to keep the windscreen clear. I cranked up the heating, hoping it would help, but that only served to make me queasy. In the end I knocked the blowers off and dropped my window instead. The rush of the icy wind was a welcome relief, and I could ignore the flakes of snow that whirled in my immediate field of vision.

As I drove I hit the speed dial on my mobile, flagrantly disregarding the law as I held it to my ear and again heard the broken tone of an engaged line.

"Shit, shit, shit…" Not the most comforting of mantras, but it was all that came to mind. I feared the worst. I considered dialling the emergency services and getting the paramedics to my address A.S.A.P.

PRETERNATURAL

Karen wasn't a vicious dominatrix, or a self-centred or spoiled bitch. She was the woman I loved dearly, the person I would die for. Normally she was a sweet, caring and supportive person. It was only over the past four weeks or so that she'd changed. But that was to be expected, wasn't it? Karen's moods, her recent mistrust and jealousy, all had a single catalyst. They began the day after she realised that she was four months pregnant with our child - one of those *hormonal things* that men simply do not have the slightest clue about. Me included. And, like most men, I could only bite down on my frustration and ride out this period of living at the crest of a hormonal tide until things settled back to normal. Apparently it could be some time. But it wasn't a bad deal; she took the pain, the swollen ankles, the aching back, I took the brunt of her mood swings.

Karen had good excuse for her behaviour.

And that's where my fear lay. The pregnancy. There could only be one reason why Karen had summoned me so desperately. Something was wrong with our baby. Karen's pleading, the unanswered phone, screamed it at me. *Something was wrong with our baby.*

I drove on autopilot, a strange sense of distraction replacing my previous frantic need to get home. It was a cold-edged sensation named dread, hating what I might discover when I arrived home. Somehow the journey passed so much quicker. I was pulling into our drive before I was even aware of having arrived in the village. Then I was at the front door of our house with no memory of leaving the car.

One thing I did notice. Well, two things, actually. There was no ambulance at the scene, and Karen's Citroen Picasso was parked under the lean-to adjacent to the house. But that didn't mean Karen was still at home. An ambulance could have been and gone. Except that a glance at the virgin snow - marred only by my tyre tracks - pretty much negated that. I had a flash vision of Karen collapsed in the kitchen, lying beneath, but out of reach of the phone, while blood darkened her trousers.

I blinked the vision away. Denial was the only weapon against my darkest fear. I charged at the front door, grabbing at the handle. The door resisted me. I stepped back, twisting at the handle again. And it still refused to open.

"Karen?" I set off around the side of the house. Shouted her name again. I squeezed sideways between her car and the wall, making for the side entrance. I saw my brother's Harley Davidson parked to the rear of the Citroen. Something registered. Why hadn't Cash called an ambulance? In all probability he was in the house. He'd been staying with us for the past fortnight, since his abrupt arrival at our door following a sudden cancellation of his six-year sojourn around Europe and Asia Minor. He gave no explanation for ending his travels, merely stating that he'd done everything and seen everything he wanted to. Since then he'd been camped in our spare room - the room designated for our child. He'd ate my food, drank my beer, left his dirty washing for Karen to launder. He'd done little else in the meantime. What on earth was he good for if he couldn't even pick up the telephone? Couldn't he repay our hospitality with that one kindness?

The side door was locked. I grabbed at the keys in my pocket, even as I banged on the door. "Karen? Karen! Where are you?"

My keys were in the ignition in my car. It didn't stop me fumbling again at my pockets, or pushing out through the small door that led out to our back garden. The snow seemed to be responding to my urgency, seemingly falling with more intent at clouding my senses against what I might find. I'd made my mind up: our baby was dying; Karen was dying. And my useless little brother was too drunk or too stoned to care.

Across the rear yard I could see the ghost of the watermill that sat astride the river. A relic of days gone by, to some a huge white elephant, but it was a buying point when I'd viewed the house. Call me an old romantic: it appeared mystical, magical, with the sunlight dappling the droplets of water pouring off the wheel as it turned with the sluggish flow of the river. I couldn't resist.

Now, through the snow, the mill looked like a misshapen ogre, way too heavy across the shoulders to remain upright for long. To my surprise, a single set of tracks dug their way through the snow towards the mill.

I did one of those cartoon double takes. Did I head for the mill or house? The tracks were too large to be Karen's. They had to be my brother's boot prints. I felt a pang of regret at judging him harshly. I'd thrown blame at him, when, judging by the tracks in the snow, he wasn't even home to offer assistance. But the pang was only momentary. I recalled our words from earlier...

"Where's Cash? Tell him to come to the phone."

"He won't. He said I had to call."

"What? Karen, put him on."

"Please, Carter..."

...His tracks were fresh. Minutes old at most. What the hell was he doing gallivanting out by the mill in this blizzard when Karen was in dire need of help? It was typical behavior of the scrounging bastard!

My mind made up, I ran towards the conservatory. The door was closed against the weather, but to my relief it gave under my hand. I charged into the conservatory, through the adjoining doors and into the living room. The leather couch was out of sync, like it had been shoved aside. I saw scuff marks on the floor. I wondered if Karen had first fallen there. But that wasn't all.

A smell registered in my subconscious mind. It was barely an undertone. Salty. Familiar, yet out of place. There was a stirring of the short hairs on the back of my neck. I should have taken more notice. My urgency made me disregard that which I knew had taken place here and I continued on into the house, shouting for my fiancée. I checked the kitchen next. The handset of the phone dangled on its cable. I could hear the *meep! meep! meep!* of the engaged tone. I slammed the phone back into its cradle, lifted it again and then hit redial.

999.

A woman's voice: "Emergency. Which service please?"

Again I slammed the phone down and ran for the stairs.

"Karen? Karen? Where are you?" My voice came out high-pitched. I hit the landing without taking a breath, lunging for the master bedroom. It was empty, the bed made, nothing out of place. I turned back, went to the next room, finding it empty. On to the bathroom. Empty. Then to my brother's room. The room we'd earmarked for our baby's nursery. A room no baby should ever be raised in again.

He'd made the room a nightmare.

I took in the details in an instant. And in the next my mind closed down against the horror. But that was before I could block the weird, hallucinogenic symbols he'd spray-painted on the walls and mirrors. There were other paintings, mostly of large penises forcing into open vaginas, raw and dripping. There were photographs of what I took to be *his* erect penis. There were also photographs of women. He'd pinned them to the walls above his bed. The women encompassed many types - Caucasian, Black, Asian, some of Eastern European descent. Many races, creeds, colours. In each of the women I saw the single factor that made them a collective group. Each and every one of them was pregnant. Or had been, before their innards had been spilled in a brutal form of Caesarean section and their wombs laid open to display the developing fetus within.

"Karen?" Her name was torn from my throat.

I descended the stairs in panic. My feet left me about three paces behind, and I ended up negotiating the last few stairs in a bumping slide on my backside that ended with me grasping at the walls to avoid slamming my head on the steps. Then I was running for the kitchen again. The phone.

Gasping, I hit redial. Not waiting for the emergency call handler this time, I bleated out my address, asked them to hurry and threw the handset away as I hurtled back through the disarrayed living room. The smell was still there, and I knew it for what it was. Semen. Man stink!

The odour of sex. Forced sex? Rape!

Jesus Christ! What had happened here?

I ran through the conservatory into the yard, my hearing deadened by the hush that accompanies snowfall. I screamed for Karen, but it sounded like my voice came from a distant place. I screamed again. Saw the remnants of the tracks in the snow. They were fainter now, the snow backfilling them as I stood there.

"Cash! You bastard! What have you done?"

In my shirtsleeves I ran through the blizzard, insensible to the cold or to what I intended doing. The mill rose out of the white curtain like a giant's castle in a dark fantasy. The creak of the slowly turning wheel sounded like a witch's laughter. Beckoning me forward.

Built of steel girders and timber when such constructions were the life's blood of the countryside, the mill had fallen into some decline. Boards in need of treatment were the mottled colour of fungus, and the mill itself stood like a lopsided mushroom, silhouetted against the trees crowding the riverbank. A central workshop area, wherein were housed the massive cogs and workings of the mill, was topped by a roofed platform, from which hung the block and tackle, and a rudimentary crane that once loaded the product of the mill onto boats and barges. From my approach I couldn't see the wheel that turned the machinery, or the river with its sluggish black water, because of the bushes that had claimed the area around it. I could see a single light in a window on the platform thirty feet above me. It wasn't the steady light from a bulb; it flickered.

The doors didn't slow my charge. I threw my weight against them and they burst inward with little resistance. Then I was in the workspace and I blinked at the sudden darkness. The abrupt change from white to black upset my equilibrium and I experienced a rush of blood to my head. I ignored the sensation, moving quickly to my left, feet probing for the rungs of the ladder that climbed to the platform overhead. I found the first rung, grasped for the ladder and began clawing my way hand-over-hand. Dizzy, nauseous, I ascended like a spastic arachnid.

It was dark, but my vision was beginning to adapt. Above me was the hatch that opened onto the platform, puissant yellow light etching its sides. I thrust against it and the trap flew up and over, the booming concussion jarring my senses as it slammed down on the floor. The notion that my entry into the attic space was too easy didn't strike me. I was simply thankful that the trap gave way. Forgetting the consequences, I began hauling myself up through the gap, my elbows locked as I took the entire weight of my body, feet swinging into space.

I was in that precarious position when Cash hit me. I didn't see him coming. I was barely aware of a shadow looming at my side, then a rope was looped around my neck and something incredibly hard caromed off my skull. Sparks danced a fandango across my vision, and my mouth was flooded with saliva laden with the essence of copper. Miraculously, I didn't immediately pass out. Perhaps it wasn't Cash's intention to knock me unconscious with the blow, maybe it was just oversight. It didn't matter. I couldn't fight back. What with the rope biting into my throat and cutting off my air, the whack to my skull making my mind whorl, it was everything I could do not to fall back through the trapdoor. A plummet to the earthen floor thirty feet below would most definitely have been the end.

Cash tugged on the rope, hauling me backwards. I was now on the platform, but was unable to find my footing as I was dragged across the rough planks. I grasped for the rope round my throat, digging in with my fingers to alleviate the choking pressure. Another jerk of the rope tightened it further. I gagged, attempted to suck in air, gained nothing. The sparks in my vision were turning red. Then black. Though I knew who was behind me, who was killing me, I craned backwards, trying to see his face. I wanted to see him and remember so I could curse him all the way from Hell. But then he struck me again. This time I felt my eyebrow open up like fruit left too long in the sun. Blood cascaded over my features, invaded my mouth. I made a moaning gurgle, shoulders going limp.

The bastard hit me again.

SIX

Connor's Island

I blinked out of my fugue. Four years and a few months later. I was surprised to find myself lying amongst tough grass and sodden moss. I was face down, my arms stretched in front of me, my hands wrist deep in brackish water that had turned my fingers numb. I pushed up, taking stock of my surroundings. Disorientation assaulted me. Past and present blended and I raised tremulous fingers to the gash above my eye, only to find the puckered scar and, not blood, but rainwater trickling from my nose. I rolled to my knees, then collapsed onto my backside, head in hands, and I moaned in dismay. Hunched like that, the rain chattered on my raincoat, plastered my hair to my forehead.

I felt almost hypoglycaemic. I shivered. No energy. I coughed to clear my throat. Finally I forced myself to stand. Out here at the centre of Connor's Island the night was as thick as tar and every bit as black. Only the crystalline shards of rain lent any contrast to the picture. I pushed through the tall grass, following the dim trail of flattened stalks that must have been crushed when I staggered from the road in the grip of my memories. It was only fifty strides-or-so to the road, but the distance felt interminable the way I shuffled along. I was relieved, at last, to find tarmac beneath my feet again. I almost set off jogging. Almost, but didn't. I was still too weak.

Judging by the row of red lights hanging on the horizon to my right, I guessed that I needed to go left to continue my trek over the island. To be honest, if the submarine tracking station lights hadn't been visible, there was no guessing which way I'd have turned. I may have ended up heading back towards Skelvoe harbour and my walk in the night would have been for nothing.

As I walked I regained some of my strength, partly due to the anger building inside me. It was many months since I'd experienced what my doctors had colourfully termed *'an episode'*. With my preparation, and the self-control exercises I'd made part of my daily routine, I had largely eliminated the memory-imposed states of mind that had plagued me the first few weeks following the nightmarish events in the watermill. To find that I was still a slave to their effects after all this time was more than disorienting; it was also frustrating. Kind of pissed me off.

More than anything I wanted to be free of the memories. Because, not only did I want to move on, to kick-start my life, I wanted to cleanse my soul of the shadow, which that day had placed on me. In forgetting that awful day, I believed I could finally be free of my brother's taint. But therein lay the problem. The son of a bitch just wouldn't allow it. And now, as ever, he chose to remind me.

"Accept it, dickhead. You are never getting shot of me. There's just no way, Carter. I'm with you all the way, bro. Like an insect caught in amber."

"More like a fucking fly in the ointment."

For once his laughter curtailed rapidly, and I was allowed to continue on my way with only the most delicate of sensations tickling the base of my subconscious. His intention was to remind me that he was still around, but in a way that shouldn't impede me. He also wanted me to know that *he* had chosen to back off, and - for which I should be grateful - that now, when I was at my most vulnerable, *he* had decided not to torment me. He intended that I understand, and appreciate, that he was upholding his end of our bargain.

His silence allowed me space to think, to consider, and ultimately…to remember. But this time I was adamant that the memories would be under control and on my terms. I recalled again the telephone call I'd received at my office at Rezpect Sports. How my fear for the welfare of my fiancée and the life of my unborn child had caused me to drive like a madman through the heart of a blizzard. How I'd arrived to a deserted home, found the room defiled by my brother's insanity, then followed his tracks to the decrepit watermill. And that's where everything changed. My life. My hopes and dreams. My *burden*.

Four years ago...

...The noose around my throat burned my skin. My wrists were raw wounds. My eyebrow was gashed to the bone. My nose, broken and also split like rotting fruit, throbbed with pain. Blood and snot gathered in my mouth, my eyes were full of tears, my hearing whistling as though I was in a wind tunnel. Total sensory overload. My mind should have shut down. I shouldn't have been able to bare the agony, the horror, or the worthless futility of it all. However, the hatred I felt for my brother would not allow me escape. Through the tears I glared at his sweaty face, desiring nothing other than the opportunity to chew it right off. If I could have, I would have done it. I'm sure he knew it, too, because he was cautious and always remained out of range of my snapping teeth.

I was bound to an upright joist that supported the roof, with my arms wrenched backwards round it, my ankles crossed one over the other and also cinched tight. The noose was round my throat, though some slack had been allowed so that I didn't choke outright. It wouldn't be much fun if I died before my brother was done with his administrations.

Cassius Bailey moved in front of me, sinuous as a leech as he sought a fresh place to bleed me. In his hand he held an ignominious-looking craft knife. The blade, diamond-shaped, no more than an inch of metal protruding from the orange plastic handle, could have as well been a samurai sword. It was every bit as sharp and able to cut strips from my body.

Not for the first time, I gathered the blood-clotted mass in my mouth and spat at him. He merely smiled through the gore plastering his features. He stuck the knife into the flesh above my left nipple and sliced downward in a vicious curve. I yelled in both agony and hatred. Mostly hatred.

Cash laughed.

"Pussy," he called me.

I gritted my teeth, then hollered directly in his face.

He laughed again. "Listen to you. You aught to be ashamed of yourself, brother, for making all that noise over one itty-bitty scratch."

"Fuck you, Cash!"

"No, Carter. Fuck you." He punctuated his retort by slicing me again. My face screwed tightly against the pain, my cry coming out in a stuttering moan. Cash snorted. He reversed the blade, drawing it upward from my solar plexus almost to the top of my sternum. Every millimeter of the way the blade tip grated on bone. I screamed, and this time couldn't halt it.

"Pussy," he said again, eyes wide, gloating.

I lunged against my restraints. The upright creaked, didn't move. Straining against them only served to tighten my bonds.

"I'm going to kill you!"

"Hardly likely," Cash said. "Considering I'm the one with the knife, and you are the *pussy* tied up and crying like a baby."

"You are going to die…"

"Not before you, Carter." He held up the knife, inspected the tip, and appeared satisfied that it remained sharp. "Kind of the nature of things. See, you're the big brother. Me, the little brother. Big brothers die before little brothers. No?"

"I swear to God-"

"Don't bother. Your god isn't here today."

"-I'm gonna make you pay-"

Cash snorted in derision. "Stop whining, will you?"

"-for everything you've done. I swear to God you'll be made to pay it all back ten times over. A hundred times."

"You know something, bro? I'm beginning to grow a little tired of listening to your bitching. Maybe I should open up your throat right now and have done with it."

"Maybe you should, you sick-minded bastard!"

"Only that wouldn't be half as much fun as making you suffer for a few more hours, would it?" He rotated away from me, lifting the knife to point across the platform. I hung my head, refusing to look at what he indicated. "Seeing as you went and spoiled what me and Karen had going on."

He walked towards her. Stood with his hands fisted on his hips as though surveying his handiwork.

"Don't, Cash. Don't touch her."

But he was of a mind to touch her. It was why he'd allowed Karen to summon me home, so that I could bear witness to his cruelty. By doing so, he was torturing me more than all his cutting of my flesh could achieve. Despite myself I looked across at where Karen was bound to the opposite upright joist. Cash stared back at me over his shoulder as he reached out with his free hand and fumbled at one of her breasts.

"Take your fucking hands off her!"

"Uh-uh, Carter. Going to have me some titty-squeezing fun."

I roared. Strained at my bonds. Dust sifted from overhead. My throat was ragged enough, but my roar of frustration left it ripped and bleeding.

"Listen to you," Cash said. He walked back towards me, sashaying his hips, flicking the blade of his knife. "All that fuss about nothing. Don't worry, Carter. I am not hurting Karen's feelings. You know she's beyond *feeling*." He stood so close to me I could feel his breath on my skin. "Why can't you be as quiet as Karen?" He put a hand over his mouth, tilted his head to one side. Hamming it up for effect. "When I used my knife on Karen she didn't make all that howling and screeching."

"Bastard," I hissed. But he wasn't listening. He was too caught up in taunting me.

"Of course, it was different when we were back at the house. Boy, oh, boy, but did she scream then. Screamed for England, the hot-arsed little bitch. See, I wasn't using this little ol' knife then." He wagged the craft knife. Then, suggestively, he dropped his free hand to his crotch, gripped himself. "Gave her nine solid inches of the Love Dagger. Cut that bitch right to the core." He leaned in closer to me. Stared me dead in the eye. "You know something? You should be thanking me, Carter. For killing her, I mean. Saved you a whole heap of trouble that was bound to come to pass. There was just no way that she'd be happy with you after she'd got a taste for the ol' Love Dagger inside her."

His face swam in my vision. In and out. In and out. But I stared beyond him at the forlorn wreckage of my dreams. In the flickering of a single lantern Karen was a pale blur against the darkness beyond. She was naked, a scarlet-edged shadow at her lower abdomen marking the debasement Cash subjected upon her and our baby. Her hair hung in tatty ribbons around her shoulders, her head lolling to one side. Our eyes met. Mine were feverish; her's were dull cataracts. And I saw reflected in them my failure. I saw loathing. Scorn. And I saw the bitter understanding of my betrayal. I'd promised that I'd keep her safe; I'd keep our baby safe. That I'd always be there for them. But I'd come home too late. And, that, I just could not live with.

Hatred drove me. It grew beyond pain. Well clear of the capacity for rational thought. Animal-like I lunged forward, clamping my teeth on the flesh of Cash's shoulder. I sank my teeth through clothing into skin, grinding into muscle with wild beast tenacity. Cash tried to pull back, but there was no way he was getting away from me without relinquishing a sizeable chunk of his anatomy. I chewed even deeper, tasting, for the first time, blood that wasn't my own.

"You frigging tosser!" Cash brought up his hands, tried to pry me loose, the knife in his hand scoring lines in my scalp. When that didn't work, he forcefully tried to tug away. I followed him, our combined weight dragging on my bound wrists. A tendon ripped above my right elbow, but I didn't let go. I hung on, savaging him. He was screaming now, and deep inside I felt a trickle of satisfaction at his pain. But it simply wasn't enough. I wanted payback. I wanted his throat.

Cash stabbed me. He thrust the craft knife into my gut, twisting it. I grunted between my clenched teeth. Didn't let go. He thrust again. Scored my hip. I chewed down, feeling tendons popping in my jaw. Frantic, Cash threw himself back, ready to give up a mouthful of his skin in order to get away from my teeth. But I didn't release my hold. Like Cash, the centuries old joist had experienced enough abuse. It gave way, snapping in an explosion of splinters and worm-ridden dust. I went to my knees, Cash under me. I aimed to hold on, but the shock of our sudden fall dislodged my teeth from him. Beneath me, Cash kicked out, his boots barking my shins. He slashed with his knife, and I earned yet another stripe across my chest. I squirmed up, and Cash propelled himself away, coming to his feet, even as I tried to rise to mine.

"You fucker!" he yelled as he swung towards me. "I'm gonna kill you."

"Do it then," I screamed at him. "But you're coming all the way to Hell with me."

I launched at him, driving forward with my feet, head down, shoulder in his guts. Barrelling him backwards across the platform even as he stabbed down at my back. Through the flimsy plank wall we went...out into space. As we fell Cash screamed. I was silent. Snowflakes swirled around us and I felt as weightless and insubstantial as they did.

Cash struck the great wheel spine first. The noise was like a gunshot. He pinwheeled away - I followed like a streamer in his wake - all disjointed and lifeless. Then we hit the flat expanse of the dead river, throwing up algae and weed and gouts of putrid water. We sank like rocks. And that should have been that.

But our ferocity was too intense. We continued to struggle even as we sank. Cash with his fingers entwined in my hair, my legs somehow snared around his by the loose rope trailing from my ankles. We glared into each other's eyes, even if by natural standards that must have been impossible. Plumes of bubbles marked our screams and curses for a short while.

Then the bubbles were no more. The dark was absolute.

The next thing I was aware of was lightning. Blue flashes that invaded my vision, flickering strobes of light the likes of which I'd never saw before. Flakes of icy snow pattered on my lashes, briefly trembling there before the heat of fever melted them to nothing. There was movement around me. Unintelligible words spoken as hands worked on me. The thunder sounded like the disembodied crackle of a radio. There were distant shouts. Another roar of thunder much closer by sounded like a revving motor.

Metal was placed on my chest and lightning struck at the centre of my being. My body convulsed, back arching.

"Whu?"

I sucked in air.

The voices were less frantic now, but no less urgent.

I felt myself raised up, a hand tugging loose the bindings from my wrists. I was placed on a raised platform. Something was tugged down over my mouth and nose. Sweet oxygen flowed down my throat like the passage of angels. A shroud of wool was wrapped around me. A blanket? My head lolled to one side.

The blue lights continued to strobe across my vision. A man in green and another in fluorescent yellow moved across the scene. They were indistinct, blobs of colour only. Yet I could see the surface of the river many yards away with superhuman clarity. The river was still and flat and murky once more. Dull as the lifeless stare of my fiancée. I blinked. The water erupted upward. Not like a geyser or a fountain, or anything else out of nature. It almost sprang from the surface like the coils of a sea serpent. It folded, rippled, and then slithered with terrific speed towards the riverbank.

I stared at the paramedics and cops around me. Why weren't they reacting? Couldn't they see this miraculous but horrifying event?

The coils crackled with violet energy, interspersed with veins of scarlet and an ugly colour like bruised flesh. Then *it* jerked, swung about fluidly, and rocketed towards me. I could go nowhere. I was strapped to the stretcher and was being bundled into the rear of an ambulance. No one was paying the ethereal serpent any heed.

I yelled a warning. My mouth didn't open. The scream was for no one's ears but mine and for the *thing* racing towards me with singular intent. The thing that wore the features of my dead brother, Cash. It jerked to a halt, rising up over me, head swaying like that of a cobra dancing to the charmer's flute. This time I did open my mouth to shriek, and the ethereal creature dove at me, screeching likewise. It forced its way into my mouth, my throat, then deep inside, coiling and tightening around my soul. Whatever diabolical rites he'd been practicing, whichever demented devil he'd been offering up the sacrifices to, it had allowed him to come back from death – but not in a way in which he had ever expected. He'd been granted immortality in spirit, but he was trapped within the mortal coil of his greatest enemy.

SEVEN

Broom's Cottage, Connor's Island

One of those ironies of life: a cobbler's child often goes barefoot. It's the same idea when you see a builder's home and there are slates missing off the roof, or there are cracks in the brickwork. The craftsman is far too busy with his workload to look after his own abode or, as it was with the cobbler, to make shoes for his children. The same could have been said for me when I was involved with Rezpect Sports; though we designed and retailed fashionable sports clothing, I was never seen in shorts and vest, and God forbid you'd see me in a tracksuit.

My point being?

Well, the last thing I expected when approaching Paul Broom's home was something like the witch's house out of Hansel and Gretel. As a writer of horror and dark fantasy tales, I knew that his imagination leaned towards the gothic and macabre, but I also knew him for enjoying his luxuries and the niceties his modest wealth brought him. This small crofter's cottage with its time bowed walls and sunken roofline came as a bit of a shock. The dilapidated building wasn't my main surprise. It was the wood and bone chimes that hung from the eaves, the ominous scarecrow in the garden, the leering skulls surmounting the gateposts that gave me pause. Not to mention the crimson pentagram etched into a panel decorating the front door.

The windows were blacked out. Or maybe he'd simply dropped the blinds and the interior was in darkness. If not for the torch Broom played intermittently in my direction, the scene would have been in full darkness. The fact that he flashed the torch over these quirks of exterior décor meant that he intended for me to grasp the overall impression he'd tried to achieve with his spooky props. I shook my head at it all, a smile dawning where previously there had been none.

From beyond the house I could hear the swish of surf on a pebble beach, and the wind rasped the boughs of imported trees in a copse partly concealing the cottage garden. The scarecrow, topped off by the skull of a deer, creaked on its pole. Also, the wind chimes clattered in discordant symphony. Above all, I could hear Broom whistling *Strangers in the Night*. The guy was such a ham.

Certain that he was aware of my approach, I called out, "Hallooo!"

"Hallooo, right back at you!" He was at the gate to his property, torch in one hand, a mug of coffee in the other. By the amount of rain falling, I guessed that the coffee would be well watered down by now. As I approached, I saw him set the mug on top of one of the gate stoop skulls. Then he strode towards me, meeting me with arms outstretched. "I was beginning to think you'd had a change of mind and decided not to come visit."

"I expected to be here sooner than this," I told him. Then, in my best Bugs Bunny impression, "Musta took a wrong turn at Albuquerque."

"But you're here, anyway," he said. "And that's all that matters."

I'm moderately tall, but Broom stands a head taller again. Not what you expect of an academic or someone who spends most of his time at a computer keyboard. He puts me in mind of a professional wrestler with his stature, his beefy shoulders and arms, and his flowing blond hair. Nothing at all to do with the bear hug he caught me in and lifted me off my feet. He squeezed me with ill-restrained affection.

"I guess it gets lonely out here, huh?"

"I am so happy to see you!" He grinned, giving me another squeeze, the torch in his hand uncomfortable against my lower spine as he bounced me up and down.

"Alright if I breath now?" I wheezed.

"Ha! Ha! Breathing is for weaklings!" he said. I swear I could feel my ribs cracking.

"Enough…pleeeaase…"

Finally he let me down. I swayed like I was back on the ferry again. Broom gripped his mug and torch in one hand and placed the other in my lower back to steer me towards the front door. I couldn't have resisted if I tried. I was propelled over a path of crushed shells, but my feet barely made a sound. In comparison, Broom's limping gait of crunch and drag reminded me that, as powerful as he looked, one leg was partially crippled as a result of a head on collision between motorbike and tree. Maybe it was this accident that left him perched in front of a computer instead of grappling in the squared circle. More likely, it was down to his gentle heart.

"Got a huge pan of soup on the stove. Thought you might be hungry after travelling all day."

"I'm okay," I said, but the thought of a bowl-or-three of Broom's homemade soup had my stomach gurgling in anticipation. I paused at the door. Nodded at the pentagram. "I like what you've done to the place. Is it all your own work or did you hire a P.R. consultant?"

"No extracting the urine, old fellow." He reached out with thick fingers and pulled loose what I now saw was contact paper. He crumpled the pentagram in his fist. "I had a photo shoot with some journalists from *Dark Empires* magazine. Had to titivate the place so it fit with their readers' expectations of 'The Master of Dark Fantasy'. I just haven't gotten round to clearing up after them, yet."

"Wasn't that about two months ago?"

Broom grinned. "Hey! I'm a busy man. Any way, it gives the residents of Conn something to talk about. For some unknown reason they think I'm a tad strange."

"Can't imagine why," I said, acerbic as you like, but Broom didn't notice. Or, if he did, he chose to ignore my wit. He pushed me into the cottage. He flicked on lights.

If the exterior was The Brothers Grimm, then the interior was Essex chic. The living room was all cream carpet, white leather upholstery, metal and glass trimmings, and a plasma TV screen mounted on the wall that would put some cinemas to shame. The space looked like a showroom for House and Home. Didn't appear lived in.

"I'm going to drip all over your carpet," I warned.

"No you're not, Carter. The kitchen is this way." He steered me to the right, up a couple of steps and into a kitchen redolent with the odours of culinary delights. The kitchen was large, as equally splendid as the living room in the way it had been decked out. The difference was the homeliness of it all, the books spread on counter tops, the dishes in the sink awaiting transfer to the dishwasher. The huge pot of soup bubbling on the hob. Broom bustled past, placing his mug amongst the crockery in the sink, the torch on a counter top.

I stripped out of my coat and Broom hung it on a hook at the rear door. My chino trousers were wet from mid-thigh, testament of the efficacy of my raincoat. Broom offered to put them in the dryer, but I declined. Didn't fancy sitting about in my boxer shorts whilst they went through a cycle.

He tossed me a towel and I scrubbed the rain from my hair. He was also streaming, his blond hair hanging in ringlets round his broad face. Big, tusky teeth set in a grin.

"I really am pleased that you are here," he said.

I sat at his table. "You didn't doubt me, did you?"

"Not for a second. But it is such a long way. I've put you to a lot of trouble."

"Planes, trains and automobiles," I said. "Not to mention the ferry ride from hell."

"And a long walk in this shitty weather."

On cue a drip formed on the end of my nose. "Is it always this wet?"

"Not always," he said, a spark of mischievousness lighting his features. "There was one day last August when the sun got out for an hour."

We both chuckled. Broom took the towel and scrubbed his own hair. Satisfied, he shook out his frizzy mane. Brian May eat your heart out. Then he set to the pan of soup, ladling enough for ten men into each bowl. He brought mine over, pushed some crusty bread at me. "Tuck in, Carter. Don't go resting on formality."

"Your wish is my command, O Master." I went at the soup like a man possessed - if you'll excuse the pun.

Broom sat opposite, spoon poised as he studied me. He sniffed. "You've lost weight. Have you been eating healthily?"

"I eat when I'm hungry." Indicating my bowl, I said, "It just isn't usually as wholesome as this."

"Burgers and shit, I bet."

A shrug of my shoulders.

"What about sleep?" Broom asked, as if he was my personal agony aunt. "Are you managing to get plenty of rest?" He lifted his spoon and aimed it at me. "And no blasé answers like 'I sleep when I'm tired', Carter."

Staring at my bowl, I admitted, "Sleep doesn't come so easy when your lodger is up all night."

"Are you taking anything to help you sleep? I could give you…"

I jerked upright. "No." Then, not so obstructive this time, I went on, "I'm still using the preparation you told me about."

My preparation. A homeopathic tonic that Broom gave me the formula to. It did allow for a more restful night than I could achieve without it. Saying that, for all I knew, the ingredients I'd had mixed for me by a Chinese herbalist could have been sugar and talcum powder. I couldn't deny the preparation offered nothing more than a placebo effect.

Broom wasn't finished yet: "It's important that you look after your health, Carter. Make sure you continue with the preparation. Are you also continuing with the exercises I set you?"

Nodding affirmative, I said, "I do them most nights-"

"Most nights aren't enough. You must do them every night."

"You didn't let me finish, Broom. I was about to say that I do them most nights, but do them *every* morning without fail." I gave him a lop-sided smirk. "Don't worry, I'm not shirking."

He placed his spoon in his soup to give me a slow clap. "Bravo. I'm pleased about that." His gaze grew intense. "It's imperative that you keep up your guard. The only way you can do that is by following the regimen of mind control exercises and meditation I set you. Show Cash the least sign of weakness and he'll exploit it."

Paraphrasing the gospel of Saint Matthew, I quoted back to Broom the verse he'd commanded I absorb and make my life ethos. "Be self-controlled and alert. Your enemy the devil prowls around like a hungry lion, searching for souls to devour."

Highly pleased at the devotion to study of his number one pupil, Broom munched vigorously at a chunk of bread. Around the mouthful he said, "Knew that I could depend on you, Carter."

He wasn't simply referring to my continued self-control practice. I asked, "Did you think for even one second that I wouldn't come when you asked?"

"Honestly?" He seesawed his head. "You don't owe me, Carter. It is your prerogative to refuse."

"How could I possibly refuse?" I held his gaze. He puffed out his cheeks, lifted his shoulders. I placed my spoon in the now empty bowl. "After everything you did for me, the least I could do was answer your call for help."

"Be that as it may. But you're not beholden to me. It's a lot that I've asked, dragging you all the way up here to the middle of nowhere."

"Broom. You can deny it all you want, but I do owe you. If it wasn't for you, I would still be stuck in a mental hospital." I exhaled. "Makes me wonder…maybe I'd be so far gone by now that I'd be permanently sedated and locked in a padded room, staring into space and drooling on my chest."

"I doubt it would have come to that."

"Possibly not," I said. "But only because I'd've taken a swan dive from the hospital roof before it got that bad."

"You're not the suicidal type," Broom argued.

"No. I'm not. But who knows what would have become of me if you hadn't intervened?"

Broom lifted our bowls, headed back to the stove. He served up another portion for ten. With his back to me, he asked, "When I first sought you out, you do realise that it was for purely selfish and not altruistic reasons?"

"I know that your doctorate in psychology gave you certain privileges. It gave you access to patients in order that you could conduct research for your novels. You told me, Broom. Right at the onset, that you wished to speak to me due to my unique case of - as you put it - disassociation-persona syndrome. You believed that it would make interesting subject matter for a character in one of your stories."

"I never did write that story." Broom returned with my second helping of soup. "I realised that you weren't half as interesting as I'd originally thought."

He was joking, and I laughed along with him.

He went on, "When I discovered what was truly plaguing you, it became my personal mission to get you out of there and on to the correct course of treatment."

"When you first approached my doctors with that in mind, I thought that you were going to end up locked in the room next to me."

Broom laughed. "I'm a little peculiar, I'll give you that, but I'm not ready for the nut ward yet."

"Nut ward?"

"Please take that comment in the spirit it was attended."

I waved it off; I'd only been joking, anyway.

"I had to pull a few strings, call in a few favours. In the end you were released into my care. It was only pertinent that I then gave you a place to live whilst you achieved some level of control over your problem. I brought you to me; I helped you because I had to as much as I wanted to. The pleasure, as they say, was all mine. Ergo, you owe me nothing."

I shook my head. "You went way beyond helping me, Broom. You saved my life. For what it is, you saved my sanity."

"But I haven't fully cured you."

I stared at him. His words hadn't been a simple disclaimer. They were loaded with a certain amount of anticipation.

"You haven't fully cured me, no," I said, wondering what it was he hadn't added. "You have given me the strength to cope, though. And that is a gift I can't begin to thank you for."

"Your thanks are given by your presence here," Broom assured me.

"Least I could do." We were going round in circles. Getting nowhere nearer to breaching his reason for asking me to his remote hideaway.

As though coming to the same conclusion, Broom set aside his food. He sat watching me. I returned his attention. Finally, his voice at a whisper, he said, "There is something very wrong on this island, Carter. Something that requires your very special skills."

A sense of foreboding tightened my chest. Unable to shrug it off, even though I'd somehow known what he was about to say, I said, "Go on."

"Something has returned."

I stared into my bowl. The residue of vegetables and meat stock was all that remained. Not the most ideal auger's scrying pool. Still, it worked for me.

"And you've asked me here as you want me to stop it," I said.

EIGHT

Near Ura Taing, Connor's Island

Catherine Stewart was beginning to worry. And there was no doubt in her mind that her concern was justified. That the house was empty wasn't the source of her unease, her children were wild spirits and often did their own thing following the school day. Daily they would arrive home like dervishes on a mission to create uproar, their shoes and uniforms discarded where they fell, their satchels slung over the backs of the chairs in the kitchen. A quick bite to eat, the dirty cutlery and utensils dumped in the sink, homework rattled off with Kalashnikov rapidity, then they would shoot off to secret parts of the island known only to them and their friends. On this remote island – where the crime statistics was practically nil - her children were allowed more freedom than if they lived elsewhere, but it came with a caveat. They had to be home by eight pm and in bed by nine. It was now nearing ten o'clock. It was the tidiness of the house that told her that her children had not returned as instructed. And that did not bode well. It did not bode well, at all.

As a single mother it had been a chore for Catherine to raise her bairns in a manner befitting the staunch moral ethics expected of an islander. She'd managed this by being very strict in her instilling of rules - even if she wasn't in fact the dragon her children often made her out to be. Her rules were simple; no thieving, no lying, no bullying, no foul language, and you only go out once you've had your tea and your homework is done. She knew Jimmy struggled with her first four commandments, but never did he shirk on the latter two. Especially not the one about filling his stomach. Bethany, on the other hand, wouldn't dare to go against her will in regards of any of the rules, and would ensure that her mother knew that she'd fully complied by leaving behind evidence of her meal, and the completed homework set out in the living room for her mother's perusal. It didn't matter that this only made Catherine's workload all the more difficult on top of the eight hours late shift she'd already put in at the fish cleaning plant down at Ura Taing on the island's southern tip.

The sink was as empty as it had been this morning after Catherine had cleaned away the breakfast dishes and seen the bairns off to school. She tasted bile in her throat. If it had been the summer months she could have easily believed that the children had been slow in returning home and had been caught up in some adventure or other. But it was full dark - had been for hours - and the rain and wind would ordinarily be sufficient to send the kids scurrying for home. Something was terribly wrong. Mother's intuition? No, logic told her so. Her children were in danger.

Her first instinct was to lift the telephone and jab out the number for the police office situated over in Skelvoe. Still, she let the receiver fall without making the call. She wasn't yet hysterical and knew that she'd be branded as such by the constable on duty if she allowed her fear to get a grip of her. Instead, she returned to the front door and looked out on the squalling weather. The rain was more a swirling mist riding the air, but the wind moaned over the crags beside the house and she could hear the faint boom of waves from the sea. The sound of childlike voices would be blanketed by the elements. But not so her loudest yell.

"Jimmy, Bethany, come on home now!" Her voice held enough of an edge that the bairns would recognise the fear riding above her anger.

Without waiting for an answer, she stepped out into the night. The rain clung to her face like spider webs. She pulled her cardigan round her body, arms crossed beneath her breasts. Her voice again battled the wind and surf, shrill and piercing.

Shuddering, she crossed the garden to the boundary fence, where she stood pressed up against the spars so that the sharp points dug into her thighs. She made her throat raw with her prolonged shouting. Still no reply. She glanced at the house, considered the phone. Not yet. She clambered over the fence onto the stunted grass marking the beaten path over the hill at the back of the house. The bairns usually used this short cut from the school bus stop. Water pooled around her feet at each awkward step.

She crested the hill out of breath. She wasn't unfit, must have been holding her breath. She made almost imperceptible noises, like a small, panic-stricken creature. Her legs ached, a mix of adrenalin and cold making her footing unsteady. She paused, eyes digging through the night. Grass, rocks, the plantation of spindly fir trees off to her right. The hill swooped down to the coast road below. Off to her left she could see the sulphurous glow of the town lights from Skelvoe reflected off the low-lying clouds. Nothing else. No movement. No hurrying children. She started down towards the road, following the trail through the grass that the children had beaten down on many previous journeys.

She shouted again. Hollered their names without realising she was doing so. Her breath came sharp and staccato, her stumbling footsteps more rapid than the lay of the land forced. Her shoes were full of water, her jeans saturated to the knees. She couldn't care less. These were only minor discomforts compared to her current problem. Contrary to everything, including the rumours regarding her liaisons with legible widower, Thomas Rington, her children were her only concern. They were all that mattered. Nothing in this world came before them.

Half skidding, she scrambled down the hillside. Loose pebbles were kicked loose, the sound of their decent muted by her pulse pounding in her skull. The noise startled a feeding crow and it shot into the air shrieking at her sudden intrusion at its banquet table. In defiance it threw itself at her face, wings beating in frenzy before it wheeled away and took up a safe distance, watching her through eyes the colour of sump oil.

The thought barely registered: a crow feeding at night…in this weather? Maybe it was the weirdness of it all, perhaps it was something subtler, some primal instinct that forced her from the path. She stepped over to where the grass grew tall. To where the crow had been gorging itself.

Before her breathing had been forced, short gasps. Now it resembled the puttering of a labouring engine. Her knees gave out and she fell onto her palms, her neck taut, her eyes bulging. The shuddering in her innards extended outwards and she sprayed vomit onto the grass, over the backs of her hands. Her stomach heaved again. Sickness splashed over the crow's dinner. Over the scuffed shoe. Over the cuff of the grey trousers. Even over the pale flesh and splintered shinbone protruding out of it.

Catherine's mind rebelled. It couldn't be true. But the involuntary reaction of her body spoke volumes.

"No," she moaned. "No, no, no, no. Not my boy. Not Wee Jimmy."

NINE

Broom's Cottage

I don't know too much about guns and the like. As co-founder of a sporting goods line, I was more inclined towards clothing and running shoes, my expertise in shooting having only fired an air rifle or two during my youth. So I had to trust him when Paul Broom showed me the SIG Sauer semi-automatic handgun that he fetched from a strongbox in his bedroom. He told me that it was a model that held nine rounds, didn't have a safety catch, and only required me to simply depress the trigger repeatedly to fire all nine rounds in rapid succession. The gun was coloured a matte black - Broom informing me with a fervent sheen to his face that this was the same model favoured by covert anti-terrorist operatives as it did not reflect light, so did not betray their position whilst waiting in ambush. Also, because of its lack of non-essential switches, it was easily concealed under clothing and could be drawn quickly without fear of snagging on cloth. 'I learned all that from reading my favourite thriller author, who I'm sure knows his stuff.'

"I'll take your word for it," I said.

"Here, Carter. Try it out."

Broom handed me the gun. There was no magazine or load in the gun, yet it still appeared surprisingly light to my hand. Some people are fascinated with guns; they relish the weight, and the power it imbues, in their hand. I'd never had such feelings before now, but I have to admit that there was something comforting about the way the grip fitted my palm. It was as though Broom's SIG had been built with me in mind. I couldn't help raising the barrel and pointing it at my distorted reflection in Broom's plasma TV screen in the adjacent living room. 'Go ahead, punk. Make my day,' I quoted in my best Dirty Harry snarl.

Broom placed a hand on the gun barrel, guided it towards the floor "Let's not have any Elvis moments, huh?"

"It isn't loaded," I reminded him.

"Regardless. Never point a gun at anything you don't intend shooting."

"What if I never intend shooting *anything*? To be honest, I'm a little concerned that you've actually handed me this thing."

Broom walked away from me, fetching a box of ammunition. 9 mm Parabellum, it said on the carton. He began feeding cartridges into a magazine.

"I said 'what if I never intend shooting anything'?"

"Sometimes that choice is not yours to make," he said.

I placed the gun down on the kitchen table. "Not my choice to make? You're kidding me, aren't you? Put it away, Broom. I won't use it. I'm not…capable."

Broom's features became chiselled planes. "Not capable? I beg to differ."

"Beg all you want; I couldn't shoot someone."

"So you think."

"I don't think it, Broom. I bloody well know it."

His reply was a disparaging chuckle. The dead eye I shot him earned little response. He merely came over and pushed the magazine into the gun. He pulled a slide, feeding a bullet into the firing chamber.

"At the expense of dousing your enthusiasm, may I take you back to that hellish night when you were being tortured by your brother? Back to the water mill. You had just witnessed Cash cutting your baby out of Karen's womb-"

"Fuck it, Broom. Do you have to?"

He held up a consoling hand. Placed the SIG on the table. "Sorry, I don't mean to be so graphic. I'm merely attempting to prove my point."

I leaned both hands on the table, hung my head. Eyes closed. Felt the buzz, the rush of hatred within.

"It's show time, bro."

"When Cash had you tied to that post and was cutting strips of flesh from your chest…"

"Okay. Enough!" I reared up, inhaling sharply. "I get where you're going with this, Broom. And the answer is yes! Without a doubt. Without fucking pause. If I'd had that gun with me, I'd have emptied it in Cash's face. And when it was empty, I'd have slammed his skull to a pulp with the barrel. It's likely that I'd have rammed the fucking thing right down his throat and made him choke on it."

"Ouch! That's brutal, brother."

Broom winked. "All you need is the correct set of stimuli."

Phlegm cracked in my throat.

"You are capable of killing," Broom went on. "You've proven that once."

I shook my head like an old dog attempting to shake a flea out of its ear. "That was different. That was an extreme *circumstance*. Nothing I could ever imagine could come close to that ever again."

"So you think."

I thumped my knuckles on the table, shaking empty soup bowls and the ammunition box. "That was the worst imaginable thing ever. I lost everything. I lost the woman I loved; I lost my baby, for Christ's sake!"

"Yeah, but you gained a soul companion."

I snatched the gun from the table. "Fuck you, Cash. And fuck you, Broom. I'm not a killer. I'm not like either of you. I couldn't shoot anyone."

"Even if that someone was as bad as Cash was?"

"Even then."

"I don't believe you."

MATT HILTON

"I don't care. I'm telling you." Contrary to my words, I lifted the gun and aimed it at an imaginary target. Broom shifted out of my line of fire. "No one could be as bad as Cash."

"Thanks, I'll take that as a compliment. I think."

Broom pursed his lips. "I hate to disillusion you, Carter. And this isn't to take anything away from your hurt, but, believe me, there are things out there that make Cassius Bailey look as sweet as a choirboy. His crimes pail into insignificance when-"

"Don't fucking say it," I snapped. "What Cash did to me…to Karen…to my son…" Words caught in my throat.

"Attaboy. You tell him, Carter." I felt heat behind my eyes. *"You put the facetious ponce in his place."*

Broom leaned against a counter top. Nonchalant, head drooping. All he needed was a cigarette hanging from his lips and he'd have done a good impression of the Marlboro Man - sans the Stetson.

"If you had to protect someone you care for," he blinked up, including himself in that equation, "or it was someone you became emotionally involved in, you would kill. It's human nature."

"I'm not emotionally involved with anyone; don't think I ever could be again. Not after what happened to Karen." But even as I said it, an image of the woman from the ferry flashed into my mind. Janet. Archaeology student. I pictured the slope of her nose, her full bottom lip, and her glittering eyes as she'd watched from the minibus as she'd been carried away from me by the ageing hippy. I shook the cobwebs loose. Stared at Broom. "Any way, who the hell do you think I'm going to have to shoot? You still haven't explained yourself. What was all that about needing my special skills?"

Broom gripped my shoulder. I allowed the barrel of the SIG to drop.

"Tomorrow morning, after we've had breakfast, I'll take you down to the beach and you can practice shooting tin cans. For now, mind you don't go and shoot yourself in the foot."

73

I sniffed, but laid the SIG on the tabletop, angling the barrel away from us. "You're avoiding the issue, Broom."

"I'm not avoiding the issue; I'm trying my hardest to soften the blow."

"I don't like the sound of that."

He shrugged, sloping away from me.

"Or the way you keep side-stepping the question. Who is it that you think I might have to shoot?"

"Didn't I hint at that earlier?"

"Not to my recollection."

"I mentioned that there was something wrong on the island."

I raised my brows, puckering the scar on my forehead.

"I told you that something had returned." He looked at me as though his enigmatic explanation should be enough. Call me ignorant, but other than the unerring pull that had brought me here with a sense that I was needed, I wasn't sure there was any basis to the feeling until the revelation had hit me over my soup bowl earlier.

He pushed his hands into the pockets of his jeans. Standing like that his height wasn't so imposing. He had the bent aspect of a frail old man, or the drooping boughs of a willow tree.

"Do you recall our conversation when I asked you to come here?"

"Yeah. Most of it."

"Do you remember how I said that you weren't beholden to me, that it was your choice, that you could refuse to come?"

I nodded. "We've already been over this, Broom. After you got me out of hospital, supported me, nursed me back to health, how could I refuse to come?"

His mouth twitched. He rolled his shoulders. "I'm no saint, Carter. As we have most assuredly ascertained, most of my reason for helping you was for purely selfish reasons."

"*Most* of your reason was selfish," I reminded him. "But you went way beyond your needs, didn't you? I know that. You know that. Then, somewhere along the way, you and I became friends. Round about the same time, your helping me became unconditional. You aren't as selfish as you like to make out."

His lips quirked. "No it isn't that. I simply realised that you were handy to keep around. It was good that I had someone to put out the rubbish, wash the dishes, iron my clothes and stuff. I didn't even have to pay you the minimum wage."

"Gee, thanks." We were both smiling now. "Now I feel really special."

"Is this where we hug and then go and snuggle up on the couch and watch some chick-flick together?" Broom laughed.

"I wouldn't say I was *that* grateful," I said. "But, really, you asked for my help with a problem. I said I'd come. Here I am."

"And like I said, you're not beholden to me." He nodded at the gun. "Does giving you the SIG change things between us?"

"As long as you didn't ask me here to kill someone."

"Not someone. I thought I'd already made that clear."

"Some thing."

"Some *thing*," he emphasised. "Contrary to what you believe, I think that your special skills go beyond anything anyone else could possibly offer."

"My special skills? You keep saying that, but I don't know what it is you're referring to."

"Oh, Carter. I think you do."

I frowned. It was just for show. Both of us knew it.

"I'm talking about your ability." He withdrew his hands from his pockets, folding them under his armpits. "Your inclination to sniff out evil."

I snorted. Made me sound like some sort of wild boar snuffling for truffles. "Now you're getting weird."

He held up a finger. "Weird is my middle name."

"Any way," I asked. "When did you come up with this idea? It's not as if I turned into a psychic over night."

"Your ability has nothing to do with psychic or mediumistic powers," he pointed out.

"I'm glad about that," I said. "I don't want to depose Van Helsing in your affections."

"That would quite simply be out of the question." He smirked at me. "Van Helsing's the main man."

"W.W.V.H.D. I remember."

He formed his fingers into a make believe pistol, aimed at my chest and pulled the trigger. Satisfied that he'd put things into perspective, he went on. "However, my good friend, I think that you come a very close second in the old demon hunting stakes."

I laughed, shook my head. "Have you been sniffing the correction fluid again or what?"

He chose to ignore me. Instead he explained, "You've been all the way to Hell and back again. Something about your experience has given you an affinity with evil."

"You are speaking in metaphors, I hope? Regardless of what I told you about Cash, I didn't have one of those near death experiences. No tunnels or bright lights for me. No harp music. I sure as hell didn't go someplace full of flames and little pointy-hoofed men with toasting forks."

"Not that you remember."

"Trust me, Broom. It wasn't anything like that." It was my turn to fist my hands in my pockets. "Only place I went was straight to the bottom of the river. Luckily my hang up call to the ambulance had brought everyone running. A young copper dove in and dragged me to the surface. I was dead. Had been for a few minutes they reckon. If it hadn't been for the paramedics throwing a few thousand volts through my heart, I wouldn't have made it. I'd have lain at the bottom of the river until nature took its course and I came bobbing up to the surface like a cork. The point I'm trying to make is this; other than being dead, nothing remarkable happened to me whilst I was at the bottom of the river. Everything was just black. No thought. No conscience whatsoever. No Heaven. Certainly no hell, either."

"Like I already pointed out. Not that you remember." Broom gave me a self-satisfied grin. "You - and you're hitchhiker - are definitive proof of an afterlife. How can you find the notion of heaven or hell so ridiculous when you believe you are possessed by the spirit of your dead brother?"

"Oh, that's an easy one," I said. "I'm as nutty as squirrel shit. And so are you by association."

Broom turned down his mouth. "Neither of us is mad."

"Not even a little?"

"Switching track," he said. "And attempting to explain myself to one obviously too ignorant to understand the implications of such a God-given gift, I believe that you did indeed see Hell. Maybe only for a fraction of a second. But that was long enough. The distillation of pure evil recognised you for a righteous man, and it latched on to you. When you were snatched from its grasp it sent your brother after you. Cash, however, was too late to drag you back down below and instead became your prisoner. I truly believe that God intervened. Came to your aid. Made you master over the beast, as is correct in His law."

I stood there looking at him. Drool threatened to pool in the ditch made by my lower jaw. Broom was weird. For a trained psychologist his overwrought imagination was downright unbelievable.

"See, Carter," he went on. "You touched the devil. Now, due to that, you have this ability to draw evil towards you, or you to it. Imagine if you will a gigantic magnet. Then imagine that evil has substance, like small, twisted fragments of metal. You Carter are like that magnet. It is inevitable. The evil will come to you."

"Y'know something, Broom? For such a noted writer you sure do use some cheesy clichés. I mean…magnets and fragments of metal?"

He jutted out his jaw. Effrontery wasn't something Broom did very well. "I was keeping it simple. I do that when talking to an ignoramus. I thought I'd already made that obvious."

"Ignoramus, yeah. But not completely gullible." I stepped closer. "Have you actually listened to what you're implying?"

"Have you?"

"I've listened. I just can't believe what you're saying."

"Surely I made it clear. Cheesy cliché aside."

I giggled, slightly too hysterical for my liking. "How did you come up with this madness?"

"I didn't. You did."

"Me?"

"It's truth or consequence time, Carter." He stepped away from the counter, towered over me. Forced me to look up to meet his challenge. "When we spoke on the phone, what was the first thing that struck you?"

I had to think. "I was glad to hear from you."

"Uh-uh," he said, his hair swaying. "That wasn't it at all."

Chewing my lip I stared up at him; a minor battle to see who would blink first, who would glance away. Broom won. I studied my boots. "I knew you would call," I admitted.

"And you knew something was wrong."

My boots blurred out of focus. "Yes."

"How?"

"I don't know. Something just felt *wrong.*"

Broom snapped his fingers, the noise shockingly loud. "There! You felt it. You felt the stirring of the evil." He clumped away, grabbing a book off a pile of volumes stacked on the work top counter. He opened the book and held it out for me. It was an atlas. I saw the chain of Shetland Islands. My eyes immediately sought out our current location. Connor's Island was an insignificant blemish on the page alongside the larger islands. "I recall you asking me how island life was treating me. This was before I even told you where I was. You knew without thought where I was."

I could deny it all I wanted, but admittedly, he was correct. I'd been conversing with Cash on the subject for five days before I received Broom's telephone call. I knew that Broom would call. Knew that I would be travelling to an island whose name I'd never heard mentioned before. My main concern, that which had frightened me most and had caused me to seek the aid of my immortal enemy while holding him chained in the desert of my mind, was in truth a feeling that something immensely dark and evil awaited my arrival on Connor's Island.

I looked across at the SIG. Reached for it. Again it fit my hand like the caress of a lover. "Whilst we're playing truth or consequence, can you tell me one thing?"

"I'll try."

"You know what it is. It's why you gave me this gun." I weighed the SIG in my palm. Now it was as heavy as a house brick. "How the fuck do you expect me to shoot evil?"

TEN

Skelvoe, Connor's Island

Sergeant Shelly McCusker anticipated an extremely long tour of duty. As it was, ten-hour night shifts could be interminable on Connor's Island, but this incessant wind and rain ensured even the most determined thief remained behind closed doors. She had been hopeful of a little excitement earlier in the evening when she'd stopped and questioned that Carter Bailey character. Disappointingly, the check of his details showed that he was clean. Nothing on record said that he was a danger, but she'd noted something in his demeanour that warned her otherwise. Maybe it was simply a reflection from the dashboard of the police car, but she was certain she'd caught a flash of scarlet in the depths of his eyes when she'd spoken to him. Uncharacteristically, this had made her turn from him, allow him to go on his way without further interrogation. When Bob Harris offered to give the man a lift across the island she'd almost swallowed her tongue. Deny it as she might, but there was something about Carter Bailey that frightened her. Not easy for a police sergeant to admit.

She'd dwelled over Carter Bailey these last couple of hours, to a point that she couldn't think straight. In the end, even Bob, supposedly her subordinate, had grunted angrily at her and sunk into his own melancholy. Now they were parked on the headland overlooking Skelvoe's harbour, their headlights ineffectively probing the dark oblivion over the sea.

"I'm going to step out and have a cigarette," Bob Harris said. Nothing in his tone suggested that he was asking for her permission. Shelly frowned, but didn't deny him his fix. Bob was your old school copper, six feet four, stocky, slightly overweight, and it was no easy task for him to extricate himself from behind the wheel. He was sparking up even as he clambered out into the wind. He stood in the headlights' beam, shoulders bent against the precipitation. His exhalations were snatched away by the breeze, wraiths dematerialising in the mist.

Shelly leaned forward, pressed buttons on the in-car radio. Anything to pass a few more seconds. The addition of digital technology ensured that reception was clear, but that only made sense if someone else was indeed doing any talking. The radio was silent. Nothing to grasp her attention. She sat back, exhaling. Long, long night. Only seven hours to go. Bob's pack of cigarettes was wedged into the space behind the handbrake. She picked them up. Read the health warning. So what if smoking caused male impotence? She drew out a cigarette, stepped out the car. "Bob?"

The constable turned to her, blinking rainwater out of his eyes. Droplets clung to his sandy lashes and to the tip of his nose. He was cupping the embers of his cigarette in the palm of his hand. "Sarge?"

"You can smoke in the car if you like," Shelly said.

He reared back a half step. "Thought it wasn't allowed."

"It's not. But who's going to tell?"

Bob Harris wavered.

"If I join you," Shelly said, holding up the appropriated cigarette, "you know that I won't be running to the inspector with any tales."

Bob forced a smile. "Fair enough, Sarge." He started round the front of the car and Shelly slipped back into the passenger side. Bob leaned down at the door. "I thought you'd given up?"

"Three months, two weeks, three days." She checked her watch. "Four hours. I'm gasping for a smoke. Get in, Bob, and for God's sake give me a light."

Bob flicked the stub of his cigarette into the night. It sparked and flared as it tumbled off the headland into space. With much grunting, Bob settled himself back in his seat. He reached for his packet, slipped out a second cigarette. "I'll have another one with you, didn't really enjoy the first one." He struck a flame from his lighter, touched it to his cigarette. He leaned across. "You sure?"

"Positive." Shelly inhaled. "Whoa! Head rush."

"Wish it still did that for me," Bob said.

"I'd forgotten what the first kick was like. Takes me back to when I was fourteen and had my first drag. Behind the bike sheds at school."

"You surprise me, Sarge. I didn't take you for a rebel."

"There are many things you wouldn't take me for, Bob," she said with a mischievous smile.

"Pray tell," Bob said as he settled back in the driver's seat. "Help pass the time with a few old war stories."

Shelly took another drag, sitting back, eyes half shut as she attempted a smoke ring. Her mind on her schooldays, a cheeky story involving boys from the neighbouring college almost on her lips.

"Echo Victor One."

The sudden intrusion of the voice almost sent the cigarette flying from her lips. Shelly blinked in confusion, searching for a safe hiding place for her forbidden ciggie. Bob was watching her, tongue on his bottom lip, eyes sparkling.

"It's just control," he said, reaching for the hand mike. Shelly swung back and forth, settled on the digital readout. TALK GROUP 1. Dispatch all the way over at Lerwick on Mainland Shetland. Echo Victor One was the designated call sign of their police vehicle.

"Echo Victor One receiving. Go ahead." Bob held the mike up as though the dispatcher's answer would emanate from it instead of the speakers in the dash.

"Echo Victor One, what's your status?"

"Mobile. North headland. Skelvoe Harbour." Bob's reply was perfunctory.

"Confirm you are double crewed?"

"PC Nine two three and Sergeant sixteen twelve."

"Sergeant sixteen twelve," the dispatcher said, avoiding now Bob Harris' presence in the car. "We have an immediate response call from a Mrs Stewart. Noble Croft Cottage. South End. Near Ura Taing."

Mrs Stewart? Shelly dredged her memory. "Would that be Catherine Stewart, Control?"

Already Bob had started the car, was reversing out towards the road. He flicked on the blue lights. The sirens weren't necessary. Traffic - like everything else tonight, excepting the rain - was light.

The dispatcher came back on. "Catherine Jane Stewart. Born twelfth December seventy-two. No warrants or locally wanted. No markers. But we've had previous calls from this address. Domestic violence. Husband is George Stewart. You want me to check him out, Sarge?"

"Negative, Control. George Stewart is deceased. The boat that sank off Quillan's Point last year." All this was unnecessary banter. Shelly mentally shook herself. "Nature of the call, Control?"

There was a momentary pause. Shelly didn't like it when the dispatchers seemed unsure. Didn't exactly give her a fuzzy feeling when the precise nature of a call for help was unclear. Forewarned is fore armed, as the saying goes.

When the radio next blared the female dispatcher had been replaced by a gruff male voice. Inspector Clift. "Report of an animal attack, Sergeant McCusker. Treat as urgent. Possible Foxtrot."

"Inspector," Shelly acknowledged. "Can you show us attending, Sir?"

The engine revving with a banshee's howl, Bob throttled along the coast road as it swung above the town. The two officers shared a glance. Shelly noted the paleness around Bob's lips, at the corners of his eyes. She assumed that her own face bore the same pallor.

"Possible Foxtrot," Bob muttered under his breath. "Shite."

"Yeah." Shelly sighed. "Shite is exactly what I was thinking." Despite the vulgarity her voice was that of a small child. *Foxtrot*. Not a word a police officer ever liked to hear. Cop code for "fatality". Read that as dead. Usually suspicious. Usually messy.

Bob drove with an unerring accuracy that made use of the natural curves of the road, making good headway. Whilst he concentrated on driving, Shelly called up Control and again spoke directly to the force room inspector. "Anything further, Sir?"

"Nothing further at this time. We received the call from Catherine Stewart. She was distraught, not making much sense. She hung up after a few seconds and we can't get her to pick up the phone."

"Did she say who was hurt?"

"Negative. She was just screaming about it looking like a wild animal…mentioned biting and clawing. That's all we have at this time."

"Thanks, Inspector. ETA is a couple of minutes. I'll update Control on arrival."

Shelly was acquainted with Catherine Stewart. Knew that she had two small children. They lived at a pretty remote location just above the village of Ura Taing. Alone, as she recalled, since George's untimely demise. "I hope it's not one of the children."

Bob squinted into the slanting rain. "I don't get it," he said. "Animal attack? What kind of animals have we got on Conn that could kill anyone?"

His question was pure rhetoric. The simple answer was none. In fact, Shelly was finding it difficult to think of anything more vicious than Andrew Clairey's elderly collie, Jip. Even the surly old collie dog wasn't capable of breaking skin these days; last Shelly remembered was fifteen years old Jip having lost all but one of its canines when it had chewed its way from its kennel to go hunting a bitch in heat a couple miles over the island.

There were other dogs. Will Gower had his Jack Russell terriers, Sam, Pip and Frodo. Rob Wallace owned an Airedale terrier - Jip's alluring femme. Grant and Heather Irving had a poodle named Chrissie, for Christ's sake! Not a one of them capable of more than a nip at a jogger's ankles.

There were of course the guard dogs employed up at the submarine tracking station at Burra Ness, but Shelly doubted that any of these dogs could be responsible for an attack at this end of the island. For a start, should one of the dogs have escaped, she would have received a call by now. The dogs were expensive commodities and the base security team wouldn't allow them to run free.

Sheep, fowl, goats, even the short, stocky, indigenous breed of pony, didn't bite or claw people to death. Neither did the two dozen-or-so cats that prowled the harbour streets, often the police's only companions during a night shift.

At the southern end of the island it was a little more verdant than the moorland at its centre. Fir trees, sustainable copses, clung to the ridge above the coast road. The rain teemed from the heavy boughs, making crazy rivulets on the road surface. Bob simply blasted through the pooling water with nary a concern for aquaplaning or otherwise. The gumball lights made the woodlands strobe surreally, a flickering pattern of shadow and hard-edged neon.

To approach Noble Croft Cottage you would ordinarily follow the road around the curve of the land, before picking up a trail that swung round a wooded hillock and adjacent to the ocean inlet that the cottage overlooked. Bob applied his brakes early. The car slewed to a halt, adjacent to a steep embankment on their right. Shelly didn't question his daredevil manoeuvre; she too had spotted Catherine Stewart mid-way up the embankment. She was kneeling in the tall grass, leaning on her hands. Her ginger hair hung in rain-soaked bunches around her face. Their harsh blue lights etched sharp planes into her features. Her eyes were huge as she stared at the police car. And even over the thrumming of the engine, the constant drumming of rain on metal, Shelly heard the keening wail issuing from Catherine's twisted mouth.

Shelly experienced a jolt in her innards, the kick of endorphins, the queasy sensation of spurting adrenalin. It had been a year or two since she'd come anywhere near as close to this trembling excitement; normally police life on Connor's Island was the stimulation equivalent to painting skirting boards. Fingers shaking, she rummaged in the back seat for her hat, grasped it and pulled it to her chest. Bob was already exiting the car. In his professional urgency, his usual awkwardness wasn't in evidence. He was three or four paces away as Shelly grasped at the microphone.

"Echo Victor One to Control," she said, clambering out, the microphone cable at its extent. "Can you show us at scene?"

"Received." The force room inspector continued to monitor the transmissions. "Please advise as to situation as soon as possible."

About to confirm the request, Shelly looked again for Catherine Stewart. She saw the woman rock back on her knees, lift something and show it to Bob Harris. The constable stumbled to a halt. He slowly turned and looked back at his sergeant. Seeking direction. Seeking a grain of understanding. But Shelly had nothing to give. Nothing in her experience prepared her for what Catherine held up.

It was the first severed head she had ever seen.

ELEVEN

Broom's Cottage

Admittedly, the bedroom at Paul Broom's house was more than marginally comfortable. Compared to the billet I'd rented at the Sailor's Hold back in Skelvoe I would go as far as describing it as palatial. Plus the accompanying sounds were the soft ticking of the central heating as opposed to chainsaw snoring, muted late night TV, and the clearing of throats I could have expected at the hotel. Didn't mean I could sleep any better than normal. More than the intrusion of Cash's constant grumbling troubled me. Obviously the madness that Broom had flung at me was a sore point. Carter Bailey: Demon Magnet. A notion as *way out there* as that was bound to give me nightmares. But that wasn't the only thing impinging upon my dreams. I also had a certain lady archaeologist on my mind.

Surely I had no right to my thoughts of Janet? We had barely met. Our conversations had been nothing more than strangers exchanging small talk during a stressful voyage. Her interest in me was simply due to me being an unfamiliar face in a familiar setting. For God's sake, the woman was married! I had to keep reminding myself she belonged to another man therefore she was unattainable. What was I doing imagining my mouth on her pouting lips, or gently kissing her trembling throat? What was I doing imagining her petite body as it might look devoid of her bulky waterproof anorak - or any other clothing for that matter? How soft that body would be beneath mine as we locked together? It was growing very near to cold shower time.

At 03:19 a.m. I gave up on the notion of sleep and slipped from under the twisted sheets to pad across the bedroom in my boxers. My bare feet whispered on the thick pile. I entered the en suite bathroom and guided myself towards the toilet without use of a light. I kidded myself that my erection was down to a very urgent need to empty a distended bladder, but it took me a good few minutes to squeeze out a few fluid ounces of urine. For reasons I can barely explain I was angry with my body for betraying me. I loved Karen. Still did, even though she was gone. I had no right experiencing carnal desire for another woman.

Finally I flicked on a shaving light above the mirror. For the second time that night I stared at my reflection. I still didn't like what I saw. My burgeoning designer stubble would require attention again. I was in no frame of mind to see to my ablutions and contented myself with scrubbing my palms through my growth and listening to the faint rasp. I'd have to borrow a razor from Broom at any rate. My meagre belongings and my shaving kit were left at my digs in town.

I allowed my fingers to trail up to the scar on my face, feeling again the risen edges. In my reflection my skin appeared pasty, the scar livid against it. Most people barely noticed the scar, when to me it looked as vivid as a motorway on a relief map. The scar, Broom explained to me, was as much psychological as it was physical. So be it. I'd wear it not with pride, but as a reminder of the night I'd failed to save my loved ones. In a way, it gave me an inkling of self-satisfaction to know that the scar was there. It proved to me that I had indeed suffered, that I had resisted Cash. In these days of cosmetic surgery on tap it would be a simple enough procedure to eradicate the scar, but I was not of a mind to have it removed. Call the scar a badge, if you will, my very own tin star.

If Broom's crazy notion held any truth whatsoever then let the demons know me for whom I was. Let them recognise me by the signs branded upon me by one of their brethren. It was cold comfort at best, but if indeed I was destined to confront evil, then let it be my face they came to despise, the last thing they saw before I sent them shrieking back to hell.

"Jesus," I muttered, an embarrassed smile on my mirror-self. "You are totally cracked, Carter."

In the mirror, the scarlet patina shifted.

"Not now Cash."

"Now would be a good time."

"Not interested."

"Despite yourself, you know that is not quite the truth, brother."

"I need to sleep."

"Is that why you're prancing around with a hard on for cute little Janet?"

I slapped my palms down hard on the sink. Water residue round the plughole shimmered. "Leave Janet out of this, Cash. I don't want you to even speak as much as her name."

"Quite difficult, Carter. Your thoughts are often my thoughts." I held my breath. *"And you just gotta know what I'm thinking about doing to her right at this moment."*

"Cash, you sick fucking parasite, if you as much as mention her again I'll…"

A scraping at my brain was Cash's laughter. *"Hey, go easy on the vitriol, will you, bro."*

"You are a pig, Cash."

"Oink! Oink!" Another scrape, an itch I couldn't scratch. *"But at least I now have your full attention. While you can't sleep, why don't you visit your little brother, huh? Have a nice little tête-à-tête like we used to have in the good ol' days?"*

"I don't want to see you, Cash. It's bad enough that I have to listen to your constant complaining without seeing your ugly face as well."

"Aw, come on, Carter. You asked for my help, didn't you? At least let me do what I promised I would."

I shook my head at my mirror companion. My reflection didn't appear to conform to the rules of nature and remained static. A twitch at the corner of his lips. Eyes like iron nuggets in a furnace. Cash playing tricks. Or maybe it was just me playing tricks.

"In those immortal words…CARTER BAILEY, COME ON DOWN!"

"What the fuck do you want?" I leaned on the sink. Stared into the plughole making stupid word associations. Like the sink, I too was drained.

"I want to talk."

"About what?"

"Us."

"There is no 'us'." I slowly raised my gaze. My reflected eyes were back to their normal hue; Cash playing it cool. "There's me and then there's you. Do I need to remind you what you are?"

He sniffed. Incredibly, I'd touched a nerve. Gave me a warm, fuzzy feeling.

"I know what I am, brother." Cash was the epitome of brash. To hear him calm and controlled, displaying just a hint of pathos, made me squint into the mirror-man's face. *"But do you truly understand what you are?"*

I had no reply for him.

"Love him or hate him - personally I think he's a pompous know-it-all dick head - but your good buddy, Paul Broom, is closer to understanding the truth than even he realises. I think that you suspect it, too. Even if you won't accept it yet."

"I'm a fucking demon magnet?"

"Hey! I agree. Shit metaphor. But good enough under the circumstances."

"Bollocks!"

"I can explain it all."

"Cash, you are a liar. Say what you want, I won't believe a word of it."

"Oh, but I think you will." He shifted in my being, a lazy stirring. *"I have no reason to lie to you about this. Whether you like it or not, we are inextricably linked. It is in my best interest to see that you survive this test. Ironic as it may seem, I want you to live. How do you expect me to gain my revenge on you if some other half-wit claims your soul first?"*

His words gave me pause. Not the bit about him wanting domination over my soul, that was a given. "What test?"

"I'll explain all, Carter, but not under these conditions. You have to come to me."

I gnawed at my cheek lining.

"Oh…and Carter?"

"What?"

"Can you make our meeting place a little more comfortable this time? I gotta tell you, that ol' Mojave Desert thing was a bitch. I'm still trying to get the sand out the crack of my arse."

TWELVE

Within

I descended steps so black that they threw back glistening reflections of my features. Drapes on narrow windows were deep purple or magenta, with sashes of roped gold. Candles flickered in wall sconces. There was no sound other than the clip-clop of my heels on the stairs that in my mind had to be formed of obsidian.

At the bottom of the stairs was a huge wooden door with metal studs, hinges and braces, formidable enough to deter a battering ram. I reached out a hand; saw that my fantasy extended to white gloves and a ruff of lace at my wrist. I blinked, dispelling the illusion and saw only my bare fingers. I twisted the ornate knob and the door opened with a satisfactory squeal of un-oiled metal work. I stepped through the doorway into shadow. Firmly closed the door behind me. Illogically, the bolt on the far side was thrown as I guided it into place by force of mind alone. Only when I knew that it was fully secure did I turn and scan the centre of the room. As I looked, a faint glow bled from its centre, blossoming slowly to show a wing-backed chair, complete with seated figure. I stepped closer, interlacing my fingers behind me and stared down on my brother, Cassius. In keeping with the gothic scene he was garbed in a white cotton blouse with ruffs at the open collar, cream breeches pushed into calf-length black leather boots. Somehow his shaved head and goatee wasn't anachronistic.

Cash shook his head. As was usual he turned down the corners of his mouth. "Let me guess…The Prisoner of Zenda? The Count of Monte Cristo?"

"The Pit and the Pendulum," I said.

Cash glanced upward. No swooping blade. No precariously balanced Sword Of Damocles neither. Perhaps these were details I should have included. He lowered his gaze to meet mine. "Vincent Price I presume? Or is it the crap remake with Lance Henrickson?"

I twisted a lip; I actually enjoyed the updated version starring Lance Henrickson. "In fact, I was going more for the Edgar Allan Poe original."

My brother settled back in the chair. "That Poe dude…one seriously fucked up individual if you ask me."

"No one's asking you."

"You have to admit, Carter. Poe was acutely disturbed."

"That's a bit rich coming from a psychopathic serial killer, isn't it?"

Cash gave me the eyebrow. "You're probably right. Thing that separates Poe and the likes of me, though, is I just didn't pussy around scribbling down my thoughts on paper. I actually had the balls to carry out my darkest dreams. Poe was…what do they call it? Repressed. He was simply play acting."

"And the better man for it, in my opinion."

In my youth I'd read the entire writing of the master of gothic horror. Since Cash hijacked my psyche and invaded my dreams, I often paraphrased Poe. "Sleep. Those little slithers of death. How I loathe them." But I had to admit, my brother had a point; Poe was a strange character and possibly as crazy as Carter Bailey in some people's opinion.

"You should be thankful," I told my brother. "I did contemplate The Man in the Iron Mask."

Cash frowned at me, weighing the probability of me slamming a metal helmet over his face. He smiled, an eyetooth glistening. "No, no, Carter. I've just gained a new found respect for Poe, if you don't mind."

I inclined my chin. One nil to me.

With a rattle of chains, he lifted his wrists. "You think that Poe shared my sado-masochistic tendencies, Bro? Maybe we have more in common than I've given him credit for."

"Who knows, Cash? The manacles are my doing. And I've definitely got nothing in common with you."

"I beg to differ." Cash smiled again. Twice in such a short time was too disconcerting. "We share quite a number of traits. For instance, we were both spawned from the same gene pool. Both products of Momma and Poppa Bailey."

I spat in disgust. "That has to be debatable."

"Are you throwing aspersions on our dear old Momma, Carter? Shame on you!"

"I'm saying that you were probably switched in hospital. Some reprobate gave birth whilst hooked on drugs and cheap sherry, then stole herself a beautiful child and bunged us your maggot infested carcass."

"Whoo-hoo! Maybe you're right, Bro. That'd explain why I was stuck with a wimp like you instead of a real big brother."

In spite of myself, I found humour in his remark. It was about the nicest thing he'd ever said to me. Maybe my dream scenario of Cash's origin had a grain of truth in it.

"I can but wish," I said.

"Nah," he said. "That kind of thing only happens in the soaps. I'm afraid you're stuck with me, Carter. Brothers united, and all that jazz."

"More's the pity."

"Yeah."

Jesus! Something we were in agreement on. I couldn't allow that to continue. Broom's words echoed in my ears, 'Be Self-controlled and alert.' I turned from Cash, nodded into the shadows and a second wing-backed chair materialised. I took my time seating myself. I crossed my legs, hands folded in my lap. Classic psychoanalyst pose I was well used to seeing from the opposite seat. I had to gain command of this meeting; the posture was patronising enough. Now for the attitude.

"You asked me to visit. Now, what is it you wanted to tell me?"

Cash mimicked my pose. The chains on his ankles made it difficult, but he persevered. He offered me a smirk. I gave him a level stare.

"Come on, Cash. Just for once, eh? None of your bullshit."

As far as his manacles allowed, he flicked a submissive hand. "I meant what I said earlier. There is something I need to tell you. Something very important regarding why you came here."

"And all of a sudden you are concerned about my welfare? Sorry, Cash. I just don't believe you."

He rotated his head on his shoulders, languid like a cat. "I told you. I don't want you getting taken down by anyone else but me. I feel a certain responsibility for keeping you out of harm's way - even if it is to ensure that, when the time comes, it's me who sucks your eyeballs out of their sockets."

"That's a reassuring image you're painting," I said.

"Just letting you know I'm deadly earnest about saving your flabby arse, Bro." He flashed a tooth. "Don't think that you'd take me serious if I came over all lovey-dovey and the like."

My lips formed a tight gash. He had a point.

"The big poofter Broom was almost right," he said.

"About my ability to detect evil, you mean?"

He clicked his fingers.

I chewed my inner cheek lining. Even in this astral-like state I retained bad habits. "That's supposing that I believe that evil is tangible, that it can metamorphose itself into a living entity. Personally, I think that's a big pile of crap. We're not medieval peasants, Cash. This is the twenty-first century. Terrorist bombs and super-virulent plagues, I believe in. They are the modern equivalent of the hobgoblins and demons of the middle ages. I do believe in the notion of evil as a frame of mind; you only have to think about Hitler, or Saddam Hussein or Osama Bin Laden for proof of that point. But, as for the embodiment of evil, take Satan or Lucifer for instance, well, I just don't accept it."

Cash sniffed. "It all depends on your outlook, doesn't it? To the Nazi's Hitler was practically a god. People are still dying fighting for what Saddam and Bin Laden stood for. Ask them and it's Bush and Tony Blair who were the evil ones. So that does nothing for proving your argument. Those are political evils only. Different ideologies: playing with words to suit the individual speaker's ethos. That's not the essence of evil we're talking about here."

"He didn't say it as such," I said. "But from what Broom was intimating, he is specifically talking about some sort of demon or something. He's actually setting me up as a kind of modern day dragon slayer. And listening to you, it sounds like you're doing the same."

His eyelids drooped as he sighed.

"Carter, why don't you take a look around you here? You are actually sitting in an imaginary castle conversing with your dead brother. If you can accept this as real, why can't you just open your mind to other seemingly impossible notions?"

"Ha!" I leaned forward, forcing him to look at me. "That's easy to explain. Because that would be admitting that I am insane like so many of my doctors told me. This," I held out a hand, encompassing the entire room in one gesture, "is all nothing but an effect of an over-wrought imagination; a coping mechanism against my grief; a way of reconciling myself with my failure to save Karen and my baby son. Who says I believe any of it is *real*?"

Cash belched, proof of his disdain.

"Psychobabble mumbo-jumbo bullshit," he said. "You don't think that this is real? That I'm not real? Tell you what, brother. If that's what you think, loosen my manacles now and see what the fuck I do to you."

We held each other's gaze, both sets of eyes as sulphurous as the other. The tableau held for an extended heartbeat before I sat back. "Good try, Cash. There's no way I'm going to let you loose. Whether-or-not you are real is purely rhetorical; I can't take a chance that this is all some schizophrenic delusion. If I was to let you loose, and your personality dominated my psyche, God knows what I would become in the outside world."

His lips formed a gloating smile. "What's up, Carter? Afraid that you would turn *evil?*"

Son of a bitch! Outflanked by the arsehole. So much for being self-controlled and alert. Bastard had only been goading me to prove a point. It was time for my eyelids to droop, show defeat. "I hear what you are saying, Cash."

"Uh-hu," he acknowledged. "The incarnation of evil does exist in the genuine world, Carter. Take your paedophile grooming children on the Internet, or the rapist who sneaks into the bedroom of a frail old woman…"

"Or the bastard who rapes and murders the pregnant fiancée of his own brother?" I finished for him.

Again the snap of his fingers. "Exactly."

"You've got a point. There are evil men in this world. Ideology and politics aside, there can't be a person on this earth who couldn't see you as evil."

"You'll get no argument from me." He raised an eyebrow. "You see where our conversation is headed, Bro?"

"You're saying that there is someone here on the island just like you?"

"Not half as ravishingly handsome or erudite as one's self," he smirked. "But, yeah. There's one bad ass dude kicking off big style."

"Who?"

"I don't know."

"Yes you do." I stood up, the advantage of height as a domineering factor not particularly useful when I was visibly trembling.

"I'm not fucking psychic, Carter."

"You said you wanted to tell me…warn me…that there was a test…"

"And I've done all of that. I've readied you, put you on full alert. That was what I needed to achieve. It's all about protecting my own interests. I told you that already, too." He folded his arms, pursed his lips, making farting noises with his mouth. When I didn't demand further clarification, he said, "The test I mentioned is still to come. It's whether-or-not you're man enough to complete it that's important."

"And what is this test?"

"You'll recognise it when the time comes. That's all I'll say on the matter." He watched me with his hateful eyes twinkling. "You can go now."

He turned his head away, finished. I could have forced him into compliance, twisted his neck so that he had to look at me, to talk to me, but I knew that it was pointless. He'd said all he was going to say on the subject - for now. Any words pressed from his lips by force of my will would be hollow, my own words in his voice. Totally worthless as far as explaining anything I didn't already understand.

I turned from him. The chair I'd been sitting in had dissolved, the room itself shimmering into light grey nothingness as I paced away. The wooden door swung open at my gesture, slammed behind me with a hollow thud. I never made it all the way up the stairs.

Instead, I snapped into full cognizance sitting cross-legged on the bed in Paul Broom's guest room.

No confusion or sense of displacement ruled, I knew exactly where I was, who I was. As was usually the case when returning from one of my visits to speak with Cash, I wasn't angry or full of hatred. I actually sensed a lightening of my spirit; oddly I had an inclination towards self-worth and value I hadn't experienced in a long time. My life had found purpose.

It was one of those epiphany-type moments of clarity.

Though I'd never have admitted it to Cash, his suggestion that there were others like him had given me a new awareness of purpose. As well as Cash's argument, Broom had also gone some way towards planting the seed in my mind. He'd said I should see my being brought back from death as a gift. A second chance to put things right. Regardless as to whether I'd ever be able to change the atrocities perpetrated by my brother, I sure as hell could stop others like him. I still stood by my resolve. There were no cloven-hoofed demons out there, but there certainly were monsters. Monsters concealed behind the innocuous masks of men. So be it. If that was the way of the world, then it was only just that I be the embodiment of the monster slayer.

Question: What is evil?

Answer: Man, by virtue of his actions and his thoughts.

Simple when you think about it.

Question: "How the fuck do you expect me to shoot evil?"

Answer: "The only way to be sure? Two in the heart and one in the head."

THIRTEEN

Near Ura Taing

It was divine retribution, Shelly decided. Had to be. Punishment for transgressing the laws of the patron saint of non-smokers. It was her own fault, she just had to go and light up. She was weak-willed, a pitiless wretch who could not abstain as she had sworn to. She had promised on the memory of her mother, dead from lung cancer these past three months, two weeks and four days. As her mum had succumbed, lying there with drips and feeds futilely urging her to hold on to life, Shelly had held her hand and made the silent oath. *No more cigarettes for me, Mum. Don't you worry; I won't touch a single one as long as I live.* Tiny and frail in the hospital bed, her skin puckered and thin enough to tear, looking thirty years beyond her fifty-five, her mother had opened her eyes. "You promise, Shell?" The surprise was outweighed by her grief at the time, and it was only later that Shelly was positive that her mum hadn't spoken out loud. That only strengthened her resolve, verified to her that there was a greater power in the universe, that, even as the big man in the sky reached down a gentle hand, her mother had heard her oath. And obviously held her to it.

The cigarette she'd smoked in the car alongside Bob Harris had been a betrayal of both her mum and the divine spirit who'd allowed them those final words together. And for that betrayal she was now being brought to bear. How else could she explain the horror unfolding in front of her now?

For a sergeant she was young in service. Less than five years. But she had worked hard to attain the position, and continued to work hard to demonstrate that she was up to the promotion. Her two years of probation, and a further thirteen months of independent patrol, had been spent on the streets and dockyards of Aberdeen. The city had highlighted the depravity to which some members of the public could stoop, had given her a shocking lesson in life's dirtier ways. But nothing of the beatings or robberies, the drug overdoses, or the drunken car wrecks had prepared her for this.

Neither, she supposed, had the last twenty-two months since she'd transferred to the Shetlands. A year on the mainland based at Lerwick, as she'd concentrated on passing her sergeant's exams, and then ten months here on Conn chasing sheep off the road and rousting drunk fishermen from after-hours 'lock-ins' at the Muckle Ram Inn. Up until *this* the most gruesome thing she'd had to contend with was - ironically enough - the drowning of George Stewart and his cousin, Alan Dougherty, when their boat had capsized off Quillan's Point last year and she'd joined the recovery effort to pull their water-logged corpses from the jagged reef.

Her heart went out to poor Catherine Stewart. To lose your husband was one thing, but to lose a child must be the most awful situation imaginable. Especially when her wee boy, James, had been literally dismembered and his body parts strewn across the hillside.

"I'm sorry, Mum," Shelly whispered as she lit up another cigarette offered to her by Bob Harris.

She was leaning against the trunk of a fir tree, the boughs heavy with needles that threatened to knock the hat off her head. The god-awful rain persisted and the trees were the only source of shelter in this terrain. The downside was the trickling runnels and the shedding needles falling down her back, which still managed to invade her waterproof high-visibility jacket at her neckline. She shivered, the reaction induced by a cold droplet worming its way down her spine, but more than that she squirmed at the realisation that her first test as a commanding officer was going to shit.

Her vow to never smoke again, which she had so easily broken - twice now - was the least of her concerns. In the big picture she could be forgiven for turning to the emotional crutch of nicotine to get by the shock of what she'd witnessed. But, how in creation was she going to justify passing out cold on the grass, causing Constable Harris to not only have to contend with a traumatised mother but also with his unconscious supposed supervisor? It was no secret among some of her staff that they viewed her as too young, and too inexperienced, to win their respect. That was always going to be a problem, and she'd worked hard to get past the misconceptions, to a point that, yes, she wouldn't win their respect but she'd damn well earn it. But now, having ended up face down in the dirt, she could kiss goodbye to that idea.

"You okay, Sarge?"

She tilted her gaze up to the bluff features of Bob Harris, searching for any sign of reproof or sarcasm. He was forced to stoop beneath the branches, and he was clasping his peaked cap under an armpit. His generally light coloured hair was much darker and plastered to his forehead. His skin appeared bleached; apart from vivid patches of scarlet creeping up from his throat as the effects of the initial adrenalin rush began to abate now that they'd won a moment's respite. The thing that struck her was the clarity of his eyes. Hers, she knew, must be bloodshot and red-rimmed, but Bob's amber gaze was as calm as a pond in summer twilight.

"You're going to tell them, Bob?"

He crinkled his nose. "Tell who what?"

Shelly lifted her chin towards the officers called in on overtime to stand guard over the crime scene while they waited the arrival of a back-up team from the mainland.

Bob made a big thing out of studying PC's Charters, McCall, Brown and McGregor, fifty percent of Connor Island's twenty-four-hour, seven-day-a-week, police resource. Of the island's team, only Jorgenson and Petrie were missing. Both of them had accompanied Catherine Stewart in the air ambulance to the hospital over at West Sandwick on the neighbouring island of

Yell. Not only was Catherine a distraught mother but she was also a suspect in the gratuitous slaying of her son, James. And possibly also that of her daughter, Bethany, who at that time was missing and presumed dead.

After a slow nod, Bob said, "I'll tell them all they need to know."

"Do they need to know about…?" She faltered. Couldn't say 'their sergeant collapsing out of fright'. She didn't need to; Bob fully understood.

"Anybody would have been shocked, Sarge. It's nothing to be ashamed of. I doubt any of them would have handled it any differently than the way we did."

There was an emphasis on 'we' that Shelly fully appreciated. She suddenly began to see Bob with a fresh perspective. All right, he could be a miserable, surly old curmudgeon, but she had to admit, she'd never once heard him joining in with the parade room gossip his colleagues indulged in with almost Olympian effort. Often he was his own man, and appeared not to resist authority but work around it to his own taste, but she couldn't recall a time when he was blatantly disrespectful of her either as a woman or as a senior officer. Maybe her secret would remain between the two of them. Only time would tell. The truth would probably come out as soon as Detective Inspector Marsh arrived from the mainland and demanded a report.

As if Bob read her thoughts he held out a clipboard that he'd secreted under his armpit alongside his hat. "Scene log, Sarge," he said. "I've also set up a single approach path and positioned the others to protect it. Can't say that the scene is easily protected in all this bloody rain, mind you."

Shelly jammed her cigarette between her teeth. Lifted the clipboard. As she'd previously come to appreciate, Bob's paperwork was always immaculate. Even under these conditions he'd taken the time to rule straight lines and the times and names on the sheet were written in small, concise letters. Shame that the rain had smudged the ink in places.

She flickered a glance at him. He was hunched over, but still came across as being an imposing figure. A casual observer would be forgiven for thinking that Bob was the superior officer in this duo. Even Shelly realised he was the image she'd always conjured of the staunch old beat sergeant when she'd dreamed of joining the force. She nodded in appreciation, more for his presence than anything else. The log made no mention of her swan dive in the grass. Bob's handing over of the log was his silent promise that only what was on the log would go into his report.

"Thanks, Bob," she said, almost a whisper.

"Nae problem," he said, and shot her a quick wink.

It seemed that allowing him to smoke in the car had won her a friend. Perhaps it was because her gesture had assured him that she was prepared to meet him on his own level, and for that he would reciprocate. More likely it was because she'd promised that she wouldn't be running to tell tales that he'd decided that she too was worthy of his discretion.

This realisation gave her strength. She sucked in another lungful of smoke, then sent a ribbon of it into the tree boughs. Perhaps in her previously shaken state she'd have automatically flicked the finished stump away, but thinking clearer, she had the presence of mind to pinch the ash off and dropped the butt into her pocket to avoid contaminating the scene. She noticed the smile building behind Bob's features as she watched him follow suit.

"Maybe you want to take a walk down to the shore and wash your hands? We don't want ol' Marshy knowing you've had a fag." Bob eyeballed her.

"Fuck him," she said, feeling the rebel all over again. "I think we've earned a cigarette or two tonight, Bob."

"Aye, and maybe a wee drink or twa, as well," Bob added.

Shelly dry-coughed. "Aye, Bob. That sounds real good right about now." She reached out and touched his wrist, an intimate gesture uncommon to them. "Later, eh?"

Bob sucked in his bottom lip, shrugged like a bashful youth. "Aye, Shelly, that would be nice."

Shelly. Not Sarge or Sergeant McCusker. The walls were tumbling down. Before they were knee-deep in rubble, Shelly decided she had to get back in gear. There was police work to be done. Her social life could come later. Much later if necessary. Until she'd found the monster responsible for the death of this child – children - she had to get her sergeant's head back on her shoulders. All thoughts of men must be put to the back of her mind. Even thoughts of her new found friend, Bob Harris. And of....and of....Carter Bailey.

Now why the hell had he invaded her thoughts again? She'd been distracted by him when this nightmare had first began, and now he was back. In particular the seething flicker behind his pale eyes. The eyes that she'd instantly recognised as those of something *dangerous*.

Call it coincidence, but wasn't it strange that his arrival on Conn correlated way too neatly with this brutal murder?

Too neatly to ignore.

FOURTEEN

Near Broom's Cottage

As the sun broke through watery clouds, I was standing on the pebble-strewn beach just above the high tide line. Drift wood, tattered netting, half an oil drum, all intertwined with decomposing seaweed in a swathe almost fifteen feet wide that stretched the length of the cove. Amongst the detritus tossed up by the sea I searched for viable targets. The half oil drum was an obvious choice, but the damn thing was buried in sand and gravel and way too much bother to attempt to haul out. Instead, I chose a tree limb that had been smoothed to a glistening sheen by the relentless motion of waves against shore. I hauled the branch out of the flotsam and carried it to the strip of land above the tide line. I drove one end into the sand and then strode away.

I over compensated with my first shot. Years of Hollywood brainwashing had me believing that the gun would jerk like a cannon, throwing it upwards as it recoiled from the blast. The gun did buck in my hand, but it was more to do with me holding it too stiffly than any recoil from the bullet leaping from the muzzle. I relaxed for my second shot. I stood with my right foot facing the target, my left foot behind and angled towards nine o'clock. I extended the gun with my right hand, cupping my elbow with the left. Instead of jerking the trigger I squeezed gently, sighting from the rear sight along the muzzle. The tree-limb sprouted a new hollow, and a puff of wood fragments drifted on the breeze. Silently chuffed with my prowess I allowed myself a sniff.

After that there was no holding back. Five more shots obliterated the upper portion of the branch, leaving splinters strewn on the sand. The gun held nine rounds and, yes, I was thinking in terms of the associated jargon already. I decided that the static target was too easily shot when standing taking aim. I shoved the gun into my waistband at the small of my back. Walked away a couple of paces. Then I turned, pulling the gun out and fired on instinct. The last I know is that the bullet flew off en route for Iceland. I was no "Billy the Kid" yet.

I went through the rigmarole a second time, and on this occasion shot the sand five feet to the right and ten feet behind my tree-limb target.

"Bull's eye," I snorted.

"No. Bull shit."

Engrossed in my practice, I hadn't heard Broom's approach through the low dunes. I looked over my shoulder at him; saw him leaning on a walking pole, bolstering his weak leg on the unstable sand. He was grinning. Not at my ineptitude, but at the very fact I'd accepted the assignment he'd set me. This target practice was an end to a means only, but indicated to us both that I was taking his theory seriously that I must become proficient with the weapon.

"I take it you slept on my words and decided I'm not as mad as I first sounded," he said.

"Didn't do much sleeping," I told him. I ejected the spent magazine and inserted a fresh one I'd earlier loaded.

Broom approached me through the sand. Around me were ejected casings. He busied himself with pressing them into the sand with the toe of his boot. "Best we leave no telltale evidence behind, eh?" He paused, lifting his gaze and flicking back his hair so he could see me. "You are aware that the SIG is illegal, aren't you?"

I lifted the gun, pressed the trigger rapid-fire and shattered the remainder of the tree branch. Nine brass casings littered the beach around my feet. "The notion had crossed my mind."

When I next glanced at Broom he was standing hunched over with his hands cupped over his ears. "Shit, Carter! You might have warned me you were going to do that."

"Didn't think about that," I said.

"Obviously not," he grunted. "Shit, I think I'm deaf."

"You aren't deaf; it's just your ears reacting to the percussion. The displacement of the air pressure causes your eardrums to react."

"Shit! You don't say, Einstein? And here was me thinking it was all to do with those loud bangs."

Leary twat. I gave him the dead eye. "You'll be okay in a minute or two."

"Says you…shit."

"Is that your word of the day?"

He returned my weary expression with a hangdog look of his own. "What word?"

"Shit," I told him. "Considering you've used the 'S' word just about every other since you got here, I assumed you were trying out as many possible variations of it to see how it would fit into your writing."

He raised his brows. He said, "Sometimes you surprise me."

"What? That I'm so astute and observant?"

He snorted out a humourless laugh. "No, Carter. If you had actually read any of my books you would be painfully aware that I never…*never*…use any form of profanity or rude words."

"Just gratuitous violence and over the top horror clichés?"

I was pulling his leg and he knew it. Didn't stop him prodding me in the gut with his walking pole. "I'm not the country's fifteenth best-selling horror author for nothing, and that is if you ignore my eBook sales. People enjoy gratuitous violence and over the top horror. They expect it. What they don't like is writing spattered with four letter words and reference to male genitalia. They can get as much of that as they want from the music they're listening to."

"Possibly," I shrugged. "But then again, maybe if you stuck in a couple of swear words now and then, you'd bridge the music and writing gap and become the country's fourteenth best-selling horror author."

He prodded me again.

"You want me to sell out and attract the pimply teenage market, Carter? Shame on you."

"Aren't teenagers the mainstay of your market now?"

He looked scandalised. He lifted the walking pole like a rapier. "Take that back, Carter!"

I dodged his jabbing pole. "Easy, Broom. I'm armed too, remember."

"I care not, lout! You have besmirched my honour. Have at you."

I was jabbed and prodded all the way back to the house. We were like a couple of kids playing at Robin Hood or an under-populated Three Musketeers. Call Broom one wacky loon but he had a penchant for drawing me out of the doldrums. Made me wish that I had a stick of my own; I'd have given him a duel to remember. Stuck with the very lethal SIG Sauer, I had to shove it in my waistband and only go through the motions of parrying and thrusting. We were breathless and laughing like adolescents on helium by the time we tumbled into the kitchen.

Another of his ploys to cheer me up, a full fried breakfast was warming under the grill. I got stuck into it with a zealousness I couldn't previously recall. Something about shooting guns and fun fighting was an appetite builder par excellence.

A couple of cups of coffee down and nothing left on my plate but gobbets of cooling fat and streaks of egg yolk, I sat back, hands on my gut.

"Want more toast?" Broom asked. "Island butter? Homemade damson jam?"

I blew out. "No, Broom. No more. I couldn't handle another morsel."

"Nonsense. You're going to need all your strength." He busied himself with loading more crusty bread into his industrial-sized toaster. I didn't argue. He would see it as a personal insult if I didn't allow him to feed me to bursting point. But not only that; his harmless remark had brought back to mind my reason for being there. Demon Magnet. Monster Slayer. Carter Bailey: The man who *feels* evil.

Watching him flutter round the kitchen like a moth round a bug-zapper, I asked, "All talk of the supernatural aside, how do you go about explaining this ability of mine to sense evil?"

He paused, raising a butter-loaded knife like an exclamation mark. "Do I detect a certain amount of acceptance in my wayward student?"

Pursed lips don't look too good on me. Apparently Broom decided otherwise.

"At last," he said. He layered locally churned butter and clots of jam onto a round of toast and pushed it in front of me. Despite my earlier protestation, I lifted the toast and took a hearty mouthful. The jam was sweet with an underlying bitterness. Excellent. He said, "You don't know how happy that makes me, Carter. Kind of validates everything I've ever done for you."

"I'm still trying to get things straight in my head," I told him. "You know that I'm not a church going man, so I have this problem accepting things like spirits and devils and stuff like that. Maybe if you can put it in layman's terms for me, I'd be more prepared to accept it."

He sat down at the opposite side of the table. "That's fine by me, Carter. Sometimes I do get a little carried away with myself. I blame the writer in me. I do get a tad verbose with everything ghoulish and macabre. But, lest you forget, as well as a fiction writer, I am also a doctor of psychology and of paranormal studies. By their very nature, I am a walking contradiction. I have offered you the horror author's version. Now…in my parapsychologist's role, are you ready for the scientist's take on the subject?"

I smiled. "As long as you don't use too many long words."

"I'll do my best," he said, sighing theatrically.

And so he began.

"Discounting individual theories and ideas, within the mainstream field of science, there have only been three major schools of thought since the seventeenth century. Other than a couple of tweaks here and there these theories about the machinations of our world, our universe, have altered little up to the present day." He counted them off on his fingers. "Isaac Newton, father of modern physics who gave us cause and effect; Charles Darwin and his theory of evolution; Albert Einstein and his theory on relativity. These paradigms have been set in the minds of modern man, and by sticking so rigidly to these 'proven' sciences, we have become disassociated from the real truth."

"That being?"

"That through this indoctrination of the scientific community, we lost sight of ourselves. We came to accept that the universe, the earth we stand on, are governed by certain laws of motion with predictable conclusions. Our world is a machine, man is a survival machine whose only intention is to copulate, eat or be eaten. Don't get me wrong; due to this thinking we have attained technological mastery of our environment, which can't be a bad thing in itself. The problem is, we have lost sight of what we are. The essence of the human on a spiritual or metaphysical level."

"And now we are back to the ghosts and ghouls," I sighed. "Already?"

Broom slapped a palm on the table. Crumbs from my toast vibrated with Newtonian predictability. "No, damn it! We're back to a profound understanding that religious scholars and theologians have espoused for centuries. Think on it, Carter. We are far more astounding than a simple assemblage of blood and bones. We are far more than a chain of genetic changes weeding out the weaker elements, where life is only about winning and getting to the top of the evolutionary ladder. We are more than a simple chemical reaction, for heaven's sake!" He sat back shaking his heavy head. He sucked in a shuddering breath.

Finally he swivelled side on and laid a forearm on the table. "For decades now a number of respected scientists from all over the world, experts in a variety of disciplines, have been conducting controlled and documented experiments that prove what the ancient scholars already knew; we, as humans, are not a chemical reaction but an energetic charge. Human beings, in fact all living things, are a coalescence of energy interconnected to every other thing, be it a rock, a tree, whatever. Call it a leap in quantum physics if you wish, but it was discovered that there exists an ocean of microscopic vibration between all things - the Zero Point Field. An unimaginable force of quantum energy that holds the key to life itself: cell communication, DNA, even ESP and spiritual healing, are all now thought to be powered by this energy.

"This in itself isn't a new school of thought. For one the Druids espoused this notion thousands of years ago. Certain Native American tribes, too. Thing is…these scientific experiments have re-discovered this truth. It flies in the face of current biology and physics, but it can't be refuted. This energy exists."

"Like 'The Force' in Star Wars?" I offered, trying hard not to sound as if I was taking the piss.

"If you like," he said. "But it is more commonly referred to as The Field.

"Have you ever paused to wonder, Carter? How does life begin? What is the spark that ignites the chemical reaction and turns a single cell into a fully formed person? How do we think? Where does our consciousness reside?" He lifted a finger. "The brain? But is not the brain powered by a series of electrical or 'energy' impulses? At our essence, we are energy. This energy is our soul or spirit. Energy - think of it as an electrical charge - can be changed. This has been fundamentally proven. But it can never be destroyed. Agreed?"

"So I've heard." I perked up then. Something grounded in science that I was familiar with.

"Okay. So if we are governed by energy, that the energy is our soul, or if you prefer, our consciousness, what happens to our consciousness after we die?"

He sat and looked at me and I looked right back. The ticking of the cooling toaster was a metronome timing our blinks.

I never could win a staring contest.

"Sounds really 'New Age' and hippy to me," I mumbled.

"So what? Those are only names used in derogatory terms these days. Forget about the images you have of pot-smoking-tree-huggers as layabouts and wasters for a moment. Okay, maybe their lifestyle doesn't suit everyone, but does this mean their beliefs are wrong? This new age thinking is based upon the Druidic wisdom, after all. And in its most intrinsic form, the Druids of Celtic times were saying much the same as science has now come to accept. This field of energy surrounds everything, impregnates everything living and otherwise."

"So what is it that you're saying exactly?" I asked. "That I am some sort of conduit for this energy?"

He seesawed his hand. "Sort of. But more specifically, you are a conduit for the dark side of this energy."

"Uh-oh. Darth Vader territory."

"Scoff all you want." He stood up, began pacing. On a roll now. "Are you familiar with homeopathy or some of the eastern medicines? Acupuncture? Acupressure?"

"Yeah, and I see where you're going. Holistic healing. The laying on of hands. Needles in energy meridians. That kind of stuff."

"Yes, in your intellectually challenged manner, that kind of stuff." Broom sat down again with a scraping of chair legs. "In the eastern disciplines of medicine, the energy - the same energy we've been talking about - is seen to be the alpha and omega of our existence, a constant flow and fluctuation of good and negative energy. Too much of the negative and we get sick. Their medical practice is based upon restoring the flow of good energy, dissipating the negative, restoring our well-being."

"Paul Broom, the Yin-Yang Man," I said, my thought process and mouth working co-dependently but way out of synch. Broom didn't appear offended. In fact he looked quite pleased.

"Yin and Yang. Exactly," he said, a gleam in his eyes. "Most aptly demonstrated when you view practitioners of certain martial arts performing outstanding feats. Tai Chi and Aikido for example are based upon harnessing and using this energy, termed Chi or Ki respectively, to blend with and defeat the negative energy of an attacker by neutralising it and restoring the balance or the Yin-Yang."

I was nodding along with him now. I was not totally unaware of eastern martial philosophy and had myself taken a few classes in Aikido as a youth. At the time, I was unable to 'blend' as my Sensei continually extolled, but I did witness some amazing results performed by the black belt students and the Sensei himself. In my western mind, I thought Sensei's almost superhuman feats were solely down to years of practice to a point his movements had become perfect and balletic, but he had explained that, no, for the art to work he had to be 'in Ki' with his attacker. At first I thought his reference was to being keyed up, full of vigour and enthusiasm, but I soon came to understand that he was referring to something subtler: the blending of mind, body and spirit of both attacker and defender. Like many youths I was too impatient to achieve results, and found that more often than not I was relying on my physical strength to power on a lock or throw. I of course thought I was The Man, but in reality I achieved nothing more than clumsy attempts at control, and gained a few pissed off training partners along the way. I gave up Aikido shortly afterwards and took up boxing instead. Putting my fist in someone's face I understood. Problem was, I received more than I gave, bringing me to understand that maybe there was more to fighting than the physical game. Dejected, I gave up on the boxing, too.

The next time I witnessed anything like 'the blend' my Aikido sensei spoke of was when I watched James Pender, my ex-business partner, on the tennis court. His movements appeared to almost predict where the ball would be next. His skill went beyond mere mechanical perfection and positioning. He was at one with his opponent. In Ki, I suppose. I didn't realise it at the time, but by definition, any competition is a battle. A banging of heads, a conflict of styles, an imbalance of the Yin-Yang.

"What you're saying is that I've become some sort of Yin and the evil is the Yang? As we cannot exist without the other we are intrinsically drawn together?" I said it without the least trace of incredulity.

Unbelievably, Broom gasped. "Bloody hell, Carter! I thought this was going to take more of an argument on my part."

"Didn't say I believed it," I said. "Just that I understand what you're implying."

"Theoretically it's a sound assumption, no?"

"Okay, and say I accept the theory, how does this explain how both Cash and I wound up in the same body?"

"All I can come up with is this: You recall how we determined that if energy can't be destroyed, then something must become of the consciousness after physical death?"

I nodded.

"Well, all I can assume is that at point of death, just as your spirit - for want of a better term - was about to undergo whatever metaphysical transformation is ordained, it was snatched back from the brink by the intervention of the paramedics' defibrillation of your heart. You were called back to your body, the physical receptacle of said energy. Cash died at the same instant. Maybe, due to his proximity, or by the very power of his hatred, or negativity, he leapt into the closest receptacle he could find. Perhaps because his consciousness was still active, he wanted to continue the battle and clung to your essence in order to do so." He paused. "I once read of a Tibetan belief that the life essence of one person can be installed within the body of another by following certain rituals. It is a practice utilised where the flesh of a body is unhealthy, but the consciousness, the wisdom, of the dying person is worth salvaging until a time that the injured body can be restored. At that point the spirit is liberated and then returned to the original body."

"Yeah, I saw a movie about that once." I said. "Steve Martin and Lily Tomlin in *All of Me*."

Broom gave me a jaded look that said he doubted my sanity. "Steve Martin? You mean the comedian?"

"Yeah. It was a good movie." I said. "Very funny." And it also reflected much more of my own possession by Cash than I hated to admit.

"Steve Martin?" Broom said again, almost a whisper, like he couldn't believe a comedian could have hit on something all Broom's much-vaunted scientists had striven to prove for decades.

"Thing is," I went on, before his mind had a total collapse, "in the movie, Steve Martin had control of only one half of his body, whilst Lily Tomlin had control of the other. Why isn't that the case with me and Cash?"

Broom waved the notion aside. "Comic license, I suppose. Probably set up a few funny walks and urinal jokes, no?"

"You've seen the movie, then?"

"Ha! I wouldn't give it the benefit of my attention." He plucked at the front of his wool sweater like he'd suddenly noticed an annoying itch. "There is nothing mentioned in the Tibetan practice that the second spirit has any influence over the first's physical actions."

"Unless said second spirit happens to be the Dali Lama," I pointed out, informing Broom that I wasn't totally ignorant about the subject of transference. "Doesn't he supposedly have full control of the new body he inhabits?"

Broom shook his head. "In the Buddhist faith, Lama is the title for those people who are believed to be the reincarnations of a *bodhisattva* or god. It is different than in your case. The *bodhisattva* inhabits the body of an unborn foetus at point of inception, at the spark that initiates life. This foetus does not have a singular spirit of its own. In effect the *bodhisattva*, or lama, is an avatar, a god made in flesh."

I shrugged. I reached for a few spilled crumbs on the tabletop and began pushing them around in random patterns. I had no recollection of finishing off the toast Broom had placed before me. But just because I could no longer see the toast, or in fact taste its lingering flavour in my mouth, it didn't mean that the toast didn't exist in my stomach. Crap metaphor for Cash's energy installed wherever it was my conscious-self resided. Call me Carter Bailey: Existential thinker for the New Age.

Broom said, "It has to be down to the relative balance of each of your energies. Because you were the original inhabitant of your body, when you returned, it was as a full balance of good and negative energy. Your field was restored so to speak. But with Cash, his negative energy won out. But as an incomplete essence, he has been weakened to a point that your energy holds him in check."

"When I go inside myself," I said, "I imagine scenarios, just as you said I should. I see Cash chained or locked behind bars. Is this really necessary? If he is weakened and I'm in full control…can he harm me?"

"Not physically, Carter. At least, I don't believe so. Whilst it is an untested scenario, best we err on the side of caution and leave things as they are. You must beware; his negative essence is at full strength. He could hurt you at a spiritual level if you allow him to do so. Keep the chains in place; they are your talismans against him. They ensure that you remain separate and distinct individuals. I'd hate to see the outcome if ever he found a way to tap into your negative energy. The imbalance then would be exponential. I don't know what you would become."

"Darth Vader territory all over again," I said. But this time I wasn't being sarcastic.

FIFTEEN

Trowhaem, Connor's Island

The overnight rain had made the archeological dig a quagmire. It would be hours before further excavation could commence, hours of shifting collapsed dirt and pumping out a few feet of accumulated water. The sputter and cough of generator-fed pumps were already in evidence, but the university archeological team was fighting a losing battle. There was too much seepage from the surrounding cliffs overwhelming the site for the pumps to contend with.

Harry Bishop, ever the enthusiast had formed a human chain of bucket wielders, but his extortions of faster! faster! went unheard by his grumbling charges. Slogging in knee deep, viscous soup wasn't conducive to either speed or enthusiasm.

Janet watched Bishop from the vantage of the cliffs above. He moved amongst the other archaeologists like a dreadlocked, bearded, stripey-pullovered titan. Spattered with mud and bellowing ill-received praise he did not portray the image of the professor of anthropological study he was. He was more like one of the Vikings of lore whose bones they now strove to excavate. All that was required was to replace his shovel with a sturdy battle-axe, his bucket with a shield, and he could be Odin come to Earth. Ironically, Bishop was blind in one eye, though he had lost his sight due to a cancerous tumour rather than pledging it in return for a knowledge giving drink at the Well of Mimir as had the Norse god.

Bishop was lead archaeologist on this dig, so it was important that he be seen to marshal his troops into activity. Results were expected of him by his financial backers as well as by the university directors back in Edinburgh. If anyone could motivate the team to action, Bishop was the man for to the task. And, rally them he would. The students working under him would give their eyeteeth for Harry Bishop. Not only was he their professor, their teacher, he was also their inspiration. Students flocked to him, and he was willing to give them back the same level of attention they lavished on him. They loved him, and he loved them right back. Especially the young doe-eyed girls who sought out extra-tuition after hours. Bishop was a good man in all respects…except that of a faithful husband.

Bishop was laughing, flicking mud speckles at Kiera McCann. Flirty Kiera, giggling way beyond the joke, allowed herself to fall up against Bishop's chest, her fingers lingering too long on his biceps than modest propriety allows. Janet shook her head and turned away.

She fingered her wedding ring. Bishop - in certain respects - reminded her of her own husband, Jonathon Connery. Watching Bishop worm his way into Kiera's pants wasn't something she cared to do. Brought back too many bad memories. Like the time she'd come home at the mercy of a virulent twenty-four hour bug, looking for hugs and sympathy from Jonathon, only to find him in bed with some slut from his office. The smarmy bastard had actually laid the blame for his infidelity on the amount of time *she* spent away from home! It was all her fault for not showing him the attention he required. Was it his fault that he had to look elsewhere to assuage his basic human needs? Those had been his actual words: *'assuage his basic human needs'*.

Well, his basic human needs were now his own problem. It didn't matter how many times that he'd come round begging for reconciliation, she simply could not get the vision of her husband and his whore out of her mind. He could plead all he wanted, or make his threats to ruin her if she didn't take him back. Anger didn't work on her either. Jonathon could go straight to hell on a one-way ticket. As could every other philandering pig like Harry Bishop.

Christ! Even Pete Johnston, her under graduate assistant, had turned out to be a two-timing creep. Pete was nine years her junior and at first his advances had been of the shy type befitting his tender years. Entrenched in rebound city, Janet had welcomed his flirtation. Only thing was, that was as far as they'd gone; the occasional light lingering touch of fingers when handing her a specific tool or paper, an embarrassed laugh shared whilst squeezing past each other, that sort of thing. He'd asked her out to dinner. She'd politely refused. Maybe another time, huh? Then he was off with Toni McNabb, and that was that. Things were too uncomfortable between them after that. Pete hadn't returned to the dig after the weekend break a fortnight ago. Neither had Toni McNabb.

That was probably for the best. Professors forming relationships with students was the kind of thing best left to Harry. And age gaps were definitely Jonathon's thing.

She kicked at a clod of soil, then walked stiffly over to the VW minibus. Thoughts of Jonathon's betrayal often angered her. Time isn't the healer some people profess. Only complete immersion in her work was. She opened the front driver's door and climbed into the seat. On the passenger seat was her laptop computer. She cobbled up the cable attachment and inserted it into the now defunct cigarette lighter, and powered up the computer. Pressing keys, she brought up a detailed map of Connor's Island. Unlike modern relief maps, this was a reproduction seventeenth century painting, showing the lay of the land as a series of less than expert brush strokes, the surrounding Norwegian Sea as a solid cerulean blue. Though less than perfect the map retained the distinctive hourglass formation of the island, and she touched her finger to the point where the western coast nipped in at the waist. Here was marked a nameless settlement, a single stone cairn surmounted with an anachronistic Celtic style cross. Before the island was renamed for Admiral Hubert Connor in 1787, following his routing of the pirate fleet working out of Skelvoe, the island had a different name. Then the wild island had been referred to as Trowhaem - quite literally Home of The Trow. The nameless settlement by default had now acquired that name in the mind of Janet, Bishop and the others at the site.

Trowhaem was the original and only major settlement on the island, built around the western inlet, where once over sleek-prowed dragon boats moored to replenish stocks of water and mutton for the onward journey to Iceland and further mystical journeys into the blue west. As a port it was an important destination for the rugged Norsemen, and it had grown to rival some of the better-known landfalls of the Shetland and Orkney islands. That was before some inexplicable turn of events had changed the fortunes of both the port and the island in general. Quite simply, the seafarers stopped coming. It wasn't a slow process; it was almost as if the port had been abandoned overnight. Plague, some scholars argued. Had to be. Nothing else could explain why it should be abandoned so dramatically. Nor with such vehemence and hatred of its name. For more than two hundred years, all who remembered the name cursed Trowhaem. Inhabitants of neighbouring Yell and Unst avoided the island and the surrounding waters as though even to approach was to attract bad luck. Trowhaem quite literally became Home Of The Trow in both act and in deed.

Ordinarily abandoned settlements became the building blocks of new villages and towns. This was evidenced on the British mainland where many abbeys, monasteries, castles, even Hadrian's Wall, had been looted for ready made building materials after fortune changed hands and others began to stamp their mark on the landscape. When people began to return to the island, people less superstitious than their forebears, they should have raided the ancient port for the dressed stone to construct their own buildings. It seemed though that the curse of Trowhaem persisted, even in these newer, more enlightened times. Not only did new materials have to be quarried, but also the arriving settlers located their new port of Skelvoe on the opposite side of the island. Scholars said that it made sense; on the eastern coast of the island, the new port was better protected from the open Atlantic weather, more accessible from the neighbouring islands. But it seemed like an awful lot of bother to Janet. For one, the town itself had to be constructed on the side of steep cliffs, and secondly, hundreds of tons of stone had to be manoeuvred out into the waters to form the promontories that formed the bay itself. Far too much effort than was necessary, in her opinion. It was as though the anathema that was Trowhaem persisted even after two centuries, and even, in some respects to the present day.

When the excavation of Trowhaem was first announced it was met with resistance. Islanders banded together in defiance, but in the end, all their mutterings of curses and bad omens held little sway in academic circles. Plus, the land making up the northern half of the island, and the swathe around the western inlet where Trowhaem was located, had been purchased wholesale in the early 1950's by none other than the Ministry Of Defence. Ultimately it was down to the government to make the decision on whether permission to dig was granted. The military aren't exactly known for their concerns for ancient curses and fairy tales. The dig began in the spring of 2012.

Ordinarily the island inhabitants would have been employed as contractors, but it seemed that old fear was more potent than the allure of wages. Off-islanders had to be drafted in for the initial work of clearing the landslide that had devastated much of Trowhaem in the late nineteenth century. Work progressed into the late autumn before the inclement weather kicked in and brought things to a grinding halt. A second phase excavation had began in May of 2013, the majority of work now carried out by field students drafted in from Edinburgh, Glasgow and Aberdeen. Trowhaem was beginning to take shape. Until this god awful weather that had plagued the island off and on these past few weeks. This latest deluge had set them back yet again. Maybe the curse of Trowhaem wasn't a product of simpler folk, after all.

Janet gave a sad smile. Persons of her educated persuasion did not believe in curses. She was a scientist and in her viewpoint only specific and proven fact held sway. There was no room whatsoever for flights of superstitious fantasy.

Not then. Not as she sat in the VW clearing her mind of the very real betrayal by her husband. But ask her again twenty-four hours later, and she would have to admit that her ethos had changed. Dramatically.

SIXTEEN

Sailor's Hold, Skelvoe

"Had I known you only intended staying the one night, I wouldn't have been so forthcoming with the rental. Missed out on a four week stint from a marine biologist who arrived on the same ferry as you, I did."

The proprietor of the Sailor's Hold was a stunted fellow, whose head, disproportionate to the rest of him, appeared far too large and heavy to carry around for any length of time. The fact I'd rousted him - and his basketball-sized head - from his easy chair in order to check me out of the hotel was probably to blame for his grumpy attitude.

He hadn't caught up with technology yet, so it was a leather bound ledger he pressed towards me for signing. I found my original signature listed second from the bottom of the page. With a name like Sigmund Van Murik being the final entry, I guessed that the marine biologist had indeed been given room and board and Mr Proprietor was telling fibs about lost revenue. Some marketing ploy, he had. I traced the column next to my name, tapping the figure scribbled to indicate the fee I'd already paid. I gave him the rheumy eye. "You can keep the difference in lieu of having lost a sale," I told him. As his eye edged towards where I indicated, I intentionally let it slip below that of Van Murik's payment. His gaze flickered away, caught in the lie.

I didn't say anything further. Handed him the key and kipper-sized fob, then hauled my backpack onto my shoulder.

"You didn't say why you're leaving so soon," the proprietor said. "Were you dissatisfied with your accommodation?"

"The accommodation was suitable for my needs," I said. There was no need to explain myself, but if I have a fault, it's that I'm not very good at complaining. If I'm eating in a restaurant, for instance, and my food is cold, I eat it and keep my complaints to myself. Karen used to get mad at me for that. But complaining was something that I remained uneasy with. "I'm not leaving through any reason associated with your establishment. The room was fine. I didn't get to eat whilst I was here, but I'm sure the food is fine, too. It's just that I've made other arrangements with a friend on the island."

"Would you mind endorsing our visitors' book with that? It's good for future business."

Carter Bailey: non-complainer. My list of nom de plumes was growing. I stood and scratched a fictional entry into the visitors' journal whilst Paul Broom stood shaking his head and tapping his toes on the linoleum.

As we walked out the hotel onto the harbour front, Broom said, "I hope you wrote that the place was a shit hole, and worth passing up for the more inviting accommodation available beneath the pier."

"I should have," I agreed. "But I'm way too polite for that."

"Way too soft, you mean," Broom said. "How you ever made it in business, I'll never understand."

"Politeness is not a weakness."

"No? Not even when you're being run over rough shod by the less-scrupulous?"

"Even then," I said. "I could always sleep soundly at night, knowing that I wasn't cheating those I dealt with."

"Maybe you're right." Broom laughed. "I recall one of your advertising strategies read 'Pay for the over-priced brand name, but get the T-shirt absolutely free'."

I chuckled. "I couldn't believe it when that approach actually worked. I think people purchased our range because they enjoyed the joke."

Side-by-side we walked along the harbour, our pace determined by Broom's dragging step. Broom ruminated. "I wonder if I could market my books along those same lines."

"Here's one for you," I offered. "Health warning: Purchasing this book may cause side effects including recurring nightmares and feelings of intense dread."

Broom didn't buy that one.

I said, "Maybe you should write about me, after all. Then you could put 'Warning! This book contains nuts'."

That one got a laugh.

Broom steered us towards a café. The place shrieked nostalgia. None of your retro-chic that had invaded the mainland high streets, this café was real oldie-style with chequered vinyl tablecloths, slat back chairs, sauce bottles growing grapes of drying spillages around the neck. Your tea came in a mug, and if you asked for coffee you got the finest instant granules available. Latte and cappuccino and espresso were from a foreign language, by God! Everything came with a side plate of chips, and if you expected a salad you'd have to make do with a leaf of lettuce, slices of tomato and beetroot direct from the jar. The café was lorded over by a gaunt old man in an off-white coat who appeared to be wearing some other person's dentures, and he stood poised at a gleaming metal dispenser, ready to pour forth hot or cold Vimto depending on your taste.

I absolutely loved the place.

We sat at a table near the entrance. Judging by the tinfoil ashtray, the smoking ban in public places didn't extend to Connor's Island. Or, if it did, the law held no sway here. Broom took out a slim cigar and lit up. Made me wish I smoked so I could join in the rebellion.

"Two of your finest bacon sandwiches and a mug of tea apiece, Stan?" Broom called to the owner.

The old man smiled around his dentures, showing gaps at the gums. He made a couple of false starts at the Vimto dispenser, before shuffling towards a side door and calling out our order to an unseen accomplice. He returned to his place at the counter, started rubbing at an imaginary ugly spot on the counter top.

"Business slow today, Stan?" Broom asked.

"That it is, that it is," Stan the café man said. He had a strange syntax that made him sound like he was about to break into song.

"Reason for it?" Broom asked. "I thought with the rain stopping, there'd be plenty of people around this morning."

Stan gave that vacant look of one who didn't comprehend what was being said. "Aye, rain's stopped."

I looked at Broom and he shot me a wink. "Conversation isn't Stan's strongpoint, but you can't bypass his bacon butties."

Broom didn't temper his volume, so Stan must have heard everything. Didn't sway his enthusiasm. The comment about his bacon sandwiches outweighed the subtle insult behind Broom's comment regarding his level of intelligence. Maybe his brain was addled with sixty plus years of hot Vimto fumes. Whatever, he continued smiling, rattling his false teeth, and rubbing at the counter top.

In a final attempt at drawing words from him, Broom asked, "Don't you normally get the lunchtime rush, Stan?"

"That I do, that I do."

Helping out, I asked, "You wouldn't do me a glass of Vimto, would you, please?"

"That I would," he responded happily, swooping on the shiny dispenser. "Hot or cold, sir?"

"Cold will do."

His face drooped, but by avoiding the hot drink I hadn't dented his self-worth. Surrounded by the gurgle and hiss of the machine, he said, "Everyone's took a drive down Ura Taing way."

"Ura Taing?" I raised my eyebrows at Broom.

"Village down the island a ways. There's a fish packing plant, a used farm implement saleroom and about a dozen houses. Don't know what's exciting enough to get everyone down there. Unless there're whales off Quillan's point again. That sometimes draws a crowd."

Stan wasn't as deaf or uncomprehending as he liked to make out. "No, it's down to some accident or other. They say some child lost his life and there's another one gone missing."

Stan's words struck me with the force of a bob sleigh with faulty brakes; very hard and icy cold. I sat blinking at him, waiting for him to rectify his statement. Perhaps say something along the lines of, 'No, I mixed that up. There are no dead or missing children.' But all Stan did was blink back at me, adjusting his ill-fitting teeth as he added the fruit cordial to my drink.

I didn't receive a retraction. I'd heard correctly. Without question a child was dead, a second child was missing. It didn't take embellishment - or Broom's knowing glance - to tell me that the *'something wrong on the island'* had just made itself known.

Fireflies swarmed in my gut. A hot fluttering sensation that could have been the spurt of adrenalin but was wholly wrong and different to any endorphin boost I'd ever experienced in my life. The heat built within, radiating out from my core, extending into the ether like seeking tendrils. It was almost as if Broom's Zero Point Field theory responded like a live and sentient being with the validation of Stan's words. I sank into my chair, feeling as though the cause and effect of the building energy was thrusting me back like I was a pilot in a fighter jet.

Broom was watching me with a mix of wonder and mild trepidation. As I noted this, the feeling within me dissipated with the abruptness of a popping balloon. Released from this unusual effect, I jerked forward. I practically slapped the table to stop from rolling directly over it. Stan, in the act of delivering my drink, pulled back, gasping and splashing plum-coloured stains on his smock coat. He did a double take direct from the silent movie era as he looked first at me, then to Broom. It was as though he was begging the question why Broom had brought such an apparent loony into his fine establishment.

"Hey," I said quickly. "I'm sorry I startled you."

Stan watched me with an ounce of distrust, but his indoctrination of servitude won out and he stepped forward to place the drink before me.

"Sorry," I said again. Then, to reassure him that I wasn't the secret odd ball Broom had been keeping locked in the attic, I said, "It's terrible, isn't it? A child has been killed?"

After a quick readjustment of his dentures, he affirmed, "That it is. That it is."

Broom asked, "Have you heard what happened, Stan?"

Stan shook his head. "It's only a rumour at this time. Police have been arriving all through the morning. CID from Lerwick. Some of those Scenes of Crime people. They've got the road closed off just this side of the Stewart place. Do you ken Cathy Stewart, Mister Broom?"

Broom shook his head, but then pointed his cigar at Stan. "Isn't that the woman whose husband was killed last year?"

"Aye, the very one. Lost her man, and now they say she's lost her son. The wee girl is still missing, too."

Quite a detailed rumour, I thought. Cagey, so not to further disillusion our host, I asked, "What else are people saying?"

In response I received a squint and a shake of the head. Stan turned his attention to Broom. "There's been talk…as *you* know."

Then Stan walked away. He returned to the steaming machine and began adjusting levers. I looked to Broom for some kind of explanation, but he remained as enigmatic as Stan. All he gave me was the smoke from his lungs and a nod of his large head.

"Talk? What talk?" I asked.

Broom glanced at Stan, then back to me, before leaning forward conspiratorially. "Tell you later."

I was about to push him further, but the door to the kitchen squealed open and a more rotund version of Stan bustled out balancing bacon sandwiches and mugs of tea on a chipped tray.

"Food's arrived," Broom announced.

He didn't appear fazed by what we'd just heard - or the demand in my eyes to know more - and tucked into his sandwich with the usual gusto he reserved for food. On the other hand, my appetite was gone.

SEVENTEEN

Police office, Skelvoe

Their shift had become increasingly long, and both Sergeant McCusker and PC Bob Harris were incredibly fatigued. The thought of getting any sleep was wishful thinking at that point in time. Something grasped at but unattainable. Out of reach.

"You should go home, Sarge. It's been a hell of a long night."

Bob slouched at the computer, elbows on the desk. His hair had dried long ago, but without the benefit of a comb it had formed curls across his scalp and over the tips of his ears. He reminded Shelly of the gruff, but softhearted, Irish-Bronx coppers that populated the black and white gangster movies of the nineteen forties.

"You've been at it as long as I have, Bob. Why don't you go home?"

"Just finishing up with this file, then I'll be off." Bob didn't make a move to add anything to the script on the monitor.

"The file can wait until you come back on duty this evening, Bob. So long as you leave a copy of your notebook for CID, the rest can wait."

Bob looked up at her. Shelly was perched on the corner of a desk, rubbing at an ache in one of her knees. Her face was pale, as much to do with fatigue, as what they'd discovered at the crime scene.

"Why do you have to hang around, Sarge?"

"I've just a little bit to do on the computer, then I'll be out the door behind you."

Bob indicated his screen. "You waiting to use this one?"

"No. It's okay. I'll use the one in my office."

132

Bob batted a dewdrop off the end of his nose. He continued to eye her. In the end he smiled sheepishly. "What is it, Sarge? You obviously want to say something to me."

"Why'd you think that?" Shelly, caught off guard, also gave an embarrassed smile.

Bob indicated the small squad room. All the others remained on duty at the scene out at Catherine Stewart's property. Even though, the room was cramped with only the two of them taking up space. "Not exactly a sergeant's hang out."

Shelly shrugged. Looked around, feigning interest. "Maybe I should spend more time in here with the team. Maybe they'd think better of me if they started to see me as one of the gang."

Bob grimaced. "Not a good idea if you ask me."

"Why not?"

"Get too close to them, they'll start taking liberties," Bob explained. "I'll guarantee you that. Best you keep the little space you have; elevates you above the rest of us."

Shelly studied Bob's face. Exhaled through her nose. "Is that how you see me, Bob? As being above the rest of you?"

Bob lifted his shoulders. "You're the sergeant, Sarge. Of course you're above the rest of us."

"In rank only," Shelly pointed out. "But not on a personal level, surely?"

Bob sat back, awkward in his own body. "I wouldn't know, Sarge. I'm not one for getting personal with those I work with."

Shelly laughed. "I just want to make a few more friends, Bob. I'm not talking about having a love affair."

The big policeman laughed also, but it was one of those embarrassed sounds that said *that* was exactly what he had been thinking. Shelly blinked, frowned. "Hang on, Bob. I hope you haven't got the wrong idea here? I wasn't hanging around to hit on you or anything. When I mentioned going out for a drink together, I was talking purely as a friend."

Bob waved a large hand. Forced out a chuckle. "I ken that."

But Shelly was studying him. Was that regret in the droop of his eyebrows?

His disappointment had a knock on effect she hadn't expected. For some reason they both cleared their throats at the same time, and Shelly found herself slipping off the desk and standing up straighter, pulling at her equipment belt. Maybe not a good idea after all, considering it tugged at the cloth of her shirt, emphasising her breasts. By the impulsive lifting of Bob's eyebrow, he too had noticed. Shelly quickly turned to riffle through a pile of statement paper. Both of them laughed hollowly.

Bob stood up, pushed his fingers into his own belt. "So…now that that's been cleared up, what was it you wanted to say?"

Residual smiles plucking at the corners of their mouths, they stood looking at each other from opposite ends of the desk.

Shelly said, "Two things really."

"Aye?"

"First thing," Shelly said. "I wanted to thank you again for keeping quiet about me passing out."

"Not a problem. What's the second thing?"

"Well, I wanted to ask you your opinion on something."

The desk creaked as Bob leaned his knuckles on it.

"What do you think could have done *that* to the little boy?" Shelly asked.

Bob ruminated. "Various things. Torn limb from limb. Bones splintered. Decapitated. Bits of the poor wee soul scattered all over the hillside. Grizzly bear. Lion. Pack of wolves."

"In other words, something that doesn't exist on the island?"

"Not that we ken about. Nothing to say that someone hasn't shipped in a large animal without licensing it through the proper channels."

Shelly chewed a lip. "I don't buy it."

"Maybe a machine, then," Bob offered.

"Wood chipper?"

"Aye, something like that." There was no sincerity to his tone. "Of course, if there'd been some kind of accident with a machine, it fails to explain a number of things. Where's the machine? Who owns it, and where have they put it? If they knew a child had been killed, why didn't they report the accident? Even if the child was killed on purpose, what happened to the little girl?"

"Bethany," Shelly said.

"Aye. Bethany." Bob straightened. "It doesn't take a CSI tech to see that the remains are those of wee Jimmy alone. Bethany has disappeared without a trace. Unless she witnessed the accident and was so traumatised that she wandered off. Then you'd have to believe that the machine owner didn't realise that he'd just shredded a bairn and didn't notice the mess sprayed over the hillside and he's took the machine away and parked it up someplace."

There was no conviction to his scenario, and if you excused the subject matter, his conjecture wasn't meant to be a serious prognosis of events. Shelly gave it the lack of regard that it was due.

"Is a man capable of doing that, Bob?"

"With enough time and the right implements? Yes, I believe a man could eviscerate a bairn."

"But what about Bethany? Could a man have subdued them both, then did what he did to Jimmy, then carried Bethany off?"

"Would take a bit of doing. But I suppose he could have knocked Bethany unconscious, maybe - God forbid - killed her first. Then cut the little lad up."

"It would explain why no one heard any screams or cries for help," Shelly said.

"Place the boy was killed, there'd be little chance of anyone hearing anything. Their Ma wasn't home; she was still at work at the plant. No other houses in quarter a mile. And don't forget the wind and rain."

Shelly nodded at his wisdom.

"Course, it's hardly likely that whoever did this carried the girl very far. There were no signs of a vehicle at the scene. Means she could be hidden quite close by to where Catherine Stewart found the boy."

Shelly asked, "You're saying that Bethany could be hidden on Catherine Stewart's property?"

"Could be. Any way, protocol made it the first place we checked. Maybe we should check again."

"Why? You don't believe that Catherine did it, do you?"

"No more than you do, Sarge."

"Who is capable? Of the men you know on this island, I mean."

Bob rolled his shoulders. "Plenty are capable. Physically, I'm saying. But there's not a man I know could do that, and carry it on his conscience."

"Not that you know of."

"True. I can't be guessing what goes on in the minds of men. No one can."

"But you don't think there's a resident who could do this?"

"Couldn't - and wouldn't - even begin to lay the blame on any of the islanders." Bob leaned forward and clicked the computer mouse a couple of times, shutting down the programme. "As you know, there are certain men around the toon who get violent when they're drinking, but its one thing fighting round the back of The Muckle Ram to tearing a wee lad to shreds."

"What about someone from off the island? There are the archaeologists over at Trowhaem, for instance. MOD staff up at the base at Burra Ness. Some visitors."

Bob nodded, but remained noncommittal.

Shelly finally breached the subject she'd been edging towards since entering the squad room. "That man we stopped up on the glen. Carter Bailey. What did you make of him?"

"Bit strange," Bob agreed. "But nothing that said he was any kind of danger to anyone."

Shelly's eyelids flickered. "You think so?"

"There was nothing on record about him," Bob reminded her.

"Doesn't mean that he's innocent, just that he hasn't been caught yet."

"Bit of a push, don't you think, Sarge?"

"Maybe." Despite concurring, and evident by the set of her jaw, she remained convicted to the idea. She remembered what she had seen behind Bailey's eyes.

"Anyway," Bob said. "Preliminary opinion is that Jimmy was killed late yesterday afternoon. Bailey said he came in on the ferry in the evening. He wasn't even on the island when the bairn was murdered."

"We've only got his word for that," Shelly said. "I think we need to speak with him, Bob. Something about him…"

"What?"

"I don't know. Just *something*. A feeling."

"Stating the obvious, Sarge, I thought we'd need more than just a feeling before we could bring him in," Bob said.

"I'm not talking about arresting him. Not yet. But it wouldn't do any harm to go speak with him."

Bob eyed her. He could see that she was adamant on this. And, notwithstanding his apparent lack of prior contact with her, believed that he knew her better than she suspected. He believed she wasn't one to be swayed once she got an idea in mind.

"You're the sergeant," he said. "You want to speak to him, then we go speak to him."

Bob stepped towards where he'd slung his jacket over the back of a chair. Shelly interjected herself between him and the coat. Pressed him back. "No, Bob. Not now. There's time to speak to him later. Right now I want you to get off home to your bed."

"I'm okay for another couple of hours."

Shelly smiled. "Of course you are." She scrubbed a palm through her hair. "But to be brutally honest, I could sleep on a washing line. And unless you get yourself away home, I can't either. You'll be keeping me from my beauty sleep, Bob. Don't think you're the type to be happy having that on your conscience."

Bob gave a bashful shrug. He said, "Don't think you need worry about that. Tired or not, you still look a right bonnie woman to me."

Secretly delighted at his unexpected compliment, Shelly feigned shock. "Constable Harris! Now who's hitting on who?"

Bob didn't know which way to look. Shelly was chuckling as he bustled out of the squad room with barely a backward glance. She would swear under oath that his ears were glowing bright red as he disappeared into the locker room. Coming out, minutes later, he avoided eye contact and left the station with only a mumbled goodbye.

Shelly went into the sergeant's office. On the island, she was the only person of rank, and unless she received a periodical visit from an inspector from the mainland, this remained solely her domain. Although it was hardly likely that any of the other duty constables would return to the station any time soon, she shut the door. What she had in mind wasn't your usual police work. Best done in private.

She had men on her mind.

Bob, for one.

Primarily, though, she was thinking about Carter Bailey.

EIGHTEEN

Near Ura Taing

Considering my bucket list, being a passenger in a car driven by Paul Broom wasn't the first on my list of things to do before I die. In fact it didn't feature at all. Trouble is, when it came to his driving, it could be the very last thing I ever did. To say that he lacked confidence would be an extreme understatement, yet he manages to drive at speeds that only professional Grand Prix drivers or F16 fighter pilots should attempt. Lack of feeling in his throttle pedal foot could explain his over use of revs, but I couldn't come up with a feasible excuse for the way he sawed at the steering wheel. Putting together the equation of speed plus erratic manoeuvres plus dodgy road surfaces, I was thrilled to arrive at Catherine Stewart's place with all my body parts intact.

He pulled his Subaru onto the verge, parking among the vehicles of a number of other sightseers. It struck me how tragedy brought out the ghoul in most people, and experienced a momentary pang of embarrassment that we'd shown up to join the group of vultures already milling in the space this side of the taped off crime scene. However, torn between mawkishness and the very real need to escape the claustrophobic confines of Broom's car, I clambered out on to wet turf with hardly a second's pause.

As Broom stepped from the car, a number of faces turned to regard us. Evidently Broom had gained a certain amount of celebrity - even here on this outpost where I'd hardly credit one of them for having read any of his books. Some gave him the star struck eyes, but I could see that as many of them gave him downcast looks before turning away and grumbling into their shirtfronts.

This island breed appeared not to have inherited any of their Viking forefathers' genetic propensities for size, and Broom in particular stood at the back of the crowd of watchers like a Scandinavian giant shepherding a band of dwarfs. Feeling awkward next to him, I moved off to the road seeking a clearer view at the place where it was reputed that a little boy had been dismembered.

There wasn't much to see. Police had arrived in numbers, and a large white plastic tunnel had been erected over the site, both as protection against the elements destroying any trace forensics, and as a blindfold to the encroaching crowd. Whatever was happening was being conducted in the poly tunnel, and the faces of the constables on guard at the perimeter gave no clue to what had been discovered. The TV crews hadn't arrived yet, so I didn't have the option of listening in to a reporter's take on the situation. Disregarding this, I fisted my hands in my jacket pockets and stared along with everyone else. Something I did notice; there was a police photographer moving around the site, and I was sure that half the photos he took were of the crowd of bystanders. I'd heard that police procedure was to pay attention to those gathering at a crime scene; it was no cliché that the perpetrator often returned to gloat at the scene of his crime.

I turned my attention from the police activity, surreptitiously glancing at the crowd. Faces meant little to me; everyone barring Paul Broom was a complete stranger. I was searching for something subtler, perhaps a gleam in an eye, or a secret smile when the person thought no one was looking his or her way. Only one face caught my attention. A tall man, with the erect bearing of a military officer stood in the tree line, surveying as I did. I took him to be one of those police observers I'd just warned myself about. His eyelids narrowed perceptibly. I skirted around him with my eyes as though I hadn't noticed him. He looked away.

"Sometimes you gotta look past the dead wood to see the trees, Carter."

I was surprised at the sudden intrusion of Cash's words, and I made a flat grunt in my chest. He'd been silent since I'd left him in the Poe-inspired chamber in the early hours of this morning. I snatched a glance to each side, wondering if the mawkish onlookers standing close by had noticed my response to his voice. Evidently not. I didn't earn as much as a lifted brow. Even the undercover cop had moved away and took no further notice of me.

In private I'd usually speak out loud in response to my brother. If I did so there, I'd probably have had half the island's police resource on top of me. I could as easily converse with him within the confines of my mind, but under the circumstances I chose to do neither.

"Cat got your tongue?"

I stepped away from the crowd, walking along the blue and white taped off perimeter. Choosing to ignore Cash's words, I concentrated on the trees beyond the poly tunnel.

"Suit yourself, but I thought you wanted me to help you."

"Leave it out for now, Cash," I finally muttered. "I get what you're saying, okay? And I know what I'm doing."

"I don't think you do, Bro. But, hey! Don't let me be the one to stand in the way of progress."

"Shush!"

"Of course, if you want to believe any of that crap Broomie was giving you on the way over…go right ahead."

Pushing him to the back of my thoughts, I found myself searching the shadows beneath the trees. Crazy, I know, but I'd taken on board more of 'that crap Broomie was giving me on the way over' than I'd readily admit. Namely the islanders' take on what had happened here. One that Broom had accepted. By default of my acceptance of the task Broom had set me that made me an accessory to his wild theories, too. Even though to admit so was ridiculous.

It had started with me demanding answers from Broom, regarding the reticence of Stan the café man's suspicions and Broom's equal resistance to further explanation.

Hanging on to my seat belt as he'd swung the Subaru through a sequence of bends, I'd asked him, "There's been talk…as you know. What the hell was Stan talking about, Broom?"

Gritting his teeth in concentration, Broom forced out a laugh. "You know what island folk are like. Close-knit. Closed-minded. Very, very superstitious."

Despite the obvious stereotyping, I nodded in understanding. I think what he meant to say was that most secular communities have very distinct and individual traditions and practices, and sometimes these customs could intrude upon logic.

Broom scowled. "You have to understand that, though it may sound as wacky as hell, some of the people here have certain beliefs that would be laughed at by people living in the modern conurbations where computers and mobile phones and High Definition television are the order of the day."

That's easy for you to say, I thought. In my own erudite way, I said, "Yeah."

In full flow - and an excuse to take even less notice of his motoring skills - Broom explained. "As you are probably aware, this island, as well as the other Shetland and Orkney islands, owe much of their heritage to Norse seafarers who settled communities here from the ninth century onwards."

"Vikings," I said.

Broom flicked his eyebrows. "We'll call them Vikings if you like, but that is a very generic term used these days to determine a number of Scandinavian races. But anyway, that isn't important for the purposes of what Stan was referring to."

"It isn't?"

"No. All you need to know is where the tales originated." For some reason unknown to me, Broom changed gear, the engine whining in protest, then changed back to the original once more. "That is in *Viking* villages and communities."

When I didn't respond, he cleared his throat. "Contrary to popular misconception the Vikings weren't all axe-wielding barbarians who had nothing better to do than rape and pillage their way across half the known world."

"Damn," I quipped. "My illusions shattered again."

Broom exhaled through flaring nostrils. "Obviously your knowledge of Norse lore is relegated to watching reruns of that old Kirk Douglas and Tony Curtis hokum."

"Spartacus?" I asked, hiding my smile.

"No, Carter. 'The Vikings'." Realising too late that he'd been had, he squinted at me. I was quick to nod his attention back to the road ahead. His driving was bad enough without taking his eyes off the road. He gave an exasperated hiss. "Most Vikings weren't hairy-arsed berserkers; they were craftsmen, artisans, traders, but predominantly they were farmers." When I didn't argue, he went on, "As do many agriculturally led communities, they laid great importance on the successful harvesting of their crops. To ensure a bountiful harvest these people adhered to strict practices that included prayer and offerings to their large pantheon of deities and demigods. Now...again contrary to common belief, there is more to Norse mythology than Odin, Thor and Loki. There is a veritable sub-pantheon of lesser-known figures, spirits who resided in the mountains and forests, in the rivers and the land. Have you, by chance, heard the legend of the Haugbonde?"

As I shook my head, he added, "Sometimes he is incorrectly referred to as the hogboon or hogboy."

Still didn't mean anything to me. "Can't say I've heard the story. What is he? Half-man, half-pig?"

"Not at all. The name is a mispronunciation of the original Scandinavian dialect. The Haugbonde has nothing to do with pigs or anything else out of nature. Basically, he was, for want of a better term, a guardian spirit of the land."

After our earlier discussion of Zero Point Field's, demon magnets and other preternatural powers, our conversation regarding Norse folklore barely raised a jitter of disbelief in my voice. "You're going to tell me that Stan believes in this 'hog boy' and that he's somehow responsible for the death of a child."

"Wait," Broom said. "Let's not get ahead of ourselves."

"Fair enough. But I'm right, aren't I?"

Broom decelerated on his approach to a corner. On our right, the craggy hillside sped by, on our left the mist-shrouded waters of Yell Sound. If Broom didn't slow down enough it was going to be a choice between hillside and sea. At the last second he gained control of the car and swept us around the bend. Back on a straight, he deemed it safe to continue. "The hogboy. Compound word, by the way, not the two the way you pronounced it. His legend is more particular to the Orkney Islands, but he also made it here to Conn, the tales carried here from the old Norse lands by the original settlers. Though generally seen as a benevolent figure, the hogboy also had a dark side. He reputedly lived in the mounds and hills, and he protected the domestic livestock from interference from the trow folk. He-"

I held up a hand. "The *trow* folk?"

"The Orkney and Shetland variant on the troll legend. Mean sons of bitches."

Inclining my chin, I allowed him to go on.

"He - the hogboy, that is - protected the animals, the land, and was even said to fix household articles left out for repair."

"Sounds like a fairy tale I heard as a child," I butted in. "The shoemaker and the elves."

Broom conceded the point with a grimace. "Could share a common source mythology. Who knows? Anyway, it's not important. The point is, the hogboy, though normally benevolent, expected reward for his protection. He demanded liberal payment by way of large quantities of ale and milk, and

144

the islanders repaid him by pouring them on to the mounds where he lived. As long as he was appeased in this manner, the hogboy was happy. Fail to give him his due, though, and it was an entirely different matter altogether."

"I've heard similar folk tales," I said. "This spirit would then turn malevolent and torment the people, bringing disease and catastrophe."

"Uh-hu. There are further beliefs that hold more weight for the islanders. You will find them hard to accept, but, as I said, the islanders are of ancient stock and hold fast to the ancient beliefs.

"Most importantly. Once dissatisfied, protection from the trow was removed by the hogboy. This left an opening for the evil little fuckers to lay waste to the land. Tales of the trow are abundant, primarily those where they stole pretty girls, or they replaced newborn children with changelings, or, if a person was sick, they stole away his spirit and hid it in the hollow hills where they lived, never to be found again."

Clucking my tongue apparently wasn't a good idea.

"I know, I know. Sounds foolish doesn't it?" Broom gripped the steering wheel with renewed ferocity and spun us through a curve in the road. "But the signs have been presenting themselves of late."

"The signs? What, like omens?"

"No. Like the unusual amount of deaths from pneumonia and such. A couple of stillborn births. The drowning of a crew of fishermen on an otherwise calm sea." He lifted a hand off the wheel to stab at the air with a finger. "One of which, by the way, is the father of the child reportedly killed this evening."

Coincidence, I thought.

Broom went on, "All of these deaths, not to mention the ungodly weather we've been experiencing of late, the islanders point the finger of blame at one thing; attracting the anger of the local hogboy."

Prudence was the best course in this matter, so I merely nodded along with Broom so he didn't labour the point any further. "It all began last year with the excavation of a Viking settlement on the island. Despite warnings from the islanders, the archaeologists disturbed land reputedly guarded by the hogboy, attracting his ire. In response, the hogboy has loosed the trow on the land. Like Stan said back at the café, Carter. There has been talk. After a delay supposedly caused by the trow, the archaeologists have recently resumed their digging; the islanders said things could only get worse. The death of this boy has borne out their warning."

I looked across at him and saw that Broom had actually bought into the madness of the island prophesy. He shrugged, bobbed his large head. "I told you something was *wrong* on the island," he said quietly.

"Yeah. But we're talking trow and hogboy's here, Broom. Stuff straight out of fantasy."

"There are more things in heaven and earth than we dream of in our philosophy," Broom reminded me by way of quoting Horatio.

Which was why I now hovered at the periphery of a violent crime scene, searching for unnatural forms creeping with malicious intent through the woodland. Trying hard to validate my actions by telling myself I did so with huge skepticism and the intention of proving how wholly *wrong* Broom was.

NINETEEN

Police office, Skelvoe

On the wall of Shelly's office, a framed photograph of her predecessor Sergeant Jack McVitie held dominance. Twenty years service on the island before succumbing to Parkinson's disease at the relatively young age of fifty-three had given him the reputation of a firm but fair authoritarian. He was loved by the officers under his command, admired by the law abiding, and even earned the grudging respect of those hard-arses whose heads he'd bashed some sense into. He was the kind of sergeant who took no nonsense, but would bend a rule to suit the ongoing peace of the island if he saw fit. Tough as old boots, but with a heart of gold, people said. Definitely not the type to faint at the sight of blood - even if it was dripping from the stump of a child's severed head.

In the photograph, he was smiling as he held up a certificate of commendation, awarded him at a civic reception. He was the kind of man who wore his uniform with pride, looking dapper in silver-buttoned tunic, his greying hair cut especially for the ceremony. His smile was genuine, but there was something in his liquid eyes that spoke of his discomfort. As if he was thinking, 'This is all well and good, but what are the bad guys up to whilst I'm wasting my time here?' Shelly couldn't meet McVitie's gaze. Because, that was exactly how she felt he'd perceive her wasting time scrutinising the internet when she should be *out there* running down this sick-minded child killer.

Clearing her throat didn't help her conscience, but it did help get her mind back on track. Ignoring the reproving McVitie stare, she bent back to the computer. The police CMIS system hadn't thrown up anything of interest about Carter Bailey that she didn't already know. His date of birth, last known address etc. was as he'd told Bob and her the night before. A call to the PNC bureau on Yell hadn't helped either. Now it was time for the less procedural route of a Google search.

She keyed in the list criteria. Various pages kicked back. A few didn't tell her too much, other than that he'd once been co-owner of a sports clothing firm. It raised an eyebrow when she saw the name of the company. Rezpect Sports. She was sure she had a pair of Rezpect training shoes in a cupboard back home. She also recognised his business partner, James Pender, as being a Wimbledon hopeful for a couple of years. There was nothing in these company editorials that gave any hint as to why Bailey was now traipsing around the moorlands of Conn looking as though permanently living out of a suitcase.

She skimmed through further pages regarding Rezpect Sports, until she noted the pages dedicated to various tabloid newspapers and magazines.

"Now then," she whispered as she clicked onto the first page and took in the headlines. "Wouldn't you just know it?"

LOCAL MAN SOLE SURVIVOR OF FAMILY SLAUGHTER.

Sucking in her bottom lip, she continued to read. Only two paragraphs in, she sat back frowning. The story wasn't going the way she had expected. Carter Bailey wasn't the perpetrator of this violent crime: he was a victim. A victim of the brutality of his younger brother, Cassius Bailey, who, it appeared, was subsequently killed during a fight between the siblings to protect Carter's fiancée and unborn child.

She recalled something about the horror of this tale. Remembered watching on TV shocking news bites centred on a derelict mill, a sudden blizzard and the disembowelment of a pregnant woman by a devil worshiping serial killer. Though taking the law into one's own hands is severely frowned upon by the police in general, Shelly could recall her own feelings that

Carter Bailey should have been awarded a medal for his destruction of his beastly sibling. The case had been debated in the squad room on numerous occasions, also over pints of beer in the bars where cops hung out after their shifts. Shelly and all her colleagues had silently, if not publicly, applauded Carter's actions in drowning his murderous brother.

Of course, as the media spin took hold, it wasn't too long before doubt crept in. Maybe it was a little too convenient that Cassius took all the blame, and that the knife used to gut the woman had ended up in the river, destroying the validity of the forensic examination. Okay, Carter Bailey had received some pretty nasty wounds during his ordeal, but it was surmised that most of them could have been self-inflicted. The scars to his chest, though ugly, weren't life threatening. The broken nose and the gouges to his eyebrow and scalp could have been a result of fighting off his brother whilst Cassius fought off his jealous brother.

This line of thinking came from two undeniable truths. The woman, even pregnant as she was, was found to have the semen of the dead brother within her. Secondly, testimony from work colleagues of Carter Bailey said that there had been problems between the engaged couple. It was whispered that Carter Bailey had fled work in an agitated state, returned home and found his fiancée and brother in the throes of passion and from there had carried out his murderous vengeance on the two that had betrayed him.

This theory was easily destroyed when it was announced that Cassius Bailey was the prime suspect in numerous similar deaths spanning a number of years and as many countries. The subsequent case file put together with the aid of Interpol had cleared Carter Bailey of all wrongdoing.

Still, ugly rumours have the power to persist. There's no smoke without fire, the apple doesn't fall far from the tree, blood is the tie that binds, and numerous other clichés abound. There were still many that surmised that the brothers were both engaged in the brutal murder spree, and it was down to a falling out over the lust for Karen that saw their fight to the death.

The theory had often been bandied around, until numerous other horrors took precedence of the news reports, and the exploits of Cassius and Carter Bailey were supplanted, effectively forgotten.

"Until now," Shelly spoke out loud.

She glanced up at Jack McVitie, his fluid gaze oozing over her like an oil slick. She grunted. "See, Jack. I wasn't wasting precious police time, after all."

She read further reports spanning the months following the incident at the water mill. Then clicked on an accompanying photograph depicting a worn down Carter Bailey stepping from a taxi parked at the entrance of a private hospital. Bailey's dark hair was shorter than he wore it now, his face thinner. The scar on his eyebrow was a dark smudge that matched the rings beneath his eyes. And the eyes themselves; caught at an angle, the sun gave them a scarlet, diamond keen edge, as though someone else peeked from behind a mask at the gathered paparazzi.

Shelly squinted at the image. Was that the same look she'd caught last night when Bailey had leaned into the car to say his goodbyes? Were those the eyes of a defeated soul or the barely repressed gloating eyes of a killer?

"What's it going to be, Carter?" she asked the image on the screen. "Are you really as innocent as they say, or were you and your brother partners in murder? Are you here now to take up where you left off?"

No sooner had she voiced the thought than doubt crept in. Perhaps it was wrong for her to place the blame of this atrocious murder at the feet of a man whose only crime was to survive something as equally horrendous. Maybe if someone dear to her had been brutally tortured the way in which Bailey's fiancée had, then she would be marked with a similar cast to her eye. Perhaps the look wasn't the Mark of Cain as she'd first suspected, but the total dejection of his spirit.

"*Deus ex machina.*" The expression leapt into her mind. 'A god from the machine'. A phrase derived from a convention in ancient Greek drama whereby a god was lowered onto the stage by an elaborate piece of equipment to solve the problems and end the play. It was the modern equivalent of the dead soap star stepping out of the shower and the realisation that his supposed demise was all *just a dream*. Or the all too handy character in a mystery novel that just happens to turn up in time for the sleuth's denouement. "Am I doing that to you, Carter Bailey? Am I making you the fall guy?"

Shelly drew in a slow breath.

"But, if that's the case, why the hell do you frighten me so much?"

TWENTY

I know you for what you are, Carter Bailey. But should I fear you? You're here to stop me, are you? Should I kill you now or later?

I stood so close, listening to your conversation. But you didn't notice me. Your writer friend has faith in your abilities to see the darkness in the souls of men, but your gaze slipped by me. Is it because you have no faith in what he says?

You should listen to him. His teaching will only make you stronger. The stronger you become, the more satisfying it will be when I finally kill you.

Serendipity, in the shape of Paul Broom, has brought you to me.

Perhaps we will have found each other regardless. Destiny decrees the inevitable. But I must say, Broom's inclusion has quickened the process, and we are going to meet soon. I watched you as you got off the ferry; I saw the look that you shared with Janet. I will be her ruination, as I will be yours.

I watch you as you slink at the edge of the crowd. You wander alone. Vulnerable. Out of sight of the others. It would be soooo easy.

Should I kill you now?

Should I kill you later?

My mind is made up.

TWENTYONE

Near Ura Taing

"This is all a pile of crap," I scolded myself.

Broom was talking allegorically. He had to be. Hogboy and trow? Those were creatures out of Tolkien or the fairy tales of The Brothers Grimm. Surely, he was using the simile to explain the mindset of the real killer? Okay, I could accept that there could be a lunatic out there that believed he was some creature of legend, but the way in which Broom explained it told me he was talking *genuine* hogboy, *genuine* trow.

That gave me cause for concern. Made me re-evaluate my take on my own mentality. I mean, it was the selfsame Paul Broom that believed that I was a vessel imprisoning the dark essence of my brother and that I had the capacity to unearth evil like I was some sort of paranormal bloodhound. It was Broom who'd supplied to me a very illegal SIG Sauer semi-automatic handgun in order to blast this evil back to hell. Kind of plays havoc with the old sanity chip, when the very same man had me out searching for hobgoblins and the like. The problem being, I was going along with him. I could stand there and tell myself that I was simply humouring my friend, that I owed him a debt of allegiance, but that wouldn't excuse me from carrying a concealed firearm if any of the nearby police officers decided I was acting suspiciously enough that it would justify a stop and search.

I wished that I'd left the SIG back at Broom's house, but following my Billy the Kid moment down on the beach, the gun's presence had felt so right that I'd automatically holstered it and pushed it down the rear of my waistband, where it now remained. Burning me like a hot coal as soon as I'd became aware of its presence once more. Glancing around in what must have been a furtive manner wasn't a good idea. At least one of the police officers standing nearby, a tall, gaunt man with silver hair, gave me the once over. I quickly turned away and continued along the road past the copse of trees.

Out of sight of the police I considered removing the gun and concealing it in the foliage with the intention of returning for it later. Not a very good idea at the best of times. Knowing my luck I'd be seen hiding the gun, subsequently arrested and locked up whilst I tried to come up with a feasible excuse for carrying the weapon. Or, worse still, the police search of the area would discover the gun and it would be presumed that it had some connection to the murdered child. Considering my fingerprints or DNA could be all over the gun, or the bullets I'd loaded, that too would mean a one-way trip to prison. Best I keep the gun on me for now and hope that my wandering wouldn't bring me to the attention of the police.

Coming to the crime scene was a mistake. When Broom suggested visiting the remote location to get a handle on the crime, I should have argued against it. Broom's suggestion that something important could come to light from viewing the scene first hand had seemed reasonable at the time, but what on earth could looking at a white poly tunnel achieve? Anyway, what the hell did I hope to find that the experts wouldn't?

"Trust in The Force, Young Skywalker."

"You're back, are you?"

"Hale an' hearty an' ready to rumble," Cash laughed.

"Okay. But while you're here, why don't you make yourself helpful for a change."

Cash sniggered.

"What's so funny?"

"You're asking for my help, yet you ignore my pointed quotes of wisdom?"

"These being? Oh, yeah, I remember. 'You can't see the dead wood for the trees'. What the hell's that supposed to mean?" I continued down the road that ran parallel to the trees, my eyes scanning, expecting *what?* to leap out. To my left the tide rumbled on a rocky shore.

"Means exactly what it implies, Carter. You're missing the obvious because you are blinded to it."

"So why don't you just point me in the correct direction?" I demanded. "Instead of giving me the old 'Confucius say's' palaver?"

"Nah, wouldn't be very fair of me," Cash said. *"See, if I make it too easy for you, you won't experience any self-worth in the solving of the riddle. You will feel most inferior, and won't be up to the coming test."*

I came to a halt. Fisted my hands in my pockets. "There you go with the test thing again. What is this test you keep talking about?"

"You will know it when it presents itself."

"But not before?"

"Not until you realise the truth."

"So, tell me."

"Nope. You have to discover it yourself, brother."

I marched on, head down. "This isn't exactly what I'd call 'helping'," I said.

"All depends on your perspective. See, to me, I'm acting like the veritable Good Samaritan."

"God help us all for small mercies," I said.

"Not my fault that you're too thick to understand where I'm trying to point you."

Kicking at loose gravel, I said, "C'mon Cash. Just tell me what you're talking about instead of messing me around."

"Wouldn't be fair."

"Yeah, you've already made *that* clear."

"Like I said…The Good Samaritan."

"Go back to sleep, Cash."

"I wish."

"Yeah, me too," I said. "Me too."

The point was Cash didn't sleep. Not ever. Made me wonder how he could remain so alert all the time. Had to be something to do with having no corporeal body. Sleep was a basic human necessity, but it was something unattainable in the spirit form. I guessed that, by now, Cash was possibly ready to trade his chance at retribution upon me for a good eight hours' shut eye. Would have been a good bargaining chip I could use against him, if indeed I had the power to allow him some respite. That, unfortunately, wasn't something I was able to do.

Whilst I was so engrossed, something large and deadly swept up behind me.

"Heads up, boyo!" Cash said. In response, I stepped on to the roadside verge, and Broom finally brought the Subaru to a halt two feet beyond where I'd been standing. *"It'd be kind of ironic if you ended up road kill. That'd put a spanner in the works."*

Broom leaned across the passenger seat to fling open the door. Almost took the skin off my shins. "Get in, Carter."

The way in which he said it didn't allow for argument. The fact is, I wasn't in a mind to argue. I'd done everything I could there, which amounted to absolutely zilch. Which meant it was pointless hanging around where the final probability would be to attract unwanted questions from an inquisitive police officer. But more than that, my mind was fixed on what Cash had just said. Was he intimating that if I were killed in an accident then he wouldn't get the opportunity at revenge? The only way for him to have a chance at dominating my soul would be through the natural process of death through natural causes?

If that was the case then it was comforting in one respect; it was in Cash's best interest to keep me alive as he'd said. On the other hand, it was quite disturbing to think that my only opportunity at peace was to die a violent or painful death. It wasn't a forecast to engender happy thoughts.

The Subaru gave a lunge like a racehorse from the gates, and we were off. Broom was chewing at his lips.

"What's up?" I asked.

"Overheard it on a police radio," he said at barely more than a whisper.

Frowning at him, I asked, "Heard what?"

"There's been another death."

I swallowed down bile. "Another death? Not the little girl?"

"No," Broom said. "Bethany is still missing. It's an adult, this time."

"Who?"

"Don't know. They didn't say on the radio." He pushed the hair from his brow, snatched his hand back to the steering wheel. "Or if they did, I didn't hang around long enough to hear who it was."

Ahead of us I saw the roofs of a small settlement. The village of Ura Taing, no doubt. I assumed that the village was the site of this latest death, but Broom ignored the turn-in towards the village and continued on the circuitous coast road.

"Where are we going, Broom?"

"Trowhaem."

I glanced at him. Trow again?

Clarifying, he went on, "At the archeological dig. They've turned up bones."

I sniffed. "Isn't that what archeologists do?"

"Yeah," Broom said. A grim smile fluttered at the corners of his mouth. "Thing is, Carter, the bones normally dug up by archeologists don't have flesh and blood sticking to them."

TWENTYTWO

Trowhaem

Harry Bishop was hardly acting like a leader under these circumstances. In fact, there was very little he was doing other than sitting in the front of his hippy van muttering nonsense into his beard. As an archeologist and in particular an anthropologist majoring in osteology, you'd think he'd have been armoured against the sight of human skeletal remains. But, as Paul Broom had so succinctly put it minutes earlier, the bones normally dug up by archeologists don't have flesh and blood sticking to them.

The remains had been discovered by pure chance. Because the flooded site was proving obstinate to further investigation, Bishop had requested a geophysics sweep of a short strip of land adjacent to where previous graves had been discovered. Conducting a geo-scan of the area, his students had reported an area of disturbed ground and what was termed a metal spike/blip. Bishop knew these anomalies could be caused by burnt stones that have become magnetised by being repeatedly heated and cooled a number of times. For instance it wasn't untoward to find magnetised stones in an old fire pit used for burning rubbish. But he was convinced instead that the shadowy readout was indicative in shape and size as previously discovered boat-shaped graves. The anomaly appeared to be approximately five-and-a-half metres long, shaped like an elongated teardrop, and it took only a few moments scraping at the dirt to discover the usual stones piled over the top. Not a good sign to the keen eye of Bishop; the stones bore the hallmark of recent disturbance and he guessed that unscrupulous treasure hunters could have previously robbed the grave.

Ordinarily the clearing of the find would have been conducted at a snail's pace whilst the dimensions and positions of stones on the grave were perfunctorily catalogued. However, due to nothing more than impatience on his part, Bishop had commanded the grave opened post haste. He was, after all, on a short timetable and had up until now shown very little in the way of discoveries to offset the spiralling costs and growing dissatisfaction of the university faculty. It was very likely that the grave had already been pillaged - he could tell that by the misaligned stones - yet he still retained hope that the robbers had missed whatever was causing the metal spike the geophysics team had located.

In lieu of a diagrammatic record, he used his smart phone to film the exhumation, intending to use the recording as evidence of any subsequent find should the need arise.

He was standing over the dig, doing his best Spielberg impression when tow-headed Davy Richardson shrieked like an adolescent and scrambled out of the shallow pit. Mesmerised, Bishop had employed the zoom facility of the camera to bring into sharp definition whatever had freaked out the young student.

As he'd studied the screen it had taken Bishop long seconds before he could fully credit what it was that he was looking at. An eyeball, milky in death, stared out the bloody socket of a human skull. With this realisation, he too gave out a startled yelp and dropped the smart phone. Bellowing like a hippopotamus in rut, he'd staggered down into the grave, tugging at stones with his bare hands, until he'd fully exposed the cranium, throat and upper torso of an adult male. The remains were practically skeletal, but not due to the natural course of decomposition. Bishop could tell that this body had been in the ground little more than a few days, and yet most of the outer dermis and a large portion of the underlying musculature had been removed from the bones. And not with the finesse of a surgeon's scalpel, either. The flesh had been literally *ripped* off.

The corpse had all the indications of a large animal attack. Bishop knew that it wasn't untoward for certain animals to conceal a kill to protect it from other scavengers. There was, of course, only one animal capable of exhuming the original Viking grave, placing the corpse within it, then piling back the stones and earth in this manner. That animal could only be Man. This meant he could only be looking at one thing: murder.

Bang goes his funding. Bang goes his reputation. Bang goes his status as leader of this dig. Bang, bang, bang, like a rapid-fire volley of mortar fire, bursting his entire well laid plans and aspirations. And with that realisation came despondency.

Standing next to the gruesome find, Janet looked over at Bishop. He was unresponsive to her glance. He was a man in his mid-forties, but for the few seconds she studied him he seemed more like a lost little boy, dressed in the beard and clothing of an old man. He appeared *diminished*. Both in stature and in command. Not the ideal scenario, really. That meant that it was down to her to take charge of the proceedings.

It was Janet who'd marshalled the students into some form of order when all around her panic was the order of the day. She had used a mobile phone to inform the police of the discovery. She had set a couple of the girls to comfort Davy Richardson. Chased Kiera McCann from Harry Bishop; he could do without the love struck administrations of the horny girl when answering the subsequent police enquiry. No doubt photographs of the professor would be splashed over newspapers, and the last thing he could do with was Kiera hanging on his arm. Janet wasn't concerned about Harry in that respect, and only intended sparing his long-suffering wife any further heartache. She hated that some people would see her actions as protection of Harry's infidelity, considering what Jonathon Connery had done to her, but she didn't intend to be the one to hurt Harry's wife by allowing his dirty behaviour to become front-page news.

Further, she'd ensured that a tarpaulin was erected over the gravesite, and that the inquisitive students kept well clear of the area so they didn't disturb the scene. Already, important forensic evidence could have been disrupted or even corrupted by

Bishop's hurried excavation. She'd damn well ensure that nothing further could be held against them for their actions. Inevitably Harry's unprofessional activity would be a sore point with the law, and this dissatisfaction would undoubtedly be reported back to their sponsors.

Now she stood a lonely vigil. Shock - more to do with the knock-on ramifications of the situation than the horrible find itself - had made Harry useless to her. And being honest, worry was impinging on her own thoughts. The murdered man was trouble in capital letters. Yet another setback to this continuously troublesome dig. Made her wonder if the curse of Trowhaem held validity, after all.

She'd always discounted the haugbonde curse as childish fantasy, but appreciated that certain islanders remained staunch in their beliefs. More than any talk of inappropriateness, she knew that the underlying point behind the resistance to the excavation was the fear that ancient terrors would be loosed upon the land. Casting her mind back, she recalled a group of vociferous islanders meeting them at the ferry terminal, demanding that the archeologists return to their university at fear of further trouble should they continue. The police had broken up the unruly protest, and the team had been allowed on their way. But that wasn't the last of the trouble. Some of the students had been targeted with abuse and threats of violence, to the point that none of them socialised in Skelvoe now. Also, whenever they travelled, they did so as a group, and were always met at the ferry terminal and ushered away before those who - eighteen months later - still resisted the team's presence on the island could descend upon them. Not without reason she believed that the murdered man had been deposited in the grave to further compound the ongoing setbacks they'd already endured. Whoever killed the man, and subsequently placed him there, was against any further excavation of the land.

Janet realised that she was holding her breath. She exhaled, hoping that this ill feeling would be expunged along with the bad air. It was a shocking thought that someone would be so depraved - or for that matter so adamant - that they would halt the excavation by resorting to murder and these awful scare tactics.

'Who could do such a thing?' she thought. 'Never mind that, who in heaven's name is the dead man?'

Frighteningly, she found herself conducting a head count of the students under her care. She double checked, meticulously listing names and current whereabouts and was relieved to find all her charges accounted for.

What about contractors, security men, caterers? They'd employed various off-island employees while the heavy work of clearing away much of the landslide that had buried the town was underway. Still, that had been last year, and since then only university staff had been on site. Her hurried examination of the corpse prior to her having it concealed beneath the tarpaulin had assured her that the man had only been dead for a few days, so it was unlikely to be the corpse of any of those workers. She also knew that a couple of watchmen looked over the site at night whilst the university team retired to their nearby shantytown of tents and caravanettes. The watchmen, Terrence and Kirk, had become well-known faces around the dig, and she could certainly remember both of them being on site when she'd arrived this morning.

Unaware of the terrible events unfolding at the Stewart home, Janet couldn't begin to guess who this man was, or who was responsible for his death. With that thought she experienced the first pangs of panic - almost to the point that she could sympathise with Harry Bishop - and it was a conscious effort to subdue the trembling in her limbs.

"Where the hell are the police?" It felt as though hours had passed since her call for help. Fair enough, travel from Skelvoe wasn't a minute or two's work, but surely the police should have descended on the scene by now? The surf made a low rumble against the nearby cliffs, and the wind groaned through the stunted trees, but above these she should have been able to detect the shriek and wail of approaching sirens. Unfortunately the only discordant tones she could detect were the screeching of gulls riding the waves in the bay.

Gulls were the dominant species of bird on and around the island, finding rich pickings in the shallow seas around Conn. Saying that, something she hadn't been aware of until now was the number of crows that had made Trowhaem their home. It was almost Hitchcockian the way in which the black plumed birds were lined up on the outcrop of land above her. She studied the birds and they studied her in return, her face reflected in their beady eyes as they cawed and nodded like wise old men ruminating over the woes of the world. Janet didn't like the birds. Not simply because they were carrion eaters and were probably grouped there as they'd detected the aroma of lunch beneath the tarpaulin, it was more for the malicious intent in their eyes and their spearing bills that made her think of the cruelty of battlefield slaughter.

It was an effort not to return the birds' stares, but she forced herself to look away. She turned her back on them, listening to the rustle as they anticipated a chance at the corpse. Their muted cawing was like the babble of eager partygoers waiting the moment the buffet is announced open.

"Disgusting," she muttered. And that one word could aptly describe everything she was currently faced with, not least the hungry carrion crows' desire to get at the concealed meat. To take her mind off the wretched birds and the intolerable wait for professional back up, she looked again at Harry Bishop. He now had his head in his hands, and the lift and fall of his shoulders suggested that his despondency was overwhelming. Trying not to feel too hard-faced, Janet told herself that he didn't deserve any pity. That, though, was more for his marital wrongdoing than any failings he had as a colleague or friend.

Maybe I should go over and offer him a hug or a shoulder to cry on, she thought.

As though sensing her scrutiny Harry lifted his face from his hands and looked at her. His eyes were red-rimmed, and his cheeks and forehead were florid. Whether from embarrassment or ingratitude, he swung his gaze from her, staring out across the few exposed walls of Trowhaem.

"Suit yourself," Janet said under her breath. Still, she found herself following his averted gaze. Primarily the site remained mounds of earth and rubble, but here and there were the squat stone foundations of buildings, marked with small flags and strings of tape. Discoveries of any significant value were very slim on the ground, and Janet wondered if this dig had been doomed to failure long before it ever started. The haugbonde curse may yet prove virulent in the minds of the current island population, but apparently the reported abandonment of the settlement one millennia ago can't have been as sudden as what was suggested. That or the fleeing inhabitants had been very rigorous in collecting their entire belongings before fleeing the town. The way things were going, the only items of archeological importance to be turned up would be the remains of the buildings themselves. That was no bad thing, of course, but every archeologist would be lying if they denied they weren't secretly searching for lost treasure. You could display all the broken crockery or dressed stone you like, but what the public really wanted to see were gold coins and jewel-hilted swords.

In her mud-clogged boots and parka smelling faintly of mildew, Janet had the sudden urge to throw it all in. Change is as good as a rest, they say. Had she finally reached that moment when her enthusiasm had finally deserted her, and she realised that this wasn't how she perceived her life would be? She was thirty-six years old for God's sake! Apart from two years whilst she'd travelled the world and worked the Israeli Kibbutz, all she'd ever known was the life of an academic. First as a student, then as a lecturer and field archeologist, finally as second fiddle to Harry Bishop on this wild outpost where all she had to show for her labour were a few stones, a broken marriage, and now…the added complication of a murder enquiry.

She didn't swear as a rule. Right now she could think of a few choice words to put a seal on her dissatisfaction. Rather than do that, she again focussed on the slow arrival of the police. "For crying out loud! What's keeping you?"

There was a billow of black feathers as the crows erupted across her vision. Janet cried out, involuntarily throwing her arms over her head. It was a long panic-fuelled moment before she realised that she wasn't actually under attack from the flock of sharp-beaked birds, and that their sudden flight was due to the intrusion of a couple of figures startling them into flight. Breathing raggedly, Janet looked at the two men striding towards her across the rocky outcrop above the grave. Stray feathers hung in the air. At sight of the men, she actually smiled in greeting, but the pleasantry was spoiled when a downy feather adhered to her lips and she hurriedly batted it away. Quickly, her smile became a grimace.

TWENTYTHREE

Skelvoe

What's worse, one hour's sleep or no sleep at all? That was the question digging at Shelly McCusker's brain as she negotiated the stairs and dragged open the front door. Right at that moment she was erring on the side of wishing she hadn't bothered with clambering into bed. You don't miss something until it's gone, she reminded herself.

Sleep, or the lack of it, made her feel awful. There was a bad taste in her mouth, as though she'd been eating liver and onions - something she had not been aware of these past three months, two weeks, three…no, correction, four days. She could actually smell smoke on her skin, or maybe the tobacco odour was coming off Bob Harris who peered up at her from the street.

Shelly's home was perched above Skelvoe, a narrow semi-detached terraced house set back from the road by a flight of steps. Bob's face was at a level with her knees, and Shelly was suddenly conscious that he possibly had a worm's eye view up the front of the terry bathrobe she'd hurriedly pulled over her skimpy nightdress. Ordinarily, such a realisation would have embarrassed her and she'd have tugged closed the bottom of her gown even as she was stepping back. Risqué or not, she held her ground, even managed to turn up the corner of her mouth in greeting.

"Bob. You're the last person I expected to see."

He was dressed in full uniform. Not the one he'd had on earlier, this was freshly laundered and pressed. In comparison, Shelly felt grimy and unkempt. Now she stepped back, tugging at the folds of her bathrobe.

"Sorry to wake you, Sarge," Bob said, averting his gaze from the flash of calf and slim ankles with more than a little reticence.

"I tried phoning, but I guess you were sound asleep. I've been banging at your door for the last ten minutes. I wouldn't have bothered you, but…"

Shelly waved off his apology, then, remembering her manners, she held open the door. "Come in, Bob. You want a coffee or something?"

Bob indicated the police car at the kerb. "I'll wait out here while you get yourself sorted."

Confusion flickered through Shelly.

Just what had she been thinking was the cause of this impromptu visit, anyway? Did she think that Bob had come a-courting? That his best dress uniform had been to impress her with how well he brushed up? She should have known that he'd come due to official police business. And what was that look in his eye about? Was he amused at her sudden discomfort, or was his twinkle and quivering smile more for his own unease when he realised what was going through Shelly's mind?

Stray strands of her dark hair were hurriedly shoved back. Attempting to make amends for her stupidity, she nodded to the living room behind her. "No. Come on in. You can tell me what's wrong while I get ready."

Bob swayed once towards the police car, then, lifting his chin in acceptance, he negotiated the stairs and stepped over the threshold. Shelly held open the door for him, and he pressed by her. Shelly felt his warmth. She also noticed that the smoky waft of his odour was actually pleasant, like rolling tobacco and a tang of citrus, a masculine fragrance that brought fond reminiscence of her grandfather to mind. Both of them smiled shyly.

"Go on in. In fact, do you mind putting the kettle on while I go and grab a quick shower?" Before Bob could answer, Shelly mounted the stairs, careful this time to keep her bathrobe tight to her body. She was aware of his perusal as she dashed up the stairs.

Bob lifted his eyebrows, finally snorted to himself and headed for a room at the back of the house that he assumed was the kitchen. Walking down the hall he called out, "It'll have to be a quick cuppa, Sarge. D.I. Marsh's been screaming for you for the past half hour."

There were a series of muffled bumps and clatters from upstairs, then Shelly's voice from behind a closed door. "What's all the panic about, Bob?"

"Everyone's still tied up at Catherine Stewart's place. The inspector apologised, but he's got no one else to pick up another job that's come in. He asked me to come get you, and said he'll meet us for a briefing at the station in half-an-hour."

"So he is coming over from Lerwick? Christ! Wonders never cease."

It was strange for Bob to have this conversation. Him pottering in the kitchen whilst a lady showered in a room above him. So very domestic. Something he hadn't been party to for over fifteen years. Not since his wife, Stephanie, had left him and went home to the mainland in order to follow her dream of achieving fame and fortune as an interior designer. There wasn't much call for her line of work on Conn, and the journey - a series of ferry, car and aeroplane commutes - hadn't made their chances of living together very easy. When she'd announced that she was moving to Inverness to be closer to her work, Bob had given his blessing. It was supposed to be a two centre home kind of thing. She'd be back at the weekend, or Bob could travel over to Inverness and stay with her. In reality, the arrangement was doomed to failure. There wasn't any anger involved, no bust up, any other love interests; they simply had separate lives, separate ambitions and requirements. The divorce nine years later was more through agreement that it made sense than any bitterness on either of their parts.

Ironically, Stephanie's dreams never came to fruition. Her plan to become the next sought after expert to dress the homes of the stars and celebrities had culminated in her opening a flower shop that sidelined in incense sticks and dream catchers. When she realised that she wasn't as talented as she'd first assumed, it wasn't so bad. She was happy enough with her lot. Flowers and alternative décor brought in a fair income, and satisfied her awareness of her self-worth enough that it didn't make sense for her to return to Conn and take up the mantle of police wife once more. The arrangement also suited Bob. He'd grown to prefer living alone. Allowed him the privacy his thoughts begged. Allowed him the freedom to be the best bobby he could be - his own life ambition.

Yet, here he was, thinking how *comfortable* this felt. So much like the old times that he ached with fondness.

"God," he whispered. "I'm turning into a lonely old man."

He put his mind to spooning coffee granules into mugs, but even this was a reminder of past times. Strangely, it had taken him a long time to shake the habit of preparing two cups; even after Stephanie had been gone for months he often found that he'd habitually prepared a cup for her without realising he was alone in the house. Such a small domestic chore, yet it brought a twinge of longing to his heart.

Above him came the sound of a hair dryer. Shelly had just accomplished something that Stephanie wasn't capable of. Steph's showers used to take ages, and getting ready to go anywhere demanded hours of preparation and pre-planning. Bob shook his head, marvelling at this subtle difference. It was enough to bring him out of the nostalgia and back to the present. He added milk, sugar, boiling water, to the mugs. Then he carried the mugs through to the living room as the sounds of Shelly's hurried attempts at dressing moved to a bedroom.

Bob's vigil didn't last long. Shelly appeared in the doorway, dressed in her regulation black and whites, tucking her shirt into her trousers as she bumbled across the room searching for her boots. She sat down in an armchair as she tugged on her high-tops and began lacing them. She smelled of chamomile soap and warmth, and her complexion was as florid as her hair remained damp. Foregoing make up, and with her hair pulled back into a ponytail, she looked younger than she was. She watched Bob from beneath the curve of flickering eyelashes as she tugged and cinched her laces. Bob ducked his head and concentrated on sipping his coffee.

"You said the D.I. was on his way over," Shelly said.

"Aye. Apparently he's commandeered the air ambulance to bring him over. Not regulation procedure, you must admit."

"Not at all," Shelly agreed. She grabbed at her own mug, took a hurried gulp. Not a bad cup of coffee, she decided. "Did the inspector give any hint at what the job is he's got for us?"

Bob gave a shake of his head. "I guess it's connected to what has already happened with the Stewarts."

"Oh, God. Not Bethany, I hope."

"Don't think it has anything to do with the wee lass," Bob offered. "CID is leading the search for her. Apparently they've asked for assistance from the MOD police up at Burra Ness to help with the search. Plus our own people are out there looking, too."

"Maybe we should've stayed for the search party," Shelly said. "It felt wrong, us leaving the way we did."

Bob chewed a lip. "We'd done all we could up until then. What good would we have been staying on duty? We'd both put in a long night; we'd both experienced a terrible shock. It was best that we got away for a while to clear our heads. The inspector kens that, too. I don't think that he'd be calling us back in if he didn't have to."

Shelly didn't miss his use of 'we' and 'us'. Small words that held so much power and compassion that she couldn't help smiling at him for his consideration. She was still reeling from the after effects of shame that her feint had brought on, and she appreciated his continued reassurance that they were in this together, and her weakness would remain their secret.

"Anyway. You about ready, Sarge?" Bob stood up. He drained his mug in a continuous gulp. Prompted by his action, Shelly also downed her drink, wishing that it were super-charged caffeine, maybe a quadruple espresso. She believed that she was going to need all the stimulation she could get.

The windows-down drive to the station was barely long enough to shake the last vestiges of sleep from her mind. The sight of Detective Inspector Marsh's troubled frown did the trick, though. The adrenalin trickling through her system gave her a buzz unlike any amount of caffeine or fresh air could ever achieve. He gave no preamble, or any explanation, but Shelly instinctively knew that what was already bad had now grown perceptibly worse. Shivering with anticipation she followed her grey-faced superior into the squad room. The cramped room was fit to bursting. Marsh had brought further reinforcements in the shape of Sergeant Alex Kelsoe, and three constables she didn't know by their faces but was familiar with through their collar numbers; Collins, Brooke and Entwhistle. All four were Tactical Support Officers. In layman's terms they carried guns and were trained to use them. She nodded at each in greeting. They obviously had been previously briefed by the inspector, judging by the grim nods they offered her and Bob.

Detective Inspector Marsh didn't play around. He jumped straight to the point. "I don't think I need expand on this, people. As you are all aware, we already have a murdered boy. A missing girl. In the last hour we have received word of the discovery of *another* corpse. There is something seriously wrong happening here on Conn." He paused for the murmur of assent only long enough to put a little iron in his jaw. "We are bloody well going to put a stop to it."

TWENTYFOUR

Trowhaem

A murder of crows.

Such a strange collective term when you think about it. Not in this situation. There was no more apt a description for the billowing flock that launched from the rocks in front of Broom and I. They flapped and shrieked in anger at our trespassing upon their turf. Some of them even dived at us in an effort to see us off. Against their sharp beaks and talons, my uplifted hands would have been ineffective, but the dive bomb tactics were all bluff and they rapidly settled to earth a short distance away, hopping to find a new vantage over the scene.

One of the scruffy beasts won a small victory over us, splattering my shoulder with fishy droppings before wheeling away and perching itself on a boulder higher up the slope. The crow made a sound like bitter laughter.

"You dirty…" Muttering, I scratched in a pocket for a tissue to clean its muck off my coat. I'm not the tissue carrying type so had to resort to using the palm of my hand.

My good friend Paul Broom was obviously impressed. "What are you complaining about? They say it's lucky."

"I never did believe in *that* old wives' tale." I scratched at the mess and only served to spread it down my chest. Finally giving up on the task, I wiped my hand clean on the damp grass.

"You should start trusting the portents," Broom said, and I was unsure if he was pulling my leg or not. "What just happened could be a sign of good luck to come."

"What are you saying, Broom? Not only am I a magnet for the evil of the world, but I'm also a shit magnet, too? And I'm supposed to be thankful?"

"One and the same thing, isn't it?"

"Uh, yeah, I suppose it is."

The cawing of the birds echoed Broom's chuckle.

Myself, I'd fallen silent.

We'd come to the edge of the outcrop of rocks. Standing directly below us was Janet from the ferry. I saw that she too had fallen foul of the damn crows; she was in the process of plucking a feather from her lips. It can't have tasted too pleasant, judging by the grimace she cast up at us. Or maybe her twisting lips were due to the mess decorating the front of my coat. Self-consciously I placed a hand over the bird muck as I returned a similar strained smile. I'd been dreaming about this woman with thoughts that would possibly earn me a slapped face if I spoke them aloud, and here we were, face-to-face once more, and me with bird crap on my clothes. Not the reunion I'd been hoping for.

I noted the flicker of recognition in Janet's eyes. Surprise, then a moment of what I took to be disappointment before she finally brightened. It lifted my heart to see the spark grow in her eyes, even though I quickly found my delight was misguided.

"You must be Paul Broom," she said, staring at my large friend. "The famous author?"

Broom stuffed his hands in his trouser pockets, affecting his bashful schoolboy look. He shared a glance with me before turning his attention back on Janet. He pulled a hand out, waggled a finger in her direction. "What? My reputation precedes me?"

She gave a sly nod my way. "Just a guess."

Broom glanced at me again.

"You two have met before?"

I nodded. "Paul Broom, this is…uh, Janet."

"Janet." Broom gave her a nod.

"Forgive me for not shaking your hand," Janet said, indicating a tarpaulin-shrouded mound between us. "It's a little awkward…"

I was astute enough to guess what it was that she was guarding. Janet remained the humorous lady I met on the boat, and I could tell now that the sour look on her face had nothing to do with our arrival, but for the stink. I was reasonably sure that she was relieved that we'd turned up.

"I'm waiting for the police," she offered. "You didn't by chance notice any police cars on the road, did you?"

Broom said, "Sorry, but you might have a long wait."

"There's been an incident near to Ura Taing" I chipped in, "and it looks like most of the police resource is tied up with it." Even as I said this I recalled the sergeant and constable who had stopped me last night and realised that they hadn't been in evidence at Catherine Stewart's place. Then again, they would most likely be off duty now, having pulled the nightshift.

Janet shook her head in mild frustration. She nudged the folds of tarpaulin with a boot. "I don't believe it. Surely this is more important? I did say that we'd found a body."

As she said this, her eyes flickered up at us, and I saw her chew at her bottom lip. She'd spoken out of turn and instantly regretted her words.

Broom said, "It's okay. We already know about your discovery here."

A small furrow appeared between her brows. Choosing not to challenge us about how we could know what was found, she instead looked over at a VW van parked nearby. It was the same one that had collected her and her colleagues from the ferry, with the self-same driver behind the wheel.

"Did Harry call you on the phone?" she asked with what sounded like a hint of derision.

Broom lifted his chin. "Is that Harry in the van?"

"Yes. Did he phone you?"

We shook our heads. Broom said, "We've never met. Is he Harry Bishop? The professor from Edinburgh? He's the one in charge here, isn't he?"

Janet scowled at the bearded man. It was all the answer we needed. She didn't say it, but I could tell she wasn't exactly thrilled with Professor Bishop's leadership qualities. Broom knew it too. He shrugged, showing Janet that it made no difference.

"Is the professor okay?" Broom asked. "He looks a little…erm, distracted."

Janet sighed. "He's okay. He's just had a bit of a shock, that's all."

"I was hoping to ask him a couple of questions." Couching his next question so that it didn't seem disrespectful to her, Broom asked, "But in lieu of the professor, who is the next best person to speak to?"

"That would be Professor Hale," she said.

Broom stared off across the archeological site, searching out a likely contender. "Where would I find him?"

"You would find *her* right here," Janet said. "I'm Professor Hale."

At my surprised look, she smiled. "But I prefer to be called Janet, if you don't mind."

"I remember," I said. "That's your formal name *and* your informal one."

We ignored Broom's quizzical frown.

Janet turned to him. "Could you tell me something, Mr Broom? What do you call your friend?"

"Carter."

Janet nodded slowly, and again Broom was left frowning at us. There were a few empty seconds between us as we each digested what we had - or hadn't - learned. Broom, being the odd man out in this triangle, said to Janet, "I've read a little concerning this dig. I have an interest in the work your team has undertaken here, so I have been following your progress in the local newspaper."

Janet shook her head. "The local paper hasn't exactly been kind to us."

"No," Broom said. "They haven't. The point I was about to make is that I haven't heard your name in connection with Trowhaem before…"

Janet inhaled uneasily. I detected a flash of her eyes in my direction as she said, "I've been misrepresented by the press. When I have been mentioned, it's been under my *previous* name."

Janet looked uncomfortable. She wasn't under any obligation to explain anything about her past to us, but I couldn't help feel that her next words were meant for me. I also very clearly recalled the way she'd hidden her wedding ring when we'd spoke on the ferry. "I've always been referred to in the press by my married name. Connery. My husband and I are separated, awaiting a divorce. I've gone back to using my maiden name."

I nodded along with her explanation, feeling warm inside. Hoping that the attraction I believed existed between us had given her cause to put the record straight. Show me that she was available and I had nothing to fear. Broom on the other hand, appeared mildly embarrassed.

"Look, Professor," he said. "I'm sorry. I wasn't prying, and hope that I haven't insulted you."

Janet smiled openly. "Don't worry, Mr Broom. If you'd insulted me, I'd have let you know."

Broom and Janet shared a chuckle. Not the most experienced man around women; I said the first thing that came to mind, "So you're a professor, huh?"

Janet blinked. Luckily for me, her question retained a little mirth. "Does that surprise you?"

"Well, uh, no. Not really. It's just that…"

"I'm not an old grey-haired guy, with bifocals and a tatty old tweed jacket?"

"No," I said. "I just don't think you look old enough."

"But too old to be a student?" Her comment was firmly tongue in cheek, and designed to poke fun at my previous attempt at small talk. It did the trick, left me kicking at loose dirt.

Guessing what must have come before concerning Janet and I, Broom decided enough was enough. He was confident around women, but wasn't *exactly* interested in them. Despite Cash's assertion, Broom was no more a homosexual than I, it was simply that he had no interest in sex, and to my knowledge had been celibate all his life. He told me once, in order to get me to open up regarding my own concerns, that he was a forty-two year old virgin and proud of the fact. He argued that what other people saw as odd wasn't important if you yourself were resolved and at ease with your life choices. Only thing was, he was like a reformed smoker in that respect, and would often belittle me for my need to find solace with the opposite sex, the way an ex-smoker will complain if someone lights up in their presence. Undoubtedly, what he saw as flirting made him uncomfortable. He was quick to get us back on track as to why we'd hotfooted it here. He indicated the tarpaulin shroud.

"Is he under there?"

Janet nodded. She gave Harry Bishop a quick glance, before she said, "No offence, Mr Broom. I'm not sure I should be discussing this with you."

Broom's shrug was expansive. "What harm can it do? I can assure you, my interest isn't purely the inquisitiveness of a writer. I had hoped to be of some assistance to you...and to the police."

"Again, no offence. But what help could you be? Despite your obvious skills as a writer, I doubt your expertise lies in crime scene investigation."

Broom gave her a happy smile. "Too true. I'm no Sherlock Holmes, I admit. My reason for attending was purely to see if I could be of assistance in identifying the body. I've been resident on Connor's Island long enough that I might recognise the dead man's face."

"I don't think that you'll be much help in that respect either." What went unsaid was much more evident than her remark.

The description I'd been able to build concerning James Stewart's death didn't bear thinking about, and I could only assume the worst regarding this latest find. Judging by Janet's aversion to what lay concealed beneath the tarpaulin, I didn't really want to look.

Broom continued to push. "I'm going to come down, if that's all right? I promise I won't interfere with the scene. I only want a quick look." Broom was ungainly as he negotiated the descent to Janet's level. I didn't share his unhealthy desire to see the body, and showed this by stepping away and concentrating on the toes of my boots.

I remained focussed on the inanity of my footwear, but only until I heard Broom's exclamation, "He's been skinned!"

Against my will, I had to take a peek. Dear God, I wished that I hadn't.

The man in the grave was like something out of a gore-splattered zombie movie. His skin and much of the adhering flesh had been torn from his frame, leaving him a patchwork of open, raw wounds and splintered bones. He was naked. Not a strand of hair remained on his skull, or any other obvious characteristic that could identify him. In fact, only through his height and build would I even guess that he was male, for even in this horrendous state I could see that he'd been of an imposing size. Feeling sick to the stomach, I stared down into the grave wondering what kind of monster could do such a thing to a man. A trow? Admittedly, I was beginning to *believe* Broom's madness.

"You see that, Janet?" I heard Broom say. "His teeth have been smashed out, his lower jaw shattered."

"I did notice that, yes." Janet's answer was barely above a whisper.

"Why do you suppose he'd do that?" Broom wondered. Then, before an answer was forthcoming, he said, "Only one reason isn't there? Whomever killed this man did so with the intention of making identification of him very difficult indeed. I believe that the skin was removed to deny us any fingerprints, or scars or blemishes, maybe even a recognisable tattoo. The teeth and jaw was crushed so that even dental records would be useless. The killer is very calculating, don't you think?"

"He's a beast," Janet offered, and I could only agree.

Broom stroked his chin with a finger. He stared at the man in the grave and I was more than slightly perturbed to note that he didn't appear that moved by the ugliness of the murder. He turned his gaze to Janet. "Other than through DNA, are there any other ways of identifying this man?"

Janet sniffed. "I thought that this had nothing to do with your curiosity as a writer; I get the impression that you are using this terrible situation to source reference your next book. I find that a little distasteful, Mr Broom. I'd be happy to discuss identification procedures with you, but not now. Not here."

Here, here, I thought. I'm in agreement with you, Janet.

Broom was nonplussed. "You know, I always encounter this problem." He gave me a pointed look. "Whenever I offer my help, people always think I have an ulterior motive. Simply because of my trade, people think that anything I offer comes with a price. I'm not Satan bartering for souls, Professor Hale. I was genuinely sharing my thoughts with one I believed would have a valid opinion."

Shrugging away the last few comments, Janet offered, "Facial reconstruction. It is a process sometimes used by scientists to reconstruct the facial characteristics of exhumed skeletons. The police also employ the same practice, but for wholly different reasons."

She didn't go into the specifics concerning the procedure, judging that we were both intelligent enough to understand what she was describing. Broom was obviously familiar with the practice, as he didn't push for further explanation. I'd watched a couple of TV programmes on the subject, and had recently viewed a reconstruction from the mummified remains of Tutankhamen, so I was also familiar with the scientific process.

"I take it that such an endeavour is rather time consuming, possibly not viable in this instance?" Broom said.

"You'd be guessing correct," Janet said. "It's more likely that the body is checked for any underlying historical traumas. For example, any mended fractures or evidence of medical procedures that could be compared with hospital records. Unfortunately, this procedure is generally used to confirm identity where the subject is preliminarily identified due to other factors. Take a train wreck or air disaster where there are a number of fatalities, perhaps they have been burned or disfigured, then this process can be used to confirm each individual."

A frown furrowed its way into Broom's brow. "Yes," he concurred. "But what you are saying is that there would have to be some reason to look at a specific individual's medical records to ascertain that person's identity. The police haven't access to some super computer that cross-references everyone's records have they?"

"No. They don't have that ability." Janet glanced once at the dead man, then back to Broom. "If someone were to come forward with…say for instance, a report of a missing person…well, then the police would be able to request access to the medical records of that person and then use them for comparison. If they had no leads, well, they'd be simply fishing in the dark."

"So…unless someone comes forward with a possible name, it's unlikely that the police would use this method?"

"The body will be minutely examined, and any identifying factors will be catalogued in the body of an autopsy report. This would be used in any subsequent inquest, or as a record for comparison as-and-when a possible name comes to light." She shrugged. 'Other than that, a DNA test will ascertain the identity, but only if the victim has been previously sampled, or they have an idea whose body it is and take comparison samples from a sibling or parent."

"I see," Broom said. Watching his face I couldn't decide whether-or-not he appeared happy with the conclusion.

Adding my own opinion, I said, "Small island like this, it's likely that someone will come forward pretty quickly. I can't imagine you can be on the island very long without someone missing you."

"Probably." Broom was wearing a whimsical smile that didn't associate with the course of our conversation. Maybe it was just me, but I found even the slightest of smiles inappropriate. I lowered my eyebrows, jutted my jaw at him. It was pointless, in fact; if anything, Broom's smile grew wider.

Grunting, I switched my focus to Janet. She appeared to have decided that Broom's interest in the dead man wasn't to her taste, and I watched her flip the tarpaulin back into place, concealing the brutally damaged skull and torso.

Wind stirred by the tarpaulin carried a charnel stench. Not so much decomposition as the stale stench of a butcher's block. I covered my nose and mouth with my hands, moving away. From the lower level, Janet followed my progress. I glanced at her. Our gazes met and stuck.

"I can understand Mr Broom's interest in this, but what about you, Carter? You don't strike me as the type I'd expect to show up here."

I fed my hands into my coat pockets. Lifting my shoulders, I said, "I'm just tagging along with Broom. Believe me, the last thing I expected when I woke up this morning was to visit two murder scenes."

Janet's pupils dilated. "Two murders?"

"Yeah," I said. "The other incident the police are dealing with at Ura Taing…" A solid lump forced its way into my throat. "A little boy was killed. His sister is also missing."

"Children? Dear God! What's going on here?"

Broom said, "The haugbonde curse."

We both turned to him. For me, I was surprised that Broom had brought up this nonsense in the presence of one as sophisticated as a professor. Janet's response seemed more like genuine shock. Her sudden fear was what I couldn't fathom. Still, her next words went a little way to clarify her thoughts on the subject.

"Don't tell me that you give that childish nonsense any credibility, Mr Broom? I'd have thought that one as learned as you would realise that fairies and trolls belong in children's books."

Her comment made me want to agree with her, but there was something in the tone of her voice that said she too had considered the curse legend as a viable explanation for the presence of the dead man.

"Take my words as analogous, if you wish," Broom said, unfazed by her pointed sarcasm. "But you must admit that the thought has crossed your mind."

Janet shook her head, but the reddening of her cheeks told the lie.

"You can deny it all you want, Professor." Broom's face took on angles and planes I was unfamiliar with. Not very often did Broom show anger and I was momentarily stunned to silence. He jabbed a finger at Janet. "This is only the latest mishap that you've had to contend with, isn't it? You've had to suffer a number of setbacks, haven't you? Confrontation from the islanders? Mechanical failures? Bad weather?" He swung his finger to point at the swamped excavation site. "Floods. And I bet you aren't the only one experiencing personal problems."

"Broom." My voice cracked like a gunshot. "That's enough."

Broom was well out of order. He had no right to talk to anyone that way. Bringing up something as hurtful as her divorce as proof of his argument was disgraceful to say the least.

Blowing hot and cold with equal speed, Broom's smile blossomed again. Then it flickered to an embarrassed grimace. "I'm sorry, Professor Hale. I shouldn't have been so personal. But all I was attempting to point out is that the signs are all there. Don't you agree that there has been more than its fair share of bad luck connected to this archeological dig?"

In a very un-professorial manner Janet said, "Shit happens all the time, Mr Broom, to everyone, everywhere. It doesn't mean that ancient curses are to blame."

Broom allowed his head to drop, his mane of hair concealing his features. He wasn't acquiescing. "Shit does happen. But how often does it turn up in the shape of a skinned corpse and an eviscerated child? Childish nonsense or not, you must see that your time on the island is up? In that respect, the haugbonde curse wins out."

Janet's mouth made a thin line. "Mr Broom. Your haugbonde is going to have to try harder than this if he expects me to leave Connor's Island."

Air stuttered into Broom's lungs. His eyes took on the intensity of lasers. "You are a very brave woman, Professor Hale. Or very stupid. You should reconsider...I cannot guarantee your safety if you stay here."

"You cannot guarantee my safety? What are you, the bloody haugbonde's keeper?" Janet fisted her hands on her hips. I liked the pose she struck. No longer the nervous, frightened woman, she projected an image of strength that named her a leader. She wasn't intimidated by Broom or the presence of the corpse at her feet. She was all the more beautiful for it. Unashamedly I watched her.

Something happened in that moment that I find difficult to describe. Recalling the incident where I'd momentarily embraced my supposed power and I'd experienced a rush of energy charging throughout my body and beyond, I saw a similar energy build around Janet. It was a pulsating aurora of yellow-orange fire, flaring like a brazier in a sudden breeze. Her skin became translucent, and her emotions were displayed as a flickering, shifting miasma of colour within.

I wasn't prepared for anything like this, and out of reaction I blinked. The colours disappeared and all that remained was the woman. Beautiful still, but wholly natural to the eye.

It was as if nothing had happened. Broom and Janet held their tableau of subtle challenge, neither of them aware of my bewildered scrutiny of them.

Broom said, "Yet again I've opened my mouth without consideration. Forgive me, Professor. I wasn't implying that I wished harm on you...or on anyone else for that matter."

"So what is it that you are trying to say?"

Broom waved a hand at me. I was probably standing there looking like I was catching flies in my open mouth. Neither of them seemed to notice.

Continuing, Broom explained, "We intend to put a stop to this nastiness. We cannot afford to be side-tracked by the need to protect anyone else."

Janet wasn't the only one who realised that Broom's words were meant more for me than the professor. Her features softened as she studied me. In response my brows crept towards my hairline, and my hands scrubbed determinedly at an imagined itch on my neck. Janet inhaled deeply, tore her gaze off me and asked Broom, "You think I am in danger?"

His head seesawed. "Not necessarily you, Professor Hale. But considering that you are standing on the very land protected by the haugbonde curse, you have set yourself clearly in his sights. I would rather you left the island, then there would be no chance that harm could come to you."

"That's very admirable of you, Mr Broom. But you sound exactly like the small-minded thugs who tried to frighten us away when we first arrived on the island."

"You should have heeded their warnings." For emphasis, Broom indicated the tarpaulin shroud. "Then this may not have happened."

Janet's nostrils flared. "You are blaming this man's death on me?"

"No. Not you. On the curse."

"But by association, that makes it the fault of my colleagues and me. If we didn't dig here, then this man would still be alive?"

Broom sniffed. "Stands to reason."

"And we're also to blame for the deaths of these children?" Janet's voice was rising in pitch.

"Not to blame. But they are a consequence of the curse."

"I don't believe what you are implying, Mr Broom."

"I'm implying nothing. Simply reading the signs. Following the portents."

Janet slashed at the air with her hand. "This man was murdered, Mr Broom. By a sick-minded killer who I believe shares your desire to see us gone from the island."

"Though my desire is only through my concern for your safety," Broom pointed out.

"Says you," Janet snapped. "I'm beginning to think that you're in agreement with whoever did this, and you want us gone. Well, sorry, Mr Broom. I'm going nowhere."

"And I'm sorry to hear that," Broom said. "All I can ask then is that you stay alert. Watch for the signs, Professor."

"What signs?" Janet huffed.

"The portents."

"Portents?"

Broom nodded.

The air filled with shrieking, billowing black forms as our audience of crows took to the air. Their racket was like insane laughter as they took off northward with single-minded intent.

"The portents," Broom repeated. "Look at the crows. The harbingers of death recognise the signs."

Janet shook her head in incredulity.

"Come, Carter," Broom said in a voice straight out of pantomime. "We are done here. We have to go north. Someone else is in danger."

Then he was clumping his way back up the slope. Janet and I shared a moment. We were each as incredulous as the other. My body language told her not to worry, that I was in control. If the need arose, I would be there for her. Her slow smile showed me she did indeed read the signs. That was all I needed. Finally, Janet lifted her fingers and gave me a goodbye wave. I returned the gesture, then slowly followed Broom. Inappropriate here or not, a smile crept onto my face.

Broom clambered up the slope, his bad leg dragging behind him. I considered lending him a hand, but following his bad manners towards Janet, he deserved a little discomfort and I decided to hang back. Unfortunately, that blocked my view of the approaching police officers, until I was mere feet from them.

TWENTYFIVE

Trowhaem

Carter Bailey? Here? Why doesn't that surprise me?

Between DI Marsh and Bob Harris, Shelly experienced a pang of inferiority. For no other reason than she was the most diminutive of the three of them, she felt like a little girl hemmed in by well-meaning adults. Ordinarily, that would cause anger to flare within her. She didn't need protection. She was a big girl. A bloody police sergeant, for Christ's sake! So why was she trembling when she saw Carter Bailey jerk back in surprise when almost walking into them?

Instinctively she caught his eye, searching for the least hint of the scarlet she'd seen flaring there the evening before. Of course, other than the brief shock, the flicker of recognition, there was nothing unearthly about the man's eyes. He had the look of damaged goods, was all. As if he was deeply sad. Considering what the man had gone through, that wasn't surprising.

She considered challenging him and his big blond friend. But then a note of caution dug in her mind. *Deus ex machina*, Shelly, she reminded herself. Don't blame Bailey, simply because he is a handy scapegoat.

Carter Bailey and his limping companion gave them a strained nod as they passed, not keen on any further encounter with the law than this brief greeting. Thinking she should detain them for questioning, Shelly opened her mouth to call them back until she realised Bob and D.I. Marsh had continued on towards the edge of the embankment they were on. Shelly watched Bailey and the man she presumed was Paul Broom as they continued on their way. Neither gave as much as a backwards glance. Then, deciding that she could always find them later, she hurried to catch up to her colleagues. Give Marsh a reason to think her tardiness was reticence to get involved and she could wave bye-bye to her position as supervisor on the island. Best she get in there and show him she was capable of her command.

She smelled the body before she saw it. Recognised death. Unlike the previous time, she bolstered herself. No way was she going to faint in front of the inspector.

There was a woman standing by the body. Shelly vaguely recognised her as one of two professors involved in the excavation of Trowhaem. During previous visits to the site Shelly usually spoke to Professor Bishop, but she'd also had passing contact with this woman. Couldn't remember her name, though. What was it? Jane? Janice?

"Janet Hale," the professor fortuitously identified herself. "I'm the one who called you."

Introductions were made, and Shelly led the way off the embankment so that they all stood alongside the professor. It was Bob's place to pull back the tarpaulin, and he crouched down with a popping of knees and the subtle groan of a man aware of encroaching years. Shelly made sure that she was ready, but still made the slightest of exhalations at what Bob disclosed. But that was okay; she wasn't the only one disturbed by what they were looking at.

"I don't think it'll take a pathology report to show this man died an unnatural death," D.I. Marsh said.

Shelly gave her superior a sidelong look, before sharing a second or two with Bob. Bob's faint smile said it all; so it's that kind of ingenuity that gets you a detective inspector position these days?

To Janet Hale, Shelly said, "You said that you called in the report; was it also you that found him?"

Marsh held up a hand to halt any response from Janet. He flicked a hand at the dead man, "Best we protect the scene first, Sergeant. We can organise witness statements later."

In the next instant, Marsh took Janet Hale by the elbow and led her away from the graveside. Turning to follow, Shelly caught a sharp glance from the detective inspector who nodded hard at the grave. Shelly gritted her teeth, but chose to ignore the obvious slight forced by her exclusion. She wanted to talk with Janet, too. Not least to hear first hand the professor's version of events surrounding the discovery of the dead man, instead of having to read it in Bob - or another constable's - report, she also wanted to ask the woman what Carter Bailey and Paul Broom had been doing here. Instead, she was left to organise protection of the scene until back up could arrive and take over. Looked like she would be on guard duty for some time yet. For all intent and purpose, she may as well forget she was a sergeant and get on with the lot usually handed the lowest ranking probationer.

Bob steepled his eyebrows. He held up a roll of blue and white crime scene tape. "What do they call it, Sarge? Groundhog day?"

"It's beginning to feel that way, Bob," Shelly agreed. "But at least it isn't raining this time."

Bob paced away from the grave, then lay a large stone on the end of the crime scene tape, and began uncoiling it as he reversed his route, before scrambling up the embankment above. Shelly began searching for further natural objects she could use to define a perimeter. She began piling loose rocks into a mini cairn. She saw Marsh and Janet Hale approach a VW van, and watched as Professor Bishop clambered out of the driver's seat and almost fling himself at the inspector. The big man appeared manic. Shelly couldn't make out what he was saying, but his voice was high with anxiety as he clutched at Marsh's clothing. Marsh, in response, took a backward step, turning to Shelly for support. Typically, he wanted the glory of being top dog, but not the commotion that went with dealing with irate witnesses.

From his vantage above the grave, Bob whispered, "Let him get on with it, Shelly. He didn't want you with him a minute ago. Ignorant bastard that he is."

In agreement, Shelly allowed her gaze to slip away as though she hadn't noticed Marsh's imploring look. She busied herself with catching the roll of tape Bob tossed to her and wedging it under a boulder.

"I'm surprised he's even bothered to turn out," Bob went on. "Since when did you hear about a D.I. at a crime scene when there wasn't a photo or TV opportunity in the offing?"

Shelly chuckled. It was a dry, humourless sound. "If the D.S. wasn't already tied up with the Stewart boy, do you think Marshy would have even come out of his office?"

"No way." It was Bob's turn to chuckle, though his laughter was bitter. Not a little sadistic.

"Two murders," Shelly said. "Here on Conn. Can you believe it, Bob?"

"You ken what worries me?" Bob straightened up, studying her with a face as flat as though moulded from wax.

"I do," Shelly said. "Bad things always come in threes. Let's pray to God it doesn't this time, eh?"

"I only hope God's in a listening mood," Bob whispered. "For Bethany's sake."

TWENTYSIX

The road to Burra Ness, Connor's Island

"What the hell was all that about, Broom?"

"What was what all about?"

"You know fine well. You had a go at Janet. It was totally uncalled for."

We were in the Subaru once more, barrelling northward. There was no hint of the flock of crows that Broom decided we must follow, but his attention was locked on the grey clouds churning on the horizon. He held his lower jaw protruding forward so that I could see saliva glistening on his teeth, sniffing harshly every other second. His tongue periodically lolled over his teeth like a squirming maggot. I could tell he was upset.

"What's wrong with you?"

"Nothing's wrong with me." Broom tone said otherwise. Adding validity to what was already obvious, he wrestled with the gear stick, cursing under his breath at the perceived sluggishness of the car's response.

"You were going on like Janet was personally responsible for what happened to that man."

"She isn't?"

Grasping at my seatbelt, I said, "No, Broom. She isn't."

"What makes you so certain?" Broom finally snatched his gaze towards me. Deep furrows knitted the flesh of his brow. "Suddenly you know everything, do you?"

I didn't answer for a moment, allowing my silence to convey my confusion. When I did speak, it wasn't premeditated. Brain and mouth out of synch. "Maybe I do. It was obvious to me that Janet is a good person."

Broom exhaled harshly.

"You're thinking with your balls," he snapped. "Just 'cause you've got the hots for *Janet* doesn't mean that she's all sweetness and light. For all you know, she's a twisted whore who tore the skin from that man's corpse."

I banged my knuckles against the dashboard. If I'd put my fist in his face like I almost did, I wouldn't have climbed from the wreckage of the Subaru unscathed. Broom flinched at the sound, then visibly shrank down into the seat.

"Enough, Broom." I shook my head. "I don't know what your problem is with Janet, but just keep it to yourself, will you."

He lifted his shoulders. "I haven't got a problem with her."

"Doesn't sound like it to me."

"I'm telling you. Janet and I are fine, okay?"

"So why were you rude to her?"

"It wasn't personal. It was just like I said: if the excavation didn't take place, then no one would be dead."

"If you believe this haugbonde story."

"I do," Broom said. "Maybe you're not fully decided…yet. But you must agree that you have your suspicions."

I showed him my palms.

Broom's exhalation was harsh. "She knows."

"Who? Janet?"

He nodded. "She knows that I speak the truth. She can deny it all she wants, but she knows that the man in the grave was put there with the intention that he would be found. He's a warning. To stop digging."

"I agree with you there, Broom. But that doesn't make Janet - or anyone else associated with the dig - responsible for the murder."

"Depends on your perspective. If the dig was abandoned before now there'd have been no need for anyone to die, would there? Okay, I'll grant you that I'm perhaps pointing the finger of blame too directly at Janet, but she has to accept some of the responsibility."

"Why, Broom? Why should she be blamed for the actions of a mad man? It's like blaming a vehicle manufacturer for building the car that a drunk driver later runs into a little old lady on the street."

"Cause and effect. Regardless of your argument to the contrary, it does have bearing on why I should blame Janet. Because her actions have loosed the haugbonde people are dying." Broom's conviction was the only thing that avoided his words sounding pathetic.

"No," I said. "That's bollocks."

"Fair enough. Let's just agree to disagree, shall we?"

I shook my head like a dog with a flea in its ear. "No, Broom. Not this time. I can't agree. Janet is blameless and I'm resolute on the issue. I *know* that she's innocent."

Maybe it was my tone that brooked no challenge. More likely it was because I was finally accepting of the power Broom believed I held, and he perceived this in my voice and was pleasantly surprised. Whatever it was, his features smoothed out and he gave me a quirky nod. "Go on, Carter."

"I saw something." I didn't expound. Not then.

Broom waited. A smile built at the corners of his mouth.

"It's not the first time," I said.

His large head bobbed, throwing his hair in his eyes. He flicked it back with a finger then grabbed at the steering wheel as the car wove patterns on the fabric of the road. Chewing his lip wasn't a product of his nervous driving, I knew. His excitement was down to anticipation of what I was about to disclose. In the end, he could wait no longer and he offered an explanation. "You saw colours, didn't you?"

"Yes." I relaxed into my seat. Admitting to Broom that I was ready to embrace what he'd promoted all this time felt like a weight off my shoulders. Confession *is* good for the soul. "And I don't know why, but what I saw I actually understood. Don't ask me to explain how."

"No need," Broom said. "Often empathic comprehension is all that is necessary. Nevertheless, whatever the explanation, tell me what you saw."

"It was when Janet was in disagreement with you," I began. "I saw colours building around her. Like fire without heat. I've never seen it for real, but I imagine it was something like St Elmo's Fire that is witnessed playing round the rigging of ships."

"What colour?"

"It wasn't black if that's what you're asking."

Broom shrugged. "Contrary to popular belief - and I know it's something I have used for dramatic effect in my own books - but the colour black is not necessarily the only colour associated with evil when dealing with the auric lights."

"Auric lights? That's what you believe I saw?"

"Yes."

"I know we touched on this when we talked about your Zero Point Field theory, but are you talking about all that spiritual healing stuff?"

Broom grunted. "First, the Zero Point Field isn't my theory, it's an accepted scientific discovery. Second, yes, some scientists have begun to accept the possibility that the Field is what makes it possible for some people to heal others by the laying on of hands. Also the Field is what generates the auric lights said healers are purported to see. As we have previously confirmed, study of this field has shown that we as humans are a collection of negative and positive energies of varying densities. These energies permeate through and emit from every living person. These particles of energy usually appear in suspension around the human body in an oval shaped field. Healers believe that by studying the colours of a person's aura they can diagnose ill-health due to the mix and prevalence of the colours projected."

Not to be outdone, I offered, "Would this also explain my vision when I was pulled out of the river when Cash died?"

"You said you saw him as a scarlet serpent, bearing Cash's face. Perhaps your vision was only a figurative expression of your misunderstanding of what it was that you did see. Your mind twisted the vision into some sort of nightmare that fed off your fears. But, yes. What I now believe you saw was his auric energy, his spirit. Scarlet, muddy red, some greens, all these are associated with anger, fear, resentment and jealousy."

"Yeah," I agreed. "They're all traits that aptly sum up my brother."

"Arsehole." The word whispered through my mind, the briefest of interaction before Cash returned to wherever it was he lurked when I wasn't holding him in thrall.

"What colours did you see around Professor Hale?" Broom asked. I noticed that it was Professor Hale again, and not Janet, so berating him must have done some good.

"Yellow. Orange." I watched his face for any negative response but only detected acceptance.

"Yellow is indicative of inspiration, intelligence, creativity and a scientific mind. Orange denotes confidence, good health and vigour. In fact any bright colours are good signs. You might say that Professor Hale's auric field epitomises everything that she is. The paranormal equivalent of wearing ones emotions on one's sleeve, huh?"

"So what's the likelihood of her being a murderer?" I was purposely sarcastic.

"Your auric field is complex, Carter. It is built of various bands of light, each band having a different meaning. What I suspect you saw around Janet was her mental aura. The mental aura is indicative of the intensity of the thought process. What is more important to defining the over all state of one's mentality is what is termed the emotional aura. This is usually seen as a rainbow-like pallet of colours. Positive feelings and thoughts generate bright colours. Naturally, negative feelings generate dark." He looked at me.

"No dark colours," I confirmed.

"Huh."

"In fact," I went on. "Janet was anything but dark. It was almost as if her skin was translucent and I was looking inside her at the very essence of her being."

A nerve ticked at the corner of Broom's mouth. His breathing became perceptively quicker. "You could actually see *within* her?"

Flexing my hands, I explained, "Well, it's difficult to explain exactly what I did see, but yeah, I could see through her and could see swirling colour. There was nothing gross about it; I could detect a faint impression of her skeletal structure, but it was nothing like looking at the skinned face on that man's corpse. It was…it was…"

"Beautiful?"

My vision hazed into the small area of space between my knees and the dashboard. "It was beyond beautiful. It was heavenly."

Wind whistled out of Broom. "Well, Carter. I have to extend my apologies to both you and Janet. If what you say is correct, there's no way that she could be tainted by the haugbonde. I still stand by the cause and effect of her responsibility in the man's death, but I accept that Janet is an unwilling party in all this. Her spirit is clean."

I gave him a sharp nod. Apology accepted. Unfortunately my satisfaction was transitional to depression. "Makes me wonder what colours I'd portray to someone else with an ability to see the auric fields."

"If only I had the ability," Broom sighed. "But I suspect that your field will be predominantly made up of your astral and celestial auras. A brightly coloured rainbow cloud and bright shimmering pastel lights. I suspect that your aura will be made up of gold, silver, and royal blue. You are, after all, a seer."

A seer? Just one more title to add to the list.

Broom said, "Your ability, though untrained at this time, is of the highest order. Makes me wonder if you are a star child."

Despite myself, I laughed. "Christ, Broom! A star child? What are you saying? That I'm a flaming extra-terrestrial?"

"No, no, no. Of course not. A star child is the term used where a soul is in its very first incarnation. Do you recall our conversation regarding reincarnation? This is the belief that our energy is never destroyed, but continues on after our physical death and is reborn in a new form. Though not commonly accepted here in the West it is a firm belief of most Eastern religions. The idea is that such souls go through an infinite number of reincarnations until Nirvana or enlightenment is finally achieved. Of course, modern science tells us that there are in fact more living human beings on the face of the earth at this very moment than have existed throughout the entirety of human existence. Therefore it is feasible to assume that new life energy must be born all the time, running concurrent to all the other old souls already in the world. Well, when a new soul is born, this is seen as a pure form of energy, untainted by the sins and failures garnered in previous lives, extremely spiritual. These people born with a pure soul are designated the term of star child, as they have been born of the unadulterated power of the cosmos."

My laughter this time was tainted with a large chunk of sardonic disbelief. "You're definitely off your head if you think I'm some sort of untainted soul, Broom. I've the same failings and ineptitudes as anyone else. I have the same faults; greed, cowardice, vanity, whatever."

Broom's head bobbed in agreement. "But you didn't possess any of those faults at inception, Carter. Those are all adopted traits, the experiences of your thirty-odd years on this planet. The product of trial and error we all must endure."

Choosing to take the conversation no further along these lines, I told him about the other time that I'd experienced the power within me. My description of the building energy that seemed to project out from me had him grinning. Breathless, he said, "I have heard of only a few other cases of living people with this power, but I have always discounted the stories as fancy and exaggeration. There are monks of the Buddhist tradition purportedly adept at expelling their inner chi in a blast of power capable of extinguishing a candle flame, but I held the belief that this was more trickery or illusion on their part."

I shook my head. "I don't think it was anything along those lines that I felt. It was more like the energy was seeking something. Like a tentacle was snaking out of my body reaching and feeling to grasp onto something. It wasn't a nice sensation. It was frightening. When I panicked, the energy whipped back at me like an elastic band. Maybe you didn't notice, but I felt like I had been knocked on my arse."

Chewing his bottom lip Broom considered this. It was a good minute or so until he said, "Unusual. Something that requires further study. Let's leave it for now. We are here."

He brought the Subaru to a bumpy halt with two wheels on the verge. The scrubby grass making up the verge stretched twenty-or-so feet to the base of a chain link fence. The fence showed signs of corrosion, but it retained the semblance of potency associated with concentration camps. Not least, it stood twice my height and was topped with barbed wire. Warning signs strung on the fence every hundred metres forbade entrance. Disclaimers made mention of guard dogs and armed personnel; a coy way of saying 'Enter uninvited and you can kiss your sweet cheeks goodbye'. Didn't take the insight of a cosmic star child to guess we were parked at the perimeter of the Burra Ness nuclear submarine tracking station.

"What are we doing here?"

Broom jerked his head, indicating a small brick and tin-sheet building standing beyond the boundary fence. It had the appearance of the small huts utilised by the power companies to house substations. Cables like a handful of eels coiled from beneath the corrugated roof and met a tall telegraph pole sheathed as high as a tall man could reach in razor wire. I followed the pole skyward to the crossbeams and saw that it was equally sheathed at the top, this time by the silhouetted forms of dozens of crows. If they were the same flock that we'd followed from Trowhaem it didn't matter, the way in which the birds actually stared down at the utility hut held the promise of dark portentous activity. Just a glimpse of them gave the impression that they were hungry to pick at whatever lay within.

"You don't mean…?" I was thinking about the missing girl.

Broom shook his head. "Not yet."

"So why all the crows?"

"It's a sign. Just like I told Professor Hale. They have foreseen the future and are prepared to be patient and await the inevitable. Someone will die here, Carter. This very evening, I suspect."

Challenging him about the power of animal precognition was pointless. It had grown so it was easier to simply agree with his fanciful notions than sit through another of his essays pertaining to the weird world of Paul Broom.

"So what's the plan, Broom? If you suspect a crime's going to happen here, wouldn't it be wise if we went back to Trowhaem and informed the police?"

"The police don't put much faith in superstition or the portents of nature. But what are the chances of them believing I wasn't a complete head case who required locking up?"

"Zero to nil, I assume."

"There's only one thing for it," Broom decided. "You are going to have to stake out the hut."

I placed fingers to my chest. "Did I just hear you correctly? You meant me? Alone? As in me, myself and I? You can bloody forget it."

Broom's sigh filled the car. "I need to return home to carry out some research. I do not have the necessary materials to hand. Don't worry, though, I'll join you later. In the meantime, it's not a good idea that we leave the hut unattended. One of us has to stay here. You're armed, so it's the obvious choice that you stay."

"I'm not hanging around here all afternoon on the whim of…" I cast my eyes around, finally settling on the flock of crows. I jabbed my hand at them. "On the whim of a load of scabby old birds."

Broom's nose wrinkled. "Carter, how would you feel if something happened while we were gone? If someone died?"

"Don't, Broom. Don't try to lay that cause and affect bullshit on me, too."

"I'm not trying to do anything of the sort."

"Yes you are. You're hoping to play on my guilty conscience."

"What a distasteful notion," Broom said. "I'm merely using logical deduction. I need to return home. You don't. I'm unarmed while you have a gun. Plus, I do not share your ability in recognising evil. It stands to reason that you should be the one to stay."

"Logical deduction my arse. You just don't want to be the one standing out here in the cold. I'm not doing it. You can forget it, Broom. There's no way you can talk me into getting out this bloody car."

I was adamant.

Set in my ways.

Defiant.

Stubborn as hell.

Still, I was the one standing on the grass verge watching with a hollow sense of disbelief as Broom's Subaru headed back the way we'd come. The fucker best had bring back the flask of soup he promised, I thought, or there'd be more harsh words between us.

TWENTYSEVEN

The Dungeon

Crying was pointless. So was beating at the door with her small fists. All either action achieved was a pain in her chest or agony in her hands. Ineffectual. She did not understand the word. So she kept right on doing what came natural. If she thought about it, maybe she'd realise the futility of it all and stop. Only thing was, it was all that her desperate senses could come up with.

She sobbed. Tears fell. Her nose ran. Her chest ached.

She banged at the rough wood with her balled hands, feeling the static-like itch from the splinters already embedded in her flesh.

The door remained impregnable. It was like the dungeon doors that populated the stories in her favourite book of fairy tales. Not surprising really, for all the ogres and monsters in her tales had dungeons where they locked away children whilst they plumped them up for the cook pot.

The walls were as impregnable as the door. Rough bricks that were slick with damp and smelled like mushrooms. Even the floor was hard-packed gravel that had resisted her attempts at digging an escape tunnel. Her hands had been *ineffectual*, the heels of her shoes quickly worn down when she'd tried to scoop away the dirt with the pawing motions of a pony.

In the gloom it was difficult to guess the passage of time. Was it night or day? Is it tomorrow already, or still yesterday? She'd slept once, but couldn't tell if the blissful respite of ignorance had been for the briefest of time or that she'd slept for a hundred years like Sleeping Beauty.

By now someone must have found Wee Jimmy. Poor Wee Jimmy. Her Ma must have missed them by now. Ma must have gone out looking for them. She'd have been mad at first, but now Ma must be beside herself with worry.

She collapsed against the door, wracked with sobs. Mind screeching.

Why hasn't Ma come for me? Has she found Jimmy? Maybe she thinks the same thing has happened to me, too. What if Ma has stopped looking?

Phlegm cracked in her throat.

Does Ma blame me?

It wasn't me, Ma. It was Wee Jimmy. He hurt the bird. Not me. It was his fault. He made the Skeklar mad.

TWENTYEIGHT

Four of nine.

That shall be your number, Professor.

Now his stupid friend has diverted that Carter Bailey, you shall be the next to die.

I have decided.

Carter Bailey does possess power. I know that now. He saw you. He looked and he recognised your spirit. As I look at you now and recognise you. He saw an angel. Not me. I see meat. I see bones. I see fear. I see a whore.

You are connected. The attachment is made, though neither of you fully realise it yet. The gods have tipped their hands and brought you together. But remember this; the gods are fickle and cruel. They enjoy the taste of your impending destruction as much as the promise of what your coupling may wring from the future strands of destiny. They care not if you live or die. They do not take sides, these grim gods. Failure or triumph, it has no bearing on their schemes, their greater plans.

They have set the scene, ordered the protagonists, then sat back to watch how the game plays out. Uncaring. Unhelpful. Full of disdain for all us lesser beings.

Forget the gods, Professor.

Carter Bailey thinks he's your protector.

Aye. But, I am your ruination.

The gods are happy with their lot. The die is cast and it us up to us to decide all our fates.

Professor, I have decided. Your fate is to die. Can you not see?

I am fate.

I am here.

You are here.

Carter Bailey kicks his heels with only the laughter of my cohorts ringing in his ears. He is useless to you now.

How do you suppose it will affect him to know that I have drank of your blood? Will it weaken or empower him? Will his righteous fury embolden him? Will it make him a worthy opponent in this game?

Will he be man enough to finish the task?

Only time will tell. Time and your death.

Hmmm? Shall I kill you now or later?

I have decided to kill you. Your number is up. You are four of nine.

It will not be easy, I admit. Not surrounded as you are. The police might try to stop me. They have weapons. But that is not why I pause. I could be among them and kill them all before they could lift their weapons. But that would not be right. The numbers would be wrong. Most of their blood is worthless to me. They are unworthy. Not of the nine.

The dark-haired woman I have marked for later. The one who carries the stripes on her shoulders, as if they have the weight of boulders pulling her down. If I kill you now, will that make her more watchful? Make her more difficult to take.

So.

I have decided.

I shall wait.

Your death will be sweeter this evening when I come for you. When you are alone. I will ensure that you are not found so easily. Sergeant McCusker will not be forewarned.

Enjoy your last hours on Earth, Professor.

Make the most of the time I have given you.

I go now.

Bethany calls.

And she is most important of all.

TWENTYNINE

Near Burra Ness

Broom's promise of a return within two hours maximum had become four hours and there was still no sign of him. For the entire time he'd been gone, I sat beside the road, uncomfortable on a moss-covered rock. I had been still so long that the crows had taken a keen interest in me. They watched me with their blank stares, their beaks partly open like peeping butlers' mouths at keyholes. Thwarting them, I lifted a hand and gave them a two-fingered salute. They shifted and grumbled. Some of them cawed in scorn.

"Friggin' vermin," I said under my breath. Not for the first time.

Evening was settling in, a purple veil lowering on the eastern horizon. Off to my left there was still a hint of the sun behind iron clouds, fingers of light tickling the Norwegian Sea like a mother's caress. Despite my dark frame of mind I could appreciate the beauty of my surroundings.

With little else to do than sit and watch the utility hut, or insult the crows, my time had been spent contemplating my lot. I hadn't been on the island twenty-four hours, but in that time I'd become embroiled in the fall out from two murders and the abduction of a child. I'd gone from being a suspected bi-polar schizophrenic to a cosmic star child with the ability to read a person's inner soul by simply giving them the beady eye. Not bad for a guy who used to sell T-shirts and tennis rackets for a living. Or it was extremely bad, depending on your outlook.

I could sit there and point the finger of blame, but what good could that serve? It was all Cash's fault, and that would never change, but it was pointless banging away at the same old drum. I tried to concentrate on the real issues at hand. Someone or something was killing people, and according to Paul Broom it was my duty to stop this thing before anyone else was hurt. According to my fertile-minded friend, the murderer was a creature from Norse mythology, a normally benign spirit of the land. However, disturbed by what was seen as desecration of its historical land, this haugbonde had grown nasty. Either it or something else acting on its behalf, was killing innocent people to ensure that the digging would stop. Preposterous, when you think about it. If it wasn't due to the very fact that I explicitly knew that I was possessed by the life force of my dead brother, I'd have been even more skeptical of this supernatural nonsense than I already was. What I couldn't deny was that something very odd indeed was happening on Connor's Island. No less, it was very strange that I was willing to sit out in the elements for four hours waiting for this thing to turn up, based upon Broom's emphatic belief that a group of mangy crows had the ability to look into the future.

If only someone of right mind was around to slap some sense into me. Maybe then I'd have recognised my stupidity, high-tailed it back to the ferry at Skelvoe and got the hell off that bloody island. Instead, honour, obligation, blind lunacy - call it what you will - for my friend made me hold my peace and see it out, notwithstanding my hope to see Janet Hale again.

With the twilight settling round me I finally decided that enough was enough. I'd had it with my rock perch, and was beginning to shiver with the onset of the night's chill. I stood up, feeling my knees crying out in protest. Stiff legged I walked across the road and approached the fence. It didn't appear to be electrified, but you never can tell. With this in mind I kept my distance, peering across at the utility hut. It took me a long hard minute before the obvious slapped me in the face. What was the likelihood of a murder taking place in a hut on the protected side of a military installation? Why would anyone bother to bring their victim there, with the added difficulty of attempting to enter a guarded MOD installation, when any amount of empty farm buildings lay scattered over the island? When, in fact, most of the island was as barren a place as anywhere on the planet?

Almost as if the crows realised I'd finally *got it*, they took off en masse, their croaks of derision sounding even more like sarcastic laughter. Hands fisted on my hips, I watched them wheel in the evening sky, then streak away to the south.

"Ever had the feeling that you've been had?" I wondered out loud.

"Sucker!"

"Oh? So you've decided to show up, have you?"

"Call it a cameo appearance, brother, my little walk on part. I just couldn't miss the opportunity to gloat."

"That's good. For a minute I thought you intended sticking around and making things truly magnificent."

"Don't be so sarcastic. Anyway, it looks to me like you could do with the company."

"I'm fine with my own company, thank you very much." After a pause, I added, "Actually, if you could find a way of clearing out completely, it'd be the best thing in the world for me."

"Hey! It's not much fun for me either, brother. How'd you like it if all you got to look at all day is your *boring life, and listen to* your *droning voice whining and blaming all your shortcomings on me?"*

"Aww, quit moaning, Cash. Things could be worse than eavesdropping on my shitty life," I said.

"Yeah, it could. You could wear a personal stereo and listen to country music twenty-four seven. Now that would *be hell."*

"There's a thought," I said.

"Don't you dare."

I laughed. Not as cruelly as you might imagine.

"I'm outa here."

"Good idea," I said. Then started singing the chorus of Rhinestone Cowboy. Cash mock screamed before sinking back to his little hidey-hole. I laughed again. Stopped singing. I genuinely did share something with Cash; a derision of hooey country and western music. Country rock I could live with, but not that my-wife-left-me-took-my-pick-up-truck-the-dog-is-dead kind of stuff. Maybe I should have loved country, my life set to music would make a million seller and would no doubt go down well at the Grand Ol' Opry.

With no other plan in mind, I headed south. I wasn't as down as I'd been moments before, and it was odd to think that my short talk with Cash had marginally raised my spirits. It was a throw back to the days when we were simply brothers, jibing and pulling each other's leg. We talked in those days without the inherent sarcasm and hatred that punctuated our conversations now. It was a rheumy-eyed thought. Got me thinking how everything went so wrong. Although there were times when I didn't like to admit it, we did share the same parents. We'd both grown up in a loving environment, experienced the same culture and upbringing. There wasn't a life changing moment in our pasts - unless you discount the early deaths of our parents - that could explain our divergence. Cash wasn't an unusually cruel child; he didn't torture insects or puppy dogs. So why he turned out to be a vicious devil worshiping serial killer who preyed on the most vulnerable of women remained unfathomable. Yeah, he'd become addicted to certain chemicals and alcohol, but those alone couldn't explain why he'd become the monster he did. Many people had their dependencies, but in general the harm they inflicted was usually to their own bodies.

Broom was of the opinion that greater powers were at work in this universe. He believed that destiny was preordained, that everything happened for a reason. No such a thing as free will in his philosophy. And that begged an important question. If it was preordained that I would become the nemesis of evil, and my powers should be a result of my convergence with Cash's life force, then wasn't it also fair to assume that Cash's murderous instincts were also engineered as a facet of the same divine plan?

That would mean that Cash had as little control over his actions as I seemed to have. Was my brother as helpless a pawn in this mad game as me? Perhaps he had no control over himself, and his mind and hands were steered to commit unimaginable torture of his victims. If that was the case, was the hatred and blame I constantly flung at him misdirected?

Was Cash a victim as much as everyone else?

"No. He is a murderous shit!"

I'd shouted out loud, and conversely, considering my remote location, I quickly looked around to see if anyone had heard me. There was no one there. It seems that some things never change on Conn.

I didn't share Broom's belief of destiny or karma or whatever: men are responsible for their fate as much as their actions and thoughts. Cash was a despicable killer, and I wasn't about to give him a get out clause. Forgiveness for my brother simply wasn't in my heart.

My mood was as black as ever. Thinking about Cash had that effect on me. Kicking the pebbles at the shoulder of the road, I pushed on. Grumbling under my breath. My ire was now directed at my absent friend. "Where the hell are you, Broom?"

There was a crooked man who walked a crooked mile. Unlike him, I walked a barren road. The coast route from Burra Ness to Skelvoe must be well worn, but it seemed that traffic on the western side of the island was very infrequent. It made sense when I thought about it. Normally the MOD and naval staff from the submarine tracking station would have no reason to travel down the western coast, and there would be very few islanders travelling to the base from Ura Taing, or anywhere else for that matter. Ergo, there'd be little chance of anyone travelling my way any time soon. My only hope of reaching Broom's house was to put on a spurt of activity, setting one foot in front of the other and pushing on.

My four hours of inactivity had a contradictory effect on me; I'd grown impatient and was ready to get moving, however, with sitting so long, I found that I was stiff and sore and the walk was tiring. I usually enjoyed walking. Gave me time to clear my head.

Not this time, though. My brain was full and threatening overload. Every time I attempted to formulate any coherence of what was really going on here, the thought was snatched from me and sent swirling into the eddies of my psyche, so that I couldn't settle any theory in my mind. Something so obvious teetered on the brink of epiphany, yet I could not grasp it fully, and was left groping for understanding. It was like waiting an elusive sneeze that tickles the sinuses, but simply won't let loose. Frustrating. Maddening.

Broom's house was on the coast below the point where the island nipped in at the waist. To get there I'd have to pass Trowhaem. I'd pass the excavation site. Maybe it would be in my interest to make a second visit and reacquaint myself with Janet. Then again, maybe not.

The thought was as much a brain fart as everything else I pondered. By now the site would be a hive of police activity, and not the best place for an armed man to be swanking around. Anyway, Janet would be too busy to spare me any time, let alone her undivided attention. In all likelihood, Janet would now be at the police station at Skelvoe giving her statement to the investigators. If I showed up uninvited at the dig, I would have a hard time explaining my interest. Wouldn't blame anyone if they tried to tie me in as a murder suspect. Not that the idea would have much validity, my alibi was strong - I'd been in England when the man had been murdered - but I could do without an impromptu trip to the cells whilst charges for carrying a concealed firearm were levied upon me. It made sense to avoid Trowhaem.

Forty minutes walking found me on the opposite side of the bay from the archaeological site. Because the dark was settling in, large floodlights had been erected, but whether this was by the university people or by forensic pathologists I couldn't begin to decide. From my position I could make out little of the bustle in the area of the dig, but I could see the shantytown of caravans and tents on the promontory to the west. Small figures wandered between the tents, moving in slow, desultory fashion. I wondered if one of the tiny stick figures was Janet. If she was even now staring out across the bay to where I stood.

Where the coast road met the ancient settlement I decided I'd have to trek inland to follow a circuitous route away from the eyes of the law. Like the rest of the island, apart from that copse of trees next to where the child had been killed, and the occasional stunted tree, the island was largely devoid of cover. Still, the darkness was my friend. I didn't have to travel too far inland before I was swallowed by shadows. I crept along like a guilty man, listening to the hushed tones of conversation and the infrequent scrape of tools. I could now see men and women in white coveralls moving at the periphery of a large illuminated poly-tunnel; a twin to the one set up at the first murder scene. From the south a vehicle approached the site. At first all I could make out was its headlights, but I knew from the distinctive diesel engine noises that this was a large van or truck and not Broom's Subaru. I crouched down for fear this new source of light would illuminate me against the backdrop of the night and watched as the vehicle swung into the lane leading to the dig. I couldn't read any writing or sign on the vehicle, but judging by the antennae and satellite dish bristling on its back, the TV crews had begun to arrive.

Whilst I'd been on Conn I'd saw no television to speak of. Which network actually covered the island was a mystery to me, so I wasn't star struck by the thought of seeing a famous TV presenter. Still, I decided to settle down and watch the proceedings for a few minutes. The van was met by a uniformed police officer. He was big enough that he could've been one of the men who had arrived with the sergeant when our paths crossed earlier. He waved the van to a halt, then guided it towards the seashore with grandiose gestures of his arms. The van crawled away to set up at a distance deemed far enough away that it didn't impede the investigation, but close enough to allow a wide shot of the excavation site. Before long cameras would be rolling, and pictures fed back to an anchorman back on the mainland.

As I watched the constable, I saw him lean back and massage the small of his back. He was standing like that when he swung his head and stared directly at me. Involuntarily I jerked down, concealing myself as best I could. It was an instinctive movement, but unnecessary as there was no possible way for the policeman to see me. Not unless he had infrared vision, which I seriously doubted. Still, I crouched there, making my body as small as possible as the man stared in my direction. I held my breath. Pulse pounding in my ears.

A smaller figure joined the man. By the slight frame, the sway of her approach, I guessed it was the same sergeant come to join her colleague. She stood very close to the man. Shoulder almost touching his elbow. Around them both I saw ribbons of light. Their colours melded and meshed together like the swirling eddies of two streams that co-join and form a river. Without thought, I understood. These two were a couple. More than mere professional attachment, too. Again I wished that my ability allowed me to see my own auric field. What would it appear like if I were standing close to Janet? Would our fields blend, as did those of the two police officers?

The thought was only fleeting. I became more concerned that the man had seen me. He lifted a hand and pointed and again I reacted by pushing myself down into the grass. I could still make them out, and could see the woman nodding.

"Shit," I whispered. Ready to run.

Then my world was filled with thunder and my body was pressed flat to the floor. The air pressure all around me became momentarily dense, then sucked out in a vacuum in the next instant. Blinking in confusion and at blades of grass whipping across my vision, I craned round, and saw the dark underbelly of a large craft pass over me. Lights blazed at the front and side of the craft, huge rotor blades whirling and cutting the night.

212

Two thoughts jerked through my mind. The police officers hadn't noticed me; they'd saw the approaching helicopter. That didn't put me in the clear; what if someone on the helicopter had noticed me crouching on the moor like a guilty man? It would only be minutes before a search party came trampling out here and discovered my hiding place.

I had to move. But the thought didn't galvanise me. All I did was stay where I was and watch with fascination as the helicopter swung in a tight curve around Trowhaem and put to earth on the promontory above the site. I wasn't familiar with aircraft, but even I could tell that this was a large Navy personnel carrier. Within seconds my suspicion was proven when men in uniform began disembarking from the guts of the craft. There appeared to be a dozen or more men. They carried rifles. Four of them with leashed German Shepherds. They all moved from the helicopter in crouching runs before taking up a loose formation fifty paces away.

Search party, I told myself. Reinforcements from Burra Ness.

The two police I feared had seen me also watched the display, then nodding in unison, they walked off to meet the party. I wondered if they'd been as surprised by the arrival of the navy people as I was.

Didn't really matter. The arrival of reinforcements didn't bode well with me staying hidden for long. Especially with the dogs sniffing around. I quickly backed away, keeping my profile low, until a fold of the land hid me. Then I set off jogging. The SIG bounced uncomfortably against my spine. It wasn't a good idea to pull it out and carry it. Not with armed military men in the area. A man carrying a sidearm may be met with extreme prejudice. Shot first and asked questions later. The discomfort of the jouncing gun was outweighed by the possibility of a round plugging my central mass so I let it be.

Keeping to the boggy moor I managed to circle Trowhaem without the might of the armed forces coming down on me. With the area a half-mile behind me I felt it safe enough to rejoin the road, continuing on towards Broom's place. My boots were sodden, so were my trousers and the front of my coat. I was cold and tired. Pissed off. Broom was going to get the length of his pedigree when I saw him. Especially if the bloody soup wasn't hot.

"Carter."

I thought I heard my name.

I stopped walking. Looked all around me.

No one around.

"What the hell?"

I should have been used to hearing disembodied voices. But this wasn't like when Cash spoke to me. For a start the voice had been that of a woman. And it was a voice I knew.

There was a series of pops.

Birds roosting in the tall grass were startled to flight.

Above the squawks of wildlife there came shouts of alarm and a single high-pitched shriek that was wholly human. "Help me."

I spun on my heel. Stared back towards Trowhaem.

Pop. Pop. Pop.

Another scream.

Other than from movies, or from the sanitised unreality of a news programme, I'd never before heard automatic machine gunfire. There was none of the thunder associated with blockbuster action movies. In fact the gunfire sounded less like rolling thunder than it did the crackling of a bonfire. Still, I instinctively recognised the noise. Someone was firing a machine gun in short bursts. Bullets were flying in Trowhaem. People could be dying.

Janet was in Trowhaem.

It was Janet who'd called out to me.

The realisation was immediate. And as quickly, I was running back along the road to the place I'd tried so desperately to avoid.

THIRTY

Why are you here, Carter Bailey?

I see you.

Hiding out there on the moor. Watching. Afraid. Wary.

Why don't you come on in? Something must have brought you here, so why don't you trust your instincts?

Do you know that I'm close to Janet? Do you know that I'm about to take her? That her life is numbered in minutes?

The police are too busy with one of nine. Or with what remains of him, at least.

They are blind.

I can take Janet from under their noses.

They can't stop me.

I have decided.

But what's this?

Helicopter? Swooping from the heavens like Odin's iron-wheeled chariot. Who is this that comes uninvited to the game?

Ah, I see now. Soldiers. With guns. And dogs.

Little matter. It is time.

I have decided.

Four of nine, I come for you now.

Wait!

Carter Bailey. Where are you going? Are you running away?

That's all right. You may go. Our time can't be now. Our time will come later.

Now it is Professor Hale's time.

I have decided.

THIRTYONE

Trowhaem

Relaxing under a hot shower sounded like a good idea to Janet Hale. The mud and the grit, even the salt-laden sea air had permeated her clothing, everything. But that was the least of it. The stink of the dead man was clinging to her clothes and her hair like a gelatinous second skin. She could actually taste the foulness of the air she'd breathed making her want to retch. Odour, she knew, was particulate. She'd actually been breathing in the rotting cells of the dead man's body. Motes of death were collected in the corners of her eyes, in her nostrils, and on her lips. Yes, a hot shower would be excellent. Plus a gallon of mouthwash and a round dozen tubes of toothpaste.

The problem being, in the caravan she used whilst living on site was the pokiest of cubicles that only played at being a shower room. To use the cubicle was a test of moral fortitude. Try banging your elbows, your hips, your head, as many times as she did without losing patience and swearing out loud like the most foul-mouthed of troopers.

As a concession to their comfort, the university had hired a cabin that they'd fitted out with shower cubicles that had been designed with adult humans in mind. It was a long walk from Janet's caravan, but she'd grown used to the eyes on her as she crossed the shantytown in her dressing gown, weighted down by towels and bath products. The thought that there were strangers in the camp tonight gave her a moment's pause, but her need to be clean outweighed the discomfort of a possible ogling from men in uniform. Under other circumstances, the thought of men in uniform might actually appeal to her sense of fantasy. But not tonight. Tonight she desired only to be clean.

Curtains closed, she stripped down to her underwear. She shrugged into her heavy bathrobe that came belted round the waist and with a hood that gave her the look of a medieval monk. She slipped into a pair of cut down Wellington boots. The camp wasn't fit for walking around in anything less sturdy. She grabbed towels and the necessary cleaning products, pondering only seconds over a bottle of bleach from her kitchenette cupboard. Instead, she took her toothbrush and paste as normal.

She was heading for the door when the lights went out.

"Damn it!" she sighed. "Not again?"

Power cuts she was used to. It wasn't the thought of darkness that bothered her. It was the thought that the water heater wouldn't be working in the shower stalls. It was going to have to be the damn shower in the caravan. Hers ran off a gas burner rather than relying on the camp's generators. She reached for a torch she kept as back up for just such emergencies as this. She found the drawer that housed the torch, rummaged inside it and pulled the torch free. She flicked the switch and weak yellow light played around the confines of the caravan.

Wind tickled her back.

She turned. Brought up the torch.

Saw the caravan door closing as if an errant breeze had plucked it open then shut it again. Furtively.

Her brows pinched.

"Hello? Is someone there?"

There was no reply.

Suddenly she was bothered by the dark. Her meagre torchlight only lent the shadows a deeper foreboding than logic could argue against. Her need to shower was no longer a consideration. She placed down her toiletries, clutched at the front of her gown.

"Hello?"

A creak. Like a solitary footfall on the step outside the door.

"Who's there?" She tried to sound confident, but even she could hear the warble in her voice.

Another creak. This time from behind her. She jerked towards the noise, her torch beam bouncing on walls and ceiling. Nothing there. Only leaping phantoms given life by the torch. Quickly she spun. Something large had loomed at her shoulder. She was positive of it. But, no. There was nothing there. The door creaked open again. Was pushed to by whatever breeze had given it life.

Janet sighed. She shook her head at her foolishness.

"What is wrong with me?" It was the discovery of the dead man, of course. She could be forgiven for feeling jumpy tonight. He was the first murdered person she'd ever seen. It would be practically wrong not to feel jumpy.

Thankfully the generators chose that moment to stir back to life. The halogen strips on the ceiling flickered, strobing momentarily, then blazed to full strength.

Janet brayed a single laugh, sounding a tad manic. She clicked off the torch. Reached for her towels and stuff. She returned the torch to the drawer and headed for the door.

The lights went off again.

Disarmed, she gave a groan. Reached again for the torch.

And that was when the darkness snatched at her.

She felt a large arm wrap round her throat, lift and drag her off her feet. Before she could scream, a hand slapped hard over her mouth and she felt jagged nails rake her cheek. Her senses where filled by a sour stench as a face leaned in close to hers. Hot breath burned her eyes.

"It is time, Professor Hale."

The voice was raw and dripping with mucus. As though the speaker was unused to speech, or was suffering a virulent and wasting disease of the larynx. The arm that encircled her and lifted her as though she was weightless had the power of a gorilla. The nails that raked her flesh were the claws of a beast.

But these things failed to register with Janet. Horror placed a clamp on her mind.

She tried to scream again. The hand was enough to stifle her, but her body rebelled, and all she could issue was the faintest of squeaks. Her fingers were useless against the corded muscle squeezing her throat. Her heels may as well have been kicking at a tree trunk. In her ears laughter tolled.

"It is pointless fighting me," the voice said. "I have chosen you. You are four of nine. I have decided."

Janet's next scream was no more effective than the first. She felt her throat tighten in reflex as panic surged within her. Air. She couldn't get air. Her attempts at screaming were serving only to push out what little oxygen remained in her lungs. It was only seconds since she had been clutched in this monstrous embrace, but already a deeper blackness than the night draped over her vision. In contradiction, blinding white spots danced beneath her eyelids. Unless she did something fast she was going to be unconscious. Then she may as well simply give up.

But Janet's parents hadn't raised a quitter. You only had to ask Jonathon Connery if Janet was a fighter. The black eye she'd given him the fateful day she'd discovered his infidelity would convince most folk.

Sucking strength from some hidden reserve, Janet thrust back with both hands. She stiffened her fingers, drove them into her attacker's eyes. She was vaguely conscious of leather-hard skin, pulled taut over ridges of bone. She dug deeper, finally feeling her nails scraping at less-resistant skin. A low growl stirred the hair clinging to her face, then the *thing* behind her pulled away, the arm round her throat loosening perceptively. Those self-defence classes she'd taken at university did hold some validity - even after all these years.

Trying to summon from distant memory what she should do next, she thrust back with an elbow, seeking her attacker's diaphragm. Whenever she'd delivered this blow on the guys she'd partnered in class, they'd all folded over, winded and gasping for air. But all she found now was a body as tough as rhinoceros hide. Pain screamed through her elbow. It didn't matter. Not after she'd won a small victory that allowed her to suck in some air. She battered back with her sore elbow a second time.

She may as well have been beating on an asylum wall. Her elbows were inefficient against the tough body bearing down on her. However, her finger jab to the eyes must have caused some damage. If nothing else, her attacker wasn't as intent on throttling the life from her. Didn't mean she was in any better position than she had been seconds before, but it did mean she could breath again. And scream.

She did so with every atom of her being.

"Silence."

Janet screamed again. Screamed at the indignity. Screamed in defiance.

Her attacker spun her, slapped her with the back of a hand.

Janet was thrown backwards. She felt weightless. Then she caromed off the caravan wall, her momentum sending her down to her hands and knees. Her head rang from the slap. She moaned. Looked up. Her attacker was an indistinct shape looming over her. Vaguely it was shaped like a man. But huge. Misshapen like the chimeras of Greek myth. Head too large and bristling with wiry hair and bony protrusions. Massive shoulders. Clawed fingers reminiscent in that split second only of a Hollywood-inspired monster, as though it wore Freddy Krueger's claws.

Feeding off the terror of the haugbonde curse, only one word went through her mind: Skeklar. The devilish trow that the islanders warned did the hogboy's bidding.

She didn't believe in the Skeklar. It couldn't possibly be true. The Skeklar was no more real than the bogeyman, the tooth fairy, or Santa Claus. The Skeklar did not exist. This shape-shifting demon that fed off the flesh of children was a figment of primitive superstition.

Which all went to prove that it couldn't lift her from the floor and fling her bodily over one shoulder. It couldn't throw open the caravan door and bound outside with her carried across its back like a sack of feathers. It couldn't lope through the campsite with her face bumping against its knobby hip with each stride.

She must be caught in a hallucination. Yes, that had to be it. Or maybe a nightmare. Perhaps she'd returned to her caravan and fallen asleep. Her preparations for her shower had all been part of the dream; mundane everyday chores lulling her before the stress of the day finally took over and brought forth this monster.

She had experienced vivid dreams before. She had dreamt in colour. Had smelled odours, which she believed was very unusual. She had even felt mild discomfort. But never had she been trapped in a dream as real as this. Not where her pain was so intense. Or where she could taste the blood in her mouth, the swelling of her jaw where she'd been struck.

There were other details, too. She could feel the sharp pinprick of the Skeklar's claws in her thighs. The rigid bones of its shoulder jabbing into her midriff. The hairs on its hip rubbing at the tender flesh of her face. And she could smell the stench of its hide clouding her senses.

It took these finer points to convince her.

This was no dream!

The Skeklar did exist.

And she was its victim.

When she screamed this time it wasn't with the same righteous fury as before. This time it was one long wail of desperation.

Caravans and tents flashed by. Behind curtains and tent flaps, shadows moved against torch and lamplights. People energised by her screams were coming to investigate. Emboldened by this, Janet screamed again. From somewhere off to her right she heard an answering yell. A male voice, followed the baying of a dog.

The Skeklar slid to a halt. Swung side-to-side. Loped to the left. Directly ahead of them, Janet saw a tent flap lift and one of her male students - Terrence? - blinked in confusion. In that moment he couldn't begin to understand what it was he was dealing with. For all he knew it was simply the latest of a long line of drunken pranks his fellows regularly engaged in. His mouth actually formed the beginnings of a smile. Then blank horror pasted his features.

Without stopping the Skeklar swiped at Terrence. There was no tempering of the blow as it had when it had struck Janet. This was a strike of full intention. Terrence's head was whipped backwards, which gave Janet a full view of the gaping wound opening in his throat.

"Oh my god," she yelped. Then her captor was beyond Terrence and leaping past his tent and all that Janet could see of her student was his twitching feet.

"Noooo…" Janet howled.

"Quiet," the Skeklar grunted. To punctuate the command, it dug its fingers into her thigh. "Your screams will not help you. All they achieve is to bring others hurrying to their deaths. Continue to scream and I will be forced to kill them all."

"Let me go," Janet whimpered. "Please. Let me go."

She did not scream. Did not want another death on her conscience. But neither did she want to die. More than anything she wanted to live. But who could protect her from this thing? No one could if she didn't shout for help. No one except…

"Carter."

The word whispered from her.

The Skeklar reacted like she'd screamed the word directly in his face.

He came to an abrupt halt. Threw her down at its feet. He remained wreathed in shadows but she could still detect the burning fury in its eyes.

"Forget Carter Bailey. He is useless to you. He is gone from here."

Janet didn't answer. Couldn't. Didn't even know why she'd spoken his name. Except that it had just felt like the correct thing to do. Like a child calling out to its mother in the night. Or like a lover caught in the throes of passion.

"If Carter Bailey was here, I would show you just how useless he is to you."

Then the Skeklar grabbed her again.

Janet flinched. Not at the Skeklar's reaching hand but at the black and tan blur that injected itself between them. The blur became a dog. A German Shepherd that leapt and clamped its jaws around the Skeklar's forearm. The Skeklar reared back and the dog was lifted off all fours, suspended in mid air. The dog didn't loosen its grip. It growled as it ground its teeth into the Skeklar's arm. The Skeklar roared. It whipped its arm up and back, shaking the dog out of its flesh. The dog rolled on the floor, but immediately renewed its attack, snapping at the Skeklar's legs. The Skeklar kicked out and the dog yowled as it was bowled over.

Janet knew the dog was badly hurt. Knew that the Skeklar would again grasp her. She kicked backwards on her haunches, scrambling through the dirt like a beetle. The Skeklar lunged at her, snatching at an ankle. Janet yelped, threw herself to one side. The Skeklar rounded on her, breath ragged in its throat.

Bang. Bang. Bang.

Gunfire.

Flashes lighting up the creature's face as it lurched back from her. A strobe effect that showed its leathery countenance and tusked teeth: Halloween mask ugly.

"Armed police," someone shouted. "Do not move or I will shoot."

Finding her voice, Janet screamed. "Help me."

"Armed police."

Another dog barked.

Three more warning shots went into the sky. Not exactly procedure. But what does an armed officer do when confronted with the unbelievable?

All around Janet there was movement. Others racing to the scene. Police. Navy. Archaeologists who had no right - or sane - reason to be there. All that was missing was the Seventh Cavalry and the tableau would be complete.

Behind her a woman screamed. Someone had discovered Terrence. Janet wanted to scream, too. She looked for the Skeklar.

It was gone.

Instead of screaming she wept.

She wept for Terrence. But most of all she wept for herself.

THIRTYTWO

The moor above Trowhaem

Intuition is a fine commodity. You don't need to be a cosmic star child, a seer or a psychic medium. All you require is the flood of adrenaline into your veins and your perception of impending danger grows tenfold. The old fight or flight response kicks in and you begin to notice things that wouldn't normally impinge on your conscious mind. Running across a moor in the dark is never a good idea. Tufts of grass, sinkholes and ditches all conspire to bring you down. But in my heightened state I negotiated all the pitfalls of a headlong run with preternatural agility. I ran with my arms pumping, swerving and jumping, making ground in a fashion I would never have credited before.

I can't remember the last time I ran at any speed; probably when I'd hurtled out of my office at Rezpect Sports that day my entire universe fell apart. Surprisingly I was in better shape than I should've been. I ran half-a-mile at almost full sprint without losing my breath. My heart was racing, yes. But this was more down to my anxiousness in reaching Janet than down to the exertion.

I'd abandoned the road a good way back, electing for the direct route to the archeologists' campsite across the moor. Now I was racing up the rise in the land that marked the promontory that formed the bay. The abandoned Viking port was to my right, the shantytown to my left. Ahead was a craggy formation of rocks that loomed against the nighttime sky like the spiked crown of a prince of hell.

It made sense that I didn't hurtle headlong into the camp. Chances were I'd be caught up in the confusion and shot at as an interloper before I could explain my presence there. I chose instead to climb amid the crags and reconnoiter the scene below before making my move.

Fortuitous that I did. There were a large number of armed men in the area. Confusion continued its reign, but at least the shooting had stopped. Most of the activity was to the extreme left of the camp, and I could see uniformed men fanning out across the moor with torches dancing through the shadows. A couple of them had leashed dogs and they had taken up pole position on the hunters. The dogs didn't seem that enthusiastic for the search, or maybe they were confused. They spent more time looking back at their handlers than forging ahead. I could hear their whimpering from where I leaned against a boulder.

Over on a grassy swathe near to the cliffs over the sea, lights were blinking on the helicopter, the rotor blades sweeping slowly. The engine was building to a high pitch, and I guessed it would be less than a minute before the helicopter joined in whatever search was kicking off. Even as I considered this men headed towards the copter, each doing a duck walk with an arm shielding their faces from the down draught.

Still unsure what was going down, I hid against the crags. It was while I crouched there, intent on the scene below that I heard the faint scrabble of movement to my left. I searched the shadows but could see nothing. The rocks and the night conspired against me. My ears were my best assets, because I again heard the scuff of a foot against gravel.

The gun. Maybe I should draw the SIG. The thought trickled through my mind, but I was sluggish to respond. What had Broom said? Trust my instincts? Only problem being, my instincts told me that whoever was creeping around was probably a member of the law enforcement community and it wouldn't be the done thing for me to greet them with a gun in my hand.

"Draw the gun."

Cash had kept his own company so long that his sudden intrusion in my thoughts startled me.

"What's wrong?" I hissed at him.

"Draw the gun."

A scratching on the rocks above me. I looked up. A bird, I told myself, or maybe an animal. Some creature of the night disturbed by my presence. Couldn't possibly be -

"Draw the fucking *gun, Carter!"*

There's a pretty good chance that my reaction was due to my heightened alertness, but Cash's warning did help. In fact, his urgency was like a motivating kick in the backside. I dropped onto my left elbow, facing the crag I'd so recently leaned against, even as I snatched at the grip of the SIG. On my side like this, I saw an amorphous shape detach itself from the rocks, then drop towards me. I caught a glint of green phosphorous. A hint of bestial eyes too large and round to be human. There were spikes and claws. But everything else was black against a nighttime sky. And all happening in weird slow motion as my mind worked faster than I could process the imagery.

My hand came up as the thing plummeted down on me. I squeezed, squeezed, squeezed. Muzzle flash. Bullets streaking into the sky. A grunt. My yell of fear tearing the ether. Then the form thumped onto the turf behind me. I rolled over to follow it, firing blindly. My eyes blinking with each shot, the flash impregnating my vision with motes of colour. Whatever it was that had tried to ambush me appeared fearful of my bullets. Or maybe, like many a wild thing, it was the thunder and lightning the gun emitted that the thing feared. Regardless of its motives, it threw itself aside, even as it swung round to face me. Half-blinded by muzzle flash I tried to follow it. For one long moment the thing was directly before me, then it dropped down as though to all fours, crouching ape-like. The bullet I fired into it found only this sudden space above its head. My mind continued to race. My reactions were out of synch with my speeding thoughts.

I did manage to bring down the gun and fire directly into the central mass. Just as the thing leapt at me. It was mere feet away from me, like shooting the proverbial barn door. Physics would dictate that the force of the bullet leaving the barrel of the gun should equal that of the bullet striking the target. If that were true, I should have been lifted and spun by the recoil of the gun. As it was, my hand barely bucked, whilst the shape was flung backwards and away from me like being snatched away on a huge bungee cord.

I tried to watch its tumbling fall. Even considered firing a few more rounds after it. That was a pointless exercise. The curve of the slope hid it from view within seconds, and all I could make out from its fall was the rattle and clatter of loose stones it dislodged.

In the next few seconds all I did was stand there.

Too many unfathomable stimuli had bombarded my brain during the space of the last dozen heartbeats. My vision remained impaired. My ears whistled to the echo of gunshot. I was still lying on the ground for God's sake.

"Carter," Cash shouted from my core. *"You'd better get your arse in gear, boy."*

I gave a languid blink. Time moved as if through molasses.

"The cops will be coming. I suggest you get the fuck outa here."

"What the hell was that?" My voice was a dry rasp that caught at my throat.

"Five years in prison for you if you don't get the hell outa here!"

There was supreme logic in Cash's frantic words. Unfortunately they weren't seeping into my over-wrought senses. I craned my neck for a better view of whatever had just attacked me. I still couldn't make it out, though, from way below me, I thought I could detect a low moan. The thing was hurt but still alive.

"Leave him to the coppers, Carter," Cash shouted.

Police, coming out of the immediate shock of hearing the volley of gunfire, were now looking my way. Without the eyes of a fish eagle I doubted they could make me out against the crags, but they must have noted my location from the muzzle flashes.

Already fingers were jabbing out my position and a number of uniform officers headed my way. They couldn't possibly know what had just transpired - probably thought that it was one of their own that had fired the barrage - and were even now trying to make sense of the gunfire. Radio chatter would be at full tilt as orders and demands ricocheted between them. Confusion reigned. My chance to escape would be short. Pretty soon someone would take charge and a concerted effort would be made to surround and trap me. I should get going, as Cash admonished. Only I just couldn't pull away. Not yet.

Two things halted my feet. Whatever had attacked me was still alive. Could I allow the police to stumble upon this savage thing without warning of what it was they faced? What if someone was injured before the thing was contained? I felt it my duty to warn them. At the same time, I knew to shout to them would seal my fate. I'd be rounded up, cuffed and loaded into a cage before I could profess my innocence. This was all a consideration, but more than that was my concern for Janet. I simply could not leave without first checking she was unharmed. It was no auditory hallucination that I'd heard. Her intense fear had reached out to me. Call it psychically if you wish. I only know that she had called for me and I had heard. I had come at her bidding: thus it remained my duty to stay until I was sure that she was safe.

"Forget all the samurai Giri *bullshit,"* Cash spat. *"You don't owe Janet anything. Right now your duty is to yourself."*

It didn't occur to me that Cash had been party to my inner thoughts. Only that his words scraped at my already taut nerves. "Shut it, Cash. I'm not going anywhere until I know she's alright."

"She's surrounded by coppers with big guns. What do you think you're gonna be able to do that they can't?"

"I'm not talking about protecting her," I said. "I just need to know that she hasn't been hurt."

"Jesus Christ!"

Cash held his own counsel. Not for long. When he spoke again there was a different edge to his voice. Almost as if he'd resigned himself to being relegated in my affections.

"All you have to do is reach out for her. See her, Carter. See her like you did the last time."

Frowning, I turned from the advancing police to scan the area of the camp. See her? Like I did the last time? All well and good, but I had no idea how I'd done it the last time.

"Christ on a bike! We haven't got time for this." Cash made a noise like he was clearing his throat. *"Relax, Carter. Don't stare. Zone out. Let her come to you."*

I did as I was told. Not easy when armed men were advancing on me. Somehow I calmed myself, controlled my breath, allowed my vision to haze out. The result was dramatic. Not only did I see Janet's auric colours, the entire camp was ablaze with a shifting pallet of reds and blues and other less-identifiable hues.

"Too many," I whispered. "Way too many."

"Forget the others. See only Janet. You've seen her before. You can *single her out from the rest."*

"I don't know how," I moaned.

"SEE HER."

Ghost-lights flickered off throughout the camp. It took me a moment to realise that my sweeping eyes were seeing and discarding the life forces of other people. Snuffing them from my view as I recognised them as strangers. Two auric fields flickered in defiance before I realised that these were the lights of the lady sergeant and her companion who I had now twice come across on the island. At this realisation I was able to block them too. Finally my eyes turned on an elongated shape that I immediately decided was a caravan. Within the caravan a beacon burned with furnace hot intensity. How I could see through solid walls remains a mystery, but it was almost as though my strange ability had given me X-ray vision. Weirdness on top of weirdness, but it didn't matter. All that concerned me was that the furnace of fire was Janet's life force. She was alive. Enraged, distraught, but alive all the same. Something else I instinctively fathomed; other than minor hurts she had no major life threatening injuries. All this I understood in a manner that is impossible to explain. I simply looked and knew it was so.

"Happy?" Cash asked. *"Can we go now?"*

"Happy that Janet's okay," I said. "But I should warn the police about the thing that attacked me."

"Fuck 'em. Let them find out for themselves. It'll stop them from following us."

Us. Not a term that rested easy with me. Made the two of us sound like a couple, or a team. Still, I had asked for his help. Maybe that did make us a co-operative, after all. I had to admit, my brother's intervention had been more than merely assistance. His coaching of me had given me the wherewithal to find Janet amid the chaos. Plus, you could say that his earlier warning had saved my life. I didn't doubt that if I hadn't been prompted to pull the gun, I would now be a steaming heap of torn flesh scattered across the crags just like poor little Jimmy.

Cash did have a point. If the police were tied up with the discovery of whatever it was that I'd shot, then they would be diverted from searching for me. I could get away.

I told myself that the thing would be incapable of harming so many armed men. I had shot it. The bullet had struck it square in the chest. I'd blasted the fucking thing right off the cliff face. If it weren't already dead, it soon would be.

After briefly witnessing what had attacked me, it was no longer such a leap of the imagination to believe in haugbonde's - or whatever the curse had made flesh. Legend or not, something I did now know: the thing had been a creature of skin and bone. When I shot it, it hurt the way any mortal creature would. Cops armed with automatic weapons would put it down permanently.

I turned away, shoving the SIG into my waistband. I made it into the shadows of the crag just as the helicopter roared overhead. Pressed up against the boulders, I watched as the helicopter swung through one hundred and eighty degrees. Searchlights stabbed out in the gloom. Thankfully they weren't primed on me. They were probing the land at the bottom of the hill. Where the thing had fallen.

Good, I thought. They've seen it.

But then I heard the screaming start, and the thought caught in my head like an angry wasp batting at a windowpane. I faltered, considered going back. I wanted to help. But, like Cash had already pointed out; what did I think I was going to be able to do that they couldn't? Instead I sprinted away from the crag, back out onto the moor. Not as nimble as when I'd ran here, but still putting plenty of distance between me and the horror transpiring at the base of the crag.

THIRTYTHREE

Near Trowhaem

The idea that her late mother was punishing her for her small nicotine betrayal struck Shelly as ludicrous now. No doubt about it, she was being punished for the transgressions accrued through a multitude of former lifetimes. It was apparent to her: she must have killed a dozen black cats, smashed a score of mirrors, judging by the way her current life was going. Yes that had to be it. Surely a couple of filter tips this side of a deathbed promise wouldn't bring this shit storm down on her?

It was less than twenty hours since the nightmare had began, but already she'd had to contend with a series of incidents that would test Dirty Harry. The list was finite, but it didn't feel that way; a murdered boy; his missing sister; a second corpse found freshly skinned but in an ancient grave; the attack on and failed abduction of Professor Janet Hale; the mortal wounding of Terrence Ross. And, now, a running chase through darkness hunting - God-knows-what? - surrounded by the frantic shouting of her colleagues.

If she'd to add the condescending manner in which Inspector Marsh treated her, not to mention her misgivings over the stranger with the odd light in his eyes - Yes, him again, Carter Bailey - then she could admit she was having a bad day. Maybe the second worst of her life next to her presence at her mother's painful passing. If she'd to attempt to balance the bad with the good, it would be uneven odds. In fact the only good that had come her way was in the shape of Bob Harris. But even Bob wasn't at his best right now. He was doing as much running and shouting as everyone else.

He was off to her right. Not too far. His large form was little more than a silhouette behind his bouncing torch, but his closeness was about the most reassuring thing she could think of right now. There were armed tactical support officers, navy personnel, dog handlers, but none she felt she could rely on to get to her quickly enough should it be her *lucky* day to come across the elusive murder suspect.

As a police officer she wanted to find the murderer, as someone with more than a little common sense she'd rather it was one of the officers carrying a gun that got to him first. She doubted her extendable truncheon or CS spray would be enough to stop this monster that'd already torn the throat out of one man, severely wounded several others. Janet Hale had to have been suffering shock. She described her abductor as a Skeklar. Not well known beyond the islands, the Skeklar was the Shetland variation of the monstrous trolls of legend. Most notorious of the Skeklar was a beast said to have twelve heads and twelve tails, upon which it bore the corpses of stolen children. Not the prettiest image to conjure in one's mind whilst charging through the night. Maybe Janet had been half-delirious from fright, and her words were simple metaphor for the terror she'd experienced. Still, Shelly didn't want to be the one to prove her right.

Through her earpiece Shelly heard a running commentary of the hunt. Nothing too helpful. Too many people calling in conflicting reports.

Two men down. No, a third. The suspect was to the west of the camp. Now the dogs had picked up a scent to the north. The suspect was armed with knives. Possibly a handgun. Suspect sighted running north. Negative, it was another officer. Shots fired. Shots fired.

"Who is shooting?" Shelly demanded.

"False alarm! False alarm! Stop firing!" Simply a disembodied voice in her ear.

"All units…STAND DOWN! Stand down!" Inspector Marsh. Angry as all hell, but Shelly couldn't blame him. "Permission to shoot revoked until further notice."

More shots.

"I SAID **STAND DOWN**!"

"Sir! Suspect is running back towards Trowhaem." A male voice. That was all, no call sign, no present location.

"Jesus…" Shelly groaned. The debriefing from this debacle was going to be historic. She could imagine Marsh's face now. Livid. Voice high-pitched. Not a single person spared his wrath. *I'll probably get my pedigree, too*, she thought.

The male officer again. "I'm in pursuit. On foot towards Trowhaem."

"Details!" Marsh shouted. "Description of the suspect, officer?"

Shelly was already veering towards Trowhaem. The crags were to her right. A group of officers were administering aid to fallen comrades. Maybe she should go to them, confirm what exactly had happened. How many were injured. Get a handle on the situation. Report back to her supervisor. Plan what should happen next. However, even though afraid of the consequences, she was as much caught up in the hunt as everyone else. She charged down the hillside, equipment belt jogging uncomfortably at her waist.

"Sixteen twelve, to last caller," Shelly shouted into her radio terminal.

"Go ahead, Sarge." Voice coming in rising and falling waves. Breathing harsh.

"Is that you, John?" Shelly asked. The voice was familiar to her, but she was unsure if it was PC 443 Entwhistle or not.

"Confirmed, Sarge. Four-four-three."

"Location?"

"I'm headed back towards the excavation site. Path down by the sea."

"Confirm you are wearing protection." Any other time, such a question might elicit a double-entendre answer. Not this night, under these circumstances.

Entwhistle's answer was perfunctory. "Vested up."

"Roger that. Are you in company?"

"Negative, Sarge."

Shelly winced. "Do not engage the suspect, Four-four-three. Wait for back up. Understood?"

A pause. Then, "I can have him, Sarge. Just ahead of me."

"Negative, John. Negative. Just keep him in sight. Wait for armed assistance."

"He's turning round, Sarge. Coming at me…" The sudden intrusion of silence was shocking. Everyone involved in the chase obviously listening in, reacting to Entwhistle's words. Fearing the worst, Shelly pushed forward, a surge of urgency powering her charge over the moor. Then the thing she dreaded, the vibrating of her terminal. She knew without looking that the screen would be pulsing red. Entwhistle had pushed his emergency button. Everyone with a terminal would receive the frantic call for assistance. It was a function of the airwave technology. When in danger an officer could depress a button, their call sign would be displayed to all other open terminals, also their microphone was opened and over-rode all others. The scream in Shelly's ear was horrendous.

It was enough to cause her to skid and fall on her backside. Like a physical punch to the chest. She flailed, trying to get her feet under her. Fell again.

"Officer in need of assistance," she yelled. Not for her own precarious situation. That was the least of her troubles. Entwhistle's scream was now a blubber of pain.

A hand grasped Shelly's shoulder. A handful of her jacket was used to yank her back to her feet. Bob Harris helped her the first few steps until she caught up with her stride. "Thanks, Bob," she took the time to say.

Bob gave her a taciturn nod, eyes scanning the excavation site for signs of movement. Shelly huffed along at his side. Bob could easily outpace her, but he was tempering his stride to match hers. Shelly was thankful again, but left it unsaid.

The assistance beacon transmitting from Entwhistle's radio stayed live until it was physically cancelled at his end. However, the open microphone was only a ten second feature. As his moan of anguish cut out, other voices interjected. Inspector Marsh shouted them down.

"Sixteen twelve receiving?"

"Go ahead, Sir," Shelly thumbed back.

"Can you update on the situation?"

"Negative at this time. I am in company with Nine-twenty-three. Approaching Trowhaem from the north. Coastal path. No sign of movement."

"Find Entwhistle. As a priority." Marsh's command was of course academic. It was exactly as Shelly intended. She didn't say as such, she knew that the inspector was attempting to take control of the situation. There were certain things he had to say. They had to appear on the running log that would already be streaming across computer screens back in Lerwick control. Others would be watching the log - people higher up the food chain than Marsh. His words were an arse-covering exercise.

Two could play at that game. "All units, all units," Shelly called. "I want a perimeter set up around the suspect's last known location. Double teamed at all times. If the suspect is sighted, approach with caution. Wait for armed back up. No one…repeat NO ONE fires without Inspector Marsh's permission." She heard responding confirmation from a number of officers before she was satisfied that her command had been heard and understood. She cut back in. "We have a man down. In need of urgent assistance. The suspect is probably armed and prepared to use force. Caution, people, caution. *But I want this man detained.*"

Whilst talking she'd never stopped running. Bob had been her guide as they'd jogged along the cinder path that marked an ancient wharf side. On her left, holes dug into the ground were a series of irregular steps leading up the hillside. Occasionally they passed a tent guarding a particularly interesting find. Somewhere above them was the grave of the murder victim. Christ, it was only minutes ago since she'd been standing there and saw the muzzle flash of a gun stabbing at the night. The nucleus to this madness. It seemed like hours ago.

"There," Bob yelled. He tugged at her clothing, urging her forward. Entwhistle was lying on his back, his shoulders propped up against the edge of the path. His knees were drawn up and he was clutching at his groin. Nothing lascivious. His posture spoke of agony.

They both slowed as they approached. Caution over-riding urgency. The suspect could still be nearby. They'd be no use to Entwhistle if they also were injured. Entwhistle's head turned towards them, and even in the darkness his face was pale. The red glow from his flashing terminal swept his features in intermittent beats, lending to his unnatural pallor. Entwhistle's eyes were wide, his mouth open in an extended 'O' shape.

"John?" Shelly said as she approached. Bob scanned around them as they moved in, his fist flexing on the grip of his extendable baton. Her guardian. Feeling safe enough to proceed, Shelly rushed towards Entwhistle, crouching down to inspect his injuries.

Entwhistle moaned. He held tight to the source of his pain. Shelly struggled with him to move his hands.

"Oh, shit," she whispered. A spurt of blood jumped a hand-span into the air. Entwhistle's injury was immediately life threatening. A severed femoral artery could kill in minutes.

"The fucker got me, Sarge," Entwhistle hissed. "So much for the stab proof vest, huh? Should have been wearing a jock strap."

Shelly's smile was more a forced grimace. Some officers expected humour in the face of adversity, but Shelly had nothing to laugh about. Entwhistle was dying. The copious amount of blood making arches across the path marked his countdown to oblivion. Shelly felt like crying.

"Put your hands back on the cut," she said, voice wavering. "Press down hard."

"No strength."

"I know, I know, but you have to try." She thumbed at her radio, hands slick with Entwhistle's blood, called in their location, requested immediate medical assistance. She shouted Bob over. "You have to help me, Bob. Press on his hands, stop any more bleeding."

Bob gave a final sweep of the area. The suspect was gone. Other officers were rushing closer. He bent down, pushing hard on Entwhistle's hands. Shelly tugged on her belt, pulling loose the Velcro on her meagre first aid pack. As she leaned down to attempt to staunch the flow with an ineffective gauze pad, Entwhistle snaked a hand loose from beneath Bob's, took hold of Shelly's hand. He gripped her.

"I almost had him, Sarge. I got him across the shoulder with my baton. But then he stabbed me. Don't ken what with. I think it was claws."

"Claws?"

"Like a bloody animal," Entwhistle said. He paused to gather himself, sucking in air. "I know it's mad, but he had claws. Honest, Sarge!"

"I believe you." And she did. Janet hadn't been wrong. She'd seen what she described. A monster. A Skeklar.

Entwhistle laughed, delirium and pain sending him half-mad. "He had claws."

Then he said no more.

He sank back. His hand felt floppy in Shelly's grip.

Bob pressed harder.

Shelly joined in.

"We're going to lose him, Bob. We can't let that happen."

"No. No. No." Bob's words were a continuous loop.

Shelly screamed for the medical assistance they needed. But she knew in her heart that any help would arrive too late.

THIRTYFOUR

Near Broom's Cottage

About four hundred metres short of Broom's cottage, the familiar shape of a Subaru drew up alongside me. I was still jogging, and I did a double take before staggering to a halt. I clutched at the roof of the car and bent down to give Paul Broom the baleful eyeball. It didn't immediately occur to me that Broom had followed my route along the road from the direction of Trowhaem, and it was only when I realised that I was glaring through the passenger side window that I noted that the car was pointing the opposite way to what I would have expected. I rapped my knuckles against the glass, motioned for him to wind the window down.

Broom shook his shaggy hair. "Get in."

"What?"

"Get in."

I pulled at the door handle, yanked open the door. "Where the hell have you been, Broom?"

"Where do you think? I've been back up to Burra Ness looking for you. Why didn't you wait for me coming back like we agreed?"

I threw myself into the seat, slammed shut the door. The SIG dug into my lower spine and I reached round and pulled it free. I brandished it like an icon of my anger. "Wait for you? You were gone for hours, you arsehole. How long was I supposed to wait for you?"

"Easy, Carter," Broom said. "Just calm it, will you?"

"Calm it? If you'd gone through what I just did you'd be anything but calm."

"I take it the shit just hit the fan?"

"And then some," I snapped. Then my anger deflated. I dropped the gun in my lap. Suddenly shattered. "You left me for hours, Broom. What the bloody hell have you been doing?"

"Important research."

"What? You've been reading books whilst I was freezing my bollocks off in the middle of nowhere?"

"Actually, I was conducting research on the internet." Broom shifted gears, bounced the clutch pedal until he was satisfied, and set off down the shallow decline towards the cottage.

"That makes it okay, then," I said.

The corners of Broom's lips lifted and fell.

"Next time you can do the stake out while I stay at home and browse porn sites," I said.

"I'd have gladly stayed this time."

"Then why didn't you?"

"Wander about the moors hunting evil? Me? That just isn't my bailiwick, Carter."

"It isn't mine, either. Who do you think I am all of a sudden? Van-frigging-Helsing? I'm only a salesman, for God's sake!"

Broom slapped his crippled leg. "Who out of the two of us most capable?"

"Or the most stupid?" I added.

"You must tell me what happened," Broom said. "I've just driven by Trowhaem, and it's like World War Three up there. I take it that's where you've just hot-footed it from?"

"You wouldn't believe me if I told you."

His shoulders lifted in a shrug. "I'm sure that I would."

We'd arrived at the cottage and Broom parked the Subaru on a hard stand next to the garden.

"Inside," I told him. "We'd better get shot of the gun. I've a feeling that the police are going to be here before long."

Broom's gaze flickered to the SIG resting on my lap. "You used the gun?"

I exhaled. Though initially repulsed by the thought of shooting anything I hadn't exactly paused to check my morals when threatened by the monstrous thing that had leapt on me from the crag. "Yeah, I had to shoot. If I hadn't, I doubt I'd be here right now."

"Who did you shoot? Please…tell me it wasn't a police man."

I gave him the dead eye.

"Then who?"

"I'll tell you inside." I shoved to get him moving.

"Did you…?"

"Kill it? No, I don't think I did." I climbed out of the car. "Come on, Broom. I don't want to be found with this thing on me when the police turn up."

Broom clambered from the car. Nodded me towards the cottage. "Go ahead. Door isn't locked. Put the SIG back in its box. I'll shove it in my safe."

"Won't the police ask to look in your safe?"

"They can ask what they want, but without a warrant they can go whistle." I'd almost reached the front door before I realised that Broom had halted. Turning, I saw that he was studying me with something akin to revulsion.

"What's wrong?"

"Tell me you haven't done something that would give them a reason to come bursting into my house uninvited."

"Don't worry, Broom. They've no reason to come after me. If anything, I did them a favour."

"Police don't always see things the way we do."

"Perhaps not," I agreed. "But if you're concerned that I shot an innocent, you can forget it. Whatever tried to jump me would have killed me if I hadn't shot it. Another thing, the police didn't come after me, they chased it. By the sounds of things they might have found it, too."

"You didn't see them catch it?"

"No." I felt cold abhorrence creep across my skin. "All I heard was screaming."

Broom lurched towards me. His bad leg seemed to be giving him extra trouble tonight. I guessed that the chilly air had something to do with it. He ushered me towards the door. "I don't think they got it."

"Why not?"

"Too much activity going on. There were groups of officers spread out all over the place, beating the grass, shining torches here, there and everywhere. They had dogs as well. And a helicopter. I guess that - if they'd caught this thing - they'd be centred on a particular area, or concentrating on gathering evidence."

We moved through the cottage to our usual hub of operations: the kitchen. The air was stale with the lingering odours of our breakfast. Christ, it seemed like days since we'd last been there.

"Hadn't they set up road blocks?" I wondered.

"Of course."

"So how come they let you through?"

"Do I look like a murderer to you, Carter?"

Neglecting to look his way, I found a tumbler and held it under the cold tap. Water bubbled into the glass. I quenched my thirst before saying, "What exactly does a murderer look like, Broom?"

"You tell me. You said that you shot at it. You must have seen what it looked like." He watched me from the other side of the kitchen; his buttocks perched on a counter top, arms folded across his chest. Was that a subtle challenge in his voice or was I simply imagining it? Made me wonder…

"I didn't get a good look at it."

"First things first. You keep referring to the murderer as *it*. Are we talking about anything other than a man?"

I thought for a moment. Shook my head at my own incredulity. "It had to be a man."

"As opposed to a woman, you mean? Or are you talking animal?"

I dry swallowed. The action prompted me to refill my glass. "As opposed to animal," I clarified. "I didn't get a good look, everything happened very quickly and it was dark. Just this thing that dropped on me from some rocks I was hiding in. I managed to dodge out of the way and I shot at it."

"Hit it?"

"I think so." I jerked my head. "No. I did hit it. At least once. I shot it square in the chest from as close as I am to you."

"But you didn't kill it? How is that possible?"

My hands raised in reflex. Water sloshed from my glass. "I don't know. The bullet knocked it off its feet and it fell down the hillside we were on. I thought that it had to be dead, but…well, the next thing I heard was screaming coming from the first policeman to reach it. I didn't stop to find out what had become of it after that. I did a runner. Didn't stop running until you caught up with me on the road out there."

Broom rocked back, tightening his arms across his chest. "Judging by the extent of the search that's being conducted, I think that guarantees that it got away." Broom blew out air. "Now you've got me calling this thing 'it'."

"It's all I can think of to describe the bloody thing."

"Not an animal, though. You said that already."

I nodded slowly. "But more than a man."

"Try to remember, Carter. What did it look like?"

My pause filled the kitchen with expectancy. Broom leaned forward, urging me on. Finally he pushed away from the counter, allowing his momentum to swing his upper body over the kitchen table. He leaned on it with his knuckles. "Describe it to me." His words were more than the intended prompt; more of a demand.

"It was shaped like a man. Big. Tall and powerful."

"As big as me?"

"I don't know," I said. "Could have been. Could even have been taller. But that's hard to judge. I was lying on the ground at the time. This thing jumped me. I rolled out the way and fired at it. When I turned over it stood up tall for a split second. Looked fucking massive, I'll tell you." I probed my memory, attempting to get a clear impression of it in my mind. "It had claws."

"What? Like a lion's claws?" Broom gave me a look that showed conflict in his own mind. Like skepticism blended with awe. The scepticism seemed to be winning.

"More like a bear's claws. Black, shiny talons. Kind of hook shaped. I don't remember much else."

"You managed to see its claws, but can't remember anything else about it?"

"I remember the claws 'cause they were what the fucking thing intended using on me," I said. "What do you think I'd have been looking at?"

"You must have looked at its face?"

"I did. But it was too dark to see its features." I frowned. "Wait a minute. I do recall something. Its head was a weird shape. It looked too big, out of sorts with the rest of the body. It had these protrusions that looked like horns." I pre-empted his next question. "Not like the horns on a bull or anything. More like growths of bone. Just knobby lumps, if you know what I mean?"

"Weird," Broom breathed.

"Weird isn't the word for it. It was totally unnatural. Couldn't be real."

Broom studied me. Then, nodded along with me. "You're saying that it was a man, aren't you?"

"Yeah, a man in a mask of some sort. A big man in Halloween get up." I allowed my words to hang in the air between us. Something that had suddenly occurred to me made me bite my tongue. Broom read my silence for what it was. An accusation.

He lifted a finger to his chest. "You think it was me?"

My face was as hard and cold as a granite tombstone. "Am I correct?"

He gave a grunt of disbelief. Stepped towards me. "Carter…you can't be serious?"

I lifted the SIG and aimed it directly at his face. "Not another step, Broom."

He lifted his hands, back peddling away from me. The colour drained from his cheeks as though a sluice gate had opened at the base of his throat. Tears shone in his eyes.

"You've played me for a fool, but no more," I said. Conflicting emotions threatened me, but I remained cool. "You must have had a good laugh at my expense."

"What do you mean? I haven't -"

My step forward was enough to snatch the words from his lips. I probably didn't need to put the gun to his chest, but I did.

"You've been playing me all along, you shit. Bringing me up here with all sorts of crazy stories about hogboy curses. What? Was I supposed to be you're fall guy for when you get finished with your murder spree? Pretty handy having a diagnosed schizoid-nut-job on the island, eh? Someone that you could point the finger of accusation at and have locked away in a mental institution for the rest of my life?"

"Carter…no, you've got it wrong." Broom's words came out like an elongated sob.

"So tell me what you did plan."

"I didn't plan anything." He was crestfallen, betrayed by the prodigal son. "I brought you here to help me stop this thing."

"Bull shit! You left me sitting in the middle of nowhere fucking bird watching. What the hell was that all about?" When he didn't answer, I gave him my take on the nonsense with the crows. "You left me there while you came back here to collect your monster mask, didn't you? Got yourself all dressed up and then went to Trowhaem with the intention of murdering Janet. Only things didn't go too well, did they? Something happened to spoil your plans. You had to run away. You were surprised, angry, when you came across me hiding in the rocks. It was a bad move, Broom; if you'd killed me like you intended, it would have fucked up any hope of using me as a scapegoat."

"No, no, no. You've got it all wrong."

"I don't think so. What is it that's going through your head, Broom? Is this all just a way of getting your kicks, a bit of excitement? Has life on the island driven you to boredom or something? You've written so much about murder and monsters that you felt it would be fun to live out one of your stories?" I flat-handed him in the chest. He outweighed me by at least a couple of stone, yet he staggered back from me as though he was a frail old man. He came up against the counter and I pressed in close, gun pushed into his belly. "Or is it something deeper? Are you so convinced about this childish curse that you decided that you'd give it validity? Jesus Christ! A little boy, Broom? You dismembered a little boy!"

"No!"

"Yes."

"It wasn't me, Carter." Broom looked down at me. Surprisingly he showed no fear. What was that in his features? Concern?

"I don't believe you," I said, sounding a little forlorn.

"Look, Carter. Put the gun down, will you? Please?" He slowly moved a hand and laid it over the barrel of the SIG, gently moving it down and away from his body. "You know it wasn't me."

"I don't know that," I snapped. I stepped away from him, half-turned away from him before realising I was offering him my back. I swung round, again training the gun on his body.

"Look at me." Broom gestured with open hands, sweeping them from throat to groin. "Look at me, Carter. You said it yourself. You shot this *thing*. Do I look injured to you? Do I look like someone who's taken a round to the chest?"

I blinked at the obvious. "I could have missed."

"Oh, no. You told me you shot the thing from as close as we are now. You said the bullet knocked it off the hillside."

"Maybe you just reacted to the shot and dove out the way," I argued, none too convincingly.

Scornful laughter broke from Broom. He thrust his hands into his hair, staring at me like I was as insane as most people thought. My gaze flickered to the floor, realising the absurdity of my argument. Broom lifted his bad leg, jiggling his foot in my line of vision. "You think I'm capable of running around the moors, climbing on rocks and leaping on people? Jesus, Carter! Half the time I can hardly walk straight."

I exhaled wearily.

Broom went on, "Damn it, Carter! What's gotten into your head? What on earth gave you the idea -"

I slammed the barrel of the SIG on the tabletop, denting the wood with a livid groove that showed the paler inner grain. "You left me twiddling my thumbs, Broom. Watching a flock of crows that you convinced me marked the location of the next murder. I must have been a complete idiot to believe you."

"I believed it, too. I left you there in good faith."

"Yeah, right."

"I promise you, Carter. I truly did believe that it was a portent. I came back here to conduct research like I said. I was excited by what you told me about the growth of your ability. I wanted to see how best to put this ability to use."

Scorn huffed in my chest. However it wasn't solely directed at Broom now. I was doing not a little internalising. The ridiculousness of my accusation was beginning to set in, even if I was too pig-headed to let it go. Many thoughts were flitting around in my mind, each vying with the other to show me how irrational I had acted, how I was still acting.

Broom said, "I can see how you got this notion in your head. I can't blame you. Out there alone, coming face-to-face with something you couldn't begin to understand. I'm sorry I left you to face this thing alone. It was wrong of me. I see that now."

"Broom…"

He waved me down. "Put the gun down, Carter. We'll leave it at that, okay? You must be tired, hungry; you've experienced a terrible shock. Believe me, I understand."

I was nodding with him, praying that his words were sincere.

"Don't listen to him, brother. Shoot the fucker and have done with it."

My teeth ground together, eyelids crinkling tight. Cash's voice was like a sudden migraine. I snorted. Misreading me, Broom flinched back. I lifted a hand at him, a cautioning gesture. Broom's frown was troubled.

"Is it Cash?" he asked softly.

Replying directly to my brother, I asked, "What are you saying?"

"Don't listen to his lies. We both know that Broom's the killer. Don't let him blind you with bullshit. Shoot him, Carter. It's what he deserves."

Broom moved towards me. I didn't know what he intended, how he thought he could physically help me. My gesticulation this time was a warning. "Keep out of this." I didn't fully know whom my words were directed at, but Broom reacted by quickly moving away. He watched me from the far side of the room. To his credit he didn't attempt to slip away while I was distracted. Or attack me.

I pushed the SIG along the tabletop, thrusting it away from me like it was something foul. Which I suppose it was. I'd used the damn thing to threaten my best friend - my only friend - in the whole damned world.

"Did you do this to me, Cash?"

"What? Warn you. Save your worthless life? Yes, I did that."

"You know that's not what I meant. I'm talking about putting these absurd notions in my mind. Broom's no murderer. You did this you sick arsehole! I don't know how, but you twisted my thoughts."

It had to be Cash's influence. Even after what I'd endured, there could be no other explanation for my turning against Broom. Intrinsically, he had faults like anyone else. But he was no murderer. All Broom had ever done was to help me. Why the

249

hell would he want to harm me now? Even if he was the killer - a big if - and my theory that I was a handy scapegoat were true, then why would he want to kill me? I'd be no use to him as an alibi if I were lying in a morgue. And another thing; I did indeed shoot my attacker, and there was no way that Broom could wander about unhindered with a 9mm slug in his chest.

I could see what had happened now. Frightened, confused, physically worn down even if my brain was on overdrive, Cash had wheedled his way into a small chink in my armour. Somehow he'd worked at this weakness, nudging and poking my thoughts, insinuating doubt in my mind. It's a simple theory I've considered since, but perhaps my fledgling ability at reading another person's aura had something to do with it. Supposing that my channelling of this ability caused me to drain my own energy, it would lower my resistance against Cash's influence over my subconscious. Before, I'd been in total control of my brother. Now it seemed that he had won a small victory over me.

I could have literally kicked myself in the backside - if such wasn't impossible. Broom had always cautioned me; be self controlled and alert. Your enemy the devil prowls around like a hungry lion, searching for souls to devour. Well, it seemed that Cash had just sampled the devil's meal. I was determined that I wouldn't give him an aperitif.

"You are a pig, Cash."

"Oink! Oink!" he laughed. *"Go on, brother. Do us all a favour. Just take that gun, stick it under Broomy's chin and blow his freakin' brains all over the ceiling."*

"Forget it, Cash. I'm not listening to you anymore." Sickened by my actions, I again aimed my words for both of them to hear. Biting my bottom lip I slow-blinked an apology at Broom. The big fella still appeared frightened of me, but he bounced his chin in a conciliatory nod.

"Sorry, Broom," I said to further mollify him.

This time he gave me a weak grin. He waved a hand at me. "Don't worry about it, I didn't take you seriously."

"Don't believe him, Carter. He's trying to get you to let your guard down. He...wants...to...kill...you."

"Go and crawl back under your rock."

"I tried to warn you, remember?" Cash said in a maddening singsong. *"I told you that there was a test. Are you man enough, Carter? Are you man enough to kill your best friend?"*

"Lies."

"I knew what it would be like when it came right down to brass tacks. I knew you wouldn't be up to it. You're a pussy, brother. A coward."

"And you are a sick psychopath. I don't care what you say; I know that Broom is innocent."

"Why don't you ask him about his interest in the man in the grave?"

"You're wasting your breath."

"Ask Broom why he wanted to know about the procedures the police use to identify bodies..."

"Cash. Would you please just let it lie?" Illogically I ground my palms against my ears; a totally pointless exercise considering his voice emanated directly from the centre of my mind.

"Could it be that the pins holding the dead dude's ankle together would give the game away?"

"Cash, for crying out loud!" I slammed my hands flat on the table. The SIG did a little jig in place, the rattle of metal on wood was like a distant drum roll. Unaware that I was screwing my eyes tight, I snapped them open and stared directly at Broom. Slack-jawed, Broom returned my stare.

"What is it, Carter? What is Cash saying to you?"

I shook my head. Cash was like a wasp in a biscuit tin, his voice an infuriating buzz. *"Ask him brother. But first pick up the gun. Once he tells you his secret he will have no option but to kill you."*

Against my best judgement, I did reach for the SIG. My fingertips fluttered over the grip. I said to Broom, "Cash tells me that you are concerned about the dead man's identity. Something about surgical pins giving the game away."

It was neither question nor explanation, but Broom was astute enough to read the fresh accusation in my voice. "What pins? Are you talking about the pins in *my* ankle?"

"Pins in the dead man's ankle," I said, echoing Cash who spoke simultaneously with me.

Broom shook his head in confusion.

"The pins prove the dead man's identity," Cash went on, and I voiced his words out loud. "They will prove that the dead man is Paul Broom."

"What? You can't be serious?" Broom looked at me as though I'd just told him that the world was indeed flat, and all that we'd been told by modern science was all a sack of hooey. But it wasn't his disbelief that made me rock back on my heels and blink at him. It was the fact that he had actually heard Cash's words. Panic welled in my chest as I considered the possibility that Cash was gaining control over me. Mercifully the feeling only lasted a second or so, for I quickly understood that it was nothing more than my own suspicion that I'd spoken out loud, that Cash's control had merely been in influencing this absurd hypothesis.

Attempting to make amends for my slip, I said, "Crazy isn't it? I think that Cash is trying to make me believe that the real Paul Broom is dead, and that you are an impostor."

"What do you believe, Carter?"

He was acting in a more reasonable fashion than should have been expected; maybe that was the true measure of his innocence, and the strength of his friendship for me. I should have left things at that, but it seemed that Cash's influence demanded an answer. Plus, the controlled manner in which Broom posed the question was the same as the delivery used by the doctor's who'd initially attempted to diagnose my supposed mental problems. Too say the least, I was insulted.

"Show me your leg, Broom."

"What? You want to see my leg to prove that I'm not some sort of pod person from Mars?"

"You said it yourself, Broom; some of these Trow have shape shifting abilities. Just show me your leg so that I can prove Cash wrong?"

"Did I say that? I don't recall mentioning…"

"See, brother, he's stalling. Just shoot the fucker now and get it over with."

"Broom, it will only take a second. Just show me your leg, and then we can get it over with." My final words were for Cash's sake.

Broom's head swung side-to-side. "How would showing you my leg prove anything? If I was indeed a shape shifter, couldn't I simply change my leg so that it was scarred in the same manner as mine is."

I sighed. "More than likely. But I don't believe what Cash is saying anyway. But at least it will shut the crazy bastard up. Come on, Broom, just work with me, will you?"

Broom gave a good old-fashioned harrumph; just what you'd expect from an eccentric author of gothic horror. Then again, wouldn't a shape-shifting creature posing as my scatty friend have done likewise? Next second he strode forward, bad leg swinging and clumping as though to emphasise his physical problem. He came round the table, and I moved away to give him clearance to swing his foot up onto a chair. His eyes flickered momentarily on the SIG before he reached for the hem of his trousers. He snatched his trousers up to his knee, then forced down the cuff of his woollen sock.

The scars on his ankle and shinbone were puckered white ridges, and a good portion of his calf muscle was gone, a striated crater marking major tissue damage. He glared at me. "Satisfied?"

I nodded. My emotions were measured in equal portions of relief and shame. More for Broom's sake - or maybe to soothe my own embarrassment - I said, "Can we now please stop the lunacy, Cash?"

Cash, of course, declined to answer. I was on my own now. He knew his opportunity for chaos had passed and he'd retreated to his dark place to leave me to endure the uncomfortable aftermath on my own. I pushed my hands through my hair.

Broom pushed his trouser leg down, concealing his horrific injury. He was supremely pissed off with me. I gave him a combined shrug and lift of the eyebrows.

"I can't believe what we just went through," he muttered.

"I'm sorry."

"Forget it. Let's just pretend that the whole idiotic episode didn't happen."

I had no words for him. All I could do was offer him a sheepish grin. Broom scowled at me in return. Then he twisted from where he stood perched on the chair and snatched the SIG into his large hand.

I stiffened.

Broom huffed. Bounced the gun on his palm. "Best I put this away in the safe."

As he stomped past me, I caught at his elbow. He spun on me, and there were still embers of anger behind his eyes.

I pulled the magazine I'd discretely removed from the gun from my pocket. "Best you put that in the safe as well."

Gazes locked, Broom took the magazine from me.

"It wasn't loaded?"

I gave him a strained laugh. "Did you actually think that I would shoot you? My best friend?"

He walked away from me swearing. But at least he was laughing.

THIRTYFIVE

Trowhaem

It was easy to compartmentalise the death of a colleague when referring to him as collar number 443. Designated only by his number he remained an anonymous figure relegated to the roll call of officers killed in the line of duty. Numbers didn't necessitate the process of grieving. You don't grieve a statistic. All that was required was a moment's respectful silence before the world continued on as though nothing untoward had happened. It was a sad fact, but police officers died the world over. Not something that you wanted, but - as part of *the job* - you accepted it nonetheless. The only thing was, that wasn't a number that was being loaded onto a stretcher. It was John Entwhistle, and Shelly McCusker knew him personally.

John Entwhistle was a twelve years veteran of the force, what was generally referred to as a lifetime Bobby. He didn't aspire to making rank, happy with his lot as a constable, and happy performing the duties of a constable. He had joined the force the way a lot of recruits did, full of ideals and a need to help and assist others. Unlike a lot of police officers with a dozen years under their belt he hadn't grown cynical or jaded with the bureaucratic red tape, or with the loss of faith in human sensibilities, facets of long service that often forced themselves in the way of ideals. John Entwhistle remained a conscientious, hardworking copper who continued to put himself in the line of fire purely for the sake of others.

Damn it! It was those same ideals that had got him killed.

He was thirty-four years old, married to…Norma, wasn't it? Father of three young children, seven, nine and eleven years old respectively. As good a husband and parent as he was a policeman. He was well liked around the station, and by the public too. He was one of that rare breed who was genuinely a nice person. No…wait. He used to be all those things. Now he was dead. The latest victim of the brutal killer who had brought terror to Connor's Island.

Shelly could think of only one way to describe John's sacrifice: a supreme waste of a good person.

After seeing that John was given the care and respect that was his due, after the report and debriefing with Inspector Marsh, Shelly had found herself a quiet place to weep. Just for a few minutes. A brief respite from the nightmare she was embroiled in. Now she was dry-eyed and ready to get back to business. Bob was by her side.

Shelly rapped on the door to Professor Hale's caravan with the butt end of her torch, before reaching for the handle and opening the door. Two of the officers drafted in from Lerwick were between Shelly and Janet Hale. The professor was sitting at the far end of the caravan, small and childlike in her ill-fitting bathrobe. Her eyelids flashed once as she peeked up at these new invaders of her home.

Shelly squeezed out a smile of greeting, before re-introducing herself.

"Please…sit down." Janet straightened a throw on the bunk opposite her, plumped a cushion. Then she sat down and folded her hands in her lap.

The two mainland constables shuffled by, exchanging mournful nods with Shelly and Bob. Shelly waited for them to exit the caravan before sitting down across from the professor. Bob remained in the kitchen area, a staunch sentinel guarding the door. Consciously or not, he stood with his thumbs hooked round the hilt of his extendable baton and the holder of his incapacitant spray; a hulking gunslinger poised to draw.

Janet gave him only the briefest perusal before turning her attention on Shelly. Something in her face said that the presence of a big well-trained man wouldn't make much difference if her attacker chose to return.

"Did they catch him?" she asked.

Shelly leaned forward, clasping her hands in mimic of the woman across from her. She shook her head slowly. "Not yet."

"Not yet." Resignation sighed from Janet.

"We are conducting an area search. I'm sure we will find him soon."

Janet's mouth formed a straight line.

Shelly said, "It's not as if there are that many places to hide. We'll have him in no time."

Unconvinced, Janet clutched handfuls of her bathrobe.

Awareness crept in to Shelly and she sat back, carefully unfolding her hands. She could be another woman feeling the same level of pain and terror as the professor, or she could be a police sergeant. The woman in her wept for John Entwhistle - and for all the other victims of this vicious killer - but the sergeant had a job to do. Primarily she had to catch the brute responsible for the murders, but equally as importantly she had a duty to reassure the victim before her.

"You don't have to be afraid, Professor Hale. We will ensure that your attacker doesn't get access to you again."

Janet looked at Bob, who stirred self-consciously beneath her gaze. Her headshake was desultory. "No offence officers, but I don't see how that could be possible. He got to me once, he could do it again."

"Not now that we are looking for him…"

"Sergeant…the camp was full of people, and he simply walked straight through them and into my home. He attacked me and carried me off. God knows what would have happened if that dog hadn't got him."

"We weren't prepared for him then. Now we are. I promise you that we will keep you safe."

Janet still wasn't satisfied. "You say you weren't prepared before…but you still don't know who it was that attacked me. Or even *what* attacked me. How can you make a promise that I'll be safe when you have no idea what it is that we're up against?"

"I'll grant you that this man is very dangerous, but there's no way he can get to you again. Not now that we're here."

Janet puffed out her cheeks. "I heard the shooting, the screaming. You didn't manage to stop him then."

Stung by the comment, Shelly slapped at her jacket, pulling out her notebook. "We underestimated him last time. We won't let the same thing happen again."

Janet looked deflated. "Was someone else hurt?"

No use hiding the truth. "Three officers were injured. Another was killed."

"Oh my God, I am so sorry." Janet's eyes shone with fresh tears.

"It's not your fault." Images of John Entwhistle forced themselves into Shelly's mind. Vividly she saw his ashen features grow alabaster white as his lifeblood leaked away. His mouth hung open in accusation, as though the finger of blame should fall directly upon the ineptitude of his supervisor to protect him. The thought was illogical, of course. There was nothing she could have done that would have changed the outcome. She batted the image aside. "As I said, we underestimated the killer and have paid sorely for it. More the reason why we won't let the same thing happen again."

Shelly felt like a stuck record, repeating herself over-and-over again. The cure for a stuck record generally called for a quick thump to the offending mechanism to skip the needle over the sticking point. Changing tact was her response. "I know you've already gone over this a dozen times, but could you describe your attacker to me again?"

"Of course. Anything that will help to catch him."

Shelly sat with a pen poised over her notebook.

"I've given it a lot of thought since then," Janet began. "Perhaps I was suffering from shock at the time." She paused, embarrassment adding colour to her drained face. "I told your colleagues that I was attacked by a monster. A Skeklar, no less."

She laughed at her apparent foolishness. "Now I realise that it couldn't possibly have been anything so ridiculous."

Shelly rolled her shoulders. John Entwhistle's words came back to her and she formed them into a question. "It was…just a man?"

"What else could it be?" Janet asked, but her words were as hollow as her conviction.

Shelly offered the alternative. "A person posing as a Skeklar?"

"Had to be."

From Bob came a grumble of assent. Both women gave him a second's notice. He lifted his eyebrows in an *I thought so* gesture, then turned his back on them and wandered to the far end of the caravan. Without seeking permission he leaned into the open door to the bedroom and checked that the window was shut. Happy that the women were safe, he stepped to the exit door. "I'll just take a look around outside, Sarge. Make sure everything's safe for you women while the two of you talk."

Shelly smiled at the manly intimation; some might think Bob's actions as ill-veiled chauvinism, but Shelly recognised his desire to protect them as a deeper and innate condition based at a gene level. Nature decreed that - comparatively speaking - the male of the species was bigger, stronger and faster than his female counterpart. Therefore, who was she to be offended by a man's need to carry out what instinct bade him do? At base level, Shelly would rather it was Bob guarding them than anyone. She watched him angle his big frame through the door, the ghost of a smile plucking at her lips.

As the door snicked to behind him, Janet asked, "Are the two of you involved?"

Shelly blinked, only then aware of the professor's scrutiny. "No. We just…work together."

Janet turned down the corners of her mouth. Eyelids drooping. "Oh."

"What gives you that impression?" Shelly asked. Unexpected warmth trembled in her midriff.

Janet shrugged. "Just the way that you look at each other. I thought…"

"That we are lovers?" Shelly laughed. It was as forced a sound as ever she'd heard.

"He seems like a nice man." Janet's stare bore holes into Shelly's. It was Shelly's turn to redden.

"Yes…"

"You could do worse, you know," Janet said.

There was a moment of silence as they both considered. The man had stepped out the room, and suddenly they were simply two women sharing intimacies. Shelly kidded herself that it was good for the bonding process, that she was winning the woman's trust. Just as a police sergeant should. So why was she feeling all girly all of a sudden?

With a slight tremor to her voice, she asked, "What do you mean by 'the way we look at each other'?"

Janet slowly lifted her head, as though seeking inspiration from the lamp glow behind Shelly. She appeared to measure her answer in the earnest way in which Shelly kept check of herself. "Pardon me for saying, but you're like a couple of love struck teenagers. Maybe you haven't realised it yet, but I think that there's an attraction that goes beyond *just working together*."

"No, no. It's simply mutual respect."

"Maybe on your part," Janet said. "But you'd have to be blind not to see the way your friend looks at you."

Waving a hand, Shelly asked, "You've noticed all this since we walked in here a few minutes ago?"

"And at the gravesite earlier," Janet added. "Please don't be offended, Sergeant McCusker. I'm only telling it as I see things. That constable is in love with you."

"No…"

"Yes."

There was little need for the lights; the glow off Shelly's cheeks was enough to brighten up a dull Sunday in Skelvoe.

"I'm sorry, I've embarrassed you." Janet screwed up the cloth at her throat. "Please. You must excuse me."

"No…I'm not embarrassed…there's nothing to excuse you for…"

Janet smiled at her. "I have embarrassed you. I'm sorry for talking out of turn. I guess it's the damn anthropologist in me. I've made a study of human behaviour, but I still don't realise how insensitive I must sound when I speak."

"Insensitive?"

"Yes. I just open my mouth, and a load of old rubbish spills out. You're here to find out what I remember about my attacker, and I'm acting like a match-maker for a dating agency."

If Shelly had a handkerchief she'd have coughed politely into it. That's what the fair maidens did when acting demurely in those Regency Romance novels her mum used to read. Shelly had to make do with concealing her bashful smile behind her pocket notebook. "Oh, my!" she said. Very Jane Austen.

They laughed. Both embarrassed now in their own way. At least the ice was well and truly broken. Shelly had won a confidant, even if it hadn't been in the way - or on the subject - she'd intended.

The warmth didn't last long. Shelly had a job to do. They both had a killer to catch.

"I've made my mind up," Janet concluded. "It was a man. Had to be a man."

"Would you please try and describe him to me?"

Janet stared into space. Her grey eyes were the colour of the mist that writhes across Yell Sound in mid-winter. "He was grotesque."

"By grotesque, you mean he was ugly?"

Janet shuddered. "As my father used to say, 'you couldn't kick putty into anything so ugly'. Sergeant, this man was about the most grotesque thing I've ever seen."

"Deformed?"

"And then some." Janet sat back, resting against the caravan wall like she'd no strength left. "Not naturally, though. Nothing in nature could be formed like that." She laughed. "Unless the government are doing secret genetic experiments up at Burra Ness that they're not telling us about."

There are no secret experiments at the military base, Shelly wanted to say, if you exclude the captured UFO that they're rumoured to be back engineering in order to develop new technologies. Of course, that would be just a little too absurd. Maybe Janet wouldn't appreciate her attempt at humour. Anyway, they had a Skeklar to catch, not little green men.

Instead she asked, "Can you describe your attacker?" She poised her pen over her notebook.

"I didn't get a clear look at it. It grabbed me from behind, carried me on its shoulder. When I was on the floor and it was standing over me, it was in silhouette against the night sky. I only got a look at it for a split-second."

The fact Janet was again referring to her attacker as '*It*' didn't escape Shelly's notice. Softly, she prompted, "Just tell me what you can recall about him. Even if it's just your impressions of what you remember."

"Okay," Janet said. She gave a single laugh. "You might think my impressions are those of a crazy woman, but here goes…Very large. Six and a half, maybe seven feet tall. Very strong. Big, big claws. Its shoulders were very bony, almost like an exoskeleton or a beetle's carapace. Its legs were hairy, like wiry bristles. Like I said, like nothing in nature."

Shelly had no need to hide her incredulity. It wasn't a factor. She'd witnessed first hand what this thing had done to John Entwhistle, and she for one wasn't of a mind to dispute Janet's memories.

"Did you see his face at any time?" she asked.

Again the singular laugh. "The face was about the worst thing about it. Like my father said -"

"You couldn't kick putty into anything so ugly," Shelly finished for her.

"Yes. Exactly." Janet scratched her hair back behind her ears. "Have you seen that sci-fi movie, The Predator?"

"The one with Arnold Schwarzenegger?"

"Yes, where he's being chased through the jungle by a huge alien hunter. Well, if I'd to give you my *impression* of my attacker, I'd say you were looking for The Predator." Janet lifted the flat of her hand. "Of course, I couldn't possibly suggest something like that. I'm a scientist for Christ's sake…I could ruin my reputation."

"Hey!" Shelly said, tongue firm in her cheek. "What's wrong with Schwarzenegger movies?"

Shelly's humour had the desired effect. Janet's laughter was genuine this time. Good, things were beginning to get too bleak again, and Shelly had no intention of getting back to the subject of unrequited love to lighten the mood.

"He must've had some sort of helmet on," Janet explained. "And goggles."

"Goggles?"

"You know like those night vision goggles that soldiers wear."

Janet nodded. Maybe their jokes concerning secret experiments weren't so far removed, after all. Who else would have access to night vision technology here on Conn, if not military personnel up at Burra Ness?

"Something else. I think he could have been wearing a gas mask or something like it. By the sound of his voice -"

"What?" Shelly asked. "He spoke to you?"

Janet nodded again. "Before you ask, I didn't recognise his voice. It's why I think he had on a gas mask; his voice was slurred and sounded hollow and his breathing sounded harsh."

"Okay," said Shelly. "Do you remember what he said?"

"I'll never forget for the rest of my life," Janet said emphatically.

"When he first attacked me, he said 'It is time, Professor Hale'. I tried to fight him off, to get free and he said something really weird: 'It is pointless fighting me,' he said. 'I have chosen you. You are four of nine. I have decided.'"

Her pen scrabbled at the page as Shelly noted down the words. "Very weird," she agreed. "Four of nine?"

Janet's shoulders lifted in a shrug. "I don't know what he meant. Unless he was talking about his victims. I was going to be the fourth?"

"But what is the significance of the nine?"

"I don't know. Maybe it's a ritual thing. I know that the number nine is significant in Norse mythology, but that's as far as my knowledge goes."

Shelly pondered. "Who is knowledgeable on the subject? Do you think that Professor Bishop would be able to help?"

"Maybe," Janet said. There was no enthusiasm in her response. "There is someone more likely to know. There's this writer-"

"Paul Broom?" Shelly squinted. "You know him?"

"Only fleetingly," Janet replied.

There was something in the way her eyes flickered that made Shelly think there was something else that was going unsaid. When she didn't expound, Shelly said, "Was there anything else of importance that your attacker said to you?"

Janet pulled her knees up and hugged them to her chest. "He told me my screams would not help me. All they'd achieve was to bring others hurrying to their deaths. If I continued to scream he'd be forced to kill them all."

Shelly grunted as she wrote. Then, "Anything else?"

"Yes," Janet blinked down at the floor. "There's this man I met, I must have called out for help or something. My attacker said, 'Forget him. He is useless to you. He is gone from here'."

"The attacker knew your friend's name?"

"He must have done. Going by what he said, I don't think that they are on the best of terms, though."

"What did he say?"

"He said, 'If Carter Bailey was here, I would show you just how useless to you he is'."

Shelly's pen stopped mid-stroke. There he was again. "Carter Bailey? The attacker knew Carter Bailey?"

Janet's pause seemed to fill the caravan. She had the look of a guilty person all of a sudden. Or of one who'd just realised that they may just have incriminated an innocent person in a crime. Finally, she said, "I told you. He had to know him. I only said Carter's first name. Never mentioned his surname."

Shelly's mind was on triple over-drive. Carter Bailey again. What was it with that man? She shook the thought away, but instantly formed another. She had reason to go and speak with Paul Broom. Why not corner Carter Bailey at the same time, and finally get to the bottom of her fears?

THIRTYSIX

Broom's cottage

How does that old song go? Oh, yeah! 'If I knew you were coming, I'd have baked a cake.' Not that I'm much of a cook, but I'd have done something. For a start I'd have at least tidied myself up.

"Janet," I said, getting up off my chair as Broom ushered the professor into his kitchen. Despite myself I was smiling unashamedly. Not all of it was to do with the schoolboy flush raging through my body; I was overwhelmed with relief that she appeared unharmed.

Janet offered me a tight smile. That's all I noted before the woman police sergeant and her huge companion wandered into the room. I shot a glance at Broom who gave me a lift of his eyebrows.

A phrase flitted through my mind, 'Uh-oh, trouble at mill, lad'. It was one of those phrases that had inserted itself into popular northern English culture, which probably didn't have any basis in a genuine quote. Trouble with me was that *trouble at the mill* was the starting point for all my woes. It made me wonder if the voice was Cash's and he was attempting to get his hooks into me again.

My smile became a tight grimace.

"Hello officers," I said. "Please, come in."

The sandy-haired constable nodded curtly. "You made it here, then Mr Bailey?"

"I did, officer. I didn't want it on my conscience if you had to traipse the moors all night looking for me." I said it lightly enough, so that it came across as a joke.

"As you know by now, we got otherwise diverted," the sergeant said. For some reason she wouldn't meet my eye. She turned away, adjusting her equipment belt in order to sit on one of Broom's wooden stools.

"Are you okay, Janet?" I asked. Janet was standing next to the counter wringing her hands.

"Fine thanks," she said without conviction.

Broom saved us all from the uneasy silence that followed.

"Can I make you some tea?"

The uneasiness lasted a few seconds before the constable said, "I'd appreciate a strong coffee please. Black, no sugar."

That opened the door to negotiations and Broom busied himself by pottering with mugs and condiments.

Sergeant Shelly McCusker introduced herself and Constable Bob Harris. Then said, "You're already familiar with Professor Hale."

The way she said it held more than a little hint of hidden meaning.

"We met on the ferry yesterday," I admitted. "Once again this afternoon at the archaeological dig at Trowhaem."

"I saw you at the dig." Shelly gave me a pointed look that immediately flickered and died. "Can I ask what you were doing there?"

"Trying to help," I said, sounding as lame as a three-legged horse.

"In what way?"

Broom jumped in. "It was my fault," he said. "Contrary to what I told Professor Hale, it was my fascination as a writer that took us there."

Janet scowled at him, then at me. I shrugged, feeling like a liar.

Janet said, "You told me that you wanted to help identify the body."

"Well…" Broom said. "I did think that I could help identify him. Unfortunately - as you know - that was not the case."

Shelly grunted. She took out her notebook and flicked through to a specific page. "Professor Hale said that you were interested in how the police could identify a severely disfigured corpse."

"Research," he said.

"You seemed to know an awful lot about our procedures already," Shelly added.

"Research," Broom repeated. "I'm a writer of horror fiction, Sergeant. Police procedures often feature in my novels. For one, I know that I am not under any obligation to answer your questions, unless you caution me first."

"If you were under arrest, then I'd caution you," Shelly said. "I'm not here to arrest you, Mr Broom. I'm here because I thought I could pick your brains for answers to a number of troubling questions regarding these murders. Judging by your earlier conversation with Professor Hale, I was under the assumption that you might have in-depth knowledge concerning this fanciful haugbonde curse."

"I have researched the curse. Yes."

Shelly turned to me. This time she managed to hold the look. "And what is your interest in the curse, Mr Bailey?"

Like any seasoned blagger, I shifted uneasily in my chair, shrugged and said, "I dunno." My unavoidable straying of eyes towards Janet gave the game away.

Shelly looked from me to Janet and I saw the hint of a smile on both women's faces. "Oh, I see," she said. Warmth flushed my features.

Then she was the sergeant again. "Since you were there this afternoon, have either of you returned to Trowhaem at any time?"

"No," both Broom and I said in unison.

"Are either of you licensed to carry firearms?"

"I have a shotgun certificate," Broom offered. "It was issued in England, however, so I didn't bring my gun here with me."

"I was thinking more along the lines of handguns," Shelly said.

It was a struggle to remain calm. Both of us managed to keep our answers separate this time. "No," I said.

"Isn't there a rule governing handguns since the Dunblane tragedy?" Broom asked. "Only persons with special dispensation are allowed to carry handguns."

"You're telling me that neither of you have this special dispensation, then?" When neither of us replied, she asked, "So if we conducted gun powder residue tests on you we would find no trace of either of you having fired a gun?"

Janet appeared as shocked as we did at the sergeant's suggestion.

"Sergeant," she said. "I agreed to come here with you so that we could ask for help in capturing my attacker, not to implicate them in a crime."

Shelly sat back. She placed her notebook into a pocket on the front of her protective vest. All the while she nodded slowly. "The person who fired the gun I'm talking about was not your attacker. In fact, off the record, he deserves a medal in my opinion."

Whether this comment was delivered with the intention of flushing out the egotist in either of us, we didn't react. Maybe Shelly was truly grateful that someone had made a stand against the murderer and it was her heartfelt feelings that forced the words. Regardless, she waved them down. "Listen, I'm not here to cast blame on anyone. I'm here because, as Professor Hale pointed out, we thought you could help us."

Throughout the discourse Broom had played mother. He brought over a tray with five steaming mugs. "I just did coffee all round," he said. "Milk and sugar's on the tray. Anyone like biscuits?"

"Coffee's fine," Shelly said, cutting off any further distractions. To Broom, she said, "Predominantly, I wondered if you have any knowledge concerning ancient Norse custom?"

Broom shrugged. "Not extensive, but I do know quite a bit."

"What about Norse numerology?"

Broom nodded. "A little. What is it you want to know?"

"If I said the phrase 'you are four of nine', what would that mean to you?"

I immediately thought of the hot Borg chick from Star Trek: The Next Generation. Seven of Nine, wasn't she called? That went to show how knowledgeable I was on numerology, Norse or otherwise.

"Are we talking victims?" Broom asked.

"We can only assume that is the case," Shelly said. "The man in the grave, the boy, James Stewart…" she paused "Bethany Stewart."

"And Professor Hale?" Broom said.

"Fortunately not," Shelly said.

"So the little girl is dead?" I groaned.

Shelly shook her head. Her face looked momentarily blighted.

Bob Harris, not wanting to be left out, said, "We haven't found the wee lass yet, but things aren't looking too good."

Not if the state of the other victims was anything to go by, I thought.

"All I can say," Broom said to change the subject, "is that the number nine is significant in Norse mythology, but no one knows why." He paused as if ordering his thoughts. Then, "Odin was hung for nine nights in order to learn nine magic spells. This is represented today by the twelfth card in a tarot deck of a man hanged by one foot from a gibbet. Heimdall had nine mothers, Aegir nine daughters. Hermod was said to have travelled nine nights to find Balder. Njord and Skadi lived nine nights in each other's homes. Freyr waited nine nights for his bride, Gerd to arrive. Every ninth night eight more rings fell from Odin's ring, Draupnir - though why eight rings, I don't know. At Ragnarok, it's believed that Thor will retreat nine paces from Jormangand before dying." He stopped, racking his brains for further tidbits stored in his unbelievable vault of useless information. "Ah, yes, then there were the great festivals held for nine days every nine years at Upsalla in Sweden where nine of every living creature - including humans, by the way - were sacrificed."

I wasn't the only one staring at him.

"Nine sacrifices?" Shelly asked for us all.

"If you believe what's written in The Readers' Digest," Broom pointed out.

Nine sacrifices. If the unknown man in the grave, the little boy and girl made three, and Janet was designated as the fourth victim, that meant that the killer intended a further five deaths before he would be assuaged. Six, considering his attempt on Janet had failed. The true scale of the horror was suddenly beginning to dawn on me; a half-dozen more brutal attacks I simply could not allow to happen.

"Suddenly you're the big hero? Who do you think you are, brother? Superman?"

Cash, ever invasive at the best of times, was under these circumstances like tomato ketchup splashed on a gourmet meal. Deliberately ignoring him didn't mean he wouldn't badger me further. To my grateful delight, that was all the input he added to the conversation. If I'd held discourse with him in front of these witnesses, likely I'd be doing a quick step to Skelvoe nick with big Bob Harris twisting my arm up my back.

Janet must have been on the same wavelength as I'd been before Cash's intrusion. "Six more people are going to die."

"Unless the sicko takes PC Entwhistle into account, plus the student he killed while attempting to abduct Professor Hale," Bob said.

"Two more people died?" My words were as wretched as I felt. Thankfully, the police didn't read them as intimate knowledge of what occurred up at Trowhaem. Aware that my failure to stop the killer had possibly lead to the deaths of other innocent victims made my stomach contents do a nose dive. It's maybe a good job that Broom hadn't brought me the promised food and drink, as I'd have likely spewed it all over his kitchen floor.

"Tell me what you know about the Skeklar," Shelly said, pointedly moving us away from the subject of further death and destruction.

"The Skeklar is a creature particular to the Orkney and Shetland Islands," Broom said. Perched on his wooden stool, his ankles crossed and a mug of coffee cupped in his hands, he reminded me of the Jackanory storytellers that held a generation of children enthralled back when TV was still innocent and boasted only three channels. Unlike those of the TV presenters, Broom's tale wasn't dramatised fiction, he was being deadly earnest. "In the remainder of the British Isles we have our own myths and legends concerning fairies and elves and such, believed to be based upon the Celtic beliefs of our forebears. These islands however pay little homage to Celtic tradition, owing more of their folklore to the tales brought here by the Norse traders who settled here. The Norse has their own pantheon of mythical creatures and demigods, probably the best known of which are trolls."

"Except here they're known as trow," Janet interjected.

"Yes." Broom nodded. "As in Trowhaem. Literally translated as home of the Trow folk. Unlike the Norse troll, the trow have gone the way of the other indigenous beasts of the islands and have grown short in stature…take for example the Shetland Pony breed."

Janet shook her head. "My attacker was almost seven feet tall," she pointed out, "so couldn't be anything to do with trow, then."

Broom mimicked her headshake. "The trow are small, I grant you that. Some, known as Peerie trow, are said to be so small that they reside under toadstools and mushrooms. However, there are exceptions to the rule. The haugbonde, or hogboy, is said to appear as an emaciated old man with grey skin, a bald head and spindly limbs."

"Sounds like Gollum from Lord of the Rings," I said. Sometimes I wish I could keep my ignorance to myself. Kind of pointed me out as the uneducated one in the room. I waved a hand in apology.

Broom was nonplussed by my less than erudite remark. "Lest you forget, Tolkien was most interested in the myths and fables of the ancient world. It is possible that he had the haugbonde in mind when he came up with his Gollum character."

"Forget Gollum," Shelly said. "You were telling us what you know of the Skeklar."

"I was," Broom concurred. "The point I was making is that not all trow are tiny sprites. In particular, our friend the Skeklar. He is a grotesque monster said to have twelve heads and twelve tails - similar I suppose to the hydra of Greek mythology."

"Twelve heads and tails. Not nine, then?" Shelly asked. "Why the inconsistency when everything else usually relates to the number nine?"

Broom could do no more than shrug. "Little is known about the significance of numbers in Norse folklore. The number nine does figure regularly but nobody knows why, as I've said. Don't forget, the Skeklar is an Orkney and Shetland variant of an older myth, so things could have become jumbled along the way. The number twelve is more important to Roman and Christian beliefs, the twelve disciples of Jesus for instance, the twelve months of the year. It's possible that the Skeklar figure has been influenced and subtly changed over the many generations since the Vikings abandoned the islands."

"Perhaps," Shelly said. "But it doesn't really help us, does it? One thing I do know: it was no twelve-headed beast that killed John Entwhistle."

Janet shook her head. "How long have you been on Conn, Shelly?"

"Not long," Shelly admitted.

"But I bet you've heard the islanders make mention of trow and Skeklar in the short time you've been here?"

"Yes, I have."

"But not in the context of a twelve-headed monster," Janet pointed out.

Shelly eyed Broom up and down. "First I've heard of it."

"That's my point," Janet said. "There will be people who've lived here all their lives who couldn't describe the Skeklar if you asked them to. They're familiar with the folk-tales inasmuch as they know it's some sort of Bogyman, but I'd bet you could ask a hundred people and get a hundred different descriptions."

What Janet said held validity. That was the fallibility of eyewitness testimony. It'd be difficult to get two people to agree on the description of a real person, never mind a creature out of myth.

"Father Christmas, Santa Claus, Saint Nicholas, Kris Kringle," Broom put in. "All the same figure, subtly altered over time and the spread of cultures. We can't even agree on his description, can we?"

"I see where we're going with this," Shelly said. "What you're saying is that the Skeklar we are up against is a modern interpretation of the beast. That he has transformed from this fantastic creature of myth into something that *could be* believable in the modern era?"

It was a little odd seeing Janet and Broom in agreement.

For my part, I said, "Only one man's interpretation. The claws, the green eyes, the invulnerability to guns, these are all things we often see in sci-fi and horror movies. Whoever is playing the part of the Skeklar has chosen his own influences and put them all together to form his own idea of what a Skeklar should look like."

Expecting plaudits for my wisdom, I was disappointed to find all eyes turned on me. Even before Shelly's words came, I realised my mistake.

"How do you know what the Skeklar looks like?"

Glancing at Broom for support I spluttered out, "I…I must have heard someone mention what it looked like."

Shelly had no reservations about staring into my eyes now. What happened to her suggestion that the mysterious shooter should be given a medal?

Again Broom came to my rescue. "At the expense of getting into trouble, I must confess that I was listening in to the emergency services on my radio scanner. It was me who told Carter what the Skeklar looks like."

Shelly frowned. "Our airwave terminals aren't like the old style radios. They can't be scanned, Mr Broom."

"Correct," Broom said. His whimsical smile was tantamount to scandalous. "But that can't be said for the radios used by the navy and M.O.D personnel who joined the hunt. They're still using the UHF band, which, as you know, is easily scanned."

She wasn't convinced by our answer. Yet, on the scale of things, it didn't really matter how I was familiar with a description of the killer. For the sake of her position, she said to Broom, "It is against the law to scan the emergency channels. I could seize your equipment and report you for the offence."

"You could," Broom admitted. "But how is that going to help you stop this thing?"

"It isn't." Shelly stood up, adjusting her belt. She placed one hand on the hilt of her extendable baton. Bob Harris stood. Like her gargantuan protector, he was silent, watching us with his steady gaze.

Janet peered up at Shelly. "Are we leaving?"

"I have to get back to Trowhaem. There are still lots of things to do."

Janet's eyes were on mine as she slowly stood up. Her legs appeared to be giving her some trouble and I wanted to reach forward and help her stand. Probably the after effects of the attack she'd suffered earlier, cramping as unspent adrenalin crystallised in her muscle tissue. She noted my willingness but shook her head. "I'm okay, Carter."

"I'm...uh...relieved."

Shelly and Bob moved away towards the step down to the living area, but the sergeant turned back. "Thanks for the coffee, Mr Broom," she said. Then to me, "Can I ask you one final thing, Mr Bailey?"

"Yes, of course," I said, wondering what in hell was coming.

"Do you wear contact lenses?"

"No," I answered, totally confused. "Why do you ask?"

She looked deeply into my eyes then, and I squirmed under the scrutiny. "No reason," she said. Then she turned quickly on her heel and moved away. I'm sure I saw a faint tremor run through her body. For Janet's benefit, she said, "I'll be waiting in the car. But we have to be back at Trowhaem soon."

Broom glanced at Janet and me, then he hurried after the police officers. "I'll walk you out. There's something else about the Skeklar I neglected to mention."

With the three of them gone, I tuned my gaze on Janet. Her face was tilted down, but she was watching me from below her upper lashes, looking both vulnerable and gorgeous.

"Are you really okay, Janet?" Stepping forward I touched her wrists. It was a conciliatory gesture, and I was surprised when she turned over her hands and slipped her fingers into mine. A little buzz of electricity shot the length of my arms, and it had nothing at all to do with my supposed abilities with auric energies or Zone Point Fields.

"I'm fine. Really." She lifted her gaze to mine. "I wanted to thank you, Carter."

"For what?"

"For saving my life," she said softly.

"I didn't do…"

She lifted a finger to my lips. "Don't say it. I know otherwise. You were there, Carter. Don't ask me how it's possible, but I know you were there to protect me. Just like you said you would."

Recalling the discussion by the graveside earlier, Broom had told her that we couldn't protect her if she remained on the island. How had she known that, silently in my own mind, I'd been promising that indeed I would be there to protect her? Was it merely intuition? Or were there facets to this new power of mine that even I was unaware of? Maybe there was more to that Star Child malarkey than met the eye.

Without thinking about the magnitude of my words, I said, "I'll always be there for you."

Janet seemed neither surprised nor offended by my forwardness. There was a touch of resignation, yes, but there was also a glimmer of faith. "I know."

It was one of those moments I've heard of but never believed: instant and unequivocal acceptance of love. In perfect synchronicity we leaned in to each other, gently touching lips in a sealing of destinies. It was almost platonic that first kiss. Yet in a way it was the kind of kiss that rocks mountains, topples empires and raises oceans to swamp continents. It left us both sated, shuddering to the core as we separated.

I'd have loved to touch her again, yet our collective destiny had an immediate need to impose itself on us. Broom's strangled shout had us running for the front door.

THIRTYSEVEN

Outside Broom's cottage

The rain had returned with a vengeance.

Huge gobbets of water flattened the grass and rattled the Halloween ornaments Broom had yet to remove from his garden. Streams overflowed the gutters of the cottage, cascading through the downspouts like they were fumaroles in a rainforest cliff-side. It was the kind of rain that drenched instantly and left the body pummelled under its weight.

But that was not why Broom cried out.

The object of his dismay was the thing crouching on the bonnet of the police car like an oversize hood ornament. Even through the deluge I saw the gleam of green eyes, the black talons extending from the malformed hands.

"Get back in the house!" a high-pitched voice yelled. Only now in recollection do I believe that the voice was that of the burly policeman, Bob Harris, his larynx nipped by fear.

His suggestion was infinitely wise, but not something I could do. Call it misplaced bravery, but I ran to join Bob and Shelly as they approached the crouching obscenity. Broom was by the gatepost, and I grabbed at him. "Take Janet back inside, Broom. You'd better get the gun, too."

"The police…"

"Get the fucking gun," I snapped.

Then I was past him and rushing up behind Constable Harris. The policeman was bent at the waist, hands flexing like a wrestler. Shelly McCusker was thumbing the mike on her radio, shouting for back up, but judging by the forlorn expression on her face she was receiving no reply. I snatched at her. "Go with Broom," I told her. "Protect Professor Hale."

She shook her head as though dislodging a beetle from her ear.

"It's come for Janet," I shouted. "Do your bloody duty, Sergeant. Protect her from this thing."

If she had slapped me across the chops I would have deserved it, but what the hell. I grabbed at her utility belt and hauled her backwards. Propelled her towards the gate. She rounded on me, hands coming up to grapple.

"Please, Sergeant McCusker," I begged. "Protect her. Just in case it gets by us."

Her face told me that I was the worst kind of bastard she'd ever met, but only for an instant. Then she blinked as though waking from one dream into the living nightmare we faced. Next instant she was running for the door of Broom's cottage, shouting again into her radio. Janet's face was a pale blob in the doorway, but for only as long as it took the sergeant to bundle her back inside.

Too many seconds had passed.

When I searched for the thing on the car bonnet it was no longer visible. Neither was Bob Harris. All I could make out through the deluge was an indistinct blur that congealed into a mass of writhing limbs as two combatants rolled in the road beside the car. Bob Harris's voice was now a throaty roar.

"What you gonna do, hero?"

Cash again. Not so uninvited this time. His words were enough to galvanise me to action. Charging for the rolling combatants, my only thought was to do *something*.

"Careful, bro. That fuckin' Skeklar dude is one scary mother humper!"

Christ! Cash actually said something I agreed with. Not that I was about to back off. I charged in, the rain stinging my features like a million hornets. Trying to determine Skeklar from cop was nigh on impossible. They were grappling so tightly, twisting and turning and changing position so rapidly that I couldn't find a clear spot to put my fist. It didn't help that they were both garbed in black, or that they both made the guttural noises associated with mortal combat where intellect and words were replaced by the savage growls of wild beasts.

Like a referee I skipped round the rolling bodies. Jerking left to right as I sought a clear shot at the Skeklar. When my opportunity came, I almost missed it.

The Skeklar gained top position for a moment, sitting astride Bob's chest as it raised a taloned fist in the air, poised to strike at his throat. Bob's hands thrust up and caught at the claw, wrenching it to one side, tussling with the beast to save his flesh. The move was so desperate that I was caught in momentary flux, torn between watching the death match and actually doing something to help.

"Get this fucking thing off me, will you?" Bob yelled.

His words snatched me into the there and then, and I lunged forward, snaring the Skeklar's head in both my hands. Yanking it backwards. The Skeklar tumbled off Bob Harris, coming to its hands and knees on the road. Then it was barrelling towards me and I'd lost my grip on its malformed head, and I felt the fire of its claws raking my chest.

There was nothing practiced about my move, I simply relied on natural instinct to lift my foot up into its groin. It was like kicking the underside of a table, but it seemed even Skeklar have testicles. It stopped in its tracks, a low moan issuing from the face hovering so near to mine. I kicked the bastard again.

I should have smacked it in the head, because it was ready for the kick this time, catching my foot between its knees. Caught off balance I had no recourse than sprawl in the rain-puddled road as it twisted by me.

"Stop it, Bailey. It's going for the women."

Bob was already struggling to his feet as I lurched up. The Skeklar was a shadow racing for the cottage. We both ran after it, but it was an unfair race. The Skeklar was at the door before we'd even made the gate stoop. It didn't stop, it rammed into the door. Surprisingly the door resisted its efforts, and it was only when I heard Broom's roar of exertion that I realised that my friend was on the other side, throwing his weight against the door.

The Skeklar raised its fists and slammed them against the door panel, cracking it lengthwise, yet the door withstood it. Then we were only feet away, and the damned thing spun to confront us. Bob Harris had his extendable baton out and he struck with all his might. There was no attempt at tempering the blow as law dictates, Bob aimed to smash the thing's ugly skull in. There was the crack of leather off willow usually associated with spring days and games of cricket on the village green, but it was the noise of the baton on the Skeklar's head.

My kick to the groin had failed to stop it, now it appeared it was as invulnerable to a stove in head. Almost without pause it threw a counter-strike at Bob Harris and the big policeman went down, his head rapping painfully off the path. Then the Skeklar leaped over him, its arms outstretched to grasp me.

Skidding on the path, going to one knee amongst the crushed seashells, I could see no way of avoiding the swiping claws. God bless him, but Broom wasn't as slow on his damaged leg as he often appeared. He came out the door and onto the Skeklar's back like a lioness protecting its cub. Neither was he a weakling. He grappled the Skeklar round the waist, lifting it like a sack of corn, and then hurled it sideways. The Skeklar landed in a flowerbed, the *Whump!* of flesh meeting earth loud even against the teeming rain.

I was neither trained nor a natural when it came to unarmed combat, perhaps it was merely the instinctive need to protect that caused me to rush at the Skeklar and kick its head rugby ball style. Catching it as it lurched to all fours, my foot connected under its chin, lifting the malformed head up and backwards on its neck. The Skeklar went over onto its backside, moaning a very human-like sound of pain.

In my mind I was propelled back to that dreadful night in the water mill. I hated this thing more than I hated what Cash had become. If it meant doing so, I would have gone tooth and nail

281

against the beast, as I had my brother. The only thing that stopped me from doing so was Bob Harris catching me by the shoulders and tugging me backwards.

Good job he did: if I'd continued forward as planned, the Skeklar's swiping claws would have disembowelled me as cleanly as any of Cash's victims.

Bob saved my life. For that I'm eternally thankful. The only problem being, it allowed the Skeklar an avenue of escape. It rose up, shaking its head to clear the effect of my kick. Then it twisted away from us.

"Get it!" Broom yelled from somewhere behind me. "Don't let it escape."

"Come here," Bob grunted as he lurched past me, grabbing at air as the Skeklar dodged away.

"It's going to get away," I hollered.

The fence round Broom's garden was no obstacle. The Skeklar vaulted it like an Olympic hurdler, then charged off down the slope towards the beach. The rain conspired against us, causing a watery screen to envelope the escaping killer, concealing its route from us.

We didn't follow. Out there, if we were separated, we would be sitting ducks against its ravening claws.

"Did you bring the gun, Broom?" I asked.

My friend was supporting himself on the fence, hair plastered across his face. His fight had been for only a few seconds but he appeared totally wiped out of energy. He glanced back at me, then to Bob Harris. "I didn't get the opportunity."

Giving him his due, Bob didn't make an issue of the gun. He had experienced first hand what the Skeklar was capable of and I could only hazard a guess that he wished he had a gun, too.

Shoulder to shoulder the three of us stared out into the rain like we were mourners searching for the wreckage of a ship lost on a storm-tossed sea.

Finally, the tinny strains of a voice buzzed from Bob Harris's earpiece.

"We're all okay, Sarge," he said into his radio. "No, I'm sorry. He's got away from us."

There was more buzzing in his ear.

"Aye, Sarge. We're going to come in now."

As we moved for the cottage the policeman grabbed me by my wrist. I stopped and looked back at him. There was a network of scratches and abrasions on his bluff face, and he had to be thankful that he was wearing his protective vest because the cloth was tattered and the inner padding showed through. He nodded slowly. "You saved me back there," he said. "My sergeant has her suspicions about you, Bailey, but I ken you're a good man."

Shoving my hands through my hair I whispered, "You saved me, too, Bob."

He gave himself a once over inspection. "I don't know how I managed that."

"Well, you did," I said, still mildly embarrassed by his words.

"Of course, I didn't do anything worthwhile," Broom chipped in.

I turned to my big friend and hugged him. "Broom, you've saved me more times than I can ever count. I owe you."

"You don't owe me…"

"I owe you an apology. After what I said…"

"I've already forgotten all about that," he said. Earnestness shone from his blue eyes like a beacon and it had nothing to do with my ability for viewing auric lights.

Bob Harris hadn't a clue about what we were referring to, but he had the good grace not to interfere. He waited until Broom and I stepped apart before saying, "Bailey. Best you don't mention guns in front of Sergeant McCusker, eh?"

THIRTYEIGHT

Broom's cottage

Shelly McCusker, Bob Harris and Janet Hale left shortly after the Skeklar fled into the sudden storm. Shelly was engrossed with forming a search party and barely spoke to us, however Bob remained grateful for our help and extended his hand to both Broom and I.

"If either of you are thinking about taking a walk on the beach I suggest you take along that *thing* we talked about," he said out of earshot of his supervisor.

Broom said, "I'm battening down the hatches. There's no way on Earth that you'll get me past that door tonight."

"I might take an evening stroll," I told the constable. "A little wind and rain doesn't bother me. If you need an extra pair of eyes for the search party, give me a shout, okay?"

Shelly McCusker turned and gave me the beady eye. "It's best you batten down the hatches as well, Mister Bailey."

"I'll let you know," Bob said. There was little conviction in his voice. What would the police want with a sports clothing salesman getting in their way? Likely Bob held some respect towards me, but it seemed I'd yet to win over the sergeant.

For all intents and purposes the area of the garden and drive where their squad car was parked was a crime scene. The rain and wind would most probably have obliterated any forensic evidence, though, so the police had no qualms about climbing into the vehicle. Only Janet came over as reluctant to get in the car. She stood at the open rear door, watching me. Finally I gave her a nod that was meant to convey reassurance. As I did so I saw her auric lights flare around her like a controlled explosion. The lights shimmered golden, then flared with lemon and then swirled into a pallet of pastel shades that changed more rapidly than I could follow. I couldn't understand what each colour meant, but instinctively I knew that the colours were those of a person guided by the highest *good*. Janet was thinking nice things about me; could I be seeing the auric manifestation of love?

If that was the case or not, I blinked and the lights were gone. Only Janet's return nod and the slow smile etching itself into the corner of her mouth told me that the colours had ever been there. She gave me a brief wave, then got in the car and off they went.

When I turned to my friend, Broom was studying me as if I was a bug on the end of a pin.

"What?"

"Something came over you just then."

"What do you mean?"

"It's hard to explain." Broom's face pinched in on itself as he considered. "When I looked at you it was as though I was looking at a stranger."

Unconsciously I touched my fingers to my face. It was the same old scarred mug I remembered.

Broom laughed. "You didn't look different. Not your features. Like I said, it's hard to explain." He seesawed his head, before coming to the conclusion, "You looked *intelligent.*"

A short expulsion of air broke from me unbidden. "Gee, thanks, Broom."

He made his way inside the house. "I didn't mean that you normally look stupid. There was just something that came over you that gave you an inner calm, a heightened perception; it made you look like you were existing on a higher plain of existence."

Following him indoors, I said, "I saw her auric lights, Broom."

He swung to stare at me again. "What? Just like that?" He clicked his fingers.

"Yeah." I clicked my fingers. "As quickly as that."

"Close the door behind you, Carter. Then come into the bedroom. There's something I want to try out."

I closed the door. "I know you said you'd forgiven me for earlier, but there's no need to show me how much."

Broom tutted at me, shaking his head so that his moisture darkened hair swung bell-like. "Just get yourself in the bedroom, will you?"

The spare bedroom I'd used last night was sumptuous, but Broom's room went beyond luxurious. It was like half-a-dozen pimps had gone crazy with faux-fur and pastel paint to create a subdued version of a hippy love nest. The divan was so deeply sprung it required a step up to it, so large it'd take an expert guide to navigate it crossways. A second plasma screen TV dominated one wall; cut glass mirrored-doors on a walk-in closet the other. Momentarily I expected MTV to turn up at his crib with a camera crew.

"And you tell me that there isn't much money in writing," I said.

"Trust me," Broom said, "most professional writers in the UK make thirty three percent less than the minimum wage. There are very few who can afford this level of comfort."

"Not unless you're the country's sixteenth best selling horror author, eh?"

"Not even if you hit the Kindle top ten," Broom said. "And actually, I'm *fifteenth* in the rankings. But most of my money comes from other business initiatives. In fact, I make more of a living from fan conventions and seminars than I do the royalties from my books."

"Looks like you're doing all right for yourself, however you make your money."

Broom indicated the bed. "Lie down, Carter."

"You want me to undress first?"

"Enough already," Broom laughed. "Then again, maybe it wouldn't be a bad idea to take off your coat and boots. Seeing as you're wet and covered in God knows what!"

"That's what I meant," I said. "I don't know what you were thinking."

"Told you, Bro. Broomy's got ideas for you."

"Aw, shut it, Cash."

My coat was a mess. It was to be expected, considering that twice tonight I'd been forced to roll on the ground to avoid the Skeklar's claws. My trousers weren't much better, but at least they weren't smeared with mud, clumps of grass and tiny fragments of sea shells. My boots had to be left outside the bedroom; the cream carpet wouldn't stand up to me treading all over it. Broom threw a towel at me and I used it to scrub the rain from my hair.

"Okay. Now lie down on the bed."

It brought back memories of lying on a psychiatrist's couch and momentarily I experienced a tingle of panic. Almost, I was transported back four years, and for the briefest time I had to fight the urge to flee screaming from the room. An illogical fear that I was going to have to live those four years over again assailed me with the force of crashing surf. Still, it was testament to my journey along the route to recovery that I was able to inhale deeply, then expunge the fear in one long ragged exhalation.

"That's good, Carter. Clear your mind."

"What exactly is it that you want me to do?"

Broom moved away, switching on a lamp in the far corner of the room. Next he switched off the overheads so that we were bathed only in the meagre glow of the lamp. "An experiment," he said. "Something I researched earlier about auric lights. Using a low light, you lie down and hold your hands out in front of you. You don't stare at them, just gaze at your hands. Then you slowly bring your hands together until they are almost touching. Apparently you will notice a blue haze appear around your finger. This is supposed to be the etheric aura. Would you like to give it a try and see what you achieve?"

"I don't know about auric lights, but I've done something similar where you bring your two index fingers close to your nose and you can see a little chipolata sausage between them."

Broom grunted. "You're not taking things seriously, are you?"

Sitting up, I said, "I don't have to lie down to see these lights Broom. All I have to do is haze out my vision. Wallop! There you go."

I was watching geysers of lemon fire erupt from Broom. Instinct told me that the lemon was an expression of fear of losing control. Blinking the colours away, I said, "I think it's all the time I've spent in front of mirror's searching for evidence that Cash really is inside me that has heightened my ability for seeing the auras. When I think back, I've had the ability for some time now, I just didn't recognise it for what it was. To be honest, I thought my eyes were just tired and out of focus."

The bed creaked beneath Broom's weight as he sat next to me. Maybe he was feeling redundant because I'd already surpassed him in both my knowledge and skill with seeing the lights. He exhaled, and I could practically detect the cogs whirring away in his brain as he pondered.

"A few hours ago," he said softly, "you made out that I was a crank for even suggesting the theories about the Zone Point Field, and yet, here you are now, telling me that, well, not only do you believe it, but that you have known about your ability all along."

"I didn't know about it. Okay, I suspected there was something there. How could I not suspect when I'm aware of my brother's spirit floating around inside me? I had a feeling, an inkling, but I didn't understand what the hell it was." I swung my legs off the bed so that I was sitting alongside him. "After what I've seen today, how could I possibly deny that I believe in it?"

His eyebrows performed a little jig of acquiescence.

"Earlier," I went on. "When I was hiding in the crags at Trowhaem, I looked across the camp. I could see everyone's auras. To me they were like fireworks going off everywhere. Funny thing is…" I paused, wondering if I should voice this next part.

Broom looked at me. "Go on."

"Thing is," I repeated. "I could identify each and every one of them. Put their auras to individual people."

"What, like you knew their names and such?"

"No. Of course not." It was my turn to ponder. After ordering my words, I said, "People I've already met - Shelly and Bob for instance - I could pick them out from the others. It was like I simply looked at their colours and instinct told me who they were. Because of the same instinct I was able to sift everything else aside and I found Janet. She was actually inside a caravan but I could still see her colours. How weird is that?"

"Beyond weird," Broom said. "Utterly fantastic."

"But it happened," I said, sounding like a small child telling tall-tales. "I know it sounds hard to believe, but I can't deny it."

"Neither should you," Broom said. "You should embrace it. Accept your gift. Can you imagine what this could mean to you?"

"What? A job in a sideshow?" I laughed without feeling remotely funny. "No. I see where you're coming from. But there's something else I have to tell you about. Something even I'm finding it hard to accept."

"You should know by now that I'm very open minded, Carter. Tell me. I promise you I'll take it at more than face value."

"When she was being attacked by the Skeklar, I heard Janet call out to me." I looked at him for signs of reproof but got none. "I don't mean audibly heard her. I mean in here." I tapped my head. "I was too far away to hear her for real. I also answered her, and Broom, I think that she heard me, too."

And it was that conversation, plus the theories of psychic power, crisis apparitions and plain old coincidence that we bandied back and forth, that led me to a point where I was once more lying on the bed with my eyes half closed while I probed the shadowy places of the island with my roving astral spirit.

It was one weird and eventful day, I'll tell you. And it was about to get even weirder.

THIRTYNINE

The Dungeon

Bethany woke up to the drumming of a marching band. Snare drum competed with bass, and the clash of a cymbal overwhelmed everything. She sat up, her breath catching in her throat. Her mind conjured images from her book of fairy tales. Had a handsome prince come at the head of an army to liberate her from the ogre's tower?

She blinked back the foggy tendrils of sleep.

The drums now sounded more like the rattle of pebbles on a tin sheet. The cymbal was the crash of surf on boulders. There was no army. No handsome prince.

Yet there still remained the ogre's tower.

Not that it was much of a tower. More a hut, really. But it was as solid as any bastion the heroes of her stories had ever assailed. It was as damp and smelly and uncomfortable as anything that any ogre would build. Except for an ogre like Shrek. She didn't think Shrek would build a place as awful as this dungeon.

Bethany was thirsty.

Earlier the Skeklar had come to her. He didn't speak. He came through the door all hunched over and flashing his green eyes at her. Bethany hid in the shadows at the corner of the room until he was gone again. Only after the door was locked and she heard the scrape of his feet walking away did she peel her fingers from her face and look for what he had brought.

There were two bottles of spring water and a bag of cheesy Wotsits. Beth didn't like cheesy Wotsits but she liked water. She drank a full litre. Only afterwards did she wonder if the water was poisonous. Had the ogre - no, the Skeklar - laced her water with poison and was waiting for her to die in mouth-frothing agony?

After that she sat for a long, long time, listening to the inner-rhythms of her body, trying to detect the signs that a vile source of corruption ate away at her insides. In the end, all she detected was an intense and urgent need to pee.

There was no toilet, not even a bucket, and though it was loathsome, she finally squatted in a corner of the room and peed onto the gravel. But that was ages ago.

Now she looked for the second bottle of water. She'd moved it away to the wall next to the door, as far away from her toilet corner as possible. She moved through the darkness as though at home with the night. Her fingers reached out for the bottle and closed round the tapered neck.

Something rustled.

"Who's there?"

Beneath the drum roll of rain - ah, that's what the noise is! - her voice was barely discernible. She tried again. First sucking in a deep breath in order to empower her shout.

"Who is there?"

No one answered. Neither did she hear the rustle again. She began to think she'd imagined it first time round. No, she hadn't imagined it. Her mind was a fertile playground for all things weird and wonderful, but she wasn't daft. She didn't *hear things* the way crazy people did.

"What if it's rats?" she wondered aloud. Now there was something guaranteed to make this dungeon the worst kind of hell hole even her furtive imagination could conjure. "Please don't let it be rats."

Her mind flitted to where her nightmare had begun. She thought about her brother Jimmy and tears moistened her eyes. She thought of how much she loved him. Ma often told Jimmy off for being vindictive and spiteful towards Beth, but she wished he were with her now. Alive and vindictive and spiteful, even if she didn't fully understand what those words meant. She

292

wanted him back more than anything, even if it was Jimmy who'd killed that poor wee bird, and brought the Skeklar out of his hole in the earth to punish them both.

Her mind filled with the terror on Jimmy's face, as he'd saw the Skeklar standing behind her. She remembered how he'd tried to make her run, and how she couldn't and how Jimmy had got between the Skeklar and her. Jimmy was neither vindictive nor spiteful towards her then. He'd been her big brother, and he had tried to protect her. And he'd died.

If only Jimmy had left the bird alone like she'd warned him.

A single droplet of blood had shivered on the bird's beak.

A thousand droplets of blood had sprayed from Jimmy's throat.

Now she was stuck, listening for a *rustling thing* in the Skeklar's prison.

Fear engulfed her.

What if the rustle were the wings of the dead bird? A zombie bird come back to taunt her for having such a vindictive and spiteful brother?

What if the rustle was Jimmy? All his bits dragging themselves back together, forming into a shapeless heap so that he could go on tormenting her? She wanted Jimmy back, but not like that! *Never like that!*

Her groping fingers found the source of the rustle.

"Oh, thank God. It's only my Wotsits!"

How daft is a crazy person, any way? She had been terrified by the sound of a maize snack falling over when she'd disturbed them by lifting the bottle of water.

Suddenly she loved cheesy Wotsits.

Not enough to eat them, yet, but enough to lift them up and hold them to her chest as if they were a talisman against this evil place.

She couldn't begin to fathom how long she'd been here. It had easily been a lifetime. Sleep had come and gone twice now, but she still couldn't guess how long each slumber had lasted. If

293

the first time had been for a hundred years, then maybe the second one was, too. Only, that was faintly ridiculous even to her fertile mind. If it was true, she would be two hundred and eight years old, and she knew even without feeling herself that she was still a little girl. Unless the water wasn't poisoned, but had been mixed with an elixir of eternal youth?

"Nah, that's just silly," she told herself. "You can't mix stuff with Wotsits and make them last a hundred years. By now they'd be all mushy."

So, she hadn't slept a century each time. More than likely she'd only been asleep for a short time. The hard ground wasn't the most comfortable of beds that you could sleep that long on it, and her need to eat and drink and pee would be much, much stronger if she'd been here for two hundred years.

She drank only a single mouthful of water. Determined this time that she wouldn't be forced to squat in a corner like her pet hamster, Nibbles. Then her thirst got the better of her and she supped down half the bottle. Pangs dug at her stomach, and she realised that she was hungrier than she thought. Maybe cheesy Wotsits weren't as nasty as she remembered. In fact, if she really thought about it, she didn't *actually* mind Wotsits, just preferred Monster Munch. Pickled onion flavour was her favourite.

She pulled open the packet and dipped into it. Placed a puffed maize snack into her mouth and slowly chewed.

Actually, cheesy Wotsits were absolutely fantastic.

She quickly ate the entire pack, going to the extent of dampening a fingertip and pushing it into the corners of the bag to mop up the last crumbs. When she sat down, it escaped her why she ever disliked the cheesy puffs. She could quite happily eat another ten packets.

Outside her prison the rain was subsiding.

The drumming on the roof didn't sound half as loud, and now and then there was even the complete cessation of noise as wind pushed the lighter rain aside. Bethany looked up at the ceiling. Her eyes had grown accustomed to the dark a long time

294

ago, yet she still couldn't define anything specific about the ceiling overhead. Like the rest of the dungeon, she'd assumed that it would be stone, but judging by the sound from above, she was actually in a building with a corrugated tin roof.

She was young, but she was neither daft nor a crazy person. She had enough sense to understand that this wasn't really an ogre's tower, but something more mundane. She was in some sort of outbuilding or farm shed. Many of the farms and houses on Conn were stone built with tin or slate roofs, so this gave her no idea of where she could be. Still, where there were farm buildings, you usually found people.

"Hello?"

She spoke out loud without conscious thought. But now that she'd done so, it wasn't such a bad idea that she wouldn't try again.

"Hello? Is there anybody there?"

There was no answer.

Not surprisingly. Who on earth would be out in that rain? She'd just have to shout louder.

"Hello…can anybody hear me?"

I hear you, Bethany.

Beth jerked in a mix of fear and wonder.

Where had the voice come from? Here in the room? No. Couldn't be. There was no one else in the room with her. Outside then? Had to be. Maybe a farmer was out in the terrible weather, after all.

"Who's there?"

Don't be afraid, little one. I'm going to find you.

"Who are you?"

I'm a friend. Don't be frightened, okay?

"Okay. But I don't understand…" Bethany put a hand to her head. "How can you talk inside my brain? Are you an angel?"

No, I'm not an angel.

"Are you an extra-terrestrial, then? Jimmy said that E.T's can talk in peoples' minds."

I'm not an alien, Bethany, so you've got nothing to be scared of.

"I'm not scared of aliens." Bethany turned full circle unable to comprehend what was happening to her. How could she hear a voice in her head? She didn't think she was a crazy person, and only crazy people heard voices in their heads. Crazy people and saints. One thing she did understand was that she couldn't be a saint. She wasn't religious enough. Not like her Ma. Did she have to be religious to be a saint, though? Was Joan of Arc religious, or did she just become religious when God spoke to her? "Are you God?"

I'm not God. I'm not Jesus. I'm just a man.

"Men can't talk in other people's heads. Unless they're wizards or sorcerers or something."

Trust me; I'm just a normal man.

"Are you sure? What if you are the Skeklar and you're using trow magic on me? Are you trying to trick me?"

If I were trying to trick you, wouldn't I have lied to you? Wouldn't I have told you that I was an angel or God or even an extra-terrestrial? Would I have told you I was only an ordinary man?

"I…I don't know." Bethany worried at the inside of her lips. "Maybe the trick is that you are saying you're just a man when really you are one of those other things."

Please, Bethany. You're starting to frighten yourself.

"I'm not frightened. I'm not scared of you." Her raised voice told more than the lie. "So you can just go away and leave me alone. Get out of my head. I know you are lying."

Please, Bethany. Just calm down…Oh, shit, Broom, I've messed up. I've frightened the wits out the poor little soul.

FORTY

Janet

Why are men always so complicated?

Okay, maybe not all men. Perhaps it was only the ones that came into her circle. But, things never seemed without complication when it came to Janet's personal life.

Take her husband for instance.

No doubt about it, Jonathon Connery was a handsome man. He was intelligent and witty. Tall and strong. He was well spoken and popular. He had enjoyed a varied and exciting life, first as a commissioned officer in the army, a Sandhurst-trained officer no less, then as a successful businessman. He had money. He owned a beautiful home. He *had* a wife that loved him. But Jonathon was not content.

For a long time Janet blamed herself for their inability to conceive the child she believed would finally make Jonathon happy. After all, her perfect man could not possibly be at fault, could he? Tests finally showed that the fault - if that could ever be the correct term for infertility - lay with her husband. He would neither accept the truth nor give up on his attempts at proving the science wrong. Love making; now, there was a term that could not be associated to what Jonathon's brutal attempts at proving his virility turned into. When his forced passion failed to produce a child, that was when he turned to the other women.

Janet could deny her husband's extra-marital affairs, but not when it came to actually catching him at it in their bed. The truth hurts, but not as much as when denial catches up and smacks you with the weight of a runaway freightliner. She had given him her best shot, both with their marriage and with the right hook that had ended it.

From Jonathon Janet had moved to abstinence, and she'd been happy in the lie, playing the part of the newly liberated woman. But, like many, she was in denial yet, and that was why she'd sought solace in the brief flirting she'd enjoyed with Pete Johnston. Then the complication factor had jumped in with both big feet. Pete preferred Toni McNabb. Janet was left high and dry and Pete and Toni were history.

Now, here she was with the biggest complication of all.

Carter Bailey.

She barely knew him. For heaven's sake! They'd met only yesterday, so why was he in her mind at every conceivable opportunity? Why did she feel as though she'd known him for an eternity? How was it that she felt so *attached*?

Like her he was damaged goods. She'd known that the first instant that she saw him on the ferry. In him she instantly recognised a vulnerability that appealed to her in a way in which she could neither understand nor put words to. It was as though she had recognised in him something for which she'd been searching for all her life. What that something could be went beyond her ability to comprehend, but when she'd sat next to him on the ferry it was as if she was drawn to him like a lodestone to the magnetic north. They were a single entity, a symbiosis awaiting connection; soul mates…every metaphor that could be culled from a badly written romance novel.

Is this love?

She *thought* she loved Jonathon.

But what she'd felt for her estranged husband was nothing like the buzz of enticement, the lightness in her mind, the trembling in her tummy she felt when sharing even the tiniest of glances with Carter. And, Jesus! That kiss. For all it was barely a step above chaste, she truly believed that she would burst like a popping soap bubble when his lips had caressed hers.

She'd played matchmaker with Shelly and Bob. Merely by observing their subtle interactions she could tell that they were attracted to each other. What did she display when she was in

298

Carter's presence? If her body language was as obvious as the strength of her emotions, she must come across as a preening harlot, or at least a giggling schoolgirl in the first flush of hormone-induced crushes.

She'd kissed Carter.

She was married. She was in love. She had no right to be. She was in love with the wrong man.

Complication.

Things, she knew, could only grow worse.

FORTYONE

Broom's cottage

There was something infinitely ridiculous about the latest twist in my abilities. To search out a missing person by strength of mind bordered on the realms of fantasy. Yeah, I'd heard of supposed psychics who used their intuition to find missing or murdered persons. It was well catalogued. Many a famous psychic had grown their fame - and their bank balance - on the back of a police investigation. My only problem with the entire psychic detective thing was that the police never, ever, placed any faith or credibility in their paranormal consultants. Generally, those famous psychics made such broad sweeping deductions that they might add a fresh nugget of evidence to the investigation, but I for one had never heard of a single incident where the psychic had led the police directly to either the murdered person or the one responsible for the crime. In my opinion, psychics weren't necessarily frauds, but clever people with a strong intuitive streak and a new perspective over a stale or jaundiced investigation. Ergo, it was all guess work, and every now and then they'd hit on a pertinent point that the investigators had initially missed.

Nothing magical about it.

Science. Chance. Maybe a little of both.

And yet, there I was with my brain chiming with the realisation that I'd just had a conversation with a missing child who until that moment had been feared dead.

It couldn't possibly be true.

Could it?

Something was certain; however, whatever, had occurred, it had left me both exhilarated and dismayed. Not to mention physically shattered.

It was like Big Ben was tolling in my brain. My muscles felt like they'd liquidised and there was a tremor in my extremities that threatened to shake the ligaments loose from my bones.

"I'll get you something sweet to drink," Broom said. "I guess that you've burnt up your sugar reserves. That'd explain why you're so weak."

I felt hypoglycaemic, so maybe a sugar rush would help. First, though, I needed answers. "What did I just do there, Broom?"

"It goes way beyond my ability to explain. All I can come up with is that not only are you capable of seeing a person's auric lights, but you can latch on to an individual life force simply by thinking about and then reaching out to them. If you actually spoke to the girl, then we must assume that you are equally able to transmit your conscious thoughts along some sort of astral umbilical cord that connects your energy with theirs."

Blinking, I said, "This gets weirder and weirder."

There was a cold sweat on my brow. Thick, oozing bulbs of perspiration. One of them trickled into the corner of my mouth and it was so bitter that I spat into my cupped palm.

"Are you okay?"

"I feel like it's the morning after a heavy session on the booze," I said.

"I'll get you your drink. We have to be careful…"

"Your enemy the devil prowls around…"

The last time that I'd employed my power to seek out Janet's energy, Cash latched onto my weakness. On that occasion he'd managed to get his hooks into me, had almost turned me against my best friend. I wasn't going to allow him to do so again. As Broom bustled out of the bedroom, heading for the kitchen, I lay back on the bed and closed my eyes.

In the past when going inside myself, I've had to go through a routine. It's a little like self-induced trance. I'd lie down, or sit, and consciously tell myself to relax. Toes first, feet, legs, torso, arms, then head, in that order. That time, all I had to do was sink into Broom's plush mattress and I was *gone*.

Past incursions into my psyche had taken me to desolate landscapes, to dungeons, to torture chambers, all figments of the bitter hatred I held for my brother. The last place I expected to find myself was striding through a swaying field of golden wheat beneath a cool, mother of pearl sky. A copse of trees, heavy with foliage danced to a vagrant breeze. Birds twittered and cooed. Somewhere nearby a stream trickled over a bed of pebbles.

A quick perusal of my clothing showed me that I was clad in my grungy coat and chino trousers. Realisation banished them, and in their place I wore a pale yellow T-shirt, khaki trousers and open-toed sandals. I frowned down at my appearance. These were clothes from a distant memory. They were the clothes I was wearing when first I met my fiancée-to-be, the woman who would carry my child. And the glade, subtly altered by recollection so that it was even more beautiful, more peaceful, was the field where I'd come across her sitting before an easel with a rigger brush dangling from the corner of her mouth as she studied the foliage of the trees before committing them to canvas. Though it shouldn't have happened in that purely ethereal state, I experienced a twinge of longing.

The wheat was taller, more golden under the sun than it had been in the real world. Plus, it stretched off to a horizon empty of the buildings that crowded the landscape of my memories. There should have stood barns and sheds and the peaked roof of Karen's parents' farmhouse. Here was only a translucent mist that moved with a sinuosity that brought a floating jellyfish to mind. It was a swirling void I recognised immediately as repressed memory. There I'd first kissed Karen, there we'd first made love, there we'd given life to our baby. The farm was a place I didn't wish to return to, neither in my thoughts nor in the tangible world. Too many memories. Happy memories that were now too painful to bear.

Looking around, I searched out the path that bordered the field before meandering its way through an area left to nature's whims, down between rugged crags to where the stream bubbled beneath dappled shadows. Without conscious volition I was between the crags. Looking down I searched for her easel. I searched for Karen. Neither was there.

The scene was sullied.

Cash stood ankle deep in the water, grinning up at me like a shark inviting me to bathe with him. He was wearing board shorts and a baggy T-shirt. "C'mon in, Carter, the water's lovely."

Squinting at him, I said, "This isn't right."

"Why not, brother? Personally I think it's the nicest outing we've shared in a while."

"That's my point," I snapped. "It shouldn't be nice."

"Aw, stop with the vitriol will you? Can't we just have a comfortable meeting for a change? Why can't we sit in the shade, dangle our toes in the water, and have a little head-to-head like we used to when we were boys."

There was a ripple in the fabric of my mind. The scene changed and I found myself sitting on a wooden jetty, my legs dangling over the edge, blue jeans rolled up to my calves as I made lazy strokes in the water with my toes. A fishing rod was in my hand, my index finger resting lightly on the line just above the reel as I waited for the telltale pluck that would signal a trout had taken the lure.

Beside me on the jetty was my little brother. Cassius, snub-nosed, tousle-haired, freckled, missing his front teeth, smiled back at me. "I want to catch the biggest fish ever, Carter," he said, the voice both high-pitched and sibilant through the gap in his teeth.

"You will, but you have to be quiet," I hushed him. "The fish can hear us. They won't take your bait if they hear you talking."

Cash squinted at me, his lips pursing. "How can fishes hear, Carter? They haven't got ears."

"Not like ours, they haven't. But they can still hear things."

"No they can't."

"They can. They feel the vibrations of your voice in the water."

Cash flicked a pebble off the jetty. A faint splash. Concentric circles pushed to the far bank of the river. "That'll confuse them," he grinned.

"You'll frighten them away," I scolded him.

"A little pebble? That won't frighten them."

"It will. Why do you have to spoil everything, Cash?"

His bottom lip protruded. "I don't spoil everything."

"Yes you do." My voice was bitter. I thumped him on the shoulder. "You spoil everything that I do. I didn't even want to bring you with me, you little twerp. Now you're going to scare all the fish away."

"I only flicked a pebble," he said.

There was only the ghost of ripples on the water now. My anger grew exponentially. "You've frightened them away. This is a waste of time. You've spoiled everything, Cash. WHY DID YOU EVEN COME WITH ME?"

Storming to my feet, I threw down my fishing rod. Cash jumped up too, but not to challenge me. He tried to get past me but I grabbed at his collar. Bigger than him by a head, he could squirm all he wanted. Thrusting him to the edge of the jetty, I demanded, "Can you see any fish, Cash? Can you? No. Because you've frightened them all away."

"I haven't, I haven't," he cried.

"Where are they then?" Shaking him. "Show me."

I pushed him. It was all it took. He windmilled his arms, his bare feet slapping at the planks in an effort to halt the inevitable. Gravity would not be denied. Cash fell face first into the river. And he sank like a stone.

If I could see my face I believe I would have been holding that fixed glare, the tight smile of one who gloats. But only for a second. Panic engulfed me. A raging tide leaped from my stomach to my throat, to the cry of dismay that I yelled. "Oh my God, Cash? What have I done?"

Craning forward I searched for my little brother. The water was as still and viscous as treacle. There was no sign of Cash. A single bubble popped on the surface. "Cash!" I screamed.

Then I was hurtling towards the water.

Splash. Tinkle, tinkle.

I landed in water that barely covered my sandals.

Blinking, I swung side to side in panic, still seeking my little brother.

"How touching." Cash's voice came from behind me. "You do care for me after all."

Gasping, I swung round to confront him.

Adult Cash stared back at me.

"What?" I demanded. "What just happened here?"

Cash hiked his shorts. "Truth hurt, does it?"

"Truth? That wasn't real. It didn't happen like that."

Cash sniffed. "Maybe not in your mind, but that's the way I remember it. You pushed me in the river, Carter. I almost drowned."

Shaking my head, I lifted a hand towards him. "That's a lie and you know it. I didn't push you. You fell in."

Cash shook his head ever so slowly. "No, brother. That's what you made me tell Mom and Dad. You promised to beat me up if I ever told them the truth."

"No," I said.

"Yes, Carter. Painful as the truth might be, you forced me to lie. I was spanked whilst dear old Mom and Dad hailed you as a fucking hero."

"It didn't happen that way…"

"It did, Carter. So did all the other times that you bullied and beat me. From my earliest memory until I was twelve years old, it was constant, brother. You pushed me, you hit me, you called me names."

"That was just kid stuff. All kids do that." Even to my own ears the argument sounded weak. "You pushed and hit me as well."

"In defence." Cash moved close to me. His eyes were on a level with mine. Behind his pale irises I saw something stir, a coiling blue shape. I reared back from him.

"Get away from me," I said. My hands came up, against his chest, shoving him away.

He stumbled away, slipping on the slick pebbles of the stream. Finding his balance he looked at me. Cash smiled. "Do you see, Carter? You're still the same now. Still the bully you were as a child."

Stooping down, Cash selected an algae-slick stone from the streambed. He lifted it in his hand. Circular, the stone was as smooth and as large as a grapefruit. It would weigh five times as much. "You know what advice is given to a person who is being bullied?"

I watched him approach with a certain amount of disassociation. One step, two steps, three. Cash was only an arm's length away. He lifted the stone like a shot putter.

"Advice is to stand up to your bully. Show them you can't be walked over," he said.

Then he swung the rock at my head.

FORTYTWO

Broom's cottage

Blood was on my face, my throat, seeping through my shirt, so that it felt hot and slick on my chest.

Cash's hurled stone must have bashed my skull open to cause the profuse bleeding I was suffering.

"Oh, my God…" I clutched at my face. My blood was hot. Steaming. It was on my fingers. Sticky and viscous and smelling of…of…*what is that smell?*

"Hold it there." The voice was one I knew. Not Cash's, though. Someone else. There was a touch of panic in the voice. "I'll bring a towel."

Round about then I realised that my blood was so hot that it was burning. "Jesus Christ!" I howled.

"Carter, try not to move," Broom shouted from the door. "Pull your shirt off your skin before it gets chance to soak through, but don't get up. I'll only be a second."

Against his command, I sat up. The blood pooled in my lap. Soaking into my trousers. "Ooooohhhhaaaaawwww!"

I leaped up, dancing across the bedroom floor, droplets of my blood spattering the carpet. Must have been the mix of red on cream but my blood stained the pile brown.

"Jesus, Carter, look at the mess you're making." I blinked at my friend who was approaching me with a towel.

"I'm bleeding to death and you're concerned for your fucking carpet?"

Broom's face twisted. "Bleeding? What are you talking about?"

I showed him my hands. He didn't seem all that concerned. "My head's split open!"

"It's not blood, you nutcase," Broom growled at me. "It's flamin' hot chocolate."

Funnily enough, the blood all over me was a bit too brown to be the lifeblood of a healthy man. And it did smell strange. Kind of sweet and…chocolaty. *That* was what the smell was.

"H-h-hot…" I stammered.

"I'm not surprised," Broom said, dabbing at my clothing, at my face, with the towel. "You knocked the whole mugful over yourself, you dozy idiot."

Reality was finally beginning to impinge. I was back in Broom's house. Not by the stream. My fingers plucked gingerly at my scalp. Other than sticky chocolate milk there was only matted hair. There was no gaping hole in my skull. "Cash didn't brain me with a rock, then?"

"Your head's fine. As long as you discount your obvious madness." Broom pushed the towel into my hands. "Here…you can do the rest. I'm going to have to put something on the carpet or else it's going to be stained permanently."

Catching sight of myself in the floor-to-ceiling mirrors, I struck a slightly ridiculous pose. Chocolate stained me from hair to groin. There were tracks across the carpet leading back to an equally large stain on Broom's bed. Had it been blood and not chocolate, anyone would believe that a serial killer had been up to his tricks.

Broom bustled back into the room, cloths and cleaning fluids at the ready. "What the hell were you dreaming about, anyway?"

"Wasn't a dream," I muttered. "I was with Cash."

"What? After what I just told you? You still went ahead and confronted him?"

"I know. I know. Bad idea. But after what happened earlier I couldn't allow him to influence me the way he did." I gave him a pointed look. "Surely it's better that it's only chocolate all over the place, rather than your blood? Don't you remember he was pushing me to shoot you last time?"

Crouching and spraying chemicals from a bottle, Broom caught himself mid-pose. He blinked at me from under his fringe. "So what happened this time? Judging by what you said, Cash tried to smash your head in with something."

"Yeah…" I said. "A big rock."

Knees creaking, Broom stood up. "How could you let that happen, Carter? You control the environment. How could you allow that maniac to pick up a rock?"

"Dunno," I answered truthfully. Wiping chocolate from my face, I said, "I don't think that I was fully in control this time."

Broom shook his head. "No, not possible. It's your mind, your thoughts. Cash couldn't have free reign without your allowing it."

Shrugging, I said, "I made a mistake. When I think about it, I hadn't done any planning, hadn't put any controls in place. To be honest I think I just dropped directly into an old memory. Maybe Cash wasn't even there with me. Perhaps it was just a dream, after all."

It was wishful thinking, of course. I knew that what I was saying was a lie. Cash had been all too real. The memory of our fateful fishing expedition had been more than a memory. It was a replay of events. And, as much as I didn't want to accept it, Cash was correct; I had been a total shit to him when we were growing up.

Was he trying to destroy me with guilt? What was he saying? Was I to blame for him turning out the twisted individual that he'd become? Had he murdered all those pregnant women in an effort at eradicating the years he'd suffered at the hands of his bullying older sibling? If so, how could cutting a living foetus from the womb of a dying woman possibly validate him? No way that I could see.

Broom returned to his scrubbing. In the end he sighed. "This is doing no good. It looks like you've cost me a new carpet."

"Sorry."

He waved off my apology. "Doesn't matter. I was getting tired of it anyway. It was starting to look soooo last year." His vanity was his way at pushing aside my embarrassment. It worked.

"One thing I learned from all this. The question as to whether Cash can hurt me when I'm inside myself? Can't be possible. I'm suffering no ill effect from having a rock slammed into my skull. Not even a headache."

Broom let out a long sigh. "Did he actually hit you, though? Or did you come out of it before the rock struck you?"

My face crumpled. "I can't remember. I just remember him rushing at me, the stone lifted in his hand."

"Then I shook you," Broom said. "I could see the terror in your face. I shook you and you sat bolt-upright in the bed, knocking the drink I'd brought you out of my hand."

Touching my head, I probed for any tender spots. "Maybe I did snap out of it just before he hit me."

"Lucky that you did," Broom said. "I suspect that Cash can hurt you when you're in the metaphysical state. You can't allow him to roam free through your memories. Never again. Who knows what could've happened if I hadn't brought you out in time?"

But therein lay the problem. If I was going to make some good of my astonishing abilities, how could I if it made me vulnerable to my brother's influence? How could I not use my power to find a missing child, even if it could mean damaging myself, or even inviting my own death? It was akin to courting the devil to perform miracles.

There was only one answer.

"It's a chance I'm going to have to take, Broom."

Go ahead, Cash. Do your worst.

FORTYTHREE

Trowhaem

Could things get any worse?

Harry Bishop didn't think so. But he also feared that he was wrong.

Police drafted over from the mainland had brought with them a contingent of Crime Scene Investigators. They had lifted and sifted like the true professionals that they were. Lifted the skinned body from the grave that is, then sifted through the debris for vital clues. But they had missed something. His eye for archaeology told him.

That was why he was standing by the empty grave alongside Inspector Marsh and a CID sergeant whose name he'd missed. He pointed at the bed of stones that the unidentified corpse had been lain on top of. "Trust me, Inspector," he said. "Those stones are not the usual feature I'd expect to see in a Viking grave. Plus, although the upper dimensions of the grave are correct, it is too shallow. If the original occupant was laid to rest at that depth, scavenging dogs and crows would have unearthed him in no time."

Inspector Marsh's eyes had a demonic caste to them as he turned to the professor. A result of the sulphurous glow cast from the lights the CSI team had installed while they worked. Marsh's black hair was greasy with perspiration and his clothing was rumpled and smeared with dirt. He was having a bad day. Possibly the worst of his professional life. "You're telling me that you think there's something else in there?"

Bishop nodded.

"Couldn't the stones have been placed there to cover the original burial?" the sergeant asked.

"Perhaps," the professor acquiesced, "but it's not something I've ever seen before. And believe me; I've excavated many, many Viking gravesites in my time."

Not to be outdone, Inspector Marsh said, "You're the expert in this field, Professor Bishop, but what experience have you in crime scene examination?"

"None whatsoever," Bishop said. "But I'm telling you…your people have missed something." He pushed by the inspector and dropped down into the shallow pit. "Here, I'll show you."

Inspector Marsh jerked forward, as if to drag the professor back from the hole. However, it was like Bishop had already pointed out, the CSI team were finished there. The crime scene was no longer a protected space. Now it was just an ancient burial place: Bishop's jurisdiction.

Marsh waved him on.

Bishop crouched down, a trowel appearing from his coat pocket. He tapped at the layer of stones. "See here. These stones are from this site, but not an original feature of the grave as I said. See how some of them are lighter on one side than the other; they are the surfaces of stones that have been open to the elements. I suspect that these stones have been removed from one of the nearby pathways we previously excavated, then placed here on top of something before the corpse was laid in the grave."

He prised one of the stones loose. "See, the underside of this stone is lighter than the top. It's obvious to my eye that - until recently - this stone lay the other way up."

Inspector Marsh frowned. He'd seen enough episodes of Time Team on television to argue with an expert. He glanced at the CID sergeant. "Colin, can you sort this for us? Maybe we'd better have CSI back here."

DS Colin Ross shrugged. "They're spread out pretty thinly as it is, boss."

"Shout them up, anyway. It can't do any harm to take a second look." He looked down at Bishop who was digging at a second stone. "You can come on up now, Professor Bishop. You've convinced me."

Bishop ignored him, lifting aside the second stone. He placed it on the edge of the grave, before turning back for a third. Marsh grunted. "Professor! Can you please stop what you're doin? I'm bringing a team back to do a more thorough search. If there's anything in there as you say, I'd rather it was not disturbed until it is fully catalogued."

Bishop swung his large head up to stare at the inspector. His eyes were demonic without the aid of the overhead lights. "There is something else in here, Inspector Marsh." He held open his hand.

Marsh had to squint to make out what the professor was showing him. "What is it?"

Bishop stood up, reaching forward. Instinctively, Marsh opened his hand to accept whatever it was the professor offered him. Then, trying hard not to recoil in revulsion, he stared down on the small item he now cupped in his palm. "Oh, dear Lord."

DS Colin Ross leaned in. He couldn't help stepping back, making a strangled shout of dismay.

In the inspector's cupped palm lay a severed finger.

The fingernail was chipped, but it was slim and elegant. Not the finger of the man that they'd already exhumed. This nail was delicately painted. Baby pink. The finger was that of a young woman.

"Get CSI over here right now!"

FORTYFOUR

The road to Trowhaem

On the journey back to Trowhaem, Shelly tried not to think about what had happened back at Paul Broom's cottage. Impossible task as it was. She couldn't get the sight of the monstrosity that had crouched on the bonnet of the squad car out of her mind. Nor could she deny how close they had all come to death if Carter Bailey hadn't intervened. She owed that man. He'd saved Bob, and for that she was truly grateful, but she could not yet shake the misgiving that he was somehow involved in all this. The only thing was *how*?

If Professor Hale hadn't been in the car with them, she'd have talked it over with Bob. But how could she badmouth Bailey with Janet sitting in the back seat? *You're not the only with an eye for the obvious, Professor Hale.* Janet Hale was in love with Bailey. Janet would argue against her suspicion that he was more than what he seemed, clouding her theory that he knew more about this whole maddening case than he was letting on.

Bob was driving.

The constable sneaked the occasional glance Shelly's way. When he thought she wasn't looking. Shelly sat with her hands in her lap. Was that where his eyes kept straying? She glanced down and realised the object of his perusal wasn't her finely shaped thighs but the fingernail of the thumb that she picked at. Blood flecked her nail and there was a shred of flesh curling from her raw cuticle. Faintly embarrassed she rolled her hand into a fist, concealing the incriminating evidence of her worried mind.

"How are you faring up?" Bob asked.

I'm a police sergeant, she thought. We have a civilian passenger in here with us. What kind of question is that to ask of

314

your supervisor at a time like this? I'm fine. Thank you very much. "I'm okay…" she said tremulously.

Bob gave a cough deep in the back of his throat.

"I could kill a cigarette," Shelly admitted. To hell with being a sergeant and keeping up the professional appearance. The image of her dying mother flickered across her vision. Sorry, Mum!

From the back seat, Janet's sob was suddenly very loud and intrusive. Shelly turned quickly to look at her.

"I'm sorry," Janet said hurriedly. She placed her hands over her face. "I don't know why I'm crying."

"It's okay, Janet. You have every right to cry," Shelly said.

"You've had one hell of a night," Bob offered.

Janet sobbed again. Then tears were rolling down her face. She couldn't wipe them away quickly enough. Shelly reached around, leaning through the gap in the seats. She placed a hand gently on Janet's forearm. "Let the tears come. It'll do you good," she said, wishing she were allowed to do the same.

"I don't know why I'm like this," Janet wept. "I've survived where maybe I shouldn't have. It's just that…other people have died. And it's all because of me."

"It's not your fault," Shelly reassured her. She turned fully so that she was kneeling on the seat, both hands now outstretched to the professor. Janet leaned into her, and very un-police-sergeant-like Shelly hugged Janet to her shoulder, patting her hair soothingly.

Bob's eyebrows did a little rise-and-fall but he didn't comment. He kept his eyes on the road.

Muffled against Shelly's shoulder, Janet said, "It's all because of me. All these people have died because…"

"Hush now. It's not your fault. Whoever this maniac is, it isn't your fault that he's fixated on you."

"No, Shelly. You're wrong. I've been thinking; it *is* my fault."

"How could it be?" Shelly said in the soothing tones of a mother cradling a child.

PRETERNATURAL

"Because -"

But that was all she managed.

Bob's bark of alarm cut her off.

Shelly loosed her, and Janet rocked backwards into her seat. Shelly scrambled round, eyes scanning for what had alarmed Bob.

"What's wrong?" Shelly asked.

Bob's face was twisted with effort as he sawed at the steering wheel.

Shelly snatched her gaze to a point beyond Bob. In the same instant as she saw the blazing headlights she realised that all of Bob's efforts at steering them clear were to no avail. Then there was the horrific collision as a vehicle rammed them from the side. The police car was walloped off its wheels, Bob tilting over her as the car was both lifted and propelled through space.

Then everything was in absurd slow motion. Shelly had no conscious understanding of what was happening, but she felt every infinitely small detail of the collision as the car began to roll. In her vision, exploding windows were like sugar glass tinkling through the air. The seat beneath her rocked and rolled. She had undone her seatbelt so that she could reach back to comfort Janet, so nothing held her from scrunching up against the roof, her head pressed nigh on down to her knees. Then she was flailing loose and uncoordinated, arms going one way, legs the other. Her chin smacked a doorpost. Then she was pressing the other way, almost smothered by the musty warmth of Bob's body travelling in the other direction. Some one screamed…maybe it was she.

It seemed like an age.

The car continued to roll, and all Shelly could do was go with it. The forces working on her threatened to pulp her in one second then rip her apart in the next, but all she could do was allow herself to ride out the worst of the collision whilst fighting against the urge to pass out.

When the car finally stopped rolling, Shelly wasn't aware. Her brain continued to spin and whirl so that she thought the torment would never stop. Neither would the shriek in her ears stop. It was a throaty howl of terror that would not curtail.

Then the screaming stopped.

She'd lost the battle.

Against her will, she passed out.

It was a small slice of total blackness. Then…

…Head ringing, she blinked awake. Where am I? Am I still alive? she wondered. Am I dead? Is this what death is like?

Is this heaven or am I in hell?

It sure smells like hell…

The smell of petrol fumes invaded her senses.

Painfully she twisted around. She was lying against the ceiling of the car, one arm jammed beneath her body. Looking up, she saw Bob's limp shape dangling next to her. Caught in his belt, he was still in the driver's seat. Only he was upside down like some huge bat.

Beyond him, there was a belch of smoke, and noxious fumes trickled through the smashed windscreen.

I'm right here on Earth, she told herself, but we'll all be in hell if we don't get out of this car.

It was an immense struggle, but she managed to force her way round so that she was close to Bob. Upside down, his face wasn't recognisable. It was loose, flaccid, and unnatural. She reached out a hand and touched him. Are you dead, Bob? Please…don't let you be dead.

Bob moaned.

"Bob? Bob! We have to get out of here now!"

The constable's eyelids flickered.

Shelly shook him. Bob moaned again, but this time it was in response to pain.

"I'm sorry, Bob, but we have to get out."

She reached for him again and this time Bob's hand moved and intercepted hers. "I'm okay, Shelly. Just…unh…give me a second or two…"

Filled with momentary relief, Shelly reached for and touched his cheek, gently tracing the lines with the back of her knuckles. "Are you hurt?"

"Feels like I've just been in a car wreck," Bob said, then hissed with the pain his chuckle brought. "I'm all right, I think. You'd think I'd ken if I was badly hurt, wouldn't you?"

Beyond him was a deflated white sack.

"I think the airbag saved you a lot of injury," Shelly said.

"Aye," Bob agreed. "Everything but my nose. I think I've broken it. How about you, Sarge? You okay?"

"As far as I can tell."

"What about Professor Hale?"

"I haven't checked yet," said Shelly, twisting so she could look behind her. The rear of the car was in darkness. No sign of Janet lying against the ceiling. Was she caught between the seats? Shelly reached with groping fingers. Nothing. A feeling of dread rose up in Shelly, pinching her throat in an iron grip. "Oh, my God, Bob. I think Janet was thrown from the car as it rolled."

They'd both been saved from the worst of the collision by the shell of the vehicle. If Janet had been flung out a window as the car rolled, there was no telling the horrific injuries she could have sustained. Put bluntly the worst-case scenario wasn't necessarily death.

"Get out the car, Sarge," Bob said. "Look for her. She might need immediate help."

"What about you?"

"I'll get out soon enough." Said he who was hanging upside down, both legs caught in a vice of mangled pedals and twisted steering wheel.

"I have to see to you first," Shelly said.

"No. See to Janet."

318

Shelly turned back to him and saw immediately the reason he wanted her out of the car. Flames were licking from the upside down engine of the car, snaking along the edge of the crumpled bonnet.

"Bob, unclip your belt. I'll help you."

"Get out, Shelly. Leave me, just get out."

"No," she cried, pushing up close to him. "Help me get you loose, Bob. I can get you out."

Bob shook his head feebly. He looked directly into her eyes. In this twisted perspective, he looked twenty years younger. "Leave me, Shelly. Save yourself."

Shelly wasn't having it. "No. No way. Help me unclip you, Bob."

Bob sighed. "I can't, Shelly. I think both my arms are broken. My legs are trapped, too. There's just no way…"

"No. I'm getting you out." Shelly began to cry. "I'm not leaving you to die."

"You have to save yourself."

There was a small noise. A subdued *whump!* But Shelly knew what it signified. The petrol had caught.

"I'm going to unclip you, Bob," she said. "You'll probably fall but there's nothing we can do about that."

"Do you think it might hurt?" Bob asked, his humour out of place but equally welcome.

Smoke belched inside the compartment. Bob coughed. Shelly's eyes began to stream at the poisonous fumes boiling around them.

"Get out," Bob said again. But Shelly ignored him. Reaching up, she pressed at the safety release on his seatbelt. Nothing happened. She pressed again. Harder. Then again, more and more frantic.

"Your weight is jamming your belt," she cried. Then she was pressing again with as little success as before.

With some effort Bob reached back over his shoulder. His fingers fluttered across her face. "Shelly. Please. Leave me. Save yourself."

"No," she snapped. "No way, you big stubborn ox. I'm not leaving you and that's that. What kind of sergeant would I be if I left you to burn to death?"

Bob coughed and Shelly could have sworn that he was laughing. Surely he wasn't laughing at her? That would be simply insane. But - madness or not - it was also galvanising. She pressed at the safety clip with all her might, and then tugged down on the seat belt. Then Bob was an avalanche of loose limbs and stocky body as he tumbled down on top of her.

It was a struggle to back out of the window, but with a lot of squirming and knocking of elbows on exposed metal, she managed. Then, limping on a swollen ankle, she made her way around the rear of the car, hands on the upturned chassis to steady her, until she was at the driver's side.

Flames were writhing from the bonnet, thick gouts of smoke belching into the night. Shelly could still smell petrol, and she realised that the tank had taken a pounding and was spilling fuel onto the ground. The earlier ignition must have been a secondary spillage. Any second now the fire would meet the pouring petrol and they would go up in a pall of flame.

It wasn't about to put her off.

Crouching by the driver's door, she tugged and pulled, forcing open the door. The metal dug into the ground making it difficult, but there was no way she was going to pit the weight of the Earth against her feeble strength and come out the loser. Yelling helped.

She reached inside, grabbing at Bob's lapels.

"Help me, Bob. As much as you can. Push!"

Bob roared with agony. Shattered bones inside his legs must have made the effort excruciating. Yet he pushed. And Shelly pulled.

Dirty yellow flames swept along the upturned chassis, writhing like evil sprites. The heat beat at Shelly's face, and she closed her eyes tightly. She didn't stop pulling, though. She tore Bob out the door with a strength driven by desperation, and it was as though the expulsion of his body from within the vehicle caused a shift in the atmosphere. Flames appeared out of the ether in the selfsame spot Bob had occupied moments before. There was an angry moan in the air as though the car itself was enraged at Bob's escape, then the flames erupted over the two of them.

Shelly flung herself down, covering Bob's face with her body.

It was a momentary belch of flame and it subsided almost as quickly. Her hair was singed and smoke was bitter in her mouth and nostrils, but Shelly realised she'd survived a roasting. She rolled over, grabbed at Bob's jacket and then propelled herself backwards from the flaming wreck. Bob was twice her weight, but she could barely feel the effort of dragging him to a safe distance. When she could feel only cool air on her face, she dropped down on her backside, gasping for air.

Her feet were splayed either side of Bob's head. Kind of intimate, but she didn't care. She crept her bottom closer to him, lifting his head and placing it gently in her lap.

"Shelly…" Bob's eyelids were flickering.

She stroked his face with her smoke darkened fingers. "Hush, now, Bob. I'm going to get us help."

"You saved my life," he said, voice small coming from such a large man.

"You'd have done the same for me."

"Of course, I would have." He tried to twist towards her. He nudged her with his cheek, then his chin. His eyes widened, finally realising how intimately close he was, and he almost sucked his head into his shoulders like a tortoise.

"Don't be getting any ideas," Shelly said to him. "It's not every constable who gets this kind of treatment, you know."

Bob smiled up at her. "I ken, Shelly."

He snuggled down as though she were the plushest of feather pillows. Shelly smiled to herself. She didn't object. She stroked his cheek again. Then she reached for her radio. Miraculously the screen showed that the radio was still in working order. She called up the communications centre, told them their situation. Offered an approximation of their location. Then she lay back, suddenly exhausted.

The rain started again. This time the beating water on her face was a blessed relief. It also brought her back to her senses.

Janet!

Where was the professor?

Was she even alive?

She extricated herself from under Bob, coming to a bone aching crouch. "Wait here, Bob. I'm going to look for Professor Hale."

"I won't be going anywhere any time soon," Bob said. Still, he reached for her with an arm that didn't look quite right. As if it had an extra elbow. His fingers gripped at hers. "Be careful, Shelly. Whoever crashed into us…he's still out there."

Shelly chewed her lips.

Bob was right.

Their car had been pushed off the road, had rolled down an embankment and had come to rest at the bottom of a steep gully. Looking upwards she could see no sign of the second vehicle's lights. Maybe they'd been smashed when the two cars had struck, but she doubted hat was the reason for the lack of lights. The other vehicle was gone.

There was no doubt in her mind who'd been driving the car.

And she knew it would be a waste of time searching for Janet.

The Skeklar already had her.

FORTYFIVE

The crash scene

There's a tradition in the Shetland Islands that I've always wanted to experience called 'Up Helly Aa'. Strong Viking traditions of the islands are celebrated in a yearly procession of torch-wielding men dressed in Norse costume and culminating in the ritual burning of a Viking longboat. It's a beer-swilling extravaganza known the world over, and it brings thousands of tourists to the islands, swelling the population tenfold over the carnival period.

Unfortunately Up Helly Aa was three months hence and not something that the residents of Connor's Island were likely to partake of. Asking Broom about the islanders' reluctance to celebrate the Viking heritage seemed a rhetorical exercise. The islanders feared the haugbonde curse, why would they celebrate anything even remotely attached to a heritage of ill fortune?

It wasn't Up Helly Aa, but I could see what appeared to be a torch-lit procession along the roadway up ahead. Beyond the bobbing lights was a pyre that lit the low clouds like a bruise on the underbelly of heaven. It wasn't barbeque weather, so I could be forgiven for conjuring up a scene more akin to this desolate place?

"I don't like the look of this," Broom muttered. As usual he was driving like someone told him that fuel was free but the petrol station fifty miles away was about to close for business.

"Best you slow down, Broom."

He gave me a look that I used to shoot at Karen when she played at backseat driver. Then, setting his lips in a grimace, he changed down through the gears, engine compression causing the bonnet to dip towards the road. My knuckles were white where I grabbed at the dashboard.

"Police?" I could see now that the torches were actually beacon lights atop three vehicles drawn up alongside the road. Conn didn't boast too many trees, but there was a small copse of sustained woodland along the western slope of the hill around which the road wound. It was these trees that had given the lights the illusion of a group of marching men as we approached.

"Gun out of sight?" Now it was Broom's turn to wax rhetorical.

As we approached, a police officer stepped into our path waving some sort of florescent glow stick. Obviously he had no experience of Broom's driving manner or he'd have never taken the chance.

As Broom slowed the car in a series of bucking lurches, I swept my gaze across the scene at the side of the road. I could tell that a car had gone off the road, and it was the source of the broiling flames just out of sight beyond the slope of the hill that led down to the sea. Stunted grass was torn and churned up to show the peaty earth beneath. Debris was strewn across a wide swathe, marking the rolling progress of the vehicle.

Something clenched at my guts.

Before Broom had fully brought the Subaru to a halt, I scrambled out of the car and headed for the wreck. The police officer got in front of me, his hands coming up.

"It's no' safe doon there," he said, his accent guttural and not of the islands. Likely he was one of the officers shipped in from mainland Scotland to bolster the struggling resources that Lerwick had to offer. "You cannae be goin' doon, sir."

"Who was in the car?" I demanded, already fully aware of the answer.

Conn didn't boast a constant traffic flow. On the western side of the island it was practically non-existent. Since Janet left with Sergeant McCusker and Bob Harris, no other vehicles had passed Broom's cottage before we'd set off on our journey. Therefore – in my mind - it had to be their vehicle that was scorching the underbelly of the clouds.

My experiences with police officers hadn't always been good. Despite that, I'd always respected the police, so the way that I grabbed the policeman and thrust him aside was totally out of my nature. I guess his experiences with distraught loved ones at the scene of fatal collisions tempered his response. Instead of bringing me down with a well-practiced rugby tackle, he jogged sideways, keeping pace with me, urging me to stop with soothing words.

"It's all right, sir. There's naebody doon there. We've got them ae by the ambulance."

I could see the vehicle now. It was on its roof, guttering flames and roiling black smoke fighting to conceal the skeleton of the vehicle within. Florescent markings were non-existent, but the shape of the structure told me that it was indeed the squad car.

"They're all okay?" I demanded, now pushing past him to get back up the hill.

"How'd you know them, sir?" the officer asked.

"We're…" I was lost for the correct term, but then settled on the obvious. "We're friends."

The officer's eyes were deep wells.

"Tell me they're okay," I said.

"There are some injuries…" the officer stopped what he was saying, as though fearful he was overstepping the boundaries of professional decorum. He stepped in close to me, and whispered. "I didnae tell you this, but I'm afraid PC Harris is no' a well man."

"Bob Harris? He's hurt?"

"Pretty badly, I'm afraid…"

"What about…?"

"Oh, she's awright. A wee bit singed. A bit of smoke inhalation, but otherwise she'll be fine."

"You're talking about Sergeant McCusker?"

"Aye, sir. Who else?"

Without answering, I broke away from him. The ambulance parked on the grass next to the roadside appeared to be the most forlorn thing I'd ever seen. As I charged up the slope Broom galumphed towards the ambulance in his own lurching fashion. Backlit by the beacon lights he momentarily reminded me of the Frankenstein monster from the old black and white movies.

Shelly McCusker was sitting on the back step of the ambulance. She had an oxygen mask held loosely in her hand and was taking periodical gulps of air. Her face was smudged with sooty oil and her dark hair looked frizzier at the back than previous. Seeing me coming, she stood up and the look in her eyes confirmed my worst fears.

"Where is she, Sergeant? Where's Janet?"

Allowing the oxygen mask to fall from her hand, Shelly stepped forward and gripped my shoulders. Broom stumbled to a halt behind me. Her eyes flicking between us, she said, "Janet was thrown from the car, Bailey. We're just about to start an area search for her."

I squinted at her. Around her head her auric lights churned a dark, muddy blue. I perceived that the lights were muted through fear of the truth, fear of what the future may bring.

"He's got her already," I said. "You know that. Why waste time looking here when the Skeklar's already taken her?"

Her chin dropped and Shelly found something on my chest more interesting to look at.

"I'm a police officer; I have to follow procedures, Bailey. You have to understand that? What if Janet's lying out there somewhere, in desperate need of medical help?"

"Fuck procedures." I quickly rotated my body, scanning the night. I allowed my vision to zone out. The beacon lights from the emergency vehicles, the blazing wreck down the slope, didn't help, but I could immediately tell that Janet was nowhere near. Snapping my attention back to Shelly, I now gripped her shoulders, so that we looked like long lost lovers reunited and unsure of whether to embrace or not. "She's gone, Sergeant. She isn't lying in the grass waiting for you to find her. *The Skeklar's got her.*"

"How could you know that, Bailey?"

"Trust me."

Her eyelids flickered, and for one indefinable second I read terror behind the look. Terror of me, because of what I was? Perhaps my talent for seeing a person's intention wasn't so unique after all.

In a softer voice, I said, "Shelly. You know as well as I do that we're wasting time here." Beyond her shoulder two medics feverishly worked on Bob Harris and immediately I wished I could take back those words. Rather than make an awkward attempt at extricating my foot from my mouth, I said, "Bob would understand. He'd want us to go after Janet."

Tears dripped down her cheeks. Shelly turned to stare into the ambulance. Bob was a shapeless form beneath a pale blue blanket. Wires and tubes attached him to monitors and what looked to be an intravenous drip. Not good.

"How is he?" Broom asked over my shoulder. For a moment I'd forgotten he was there. I nodded at Shelly, asked, "Is Bob going to be all right?"

"Until they get him to hospital we won't know the extent of his injuries." A grimace tightened her features. "Bob thinks both of his arms and legs are broken. We can only pray that they're the worst of his problems. The paramedics think he might have some internal bleeding…"

I felt as though I'd been jabbed in the testicles. I liked Bob Harris. This should not have happened to such a good man.

"What happened?"

She shook her head and I caught the scent of smoke off her hair.

"It happened so fast," she said tremulously. "Nothing I could do to stop it."

"No one's judging you, Sergeant," Broom said.

Shelly turned back to us, and for a fleeting moment there was a look of resignation. "You don't know Inspector Marsh."

"He's a donkey's arse," came a voice, and to my surprise I saw that Bob Harris had struggled up to a seated position. Wires were tangled in his bedding and the medics were losing the battle to lie him back down. "Give me a second or two," he grunted at them. "Sarge, could you come here please?"

Shelly scrambled into the ambulance and joined in with the gentle coaxing of the medics. "You have to lie still, Bob. It's for your own good."

"I'm just bashed up a wee bit, I'm not a flamin' invalid," Bob argued. Still, he lay back at the pressure of Shelly's hands on his chest. When he was the good patient, Shelly stroked his hair back from his forehead and then leaned forward and kissed him on the cheek. I'm pretty sure that his smile was of more than contentment.

Standing at the door, I felt like an interloper and I stepped away, pulling at Broom's wrist to take him with me. Broom lingered a moment longer, then he followed me as we headed back towards his Subaru.

"He's going to be okay, Broom. We have to get after Janet." My words were rhetoric, but I felt the need to say something - if only to cover the awful feelings of responsibility I felt for Bob Harris being as injured as he was.

"You think we can do this without the help of the police?" Broom asked.

Stopping in my tracks I swung round to look back at the ambulance. "The police don't know what we're dealing with. You can't stop a monster by following fucking procedures."

Broom made a low noise in his chest that sounded like disagreement. But he stepped past me, pulling the car keys from his pocket. I grabbed them from him.

"Sometimes you just have to do things yourself," I told him. "I'm driving."

"Okay. You can drive. Just…well…be careful."

Coming from a man who drives as if he's in a fairground bumper car, it made me shake my head. "It's been a while," I told him. "But don't worry, they say it's easy. Like riding a bike. You never forget."

"No, but it's still easy to fall off."

"I think you're confusing your metaphors, Broom. It's a log you can easily fall off."

"I'm not confused. You can also fall of a cliff," Broom added. "Something Connor's Island has in abundance."

"I'll be careful, okay?"

"Please do. Even the country's fifteenth bestselling horror author can't afford to buy a new car every five minutes of the day."

Nervous tension does cause a person to talk drivel. Yet the pointless conversation was doing a fine job of keeping our minds off what we were genuinely afraid of. His Subaru was Broom's way of recapturing his boy racer spirit, a way of grasping at his fading youth, but he wasn't really concerned that I was going to scratch his paintwork. No: it had finally set in that we were both in terrible danger. If the Skeklar were prepared to take Janet from under the noses of the police, then we wouldn't trouble it. Not when it was capable of taking us out in an instant.

To give Broom his due - frightened or not - he clambered in beside me and settled in the passenger seat.

Fear could be debilitating. But it could also be the spur one needs to galvanise you to action. When Karen called me that time I didn't stop to think: "You have to come home, Carter. Please…come *now*." Looking back, it was fear that drove me then. It made me race home; and in contradiction it also gave me the courage to fight Cash for everything I loved. Without that fear I would not have possessed the strength or the determination to break free and take Cash to his watery death.

It was the same fear that had controlled me to this point. How could I not be afraid with the knowledge that I was either one of two things; insane or the vessel carrying the vile spirit of a serial killer? Four years in such a constant state of horror would be enough to put some people in their grave. Yet, there I was. Seeking to bait a monster in its lair. Somehow I'd managed to embrace that fear. In comparison the prospect of dying under the slashing claws of a mythical trow meant nothing to me.

Adjusting the driver's seat to fit someone of lesser proportions than Broom, I glanced back over at the ambulance. The back door was closed now and the ambulance was driving down the incline above the road. Once on the road, it took off with urgency uncommon to this island, blue lights flashing, sirens wailing.

Wondering where they'd take Bob, I watched the ambulance move off along the road. The nearest hospital was on Yell. I hoped that Bob wouldn't have to endure the ferry trip back over to the mainland, and one of the helicopters would be requisitioned to get him the urgent help he deserved. At least Sergeant McCusker would ensure he'd be given his due. There was no way she was going to watch him suffer needlessly, not when she was accompanying him to the hospital.

There was a bang on the window.

Shelly McCusker stood with one thumb hooked through her equipment belt, staring down at me. Before I could crank down the window she pulled open the rear door and slid into the seat behind me.

"Don't say anything, Bailey. Just drive."

"What about Bob?"

"Bob told me I had to come with you."

Watching her in the rear-view mirror, I said, "You know what I intend to do if I find this thing?"

Her sneer told me everything I needed to know.

I started the engine. "What about your police procedures?"

"Fuck procedures," she said, eliciting a smile.

It was some time since I'd been behind the wheel of a car. But like I told Broom, you never forget. I gave the Subaru throttle, peeling around parked emergency vehicles and following in the wake of the ambulance.

"Are you armed, Bailey?" Shelly asked.

Broom gave a warning cough that I chose to ignore. Shelly wasn't a police sergeant now. "Yes, I'm armed. This thing has to be stopped."

"You won't get any argument from me," she said.

"Me neither," Cash chipped in. *"But have you got what it takes, brother?"*

FORTYSIX

Near Burra Ness

It had turned out to be one unbelievable day. It was difficult crediting how so much had been crammed into so few hours. Arriving back at the deserted brick structure on the fringe of Burra Ness submarine tracking base, it felt as though weeks had passed since last I stared through the chain-link fence at it. The crows were gone, but even without their subtly menacing presence the hut still exuded a form of malevolence. Against the backdrop of the night sky it squatted like a malformed *thing*, the ancient telegraph pole jutting from its back like the rearing head of a serpent.

"Why have you brought us here?" Shelly asked.

Switching off the engine, I settled back in the seat. I quickly glanced at Broom and saw him bobbing his head in understanding.

"Call it a portent," I said. "Something tells me that this place is important."

"What? Like you're a clairvoyant or something?"

"Or something."

From behind me, I could detect the grumbling of an unbeliever. Not that I bothered explaining: to a believer no proof is necessary, to an unbeliever no proof is possible. In plain speak, even if what I was waiting for did transpire, Shelly wouldn't accept it for what it was. In days to come she might attempt to make sense of what she'd witnessed and come to the conclusion that it was all down to chance and coincidence.

"The M.O.D. police have already checked this place," she pointed out.

"When?" I asked.

"Earlier. I was updated, along with Inspector Marsh, when the naval staff joined us at Trowhaem."

"What were they looking for?"

"Bethany Stewart. Who else?"

"Bethany isn't here. She never has been."

The silence became tangible. No doubt Shelly was debating how the hell I could know, unless I was somehow involved in Bethany's abduction. It seemed an age before she stirred, clearing her throat and leaning forward.

"So why are we wasting time here, Bailey?"

"We're not wasting time. I told you…I'm waiting for a sign."

She laughed. It was a bitter sounding hack in the back of her throat. "What are you expecting? Divine intervention?"

I exhaled slowly through my nose.

"I've been there, Bailey. Believe me, you'll be waiting forever."

An image flashed into my mind.

A woman was lying in a bed. Frail, barely an ounce of fat remaining on her bones, life support machines all that kept her on this side of the great divide. Beside her sat Shelly. Not in uniform but jeans and a shapeless green sweatshirt. Her hair was lacklustre, and there were dark rings beneath her eyes. I knew that Shelly had sat in that selfsame place for many days.

Then I heard Shelly's voice, barely a whisper: "No more cigarettes for me, Mum. Don't you worry; I won't touch a single one as long as I live."

On the bed the woman's eyes fluttered open. "You promise, Shelly?"

Shelly jerked upright, glancing around in mild panic. Then she leaned over the woman. "Mum? Mum?" Shelly stood up, shouting now: "Nurse! Nurse! She's awake, my mum's awake!"

A steady flow of nurses entered the private room. One of them began switching dials, checking vital signs. Another took Shelly by the hand and sat her down. "I'm sorry, Shelly. You know that can't be possible. Your mum has already gone. There was no electrical activity in her brain." Out of sympathy she didn't mention the dreadful term 'brain dead'. "It's been more than an hour now."

Shelly blinked back tears. "No. No. She spoke to me."

"Sometimes God hears our prayers," another nurse offered.

Divine intervention?

Blinking, I was back in the Subaru, my eyes tracking the raindrops down the windscreen. Unsurprised by what had occurred, I barely stirred. Paraphrasing a certain Wonderland character, things were definitely getting curiouser and curiouser. I wasn't a psychic in the true sense of the term, but it was as if my intuitive streak was working overtime, and I'd just picked up on a traumatic episode from Shelly's past.

"I'm surprised you'd say that," I whispered to her.

Shelly sat back with the faintest of sobs.

Broom grumbled beside me, but I kept my eyes on the rain-washed screen.

It was a tableau that held for some minutes, each of us lost in our private thoughts. I don't know about the others, but my mind was in a dark realm. Intuition, mediumship, whatever you wish to call it, my reading into a very personal incident from Shelly's life had given me pause to consider. If indeed there was a higher spirit at work in the universe, something distinct and all seeing - God - then couldn't it also be true that demons did walk the lower dimensions? Could Satan, Lucifer or the Skeklar be real too?

Was evil a tangible force?

Could evil attach itself to a thing, animal, beast or inanimate object?

The utility hut we stared at certainly gave the impression of being an evil place.

Nah, just bricks and mortar, I told myself. Places aren't evil. You have nothing to fear from bricks and mortar.

What is evil?

Man, by virtue of his actions and his thoughts, I decided.

I reached beneath the seat and drew out the small strongbox containing Broom's SIG Sauer. Placing the box on my lap, I slowly opened the lid and took out the gun.

My companions on this nightmare quest took in a collective gasp.

Not because I'd armed myself, their astonishment was more for what I too had noticed.

The door of the utility hut opened by tiny increments, as though the door had taken on a life of its own.

Breathless we all watched.

Within the open doorway, the interior of the hut was all raven shadows, but something stirred there, a writhing, coiling shadow against the darkness. Like smoke it issued from the hut, indistinct against the grey walls. Then it curled towards us, moving to and then through the chain fence.

Most pragmatic of the three of us, Shelly swore, "What the fuck is that?"

Neither Broom nor I had the words to explain. We could only watch as the sinuous form made its way across the road like water seeking the route of least resistance.

"What the fuck is that?" Shelly said again, but ten times more strident.

The smoky thing reached the bonnet of the car, writhed up it, becoming a shapeless mass of billowing mist that hovered there as if studying us.

"Get us out of here, Bailey," Shelly commanded. "Get us out of here now!"

"No. Just wait," I said. "Let's see what happens."

Broom was moaning but I couldn't say if it was fear or awe that motivated him. Shelly pushed herself as far into the furthest corner of the backseat as she could find.

The smoke dipped, like a swan delving beneath a river surface. It disappeared beneath the car.

Shelly let out an undignified yelp, scrambling to get in the front. I gently pushed her back into her seat. "Stay calm. Please. It isn't doing us any harm."

"Not yet," she screeched. "What is it?"

Broom repeated over and over, "Ohmigod, Ohmigod, Ohmigod…"

Craning my neck down the curve of my door, I said, "I can't see it. Can either of you see where it's at?"

Still praying, Broom gave a quick glance out his window. "I think it's still beneath us."

"No," Shelly cried. "It's behind us!"

I twisted round, and through the misted rear window I could see something moving. The condensation on the window twisted the shape somewhat, but I wasn't looking at insubstantial smoke. Something very solid stood surveying us from less than a few feet away.

"A man," I whispered to the others. "There's a man out there."

Shelly slapped at the central locking, and all four locks engaged with a clunk.

"Get us out of here," she commanded again.

"Just wait…" I cautioned. Still, I familiarised my finger with the SIG's trigger.

"Is it the Skeklar?" Broom squawked.

Shelly batted at the condensation on the window before jerking back from what she saw. "It's…it's…"

Then the figure moved around the car. Almost languorous in his movement, he stepped up to the side window and peered in at me.

"It's…just an old man," Shelly finished, and I swear I felt the atmosphere inside the Subaru shrink as she sucked in a deep inhalation.

But I wasn't staring at an old man.

At first glance the figure could be mistaken for an elderly man.

He was small of frame, bent at the shoulders, his head balding with only the barest scrap of hair sticking out in tufts over each ear. His skin was wrinkled. But there the likeness to an elderly man ended, and something truly strange began.

His flesh was of an unnatural pallor, slate grey, laced with blue veins that twisted beneath his parchment-like skin. And he was thin. Beyond thin; he was emaciated. Every bone of his entire skeleton was visible as though his skin was hung loosely over a frame of sticks and poles. And he was as naked as a newborn.

Strange enough, but the thing that told me that I peered back at something supernatural was his eyes. He had no irises. His eyes were blank orbs, a pale mauve and sickly yellow, the colours of a fading bruise. They were the blind eyes of something that dwells in the unlighted depths of caverns and forgotten places.

Yet he could see me.

And he smiled.

I experienced the same sensation that a goldfish must when a starving cat paws at his bowl.

Shelly, firmly entrenched in twenty-first century policing obviously wasn't seeing what I was seeing. Plus, she can't have made the correlation between the disappearance of the strange mist and the arrival of this thing.

"Who is he? What the hell is he doing here…nude?"

She pressed at the door locks, a second from getting out the car and confronting the thin grey man. What was she going to do? Charge him with indecent exposure? I slapped at the lock again, saying, "Don't!"

"What?" she asked, but it was Broom who answered for me.

"The Haugbonde."

"The hogboy? You have to be kidding me?"

"Does that look like a joke to you?"

The thin grey man, as though we were beyond his concern, walked to the front of the car. Bending, he laid both of his clenched fists on the bonnet of the car, and then craned forward.

Staring at us. While Broom screwed his eyes tight, and Shelly scrambled to see what was happening, I returned his unnatural stare.

His thin lips puckered.

I remained stock till.

Again he smiled, but this time it was different.

The grey man reared back. He threw out both arms, and even from inside the vehicle I heard his ligaments and tendons creaking. His head lolled back on his shoulders and he emitted a high-pitched scream.

"What the fuck?" I'm not sure who said that. Maybe it was all three of us.

The scream curtailed until it was pitched beneath the ability of human hearing, and yet he still stood with his mouth stretched wide. How long that tableau held I couldn't say; we all just sat there watching the uncanny thing screeching silently at the heavens. Finally, his head slipped forward, and again his sightless eyes sought mine.

He stood there, head nodding slightly.

I nodded back at him.

This thin grey man, this elemental spirit of nature, was not a threat to me. I can't explain how I knew, I simply did.

The grey man lifted an open palm as if begging alms from a passing stranger.

"What is he doing?" Shelly whispered in my ear. "I should get out, Bailey. Ask him what he's doing here."

"Just wait," I whispered.

"I don't recognise him as an islander. Maybe he knows something about what's going on." Shelly was rabbiting. What was wrong with her? Couldn't she see that this wasn't some old hobo-cum-naturist who'd wandered off the beaten tourist path? What did she expect him to say? In fact, what would she do when he peered into her soul as he just had mine?

We heard the noise first. A fluttering, flapping sound, as though a canvas sail was being torn by hurricane winds. It was distant at first, but growing in volume as something approached. It was dark, the rain clouds blocking the moonlight, and the Subaru's headlights were inefficient at pushing back the darkness. Still, the night suddenly became much, much darker. The shadows were solid; all that I could see through them was the thin grey man. He shone with his own luminescence under the headlight beam. Then he disappeared as the blackness thickened.

There were dozens of them, hundreds, maybe thousands. More crows than I'd warrant that the entire Shetland island chain could sustain. Ravens, too. Rooks and jackdaws. The occasional flash of white could have been from the plumage of magpies. There was all manner of carrion eater.

They flew in frenzy around the car. Wingtips and claws battered the metal, the windows. Small, rolling eyes peered inside. Beaks opened and shrill cries broke over us. The drumming of bodies on the metal work was like thunder. Reflexively, the three of us threw our hands over our heads, pushing deep into our seats. Broom and Shelly cried out, but strangely enough I stayed silent.

There was an understanding between the thin grey man and me. These birds had come at his bequest. They weren't there to harm us.

"Stay calm," I told my companions. "It'll be over with in a second."

With my words there was an immediate cessation of the clamour. The massive flock of birds cartwheeled skyward, leaving behind nothing of their passing but the odd streak of shit on the windows and some slowly drifting feathers that the wind caught and plucked away.

The headlight beam grew in brightness.

Standing in the light was the grey man. Untroubled by the birds he stood with that faint smile on his puckered lips. On his outstretched palm stood a single crow. It watched us with the same flat-eyed intensity as its master. The grey man spoke to the bird, its head cocking as though listening with rapt attention to his words. Then it hopped off his hand, swooped the few feet and landed with a chitinous clatter on the bonnet.

We all watched as the bird hopped forward and then beat its beak on the glass. Once, twice, three times. Then it streaked heavenward and we all craned our necks to see where it was going.

Twice it made a full circuit of the Subaru, before flapping off to the southwest. The bird cawed once.

"It wants us to follow it," I said.

"It's a fucking crow," Shelly pointed out. "Not Lassie the fucking Wonder Dog."

I clucked my tongue in exasperation, and shoved the gear stick into reverse and swung the vehicle round.

"Bailey…?" Shelly began.

Broom said, "Open your eyes, Sergeant. And your heart. Suspend disbelief if you have to. Only…let Carter do what has to be done."

She snorted, but didn't argue. "Crazy." Whether she meant me, the notion of our animal guide, or her own frame of mind, she didn't make clear.

As I drove in pursuit of our feathered guide, she did ask, "What about that old guy?"

"He's gone."

She craned round to search for the thin grey man. The road was empty.

"The Haugbonde's gone," I clarified. Back to the smoke and the earth that gave him birth.

FORTYSEVEN

The road south

Broom's Subaru was no Mystery Mobile, but all we required was a cowardly Great Dane with a penchant for over-sized snacks and we'd have been directly in the middle of a Scooby Doo cartoon. The blond jock was Broom. Shelly was the spunky Daphne. That would make me Shaggy - my unshaven chin and rumpled appearance only adding to the image. And, yep, Janet had to be the bookish Velma.

Anyone familiar with Scooby Doo knows that Velma often found herself in trouble, and it was up to the gang to save her. Usually she was resourceful enough to end up saving herself and solving the mystery while the others got themselves into various spots of bother. Made me wish that this was a children's cartoon; at least then there would be some hope of finding Janet alive.

Instead of a goofy Great Dane we had a bird for our animal companion. The crow flew low, beneath the low-lying clouds. It didn't deviate from the road, and flew only fast enough that we could keep pace. Periodically it turned its beady eye to us and cawed as if spurring us to greater speed.

Perhaps I was humanizing the bird. Maybe the only thing that attracted the crow to the Skeklar's hiding place was the stench of death; it was a carrion eater after all. Maybe its occasional glance back and strident screech was to tell us to go away. We weren't invited to dinner.

"This is just so insane," Shelly said for about the umpteenth time. "We're gallivanting about the countryside following a bloody bird!"

"Please, Sergeant McCusker…" Broom pleaded.

"No, no, no. Please don't call me Sergeant. I'm not a sergeant. Not now. Not here. Not following a flamin' crow." She sighed melodramatically and flung herself back in her seat. Under her breath, she muttered, "Wish I'd had chance to get out of this bloody uniform. Anyone sees me and realises what we're doing, I'll be drummed out of the force. Probably chased by a mob of angry islanders armed with pitchforks and blazing torches."

"Probably." I laughed. "Welcome to my world, Sarge!"

"It's not funny," she snapped from the back seat. "Do you realise what we're doing here?"

"Following a flamin' crow," both Broom and I said in concert.

"It's insane."

"We've already established that." Rain splattered the windscreen and I flicked on the wipers. "But at least it's something. As insane as it seems, it's positive action."

We passed Trowhaem. The site remained a hive of worker bees in yellow and black jackets. Somewhere among the activity were the reinforcements we required, but I knew there was no way Shelly was about to round up a posse of her colleagues to join the Great Crow Chase. In fact, she scrunched down so that no one would see her in the car with us. Already I'd noticed her playing with buttons on her radio. Likely she was turning it off so that she had an excuse for not reporting back to Inspector Marsh.

In many respects I couldn't understand why she was with us. She thought we were both mad men. She - despite her current actions - was a dyed in the wool police officer, who staunchly followed the dictates and procedures laid down by her force's policy. And I knew that she didn't trust me. That was putting it lightly; not only didn't she trust me, she *feared* me almost as much as she worried about jeopardising her career.

Bob Harris must have had a lot to do with it. "Bob told me I had to come with you," she'd said. I wondered what else Bob said. Or, more likely, what had went unsaid between them. As his supervisor she wasn't obliged to do his bidding. She wasn't acting out of police duty, but something else. Were they an item? There was certainly something between them that went further than friendship. It was nothing to do with professional support when she'd leaned over him in the ambulance, brushing back his hair and kissing his cheek.

I was a bloke's bloke. I liked sport and cowboy movies, a pint or two of beer when I could get it. I was never into the lovey-dovey stuff that women enjoy. But even I could see that Sergeant Shelly loved Constable Bob. Love makes us irrational and reckless. Against all training, all logic and sensibility, I decided that Shelly was along for the mystery ride simply because - male chauvinist pig that I am - the man she loved told her she had to come with us.

I supposed her motivation was no different than mine. I too was on that crusade because of love. Or, more rightly, fear of losing it again.

We passed Broom's cottage. He still hadn't got round to removing those stupid Halloween gimmicks from his garden.

Then we were on to the sweep of the cliffs overlooking the Atlantic. Beneath the storm clouds the ocean undulated like an uneasy beast and I could hear the boom of surf on the rocks. Beyond the curve of the island Ura Taing lay out of sight. Here the island was simply bleak, part of the expanse of the moor Bob Harris had warned me away from when first we met.

Our feathered pathfinder stopped. The crow perched on a fence post jutting out of the terrain like an accusatory finger. I might have missed it in the dark but its eyes flared in the headlights before it turned away and stared across the moor. I brought the Subaru to a halt. The crow ignored us. So I got out and walked around the front, the SIG pressed to my thigh. The crow glanced at me once and then launched into flight. It fought the breeze, hovering there like an overgrown kestrel.

Broom's window whispered down. Without taking my eyes from the bird, I said, "It looks like we walk from here."

Broom cursed. Not that I blamed him; it would be hell traversing the boggy earth with his dodgy leg. Still, he clambered out. I walked forward, stepped over a small wire fence and onto the spongy grass. Behind me there was a short conversation in hissed tones, but Shelly and Broom followed me on to the moor. Both their faces were fixed with stern expressions, each for their own brand of personal dissatisfaction.

The crow headed off. This time it didn't wait for us slow coaches. Not that it mattered, through the gloom I could make out its destination. A tall, tapering spire etched itself against the clouds.

"Is that a church?"

"No," Shelly said. "It's a chimney."

"A chimney? Looks too tall."

"It's from the old tannery," she explained. "They built it tall so that the stench wasn't as bad when they burned the spoiled meat."

"I didn't think Conn would need a tannery," I said. "It's not like you have an abundance of livestock, is it?"

"It wasn't cows that were skinned here, Carter. Seals. It's why the place has been abandoned all these years, since culling was *supposedly* banned."

"Strange place to have a factory."

"When it was in full swing, the stench was horrendous. Would you want that in the village where you lived? Want to smell death every given minute of the day?"

Lovely place, I thought. Blood and guts and bones. The ever-present spectre of cruel and violent death. Just the kind of place a Skeklar would hang out.

"We've already searched here," Shelly pointed out.

"When?"

"This morning. Once the team finished up at Catherine Stewart's I had them come here. It was one of the first places I thought of."

"You must have missed something."

Shelly sniffed. "Who's going to argue with a crow?"

Ignoring her sarcasm, I pressed on across the moor. From a distance, the chimneystack stood out against the horizon, a black slash against the rain-swollen clouds. Approaching over the undulating land, the stack both diminished then grew in size, once fully lost from sight as we marched through a deep valley. We splashed through streams, stumbled on rocks hidden in the grass, but pushed on against the discomfort.

Rain hissed through the reeds beside a pool of stagnant water. The wind picked up, tugging at our clothing, just a regular bracing evening constitutional walk for the likes of me.

"We should've taken the service trail from Ura Taing," Shelly muttered.

Broom groaned. His limp, I'd noticed, had become more pronounced these last few minutes. "You're telling me that there's a road we could have taken?"

"You don't think that they hauled the seals all the way over the moor do you?" Shelly said equally bitterly.

"We're almost there," I pointed out. "A few hundred metres as the crow flies. It doesn't matter now."

"We could have taken the car," Broom said petulantly.

"Better that we didn't. It would have announced our arrival." I lifted the SIG. "From here on in we're going to have to be as quiet as possible." I searched the faces of my companions. "We're only going to get one chance at this. Are you both ready?"

Shelly racked her baton. "Ready."

Broom was weaponless. He'd have a slugger's chance if nothing else. He gave me a slow smile. "As I'm ever going to be."

FORTYEIGHT

Near the old tannery

"Did either of you see that?" Shelly asked.

Spying out her unlikely comrades, she noted that the bigger shadow of the two was nearer to her. Paul Broom, crouching in the lea of a semi-collapsed wall. Rain pitter-pattered on his wide shoulders.

"See what?" he whispered.

"A light. Or else, I think it was a light. Could be my eyes playing tricks." Using her baton as a guide, she pointed towards the blocky structure ahead of them. The two-storey building, squat and ugly next to the towering chimney gave back no hint of life. Aptly enough, it was known thereabout as the Death House. "Top window on the right. For one second-or-so, I'm sure I saw the flash of a light."

"A torch?"

"Looked like it," Shelly agreed. "As if someone switched it on and off again very quickly."

Further away, Carter Bailey was moving in a crouch towards the entrance door. Not for the first time, Shelly had her misgivings concerning the man. Still, she had to admit, she was beginning to warm to him. According to the files she'd perused on the internet, Bailey had been a successful businessman prior to the horrific incident where he'd lost his fiancée, unborn child, and his brother. Nowhere did it give any hint that he had experience of hunting killers in the dead of night. Yet, there he was, entering the possible domain of a vicious murderer with hardly a backward glance. He was a brave one. And caring. The most endearing traits she found in men.

He was a lot like Bob Harris in that respect.

She had joined Bailey and Broom at Bob's request. Even if Bob had argued against it, she'd have still clambered into Broom's Subaru. In effect, she should be off duty by now - hours ago - but duty had figured largely in her jumping aboard this crazy adventure. There was still a small child missing, a woman kidnapped and a murderer on the loose. Which police officer wouldn't try to save the innocents and bring down the killer? She had to prove herself. What better way could she think of than the route she'd taken?

Inspector Marsh wouldn't approve. Likely a severe dressing down was in store for her, probably disciplinary action. But she didn't care. "He's a donkey's arse," Bob had said of their vaunted leader, and she couldn't disagree.

She thought back to her heroic predecessor. What about you, Jack McVitie? Would you have joined Carter Bailey if you were still policing Conner's Island? Would you approve of what I'm doing?

Once over she'd considered that Carter Bailey could be the killer they were looking for. He was her *deus ex machina*, as she recalled, her god from the machine. Bailey was the odd stranger with a strange caste to his eyes that simply *must be* guilty of something. Now she knew otherwise. His only crime was that he'd had enough gumption to run directly into the lion's den to save his fiancée and unborn child. Yes, he'd killed a man. But Cassius Bailey was the kind who needed killing by anyone's estimation. And now, here he was rushing into danger for the love of another woman. How could she not warm to him?

Broom whispered, "I don't see anything. You're sure it was a light?"

"No. I'm not sure about anything. It could have been nothing at all. I wasn't looking directly at it; maybe it was just a play of the shadows on the windowpane."

"We should warn Carter."

"I'll do it," Shelly said, starting forward from her hiding place. She had to pass Broom to reach the doorway that Bailey disappeared through. The big man gripped her sleeve with a hand too massive to be the elegant fingers of a master of literature. It was a hand definitely suited to the bludgeoning prose of a horror maestro. She could imagine that hand squeezing throats and wielding a blood-clotted axe.

"I'll go," Broom said.

Shelly shook her head. "It's my place to do this, Broom. Not yours."

Broom twisted his mouth. "It's better that you wait outside, Sergeant. You're the only one with a radio. If anything happens to Carter and me, it'll be down to you to bring reinforcements."

Twisting free of his grasp, she said, "I appreciate what you're saying, but I can use a radio wherever I'm at. In fact, I could leave it here with you for that matter. Using it isn't rocket science; you just press the button and talk."

"Yeah, but who's going to take me seriously? If they hear your voice, they'll come running."

"Who's going to take *me* seriously?" Shelly demanded. "I've royally fucked up. Don't forget, Broom, we came here 'cause some old grungy man has trained a bird to fly back here. If I tell my bosses why I'm here they'll laugh in my face. If anything, we should have locked the old man up and questioned him about what the hell part he's playing in all this."

Broom gave her a quizzical look. "You'd arrest that old grungy guy?"

"Yeah, that old tramp up at Burra Ness."

Broom's frown grew exponentially.

"What?" Shelly demanded.

"Nothing."

"Tell me."

"You only saw an old man?"

"Didn't you? He was right there in front of the car. Before all the birds came. The crow we followed landed on his outstretched arm not ten feet from you."

"Yes, yes," Broom said. "I saw the old man. But he wasn't *just* an old man. You do understand that…don't you?"

"Bailey said it was the haugbonde," she snorted. "But you don't really believe that? Not an intelligent man like you?"

"I'm not sure if you're insulting me or not, Sergeant."

She strained out a smile.

Broom said, "Did it not occur to you that he was more than an ordinary old fellow when he materialised out of the mist? Or when he called down the birds from the heavens in their own voice?"

Shelly decided not to argue. She'd seen the mist, yes. Then she'd seen the man. It didn't mean that they had to be one and the same. Maybe Broom's eyes were failing after so many hours in front of a computer screen. Or maybe it was her eyes that had played tricks on her – because she'd be lying if she didn't accept that, actually, she had been first to see him materialise out of the very mist. Perhaps she was suffering a mild concussion after the crash and she wasn't remembering clearly. It didn't matter. The important thing was finding Bailey and warning him about the light she'd spotted in the building. Unless that flash of light had been another effect of the drubbing her brain took as the car rolled.

"Wait here." She began unclipping her radio off the front of her coat. "If I'm not out of there in the next ten minutes, just switch on the power." She told Broom the code number to patch her radio into the network. "Then, like I said, all you do is press this button and talk."

He accepted the radio from her, but then he stood up. "I'm coming in with you."

"No. It's not safe."

"I don't care. Carter's my friend. I'm not letting him down." He lifted the radio. "And, like you said, the radio can be used anywhere. Just press and talk."

How could she argue?

"Okay. But you stay behind me."

Broom shrugged. Then he stared at the open doorway of the building. When Bailey entered he'd left the door slightly ajar. It was like he was staring into the doorway of a haunted house. His whispered an acronym.

W.W.V.H.D? What the hell did that mean?

Whatever the meaning behind his enigmatic words, it seemed to do the trick. Broom sucked it up and stepped forward.

FORTYNINE

The old tannery

My impressions of seal culling had always been tinged with the cruelty and horror of the activity. It had been a number of years since I'd watched TV bulletins showing men clubbing to death harmless baby fur seals. Still, I had vivid memories of the soft, pleading eyes, the raining blows of heavy clubs, the splash of crimson on pristine snow. It was barbaric and horrific, and I'd tried to blot those images from my mind. My coping mechanism was to deny that such cruelty could possibly exist in this modern era. Like the thinking of an ostrich with its head in sand, it wasn't happening if you didn't accept it. Sad to say, but the slaughter had continued. Culling was a necessity, they said. And, contrary to what the uneducated thought, the culling was humane. The pups didn't suffer.

Yeah, right.

Slaughter is slaughter however it was dressed up. Be it humane or otherwise. There was nothing in the practice of beating seal pups to death that I could accept. Maybe I wasn't educated, but to me there was nothing kind about having your brains smashed in.

Horrified by the practice, I'd always dwelled on the act of culling. I never considered what had become of all those pups that were beaten to death on the ice. It was bad enough that their carcasses were left for the wildlife to feast on, but it had never occurred to me that a profit was gleaned from their pelts. I didn't know that such places as the tanning factory on Conn existed.

As I entered the building, the gruesome reality hit me like a punch in the chest. The tannery was the most despicable place I'd ever been in my life, and my resolve to search it almost deserted me. I nearly retreated outside again. Pushing down the urge to vomit, I told myself, "Janet is here. Little Bethany Stewart is here. There's no turning back now."

I went forward.

"You may as well put the gun in your mouth and get things over with quickly."

Cash was back. Come to gloat now that things were about to get desperate. "Won't that spoil your plans for me, Cash? I thought you only get your chance at me if I die a natural death?"

"Did I say that, brother? I don't recall."

"You said it all right. Said you were going to keep me safe so that you could have me all to yourself."

"I think you're misquoting me, Carter. Your death needn't be natural. There's no problem in you blowing out your own brains. In fact, it's even better that you do. It practically guarantees that there'll only be the two of us around. I'll have you all to myself."

"It isn't going to happen."

"Oh, but it will. Now or later, me and you are gonna get down to a little unfinished business."

"I look forward to it. I'll kick your arse whenever it happens."

Cash's laughter was like fingernails on a chalkboard. *"You're such an arsehole, Carter. Do you know that? I showed you. It was one thing pushing me around when I was the kid brother. Quite the opposite when I was standing in front of you, all grown up and pissed off."*

It was my turn to laugh. "So you say, Cash. But I'm the one walking around in the flesh. I fucked you up, smashed your spine and left your carcass belly down in the water. Believe me, when the time comes, I'll do an even better job on your skinny arse." Hoisting the SIG, I stepped into the tannery. Cash's taunting had actually helped bolster me against what was to follow. "Now, if you don't mind, shut the fuck up, and let me get on with what I came here to do."

He chuckled once, and I felt a squirming sensation at the core of my being, as though he was settling down in a favourite comfy chair to watch a movie. *"Go for it, Bro. If you're man enough."*

He was starting to piss me off with all that talk of tests and being man enough. Well, there was only one way to shut him up. "I'm man enough, Cash. Bring me the Skeklar and I'll show you."

"I can't bring him…it's down to you to find him. Should be easy enough. I can smell the stink of fear from here. Can't you, Carter? Can't you smell Janet's piss as it runs down her legs?" Cash made a deep inhalation. *"Mmmmm. It has been a while, Carter, but it's a scent I'll never forget. Reminds me of when Karen-"*

"Shut up."

He laughed once more, but blessedly fell into silence.

Abandoned for years, the building was anything but storm proof, and I found myself stepping through pools of scummy water. Around me was the ticking of rain that wormed its way through the structure and dripped to the floor. The stench was that of mildewed wood and rusted metal. The air stirred my hair as a gust of wind found egress to the building. All my senses were on hyper-alert. All but my vision: I could barely see my hand in front of my face.

If it had been safe, I'd have stood still. Time my breathing so that I was in sync with the building, the storm. Send out the feelers and latch on to Janet or Bethany's essences. But to stand still would probably invite ambush from the darkness. I was no use to either of them if I died there.

Probing my way with my free hand, I kept the SIG close to my hip. If the Skeklar were lurking in the darkness, at least it wouldn't be able to snatch the gun from my hand before I squeezed off a couple of rounds.

I was in an open space. Above me came the rattle of chains. Jerking my head up, I scanned the gloom for movement but the darkness was impenetrable. Why the hell didn't I bring a torch? Not that I'd have used it. It would have given away my position.

353

But if I needed it, having some form of lighting would have been comforting.

Deciding that the rattle of chains was caused by the squalling wind, I ignored it. I listened instead for something that would give a hint of life.

A wall of thick planks blocked my way. Feeling it, I found the wall stood barely five feet high. Edging along it, I discovered the wall made a right angle, then opened to a void. A livestock stall of some sort.

I considered stepping into the stall, to check if there were any trussed forms lying on the floor, but immediately discarded the idea. For one, I believed that I'd have sensed them already. Secondly, and more important, I was wary about being trapped in the enclosed space.

Turning away I made for where I believed a staircase to the upper floors was.

"Chicken shit coward," Cash muttered.

Choosing to ignore him, I groped my way to the far right corner of the building. True to expectation, there was a doorway into a stairwell. It was still dark, but ambient light leaked into the building through a window mid-way up the next flight. The steps were preformed concrete, so didn't echo my footsteps as I mounted them. Holding the SIG braced across my chest, I lead the way left foot first, crabbing upward.

The stairwell was haunted house creepy. Sweat trickled between my shoulder blades. Over the stink of the building I could smell my own fear. I went up the stairs as quickly as sense allowed. At the first floor, a door opened onto a landing. Stepping into the hallway I searched the shadows for movement. Dust motes sifted down through the dimness, the only movement.

What had caused the dust particles to fall? They'd been disturbed from the ceiling above. Someone - something - was moving above me.

Returning to the stairs, I mounted them. At the top the darkness was absolute. The only sounds were the tapping of rain on the roof, the thrum of my heartbeat in my ears. For the briefest of seconds I faltered.

Did I have what it took? Was I man enough?

My thoughts were cast back to that dreadful night in the watermill. When my fiancée and unborn child were torn to shreds by a monster. I was too late to save them. I couldn't allow another woman and child to die.

Yes, I did have what it took.

But I wasn't going to be stupid about it.

"Be self-controlled and alert. Your enemy the devil prowls around like a hungry lion, searching for souls to devour."

Broom's words of advice resonated in my skull, only this time my brother spoke them. He wasn't warning me to be careful. Whatever the outcome with the Skeklar he told me I would forever be in danger from my most evil of enemies.

FIFTY

Inside the old tannery

An extendable baton seemed an ineffective weapon against something that had survived gunfire. But, Shelly decided, it was all she had. Given the opportunity she'd gladly accept the opportunity of putting the Skeklar and her baton to the test. Home Office procedure dictated that the baton should be aimed only at the limbs or body, but never to the head of an assailant. Under these conditions she couldn't be criticised for ignoring procedure, though. The Skeklar had already attacked and killed another officer, and for what the bastard had done to him and to Bob she owed the monster the beating of all beatings.

She moved through the tannery with the baton clutched like a sword of vengeance, feeling like a heroine from some grim fairy tale. If she was the warrior woman, what did that make of her companions? A quick glance at Broom assured her of one thing: he shambled through the darkness like the friendly giant. Given his muscular stature and flowing blond hair, he could even be the Viking demi-god, Thor. So what would that make Carter Bailey? Staying with the fantasy scenario, she saw him as the flawed hero. He was a man of two halves; Frodo Baggins torn between his noble heart and the dark power of the One Ring. She'd accepted that - intrinsically - Bailey was a good man, but she would never shake the feeling that there was something *wrong* with him. Her first glance into his eyes told her. Nothing would change her opinion - what she had seen lurking in his gaze was *evil.*

There were of course shades of evil.

Compared to the Skeklar, Carter Bailey hardly made the scale.

Sometimes a little necessary evil wasn't a bad thing. Murder was the greatest sin. But if the murder of the Skeklar meant that innocent lives were spared, then she wouldn't complain. She'd be rooting for Carter Bailey to put a few well-placed rounds into the Skeklar's skull. After she'd battered said skull to a pulp with her baton.

These were unwholesome thoughts for a police officer, but at that moment she didn't care. All that mattered was that the Skeklar was stopped. That Janet and Bethany were saved. Yes, a little necessary evil was in order.

Hell, she could smoke a cigarette.

Another necessary evil.

Her mother's face flashed through her mind's eye.

"Okay, forget the cigarettes," she admonished herself.

Broom came to a standstill.

"What is it?" Shelly whispered.

"We have to go up."

Broom peered into the clotted shadows of a stairwell.

"Okay, but you stay behind me," Shelly said. "Let me get up to the first floor before you follow."

In his large hand the radio looked tiny.

"You remember how to use that?" Shelly asked.

"Key in the code. Press the button. Pretty simple," Broom reassured her.

"So is breathing," Shelly told him. "But I bet before we're finished here you forget how to exhale. You'd better switch it on now. Just in case."

Broom complied. "What about the glow from the screen? Won't it give away our position?"

"A necessary evil," Shelly said, giving voice to her previous thoughts. "Any way, don't you think he knows we're already here?"

"Suppose so," Broom said, but he still slipped the radio into a pocket so that he didn't become an easy target.

Shelly moved up the stairs. She stepped into a puddle of water and to her over-active senses the splash sounded like a rhinoceros had taken a high dive into a swimming pool. When she was safely up the first flight, Broom followed. Shelly smiled to herself: Broom was holding his breath already.

FIFTYONE

The Freezer

Standing at the threshold of hell I had to give myself another mental hitch to get moving. Hell was a long way down, but it would take me only a couple of missteps to fall there.

I faced a metal door. It wasn't unlike the doors seen on industrial sized freezers. Probably was, considering I was in a processing plant where animal pelts were once stored. Why it would be at the highest, least accessible point of the tannery I had no clue.

To enter the room beyond meant sucking up my fear. If I was on the wrong track I could be stepping into a prison with no hope of escape. Not that I'd freeze to death: there was no power to the building. My fear was the door slamming shut and then dying a slow, torturous death starved of oxygen. It'd be like drowning on dry land. I'd already drowned once, and it was the last thing I wanted to do again.

The fear was irrational. I could already hear Broom and Sergeant McCusker mounting the stairs below me. They'd come to my rescue before I suffocated.

Grasping the handle I pulled the door towards me. Though huge, it was counterweighted so it moved with ease. Thankfully there was no sucking noise associated with breaking a vacuum-seal. Meant it wasn't airtight. Exhaling gratefully, I moved through the doorway and into a wide, open space, two-thirds the dimensions of the uppermost floor. The ceiling was low, and I could tell even in the darkness that it was wood and not the galvanized metal of a conventional freezer unit. The floor was metal though, dimpled with non-slip studs.

After crossing the threshold, I paused.

The darkness was too deep to see anything clearly. But the smell, no amount of sense deprivation could cover that. It was the acrid stench of human waste, urine, faeces and stale sweat.

There had been people here recently.

"Janet!" I whispered loudly. "Bethany!"

No one answered, only a faint echo of my own voice.

But there was a clink! As though something metal had struck the floor. In that slowly disintegrating building it didn't mean anything. My weight on a loose board beneath the metal flooring could easily have transposed itself to a far corner of the room, dislodging something. Anything could have fallen from the mouldering structure. But then I heard a shuffle.

Could be a rat, I reasoned, but only if it was wearing shoes.

"Janet!" I said again, this time louder.

A door banged shut.

Jerking forward, I raced through the room towards the reverberating echo of the slammed door. It was a stupid reaction. In hindsight I should have negotiated the open space with more care. I wouldn't have run headlong into the upright steel pillar, bounced off it and went belly-down on the cold floor.

I wouldn't have dropped my gun.

With my head ringing from the impact, I clambered up. It was like I was back on that damn ferry, the floor pitching and yawing beneath my feet, and my guts did a somersault, threatening to spill their contents on the floor. But a heaving stomach was my least concern. I had to find the SIG. If I had any hope of defending myself against the Skeklar I needed the gun.

As I'd hit the floor I was faintly aware of it clattering away from me into the shadows. Standing up I'd become disoriented and had no idea which direction the gun had slid.

Wishing again that I'd fetched a torch, I groped for the pillar I'd run into. At least it would be a starting point. From there I'd just have to make an ever increasing circle, search the floor with my feet until I located the gun.

A shriek rang out.

Janet.

I forgot about the gun. Forgot about caution. I lurched into a run towards the far end of the room.

FIFTYTWO

In Carter's footsteps

"Was that a scream?"

Broom's rhetorical question floated out the darkness below Shelly. A second before it she'd heard the howl of a woman in torment. She didn't bother answering. She'd already heard Bailey's answering shout, then the thud-thud-thud of his feet as he raced to the rescue.

"Broom. Get on the radio and call for help," she commanded. "Do it now!"

Then she clattered up the stairs, all caution thrust aside now there was no doubt Janet Hale was here. Her scream meant that Janet was still alive, but without immediate intervention that might not be the case for long.

Broom's voice was an urgent bleat as he shouted demands and instructions to the police control room over in Yell. But he was running, too. He was coming to help.

Shelly came to the metal door. She didn't stop to worry about entering the room beyond. She was beyond fear now and was wearing her police head once more. Doing her duty as befits a police officer, but more than that, doing the duty of any human being. She had to stop the Skeklar. She had to save Janet and Bethany. And if necessary she had to save Carter Bailey.

Running into the room she saw a dark figure ahead of her. She could barely make him out in the darkness but she thought from the pounding of feet that it was Bailey. She slid to a stop, listened as the timbre of his footsteps changed. He was mounting a further set of steps, wooden this time.

She briefly surveyed her surroundings. The room was windowless. But she recalled the flash of a torch or lamp in an uppermost window when she'd crouched outside. This had to be a room within a room. Bailey had obviously found egress to those outside this inner shell. In one of those rooms he'd possibly find Janet and Bethany. Likely he'd also find the Skeklar.

Behind her Broom charged in. He was still bleating instructions into the radio. The answering communications operator was asking needless questions of him. Shelly spun around and snatched the terminal out of his hand.

"Sixteen twelve to control," she shouted. "I require immediate assistance. Now." She hurriedly gave their location and a brief explanation of what she'd heard.

Inspector Marsh cut in.

"Sergeant McCusker. I want you to back down immediately. We have a task force en route to you now. Stand down until we have AFO's on scene."

Janet Hale screamed and there was a crashing noise from where Bailey had charged through a second door.

"We haven't time to wait for Firearms to get here, sir," she shouted back. "I have to do something *now*."

"We know who we're up against now," Marsh said. "We've identified the killer. He is too dangerous, Sergeant. Stand down."

"No," Shelly shouted as another scream rang out - this time the high-pitched squall of a child. "I can't stand around listening while people are dying."

"I'm ordering you -"

"I don't give a damn for your orders," Shelly snapped.

She tossed the radio back to Broom. "You guide them in, Broom. I'm going up."

"Not without me you're not," Broom said, moving up alongside her.

There was another crash, as if ill-stacked furniture had toppled to the ground. Carter Bailey shouted. A woman and child screamed.

Somewhere at the back of her mind Shelly was aware that Inspector Marsh was still relaying orders to her. But she didn't give a rat's arse. The only good thing from his constant use of the radio was the screen's glow illuminated the way ahead.

And she saw what was on the floor.

Stooping, she grabbed the dropped SIG Sauer.

She turned and showed it to Broom.

"Shit. He's gone in there unarmed," Broom hissed.

"He won't stand a chance."

FIFTYTHREE

The Gibbet

At the end of the big room was a flight of wooden steps that lead upward to a raised platform. I took the steps in three bounds then was onto the reverberating decking. In front of me was another door. I didn't stop, just charged forward and yanked it open, and lurched into an empty office.

Janet's next scream was louder.

"I'm coming, Janet," I shouted.

At the other side of the office was yet another door and I didn't stop to think. I sprinted across the room, almost knocking the door off its hinges as I threw my weight against it.

Sense would have told me that there was another flight of stairs at this side too, but I wasn't thinking straight. The office was on a raised deck from where the supervisors of old could keep an eye on the workers either side of the office. As I blasted out the door, I found that I was sailing through space. It wasn't a long drop, and I twisted in mid-air so that my back crashed into a desk, upon which were stacked a couple of worm-eaten wooden chairs. My momentum pushed the desk over, scattering the chairs on the floor, and I fell with them.

Something popped inside me: a rib cracking.

My face battered against something solid and blood instantly poured from a fresh wound on my face.

Surprisingly neither injury caused me to wince. I was beyond pain at that moment, existing on a tide of adrenalin. If I lived through the next few minutes I knew the pain would grow unendurable, but then I neither felt nor cared less about my injuries.

"Where are you, Janet?" I yelled, scrambling up and spinning full circle as I sought her.

"Look out, Carter!" Janet shouted. "Don't come any closer."

I followed the source of her voice.

There were windows there. Some dim light leaked into the room and I could make out an amorphous shadow towards its rear. The shape was unnatural. It was too large to be Janet. Skeklar! My mind screamed.

But then I realised, no.

The shape was made up of two forms. They were hanging from a construction that reminded me of a medieval gibbet, their feet placed precariously on a narrow cross spar.

Jesus Christ! The Skeklar planned to hang them.

I lurched forward.

Janet and Bethany screamed.

It took me a second or so to realise they weren't screaming in agony. It was to halt my mad rush.

"Don't come any nearer, Carter," Janet pleaded.

"Not unless you want me to kick loose this plank," said a voice I didn't recognise. Guttural and wheezy it asked, "Do you want them to die?"

Then I saw him. The Skeklar. He appeared out of the shadows like some great simian. He balanced on the same crossbeam that separated Janet and Bethany from a neck-snapping drop. He gave a little hop and the beam bounced beneath him. Janet and Bethany swayed precariously as they fought for balance. The Skeklar laughed.

"You bastard," I yelled at him. "Let them go."

The Skeklar laughed again. He placed a finger against Bethany's chest. "All it takes is a tiny little nudge and that would be it. She'd fall and her neck would stretch; maybe her head would pull all the way off. I think that would make a pretty image."

"You're insane."

"Most probably," the Skeklar agreed. "So you'd best believe that I would do it."

Clenching my fists, feeling totally futile, I stared up at the nightmare creature.

The darkness still disguised his true form. But this was my first opportunity to study him.

He had the malformed head, the weirdly glowing green eyes, the spikes and knobs on his torso, the claws on his hands that I'd sensed from those previous encounters. But I could see now that the Skeklar was *just a man*.

"Who the fuck are you?"

The Skeklar didn't answer immediately. He pressed by Bethany, situating himself between his two captives. Standing with a hand on each of their heads he said, "I am vengeance."

"You are mad," I told him.

The man wore some sort of weird Halloween costume. It was constructed mainly of woven straw, giving the trousers and shoulders a spiky look, almost like quills or rough hairs. Some of it, particularly across the chest and back was covered in black fur. But the costume also consisted of equipment gleaned from military sources. He was wearing a Kevlar vest. His head was swathed in a hood and respirator, and over his eyes were faintly glowing night vision goggles. His claws were those ridiculous climbing claws I'd seen during the Ninja movie boom of the 1980's, though the addition of longer blades welded onto the metal wristbands enhance their cutting ability.

Realising my enemy was only a man in a suit didn't lessen any of the menace. Crazy fucker in a makeshift costume or not, he was a killer and - as my previous run-ins with him attested to - a very capable and dangerous fighter.

"Why are you doing this?" I asked.

He'd said he was *vengeance*. Vengeance for what: the defilement of an ancient burial ground? Or was his need for vengeance more obvious than that? More mundane? It didn't matter. Mad men didn't need a cause to justify their actions.

"I do what I do because I choose to do so." The Skeklar turned to regard Janet through his goggles. Directly to her, he repeated, "What *I choose* to do."

"It's over now. This is at an end. Let them go." My words strung together as I hurried to get them out. "Killing them won't achieve anything."

The Skeklar laughed at my pitiful argument.

Then he said, "The *haugbonde* demands nine sacrifices. It is not over until I have given back the blood of nine to the mound-dweller."

"The haugbonde is nothing but a myth," I shouted at him, though I knew differently. "A fairy tale told to children. You're fucking delusional, man. Your vengeance is nothing but a sham."

The Skeklar shook his large head, turning once more to Janet. "What do you say, Professor Hale? Is my vengeance a sham? I don't think so."

"You murdered them for nothing," Janet whispered.

"No…every last one of them deserved to die. The boy. He harmed a messenger of the haugbonde. He was evil and spiteful. I did only to him what he did to the bird. The policeman? Entwhistle, was it? He tried to stop me from taking what was rightfully mine. As did Pete Johnston."

"Pete took nothing from you."

"Oh, but he did, Professor *Hale*."

"What about Toni? His girlfriend," Janet cried. "She did nothing wrong. Why kill her?"

The Skeklar shrugged. "I had to kill her. I used her death to punish Johnston before he died. It made the entire torture so much sweeter."

Whilst they conversed I stood watching the interaction with dawning comprehension. As I watched, the light emanating from the Skeklar's night vision goggles appeared to brighten, then flare in a putrid green cloud that surrounded his entire head.

It took me a moment to realise that it wasn't light from the goggles but a brightening of his auric field. Green with jealousy took on a whole new meaning.

To confirm my suspicions, Shelly McCusker chose that moment to come bursting into the room.

"Jonathon Connery," she yelled. "You're under arrest."

Jonathon Connery.

Janet's estranged husband?

FIFTYFOUR

The old tannery

Moments earlier Inspector Marsh's words were spurred more by urgency than they were by anger. Broom finally grabbed at Shelly, and said, "Maybe you should listen to this, Sergeant McCusker."

Taking the radio back from him, she keyed the button. "Sir, no disrespect intended, but unless I do something immediately then innocent people are going to die."

"The firearms team are still at least ten minutes away from you," the inspector agreed with a note of resignation to his tone. "Attempt to contain the situation if possible. Initiate a rapport with the suspect until we arrive on scene. If that is not possible then you must dynamically risk assess the situation and take appropriate action as you see fit. Do not - I repeat DO NOT - engage the suspect unless absolutely necessary."

"Of course, Sir," Shelly said.

Dynamically risk assess. That was police speak for using your common sense. Well, her common sense told her that unless she got her arse in gear a small child and woman were going to die horribly. Obviously engaging the suspect *was* absolutely necessary.

"Sir, you said earlier that you have identified the suspect. Who is it I'm dealing with? Why is it he's so dangerous?"

"At Trowhaem," he said, "Professor Bishop discovered a second body concealed beneath the first. It was a female we have identified as Toni McNabb. Both she and her boyfriend Pete Johnston went missing. This was shortly after Johnston and Janet Hale were briefly romantically involved. It seems that Janet's estranged husband was enraged at Johnston's closeness to his wife and he murdered the couple. We suspect this whole

Skeklar madness is a scam invented to cover the crime. He was trying to scare off the archaeological team so that their corpses lay undiscovered." He paused. "Sergeant, Jonathon Connery is more than just an insane ex-husband, he is also ex-military. Be very, very careful."

"Roger, noted," Shelly said. She clipped her radio back to her jacket. Now she understood what Janet had meant when she sobbed that it was her fault the murders had happened. The professor had come to the same conclusion about whom was responsible for the murders, and had been about to say so just before their car had been rammed off the road.

Subsequently, their run had taken them to the raised platform, and Broom was already making his way up the stairs. In this urgency his limp was barely noticeable. Shelly had to spur herself up the stairs to catch him as he entered the dilapidated office space. From the open door opposite she heard Janet Hale sob, "What about Toni? His girlfriend. She did nothing wrong. Why kill her?"

The next voice was human, though forced as though through a gas mask. "I had to kill her. I used her death to punish Johnston before he died. It made the entire torture so much sweeter."

Janet sobbed again. Beyond her deeper sobs came the whimpering of a terrified child.

Dynamic risk assessment time, Shelly told herself.

She glanced down at the gun in her hand. Never in her life had she fired a gun, let alone a semi-automatic handgun. Couldn't be too difficult she thought. Point and squeeze: what more could there be to it?

Okay, she thought, I'm to develop a rapport with the suspect. Contain the situation. Act only if absolutely necessary.

She stepped through the door with no real idea what she might find.

Momentarily the absurdity - and the desperation - of the scene made her falter. But then she was swinging up the SIG

Sauer and pointing it at the monstrous thing threatening the two captives.

"Jonathon Connery," she yelled. "You're under arrest."

And even as she did so, she realised she'd made one hell of a mistake.

FIFTYFIVE

At the gibbet

I'd shared only the briefest of intimate moments with Janet, but I had to wonder if the Skeklar - her estranged husband, Jonathon - had witnessed us together, which would explain his reason for attacking me. Made me wonder if it was his overwhelming jealousy that was driving him or if there was an outside force compelling him, driving him, to commit these horrific killings. Why the Skeklar charade? Why the Grand Guignol settings to his crimes? If he was jealous of Janet, why hadn't he simply acted out his madness on her, away from this island, without all the other murders and depravity he'd committed along the way?

Recalling the thin grey man who'd sent us to this out of the way killing ground, I had to wonder what weird powers were guiding not only the killer, but also the rest of us that had been drawn into the plot. Maybe there was more to this haugbonde curse than any of us suspected.

Were the rest of us agents of the haugbonde as much as was Jonathon Connery?

Those thoughts went spinning through my mind, even as I lurched forward. As Jonathon reacted to Sergeant McCusker's sudden appearance, I acted, or Bethany would be dead.

Jonathon, the Skeklar, didn't put up his clawed hands in surrender. He did as he'd promised only seconds ago. He gave Bethany a shove. As the girl swayed, then toppled from the board, he spun so that he was balanced precariously, his feet bracing those of Janet, one arm encircling her throat. He glared beyond me at where Sergeant McCusker and Paul Broom stood.

The small girl fell. Her wrists were bound before her, her hands clasped as though praying. A second rope was around her tiny throat. The slack didn't equal the space left beneath her feet.

Slow motion enveloped me, as though I was running against deep water. Bright auric colours exploded from Bethany even as she cried out for her mother. She was quickly approaching the extent of the rope noose, and I couldn't see how I'd reach her in time.

The slow motion effect imploded in on itself, and I hurtled across the last few feet, my arms snatching at her tiny body. I felt Bethany convulse, and I let out a shout of dismay. Then I hauled the girl high in my arms and stared into her fully lucid eyes as she blinked back at me in astonishment. I'd grabbed her out of the air just at that precise moment before the noose jerked tight. Bethany was still alive. But I didn't know for how long.

I felt the tug of the rope.

Snatching my gaze upward, I saw that the Skeklar had snared the rope with one of his clawed fists and was hauling on it. Around Bethany's neck the noose cinched tight. She gagged, eyes going round. I grabbed at the rope, too. Tried to pull it away from the beast but he had more vantage, and cared not for the girl's life.

"Let her go," he growled down at me. "Let her go or let Janet die."

He grabbed Janet by her ponytail, pulling her head backwards. One of her heels skidded off the board.

So there it was at last.

The test my brother had taunted me with so long.

"What's it gonna be, Carter?" Cash gloated. *"Are you man enough? Do you sacrifice the woman you love for the sake of a child?"*

"I'm man enough," I croaked, "to save them both!"

Shelly McCusker saw my searching glance. My short nod. She new instantly what she had to do. Her aim was true.

I lifted Bethany high into the air, lessening the pressure of the noose round her throat, even as with my other hand I snatched the thrown SIG out of the air. It was a desperate move, but I was about as desperate as anyone could be. Raising the gun, I fired.

Blood vapour misted the air where my bullet struck Janet's shoulder. Then more blood splashed from the Skeklar's throat as the bullet continued its almost unchecked flight and found flesh above the protection of his Kevlar vest.

The Skeklar staggered. Then his feet slipped off the board and he went over backwards. He landed with terrific, body numbing force on the floor just beyond me, and I saw a putrescent haze of auric light cloud around him as though his entire being had self-destructed.

There was no time for satisfaction.

Shot through, Janet had no way of fighting off the wave of nausea and pain spilling through her. She was swooning with agony, her balance truly gone this time. I quickly dropped the gun, snatching an arm around the back of both her knees and toppling her over my shoulder.

"I could do with some help over here!"

My scream was answered by running footsteps, then Shelly McCusker tugged the rope from Bethany's throat, even as Paul Broom helped me support Janet's sagging body.

Bethany coughed and gasped, but she was going to be all right. Shelly enfolded her in an embrace, moving quickly away, hushing her, consoling her. The little girl cried, but that was a good sign.

My concern was for Janet.

To stop the monster killing her, I'd shot her. What if I'd inadvertently struck a major blood vessel and had killed her myself?

Broom and I laid her on the floor and I leaned over her. I searched for the wound, dreading what my fingers would find. Going in a bullet makes a tiny hole but coming out was different. Worst case scenario would be that half her back was missing.

Tugging open her jacket I saw blood. It was rich and bright in colour. But not spurting, just a slow seeping. I pulled open her blouse and my heart did a little skip.

The bullet had barely scored the flesh above her right collarbone. The wound would hurt like a bitch, but Janet would be okay. Even as I formed the thought, Janet's eyes fluttered open. Her gaze was unfocussed for a second, but then the colours sharpened, her pupils dilated, and Janet asked, "Is Bethany safe?"

"Bethany is going to be okay," I told her. "What about you, Janet? I'm sorry I shot you. I'm so, so sorry."

"I'm fine," she said, but then lapsed again into a deep unconscious sleep.

I hung my head. But it wasn't in shame.

"You are one lucky mother fucker, Bro," Cash's voice impeded in my thoughts.

"You think so?" I asked him. "I'm still stuck with you."

"Mmm, yes," he said. *"But maybe not for long."*

FIFTYSIX

At the place of death

Jonathon Connery wasn't dead.

He was shot through the throat, was spurting blood from a severed artery, but he still retained enough strength to rise up behind me. It was awkward staunching the blood with his clawed hand, but he was managing to hold on to enough of it that he thought he could still win the day.

A breathy roar came through the filters of his mask, and then he leaped towards me. Caught while crouched over Janet, I wasn't in the best position to defend myself. So instead I protected Janet from her estranged husband's vengeance. I felt the steel claws rake my back.

"She is mine!"

I don't know if Jonathon screamed those words. More than likely it was me. Striking backwards with a clenched fist, I contacted with the night vision goggles, knocking them loose. I caught a momentary glimpse of his seething eyes and they appeared to be burning with witch-fires, but then Broom had hold of Jonathon and had lifted him bodily. Broom caught him in a bear hug and his arms crushed ruthlessly.

The blood jetted from Jonathon's neck as he released his hold on the wound. He clawed backwards at Broom but his attempt at gutting my friend was ineffective. Broom squeezed harder. The jetting blood lessened.

Lessened.

Stopped.

Broom let the cadaver drop to the floor.

I spied up at my big friend, thankful for more than one reason that he'd chosen to champion me.

He gave me a lopsided grin. "W.W.V.H.D?"

"Are you fuckin' kidding me?" Cash wheezed.

I ignored my brother. Instead I stared at the dead man lying at Broom's feet. I knew the face: instantly recalling where I'd seen it before. When I'd visited the murder scene near Ura Taing, the man had been standing in the crowd. Ironically I'd thought he was an undercover cop, observing the crowd for possible murder suspects. Right then I should have known, but at the time I wasn't confident in my abilities. Now I was. I'd found the evil one. Stopped him. For the briefest of moments I expected him to rear up again like the killer from a slasher movie. But this time he was dead. The cataract stare of the eyes told me. So did his rapidly diminishing aura that dissipated like river mist in the sunlight.

"Fuck, fuck, fuck," Cash muttered.

"Not now, Cash," I said. I wasn't in any mood for his opinion. There were two dead men in this room, and now neither of them mattered. I was more interested in the living.

Picking Janet up I cradled her in my arms. She mewled like a kitten and her eyes fluttered open again.

"I'm going get you out of here," I said.

"You heard me," Janet said. "You heard me and you came for me."

"I'll always be there for you."

After

We took a drive up to Burra Ness in Broom's Subaru. Broom was his usual reckless self, but I didn't mind. I was too cozy, snuggled in the back with Janet to worry about crashing and burning on the desolate road. After the horror of the Skeklar, nothing as mundane as a car wreck would worry me again. Not now that Janet was safe in my arms and Cash had resided in a sulk to a very deep corner of my subconscious.

Saving Janet and Bethany, I could lay to rest the bitter feelings of failure that had haunted me since that wintry night in the watermill. The ghosts of Karen and my unborn child could sleep easy now. Holding onto Janet's hand, I was no longer afraid. The past was behind me, the future felt good.

Shelly McCusker was being hailed a hero for her part in bringing down the murderer, but - even though I suspected that she'd yearned for the acceptance of her colleagues - she wasn't the kind to make a big thing of the accolade. She was only happy sitting by Bob Harris' bedside, cajoling him toward a rapid recovery.

It turned out that Jonathon Connery had possibly been suffering an undiagnosed form of bi-polar schizophrenia, a condition that had been exacerbated when Janet had shown him to be a misogynistic pig. When Pete Johnston had shown his wife the least bit of notice, he'd acted out his jealous rage by not only murdering the man, but also torturing his current girlfriend, Toni. Jonathon had concealed the bodies at Trowhaem, and that was when he'd truly gone mad. Clutching at the fears of the islanders - the hogboy curse associated with Trowhaem - in his delusional mind it was the ideal platform from which he could cover up his crime. And there was the added bonus: he'd found an ideal form of revenge, aimed at the wife who'd first denied him a child, then spited him when he'd tried to impregnate another. It wasn't enough to hurt Janet physically; he wanted to hurt her career, her reputation, the way he perceived she'd hurt his. What better way than closing down the dig, and with it the associated funding? His insane plan ensured that the Skeklar had been given birth. Murdering little Jimmy, snatching Bethany, had been crimes of opportunity, but they had struck terror into the hearts and minds of the islanders. Everything else following had been conducted with the malicious intent of the monster Jonathon truly believed he'd become. He had fully planned to carry out nine murders to strengthen the hogboy myth, and had most likely planned to keep Bethany for last. Even if she'd survived his planned murder spree, Janet's career would be at an end. She'd never work in the field she loved again. If not for the timely intervention of Sergeant McCusker, Connery would have succeeded. To cover up my, and Broom's, part in his killing, Shelly said she had taken the illegal sidearm from Connery, shooting him with his own weapon. If anyone suspected she was lying to save us, they didn't say.

The theory concerning Connery's actions was all conjecture.

For my part there were still some things requiring answers.

So that's why Broom again parked opposite the utility shed where I'd held my vigil with the crows, and later experienced that unreal episode with the thin grey man.

Leaving Janet in the car with Broom, I stepped out onto the road. The sun was high in the sky, but it was weak at this northern latitude. There was enough light to make out the lone crow sitting on the roof of the building. It rolled a beady eye at me, then struck out for the heavens cawing its evil little laugh.

In my hand was a pair of wire cutters with rubber handles. Using them I rattled the wire. If the fence was electrified the least I could expect was a tingling of current through the rubber but I felt nothing. I set to snipping away enough of the fence for me to pass through.

The door of the hut stood slightly ajar.

Stepping into the darkness, I paused while my vision adjusted. The hut was larger than its outer dimensions would suggest. Metal steps led down towards a sub-cellar. The floor was beaten earth, and I saw an old rusty bucket, water bottles and empty Wotsit packets strewn on the floor. Feeling a pang, I realised I'd been wrong, that this was where Jonathon had first held Bethany. This was where she'd been when I'd searched out her essence. She had been there all that time while I'd sat on my arse at the side of the road. Maybe I should have listened closer to Broom, to the portents, and then Bethany and Janet wouldn't have had to suffer the terror the Skeklar had ultimately put them through.

One questioned was answered.

But I still had another.

"Where are you?"

There was a shuffle as though small animals moved through the shadows.

Then he was standing before me.

The thin grey man.

His translucent skin was the colour of parched earth.

His eyes were deep pools of ancient wisdom.

"I just wanted to thank you," I said. "Without your help I'd never have found them. Two more innocents would have died. Those other murders, they were never demanded of you."

The thin grey man said nothing. His lips peeled back from sharp teeth, but there was nothing frightening in the gesture. He was smiling.

From my coat pocket I pulled out a small plastic carton and a tin. I popped their seals.

Milk and beer I poured onto the floor.

Giving them back to the earth.

Traditional sacrifices - the only sacrifices - demanded by the haugbonde.

PRETERNATURAL

Acknowledgements and Thanks:

My grateful acknowledgment goes to Lynne McTaggart whose book *The Field; The quest for the secret force of the universe*, allowed me to explain (if only in part) Paul Broom's personal notions concerning Carter Bailey's ability to detect evil as a source of negative energy. I hope nothing I have culled from her thought provoking treatise on The Zero Point Field has been used out of context.

Thanks to the people of the Shetland Islands for allowing me the lassitude to wholly invent an island that doesn't actually exist in their lands. Any mistakes regarding the traditions or history of the islands should be taken wholly as my fault, and merely hiccups in the process of writing this novel. My apologies to any similarities in any family names, companies etc.: all those named in the book are figments of my imagination and bear no intentional resemblance to any person or business in the real world.

Thanks to Graham Smith and Kirstie Long for their insights into making this book a much clearer read.

About the Author:

Matt Hilton quit his career as a police officer with Cumbria Constabulary to pursue his love of writing tight, cinematic American-style thrillers. He is the author of the high-octane Joe Hunter thriller series, including his most recent novel **'The Lawless Kind'** – Joe Hunter 9 - published in January 2014 by Hodder and Stoughton. His first book, **'Dead Men's Dust'**, was shortlisted for the International Thriller Writers' Debut Book of 2009 Award, and was a Sunday Times bestseller, also being named as a 'thriller of the year 2009' by The Daily Telegraph. **Dead Men's Dust** was also a top ten Kindle bestseller in 2013. The Joe Hunter series is widely published by Hodder and Stoughton in UK territories, and by William Morrow and Company in the USA, and have been translated into German, Italian, Romanian and Bulgarian.

As well as the Joe Hunter series, Matt has been published in a number of anthologies and collections, and has published three previous novels in the horror genre, namely **'Dominion'**, **'Darkest Hour'** and a young adult novel called **'Mark Darrow and the Stealer of Souls'**. Matt also collected and edited both **'ACTION: Pulse Pounding Tales Volumes 1 and 2'**.

Matt is a high-ranking martial artist and has been a detective and private security specialist, all of which lend an authenticity to the action scenes in his books. He is also very interested in the paranormal and has accompanied Ghost-North-east and Near Dark Paranormal Investigations on a number of their investigations.

Matt is currently working on the next Joe Hunter novel, as well as a stand-alone supernatural novel.

You can find out more about his writing here:

www.matthiltonbooks.com

PRETERNATURAL

9751909R00226

Printed in Great Britain
by Amazon.co.uk, Ltd.,
Marston Gate.